## Praise for *Beyond the Ghetto Gates*

"Michelle Cameron's powerful novel *Beyond the Ghetto Gates* is a passionately compelling saga of an ancient way of life on the threshold of radical change. Young Mirelle longs to dedicate her life to running her aging father's workshop, but her rabbi forbids her on account of her sex. Chafing against the constraints of both her gender and the suffocating strictures of the Ancona ghetto, Mirelle sees no way forward but dutiful marriage. Yet Napoleon's armies, sweeping across Europe, threaten to change her way of life forever."

—Mary Sharratt, author of *Ecstasy* and *The Dark Lady's Mask*

"What forces are unleashed when the world turns upside down? In *Beyond the Ghetto Gates*, Cameron tells a story of sweeping romance at a moment in history when the world really was turned upside down—Napoleon's 1797 conquest of Italy. The campaign challenged the established order of nations and the power of the Church and forever changed the life of Italy's Jews. In this novel, Cameron vividly imagines the impact these events have on a young Jewish woman of Ancona in her search for love and an independent life. An intimate tale of love vs. duty, of passion vs obligation, set against the backdrop of epic events. This is a historical novel with deep contemporary relevance."

—Michael Goldfarb, author of *Emancipation: How Liberating Europe's Jews From the Ghetto Led to Revolution and Renaissance*

"Against the backdrop of Napoleon's invasion of Italy, Cameron weaves an immersive tale of a young Jewish woman torn between her filial duty and passion for a young Catholic soldier. Her portrait of Jews and Catholics grappling with social upheaval in an 18th-century harbor town shines a light on the challenges of nationalism and bigotry that still plague society

—Talia Carn

"In this sweeping saga, Cameron draws a compelling portrait of life in late 18th-century Italy, when the citizens of war-torn Ancona face the challenges of their world transformed by Napoleon's liberating army. From the Jews who are suddenly freed from the restrictive confines of the city's ghetto, to the Catholics whose deep devotion is set on fire by a miraculous weeping portrait of the Madonna, *Beyond the Ghetto Gates* captures the double-edged sword of passion and faith."

—Judith Lindbergh, author of *The Thrall's Tale*

"I devoured this engrossing, passionate story of a young Jewish woman in 1796 who wants only to work with her beloved father in his workshop. But even after Napoleon invades Italy, liberates her city, and breaks down the ghetto gates, customs still enclose Mirelle both as a Jew and a woman. And outside the gates are waiting the riots of anti-Semitism, tragic loss, and a difficult love. These pages are splashed with brilliant colors between the dark corners of this lost world where ghetto buildings are built so close and high that people cannot see the stars. You will live and breathe this young woman's struggles to have what she wants and still honor her family until the unexpected last paragraphs—and then for a long time after."

—Stephanie Cowell, author of *Claude and Camile, Nicholas Cooke, The Players: A Novel of the Young Shakespeare* and others

"Cameron's vivid page-turner delivers a shattering portrait of love, lust, war, betrayal and faith inside the gates of a famed Jewish ghetto in late 18th century Italy. Best of all, *Beyond the Ghetto Gates* gives us Mirelle, a brave and brilliant young heroine who learns that faith in one's self is the greatest faith of all."

—Laurie Lico Albanese, author of *Stolen Beauty*

# BEYOND THE
# GHETTO GATES

# Beyond the Ghetto Gates

## A Novel

## Michelle Cameron

She Writes Press

Published 2020
Printed in the United States of America
ISBN: 978-1-63152-850-7 pbk
ISBN: 978-1-63152-851-4 ebk
Library of Congress Control Number: 2019913583

For information, address:
She Writes Press
1569 Solano Ave #546
Berkeley, CA 94707

She Writes Press is a division of SparkPoint Studio, LLC.

*For Alex, my Muse*

# PART ONE

## MARCH 1796–FEBRUARY 1797

# 1

## March 27, 1796
## Ancona, Italy

Mirelle sat at the desk in her father's office, staring blankly at the open cash box. Where was the money? Her heart hammered in her chest. Three people had the key: herself, her father, and the ketubah workshop foreman, Sabato Narducci. It was inconceivable that her father or Narducci would have taken anything without a reason.

But it was nearly April, when Mirelle divvied out the men's quarterly wage packets. And there wasn't enough money in the box to pay them.

The irrational thought that she had somehow miscounted made her scoop up the bills and coins again, hands trembling. The total was the same. *Where is the money?*

Drawing a shaky breath, she pushed her hair out of her face and swiveled around to take the oversized ledger off the cabinet behind the desk. She let it fall open and spied a few notations in new columns on a fresh page in her father's cramped, somewhat untidy handwriting. She turned back a leaf and, sighing in relief, found the culprit.

*Scarlotti.*

After reading the amount Papa had paid the man—853 scudi—she walked into the workroom, cradling the book to her chest, to find her father.

"Papa? May I talk to you?"

Simone d'Ancona looked up, clearly annoyed at the interruption. He was doing the work he loved best: illuminating a ketubah at his narrow standing desk at the back of the workshop. From there, he explained to his wife and children, he could watch over his men and still keep his hand in the work.

But Mirelle knew that once engrossed in his craft, he did very little supervising; that role was generally left to Narducci. She didn't blame her father, however. She, too, knew the magical pull of immersing herself in the tasks she loved. For Papa, it was art—for Mirelle, numbers.

"What is it, child?" The look of irritation faded, replaced by a fond smile.

Mirelle glanced at the bent heads of the men in the workshop. "Let's go into your office."

He followed her back to the tiny office. Once inside, she opened the ledger. "I thought we agreed to let me handle the accounts," she said gently, pointing to the suspect entry. "And the payments. But you paid Scarlotti for this quarter's shipment of parchment, didn't you?"

"He was pressing us for payment—said we were late, and he needed to pay his suppliers. You weren't here. What was I supposed to do?"

Mirelle shook her head as she moved her finger up the page. "Look here."

An identical payment was neatly recorded above. "You paid him twice," Mirelle said, looking into his stricken face. "Mama took me to market yesterday, remember? We saw Scarlotti there. He must have come here afterward to—"

"Cheat us!" His face turned plum red. "A whole quarter's supply— more than eight hundred scudi!"

Mirelle nodded. "You must get it back, Papa. So we can pay the men. And Papa . . . stay out of my books."

Her father averted his gaze. "I'll be more careful, that's all," he muttered.

Mirelle bit her lip. She could never convince her father that numbers befuddled him, that the accounts always became snarled when he touched them. Generally, she didn't mind rechecking his work and adjusting his errors. After all, it was his workshop. But this last mistake? If she hadn't caught it in time . . .

She took a deep breath. "Tell Signor Scarlotti to return our money. Today." Looking out the open office door, she lowered her voice. "I'll calculate the men's pay packets so they're ready to fill when you return."

"This afternoon," he said, his head still turned away.

She bit her lip as he moved to escape the office, looking like a trapped rabbit. She knew he hated confronting anyone, even though Scarlotti was just a blustering bully who would back down once faced with proof.

Before he reached the door, Papa swiveled back. "I'm grateful, child."

She nodded and, as soon as he slipped away, turned to her figures. Adjusting her father's mistake, she wrote new totals at the bottom of the two columns. Deductions for parchment, ink, paints, cleansing oils. She wrote out the men's pay packets, then balanced expenses against the income from the commissions, most paid in soldi and lire, some in foreign coin—rubles and pounds sterling and francs. She'd created a list that helped her translate sums sent from as far off as Russia and the Americas.

While she was absorbed in numbers, her father came back in and sat down at the corner of the desk to write letters. Soon the only sound was the scratch of his pen and the tick marks Mirelle made in the ledger.

They worked companionably for an hour before Narducci appeared in the doorway.

"We're almost ready to send the new ketubot to that American city—Savannah, Georgia," the foreman said. "I wanted to show you the one designed for the rabbi and his bride. The men outdid themselves."

He held up a sheaf of parchment. Papa shuffled his letters into a neat pile and placed them on his lap. Narducci laid the illuminated marriage certificate on the desk while Mirelle rose to stand behind the two men.

Mirelle was used to ketubot of all types, decorated with flowers and intricate spirals, biblical heroes, medieval creatures, signs of the zodiac, and exotic animals. Colors ranged from vivid crimson and sapphire, rich violet, and deep emerald to lighter pastels—soft pinks and yellows, celadon green, and sky blue. Some took on a darker aspect: inky black backgrounds overlaid with lacy patterns bemusing the eye. Others were spare, the white vellum untouched, a single sprig of wildflowers, per- haps, or a simple scroll. But all encircled the same text, which read:

> *Be my wife according to the law of Moses and Israel. I will work, honor, feed, and support you in the custom of Jewish men, who work, honor, feed, and support their wives faithfully. I will give you the settlement of _____ as well as your food, clothing, necessities of life, and conjugal needs, according to the universal custom.*

Mirelle stared at the blank space following "settlement of." That amount, as well as the wife's dowry, were negotiated by the match- maker and the parents of the young couple before the betrothal cere- mony. She wondered idly what her own worth might be. Five hundred scudi? A thousand? Her mother's voice echoed in her head: *"How ironic: the daughter of Europe's foremost ketubah workshop remaining unwed and unsought!"*

Mirelle tossed her head. From what she'd seen of her mother's life—cooking, cleaning, trailing the men like an obedient bird, dusting tables, and sweeping crumbs—following in those footsteps was the last thing she wanted.

"Exquisite," Papa said now, chasing her reverie away.

"It's a good thing you finished on time," Mirelle teased the foreman. "Papa was nervous that you'd miss the frigate." She ran a careful finger over the ragged edge of the parchment, adding softly, "It's lovely."

Simone d'Ancona was always in a hurry. How many mornings had Mirelle seen her father drink his morning coffee standing, shrugging on his shapeless overcoat as he took his final gulp? The slowness of his best workers often irritated him, but when he saw their gorgeous work, his impatience vanished, replaced by lavish praise. The ketubah workshop was renowned worldwide, Mirelle knew, because of the quality of their craftsmanship.

"I'll get the packing materials." Mirelle enjoyed wrapping the final ketubot for shipment, especially those that had far to travel. As she carefully rolled them into a tube, she loved to picture their journey—posted overland in a courier's satchel, placed in the hold of a merchant ship. And to imagine, at the end of the voyage, the bride and groom's delight, the pride with which they would display the beautiful certificate in their new home.

Stepping into the workroom, Mirelle breathed in the combination of oils, paint, and ink sharply flavoring the air. The shop was filled with lines of tables surrounded by men on stools, hunched in concentration. Most rolled up their shirt sleeves or covered them with splattered work sleeves, tied at the neck. Each man had a favorite set of implements—pens and ink, brushes and paint—which they placed upright in jars or laid in flat trays. Three-quarter windows on either side of the room let in the daylight—a rarity in the ghetto, where most buildings were constructed so close together that the sun couldn't seep inside.

Mirelle deftly bundled the marriage certificates into a neat package. Just as she finished, she felt a hand on her shoulder, and turned.

Papa stood before her, his face solemn. "Come with me."

Mirelle followed him into his office. Reaching the door, she reared back in surprise. Rabbi Fano and her mother filled the space, the rabbi occupying the place of honor behind Papa's desk, Mama hovering in one corner, a shopping basket hanging on her arm.

Papa couldn't shut the door—it was permanently stuck behind a cabinet—but the men who worked close by had moved off, giving them a semblance of privacy.

Papa cleared his throat, looking everywhere but at Mirelle. The rabbi waited a second, watching him, but when he didn't speak, he fixed cold eyes on her face.

"Mirelle," he said slowly. "I hope you are well, child."

"Thank you, Rabbi." She bobbed a small curtsey, inwardly fuming at being called a child.

When he nodded, his gray sidelocks swayed gently against hollowed cheeks. "Simone, would you explain to Mirelle why we're here?"

Papa cleared his throat, eyes on the floor. "Rabbi Fano and I talked last week. He reminded me that you are of an age to think of marriage. When you were a child, no one worried that you might distract the scribes. But the rabbi pointed out the holiness of their work. And that it's forbidden that a woman might . . . You're a very pretty girl, you know."

"No one in the workshop thinks of me like that," Mirelle said, an embarrassed flush rising to her cheeks. "After all, I've known most of them since I was a child."

"But not all," Papa replied. "We've brought in some new apprentices lately—and some younger workers."

She knew; she was the one who had drawn up the contracts for their employ. She gripped her hands in a tight knot. "Yes, but—"

"The Talmud clearly states that young men should not be placed in danger of sinful impulses," the rabbi interrupted, eyes slitting as he looked her up and down. "They need to remain pure, especially when engaged on a holy task. You simply cannot be present here, cannot work in the same rooms as scribes."

"I would think," Mirelle retorted, "that if the scribes were truly committed to their holy task, they would learn to look at me without their minds straying from their paper!"

The rabbi gasped. Papa clapped a hand to his mouth, eyes widening at her impertinence.

"I've never liked you working here!" Mama cut in, looking afraid of what Mirelle might say next. "I always told your father he was ruining your chances of a good marriage. No suitor wants a wife who works in an office, doing a man's job!" She turned to the rabbi. "Do they, Rabbi?"

Mirelle knew what her mother wanted for her: marriage to a rich husband. Her young brother, Jacopo, who apprenticed at the manufactory after school each day, would someday take ownership of the workshop. She realized no woman could expect to inherit this peculiarly religious enterprise. But when she thought of her future, it was always working side by side with her brother. Jacopo was a brilliant craftsman, like his father and grandfather before him, but a slow study in business, with no head for numbers. Not like Mirelle. She wanted to run the workshop alongside him, managing the staff, the accounts, the commissions—work the rabbi could never fully understand.

"Mama, we've talked about this." The words spilled out, almost of their own accord. "I've told you a thousand times that you and Papa will find a husband who won't mind my working here. Someone like Papa, who is glad of my help." She looked pleadingly at her father. "You *are* glad, aren't you, Papa? Think about the error I just caught. How would you have felt when you realized you couldn't pay the men's wages—and didn't know why?"

"Mirelle." The rabbi's voice was ice cold. "You talk like a wayward child. This is man's work—holy work—a world in which you do not belong."

Mirelle drew a deep breath to steady herself. "But you don't understand. The workshop needs me."

"You delude yourself." The rabbi sneered. "A woman should not take a man's role. Besides your unfitness for the task, you deny a deserving man a good living."

Mirelle knew he wouldn't understand that it was more than that. No one else could enter into the heart and soul of the workshop the way she did. But she would have to argue that when the rabbi wasn't there, when Mama wasn't bolstered by his presence. "All right," she acquiesced. "I'll work from home. Papa can bring the accounts there."

But the rabbi shook his head. "Did you not hear? This is a man's place. A man's job. Besides, it's unwomanly for you to fritter away your time this way. You must learn from your mother to become *akeret haBayit*—the mainstay of the home. The Torah commands you to make a Jewish home, keep kosher, take part in such commandments as candle lighting and baking challah for Shabbat. When you intrude yourself in the realm of men, puff yourself up with pride and immodesty, you commit a sin. It's contrary to Torah. Don't you want to command your husband's respect so he will bless you every Friday evening, call you a woman of valor, praise the fruit of your hands?"

"But I *can* do those things!" Mirelle cried. "I can do all that *and* manage the accounts for the workshop."

Rabbi Fano reared back, shock darkening his face. "Simone, this is exactly what I was afraid of. You've made her headstrong. Prideful. Immodest."

Papa frowned. "She's not really—"

"She spends nearly all her time here," Mama declared. "It's wrong. What husband will want her? I've told Simone . . ."

Mirelle glared at her. "Papa understands, even if you don't."

The rabbi gasped in horror. "Honor your mother!" he boomed, finger wagging.

"I do, Rabbi Fano," Mirelle snapped. "I also honor my father."

The rabbi's fist struck Papa's desk, making Mirelle and her parents jump. "Enough! I will not tolerate this nonsense any longer. Mirelle, I have told your father what I will do if you do not obey me. And I will not shirk from my duty!"

Abruptly he stood, moved around the desk, and laid a hand over her head—heavily, forcing her to bend her neck. Mirelle's skin crawled at his touch. He muttered a blessing under his breath and, with a brusque nod at her parents, eased out of the office.

Mirelle watched his retreating back, a squeezing sensation in her chest. She whirled on her father. "What does he mean?"

Her father reached over and pulled her close, kissing the top of her head. "My love, no one could manage the workshop better than you," he said—in a whisper, as if afraid Rabbi Fano would overhear him. "But the rabbi may be right. We must consider the future."

"What threats has he made?" she demanded.

"He will put the workshop under interdict if you continue to work here."

"Interdict? What does that mean?"

Papa's jaw clenched. "It means he won't perform a marriage ceremony if the ketubah comes from our workshop. And he'll convince other rabbis throughout Italy to do the same."

"But that would ruin us!" She couldn't believe the rabbi—a rabbi, of all people!—could be so malicious. "He's bluffing, trying to frighten you. He can't mean it, Papa."

"I'm afraid—"

"He can't mean it," she repeated.

"Don't interrupt your father," Mama admonished, tsk-tsking.

Mirelle turned away, hunching a shoulder.

"He's not bluffing." Papa ignored the tension between wife and daughter. "He has a list of the next couples to marry in the ghetto, said he'll visit them all if you don't comply."

"Mirelle." Her mother spoke softly. "Stop being selfish. Don't you understand what will happen if you insist on remaining here? You'll ruin the workshop, your father's hard work, the scribes, the artists. You'll ruin all our lives. You must see that."

Mirelle felt a pang for the workers. Mama was right—an interdict would ruin them.

Papa's shoulders slumped. "I want you to know that I tried to change Rabbi Fano's mind. I even had David Morpurgo try—you know how persuasive David is. But the rabbi is adamant. You can't work here anymore."

Mama handed Mirelle the market basket. Absently she took it, staring dully at her father's defeated figure.

"I know you think I'm to blame, Mira'la," Mama said briskly. "But this is best—for the business, for the family. Even for you." She waited a moment for Mirelle to reply, and when she didn't, continued. "You'll stay home with me. There are still one or two things I can teach you. Right now, I want you to go to market. The list of what we need is in the basket. Come straight home afterward. There's work for you there."

She reached over to kiss Mirelle's cheek, but Mirelle hunched a shoulder again. Mama hissed between her teeth and left without another word.

Papa shook his head. "I'm sorry, daughter. If only . . ."

Mirelle knew what her father wasn't saying. If she were a boy, she could work with him, help him run the business. For a moment, she hated him, along with her mother and the rabbi. But looking into his woebegone face, she recognized that he was trapped by the traditions of his life and work. A lump lodged in her throat. In a moment, she'd burst into tears.

No, she wouldn't. She refused to break down, at least not there. She walked stiffly away, the straw container banging against her leg. She took some comfort from Narducci's sympathetic glance as she passed his workbench, but her mood plunged again as she noticed how many of the men averted their eyes.

Out on the stoop, she reached instinctively to touch the blue-and-green enamel mezuzah attached to the front doorpost, which contained a parchment inscribed with the Shema: "Hear, oh Israel, the Lord our God, the Lord is One." She hesitated for a long, angry moment, then kissed her fingertips and stalked off.

# 2

Tall buildings loomed on either side of the street. Mirelle was used to the narrow space, but today the air seemed more fetid than usual, the close-packed homes more menacing. The buildings— many built centuries before and precariously expanded upward— were crumbling at their foundations. Apartments exuded the smells of a hundred cooking pots, paint curling under the sweat and filth of packed living.

The sounds of boys chanting their lessons—her twelve-year old brother, Jacopo, among them—rose from the tall schoolhouse. Her brother had described how the boys crowded onto splintering benches and spilled into the hallways to find room to study, how they squirmed over their books while the headmaster moved among them, swishing his cane like a whip. Mirelle threw the building a black look, her mind full of the rabbi's threats. *Interfering fool.*

Toddlers played in the streets, ignoring the refuse running down the center sewer. Housewives stopped to gossip, straw baskets crushed against their sides. The market was bustling, with vibrant oranges and lemons piled into pyramids, cut citrus samples sharp in the spring air, bundled chard and spinach, flowery clusters of cauliflower and broccoli, and long spears of artichokes piled high. Crusty breads, fruit-filled flans, and boxes of biscotti wafted enticing odors. But today all Mirelle felt were the centuries of dirt and sweat trapped inside the enclosed ghetto. The walls pressed in on her, making it difficult to breathe. On impulse, she decided to visit a different market—the one outside the gates, where she could feel sea breeze and sunlight on her face.

During daylight hours, the ornate, wrought-iron gates at the ghetto entrance were flung wide. Because her friend Dolce often designated them as a meeting spot, Mirelle knew their every nook and curve. As she'd wait, she'd run her fingers over the peeling patterns, twisting and curling. From dawn until nightfall, ghetto residents moved freely through the stone archway into the city of Ancona. As the sun dipped behind the horizon, however, city guards slammed the gates shut and chained a heavy padlock to the bars. The clang of the closing gates always raised the hair on the back of Mirelle's neck.

It affected her generally carefree brother even more. Jacopo often railed against being imprisoned inside the ghetto. "Just once, I want to see what the sea looks like under the stars," he'd said one night as they stood outside, straining to see more than a few inches of night sky. "Just once, I'd like to walk freely out of the gate and not have someone stare at me because I'm Jewish."

Something had stirred in her chest as he spoke. She felt the same when a packaged ketubah left the workshop to travel to a distant shore. A whole world existed outside the ghetto. If only they could both walk out of the gates freely!

But they were trapped. Day or night, whenever the Jews left their homes, they were required by law to don the yellow hat and armband that branded them as different. For as long as she could remember, Mirelle had covered her brown locks with a yellow kerchief before walking in the streets. She always wrinkled her nose in the mirror as she adjusted the badge of her faith. *They make us wear yellow because it is the color of urine*, she'd think distastefully. *And of cowardice.*

Her brother might feel caught inside the enclosure of the locked ghetto gates, but she felt doubly trapped—as a Jew and as a woman.

Catching sight of the open gateway, she tossed her head high and walked through. The street led straight to the quay, where the Gentiles gathered to sell their produce. She would have to buy kosher meat and bread on her way home, but at least she could buy fresh fruit and vegetables and eggs here.

As she neared the water, she took a deep breath. Early spring air mixed with the salty tang of the sea. The piercing cry of gulls and the shouts of men working on the docks drifted up. The quay was alive with the bustle of sailors and housewives, beautiful, glass-fronted shops, and busy coffeehouses.

Mirelle made her way toward the market stalls. She'd just started to select some brown eggs from a smiling woman when a man rudely elbowed past her.

"Francesca Marotti!" he cried. "A word!"

"Good morning, Signor Russo." Signora Marotti's fingers, gripping the wooden cross at her neck, belied her calm tone. "I'll attend you after I wait on this customer."

Signor Russo, a rough-looking man with a sour expression, glared at Mirelle, cold eyes lingering on her kerchief and armband. He sneered. "She can wait."

Mirelle felt a protest rising but closed her lips tightly against the rush of words. Anything she said would just sharpen his hatred. She was nothing more than dirt beneath his feet, all because she was a Jewess and he a Catholic.

Even the market woman, noticing the man's scornful glance at Mirelle's Jewish insignia, lost her kind smile. "You'll have to wait," she said to Mirelle, without a trace of apology in her voice. "What is it, Signor Russo?"

"Where is your husband, Signora Marotti? I've been looking for him for three days."

The woman squared her shoulders. "Where should he be but at home, tending to our acres?"

"Do you think me an idiot?" the man spat. "I've been there already. He's not home."

"You're mistaken," Signora Marotti replied. "He promised me—"

"You're a fool." Signor Russo laughed humorlessly. "I trusted his promises, and where did they get me? He owes me, Signora. He owes half of Ancona, I hear, but I'm the one he'll pay."

"Talk to him." The woman's hand clutched her crucifix, knuckles turning white. "I can't help you. Why are you bothering me and my customers?"

"Your customers?" Signor Russo looked Mirelle over, disgust writ large on his face.

Once again, Mirelle bit back her words.

"I'll take whatever money you've earned this morning, Signora. And I'll be back later today to collect the rest. As part payment of what's due me."

Signora Marotti gasped in anger. "You'd rob an innocent woman— pregnant besides"—Mirelle's eyes went to the woman's slightly protruding midriff—"and her young daughter?"

"I'll have what I'm owed. Let it be a lesson to you."

He extended a hand, and Mirelle watched as the woman slowly reached into her apron to retrieve the few soldi she'd earned that morning.

"And you," Signor Russo said, pocketing the money and turning on Mirelle. "Give me the money you were going to pay for the eggs."

Mirelle thought fast. "I already paid her."

"That's right, she did," Signora Marotti agreed.

Their eyes met for a second, then both glanced away.

"Pah! This is all you've made this morning? Pitiful. I'll be back this evening—and you'd better be here. And tell your husband that he has until the end of the week to finish paying off his debt—or else." He stomped off.

The women watched his retreating back. When he'd turned a

corner, Mirelle counted out the coins for the eggs. "I'll take some artichokes, too," she said, though she hadn't planned to.

Signora Marotti nodded, her face pale. She slipped the coins into the neck of her blouse. "Thank you," she whispered.

*Maybe she doesn't have to wear yellow, but she's as trapped as I am*, Mirelle thought as she made her way back to the ghetto. *Jew or Gentile, we women must do as we're told.*

# 3

# MARCH 27, 1796
# NICE, FRANCE

Daniel had never been so hungry.

He daydreamed about his mother's Friday night dinners: chicken and fried potatoes, beef stew with dumplings, grilled fish with olives and onions. Like all Jews, he was no stranger to hunger. Every year on Yom Kippur, the Day of Atonement, he and his family fasted from sundown to sundown, and he remembered how a day's missed meals made his stomach ache. But you didn't have to be Jewish to know hunger. During the Revolution and Terror, hands on Paris streets had stretched out, begging for food. His family had survived only because, even in the hard times, Mama had made magic out of the sparest of ingredients, turning chicken bones into savory soup and bean husks into rich stews.

But this was nothing like Yom Kippur, when he only had to wait for the setting sun and three stars. Now he was just another lowly soldier in France's Army of Italy, and every fiber of his body protested this enforced starvation.

He looked down the line of small white tents that marked the boundary between the senior officers and the men they commanded. Enlisted men lay listless on their bedrolls. Trails of smoke curled upward from useless cooking fires. An orderly folded clothes into neat stacks on a nearby boulder, peeling them off a laundry line heavy with long under-wear and graying shirts. The camp stunk of horse dung, smoke, and the refuse of thousands of men. Watching the mess sergeant turn over his stew pots, Daniel felt the now-familiar grip of hunger tighten in his gut.

Cries of protest about lost food carts spread through the camp.

Daniel didn't join the outcry. Instead, he rummaged through his kitbag, digging deep for a clasp knife and trencher, then walked past the tents to the open field behind them, looking for Sebastian. Sebastian, who'd served in the wilds of America—at thirty-three, the oldest soldier among them—knew how to forage for food.

Daniel squelched through mud that seeped through the holes in his boots until he found the broad-shouldered man digging in the dirt, tossing early dandelions into a bucket.

"We'll make a soup of these," he told Daniel. "Better than nothing."

Daniel wasn't so sure—the last time he'd eaten dandelion stew, he'd retched up the green mess—but he bent to help. As he dug, his knife clogging with mud, he thought of his family's warm kitchen and the smell of freshly baked bread wafting up from the bakery downstairs. Suddenly, he remembered when Marc Baker had nearly been lynched in the early days of the revolution. An angry mob had dragged Marc into the street, clamoring to hang the baker for the imagined crime of hoarding bread.

"Look how this Jew fattens upon your misery!" a wild-eyed Jacobin had cried. Even now, Daniel quaked to recall how the epithet "Jew" had sounded so damning to the crowd.

He shook himself. It was long past. As the Terror wore on, rage against the Jews had lessened. Today, as citizens of France—citizens for the first time ever in any European country—they were granted the same rights, duties, and protection as any other Frenchman. This newfound citizenship was what had prompted Daniel to volunteer for the army at the age of seventeen, before he was liable for the draft. But he knew that patriotism wasn't really why he'd enlisted.

"Good enough," Sebastian said, hefting his full bucket. "Have I ever told you how those American redskins taught us to cook greens and berries? After the skirmish at Jumonville Glen, those of us left alive fled from the British. No time to hunt—all we had in our kit bags was some hardtack." He laughed. "If the savages hadn't taught us to scavenge, we'd have starved for certain."

Daniel let Sebastian's story wash over him as he shook off his painful memories and hauled their modest harvest back to camp.

Sebastian clapped a hand on his shoulder as they neared the tents. "I can always count on you," he said. "You're quiet, but always there when you're needed."

Daniel shrugged, but the praise warmed him.

Still grumbling over the lost food carts, the soldiers boiled a kettle of the dandelion stems and roots over the campfire. The dense, green smell made Daniel queasy, but he forced down a cupful anyway. The slimy mess slipped reluctantly down his throat; still, the act of chewing and swallowing eased the empty feeling inside him.

He settled back after eating, his seat a rough, cold circle of grass, his spine propped against a heavy boulder. *Not the soldier's life I thought I'd be living*, he reflected. Silly as it was, he'd imagined himself the hero of hard-won battles, medals of valor pinned to his chest. He'd come home and Mama, Papa, even his devout brother Salomon, would heap praises on him. Salomon would compare him to the great warriors of Jewish history: Joshua, King David, the Maccabees. His neighbors in the Jewish Quarter of Le Marais would cheer, and the matchmakers would suggest the richest, prettiest girls, the ones fit for a hero's bride.

But none of that had happened, not yet.

"So I've seen him," said a familiar voice.

Daniel looked up at his childhood friend, Christophe, a cavalryman from III Corps. "You did? What's he like?"

The other men gathered around. Christophe was tall, broad-shouldered, and fair, with tightly clipped hair the color of straw and a thin, carefully groomed moustache. Daniel, in contrast, was shorter and thinner, his skin olive-hued, his hair an untidy mass of brown curls. His dark eyes were more serious than his friend's brilliant green ones, his mouth slower to smile, and he preferred to keep his face clean-shaven. He and Christophe had apprenticed together at the age of nine at Lefevre Printers in Paris, owned and managed by Christophe's uncle Alain. Christophe's obsessively Catholic mother, Odette, had encouraged her son to despise all Jews—Daniel included. But during eight long years of apprenticeship, the two had become unlikely friends, mastering the intricacies of the printshop together— until they'd decided to enlist.

"Who?" Sebastian asked now. "You mean the new general?"

Christophe nodded. "I was on guard duty," he said, sprawling on the ground next to Daniel. "Outside the generals' tent."

They were talking about the new commander, just arrived to lead France's Army of Italy, a scrawny fellow with a beaky nose.

"The other generals didn't think much of the newcomer," Christophe said now. "You should have heard them grumble."

"Who was there?" Sebastian asked.

"Augereau, Laharpe, Masséna, and Sérurier."

Daniel nodded. These four were well known—and disliked—by the men. All battle veterans, all bred in the old king's service. Many of the general staff were still loyal to the royal family, and Daniel supposed it wasn't easy to just replace them. But it still didn't seem right.

"They were saying how much they held this upstart in contempt." Christophe gestured grandly with both hands. "How he was born on some island outside France and barely blooded. Someone claimed the only reason he got the post was because he married Director Barras's mistress."

"I've heard that, too," Pierre said, reaching into the empty pot for any food stuck to the sides. "Both Barras and his lady friend were *aristos*, you know. Barras wanted to be rid of her. I hear she's a tasty enough piece. But old. With two grown children, no less!"

"I was standing by the flap of the tent," Christophe continued. "He strode right by me and stood before the old generals. They refused to budge, wouldn't even remove their hats."

"Damn rude," said Sebastian. "Respect the rank, even if you don't respect the man."

Christophe looked amused. "The general went up, his small, simple bonnet tucked under his arm, and stared each one in the eye. Without a word, he forced them to introduce themselves and remove their great plumed hats. Then he put his own hat on his head and pelted them with questions. Where was each of the divisions? How much manpower did they have? What condition were the munitions in? What was the condition of the men?"

"He asked about us?" Daniel was surprised. Despite his slight army experience, he already knew generals rarely interested themselves in the welfare of the troops.

"And our morale. Were we in good spirits? Were we ready for the campaign?"

"The campaign! Ha!" Sebastian spat into the fire. "We've been stuck here for months. I don't see how some bantam cock of a general can change that."

"He thinks he can," Christophe said. "He told the generals that we would be marching on the enemy in four days."

Sebastian spat again, this time onto a rock near the fire.

Marching on the enemy in four days? What would that be like? Deep down, Daniel knew he'd only enlisted to escape the tedium of the printshop. In line at the National Guard office, he and Christophe had laughingly imagined their army service as a grand adventure. Daniel's stomach grumbled again, this time with a hint of fear. Would the adventure feel so grand when facing live bullets and cannonballs?

"That's just posturing," Sebastian said. "When you've been in the army as long as I have, boys, you'll learn not to trust new brooms that claim they're going to sweep clean. They only end up hanging in the corner."

"I don't know," Christophe mused, eyes intent on the fire. "This one seems different."

Daniel thought about that for a moment. Christophe, like his uncle, had a canny sense of people. He was rarely wrong.

The men's talk subsided. Sebastian brought out his pipe and filled it with a tiny bit of the tobacco his wife sent every month. Daniel settled back on the grass.

Without warning, one of the aides de camp appeared before them. "Formation in five minutes," he barked.

"What's going on, sir?" Sebastian asked, rising and doffing his tall shako cap. Like many of the men, he'd pinned the tricolor rosette of the Revolution next to his upturned brim.

"Get into formation and you'll find out." The aide de camp moved briskly onward.

Christophe carelessly waved his hand and marched over to his own unit. Not for him the slog of an artillery company. Daniel smiled, remembering how his friend had convinced the recruitment officer to assign him to the cavalry. If Christophe was going to be a soldier, he'd damn well be a dashing one.

Daniel settled in line next to Pierre, two men back from Sebastian. When the general inspected his men, he would find them a tattered, barely booted, dirty bunch, famished for food and hungry for some kind of action.

The general stood before the men, legs spread wide. He wore a simple jacket distinguished only by the gold leaf embroidery reserved for generals. He'd left his collar open.

Disappointment twisted Daniel's stomach. *Someone in Paris must think the Italian campaign is a joke.*

But when the general spoke, he seemed to grow two feet. His voice boomed out over the ranks. "You are naked, you are underfed. The government owes you much, yet can give you nothing. Your patience in supporting deprivation, your bravery in facing every danger, makes you the pride of France. You have neither shoes, nor clothes, nor bread, and our storehouses are empty. Enemies who boast that they will crush our young Republic abound on every side. I will lead you to the most fertile plains in the world, and there you will find honor, glory, and riches."

He turned and walked away, the other officers trailing behind him. A buzz of excitement rustled through the camp. No one had ever spoken to them like this before.

Then the general swiveled around. "Finally!" he shouted, facing the men again. "Officers, enlisted men receive their portion first!"

Daniel's pulse raced as the food carts rattled up. A cheer rose from the troops, and rumors flew through the ranks like wildfire. It seemed the new general had searched out the wagons before he arrived at camp and made sure the soldiers driving them knew where to go. There was enough food, the men exulted, to last at least a week.

"Small portions, men," cried another officer, to boos and catcalls. He turned to the general. "Too much food after so many days' privation will make them sick, sir."

"Bread and cheese tonight, meat tomorrow!" the general ordered.

Daniel scrambled into line, eager to grab his small loaf of bread and cheese. After receiving his portion, he closed his eyes and muttered the prayer for bread, inhaling its fresh yeasty smell, along with the cheese's sharp, pungent tang. Then he twisted off the crusty end and crammed it in his mouth. Nothing had ever tasted so good.

"Looks like your friend Christophe was right." Pierre poked Daniel in the side, spraying crumbs as he spoke. "Maybe he's different after all, this General Bonaparte!"

# 4

# MARCH 28
# ANCONA, ITALY

Mirelle woke to the sound of her mother's footsteps. Mama flung the heavy curtains open and a sliver of light teased Mirelle's eyes.

"Mmmpf," she muttered, squeezing her eyes shut. What was the point of getting up, after all? Her hand moved over her quilted coverlet, tracing the swirls of embroidery, fingers snagging the loose threads.

Her mother's fingers closed over hers. "You'll tear it," she scolded. "And it's time to start the day."

Mirelle pushed her feet under the covers and stretched, eyes still stubbornly closed.

Mama reached down and turned back one corner of the heavy quilt. Groaning, Mirelle slipped from bed, her cotton nightgown dropping about her ankles. Ignoring her mother's pointed glance at her slippers, she moved barefoot across the wooden planks, grasped the pitcher on her dresser, and poured some water into the ewer beside it. She paddled the tips of her fingers in the water, then plunged her hands in and splashed her face. Looking at the mirror on her dresser, her face still flushed with sleep, she grimaced at her chestnut brown hair and reached for a comb to untangle the long curls.

*So Mama thinks marriage is all I'm good for? What would a suitor think?* She stared at her reflection. High cheekbones; a small, pointed nose; delicate lips. She pursed them in the glass, pondering what Papa would have been offered for her in Biblical times. Two camels and a goat? Making a face, she turned from the mirror and reached for her pale blue walking dress and matching pelisse. *It brings out the pink in your cheeks*, Dolce had told her once.

Once dressed, she went downstairs. Papa was preparing to leave for work. He placed long fingers on her shoulders, his worried eyes scanning her face. "I suggested to Mama that you should visit Dolce this afternoon. You'll like that, won't you?"

Mirelle nodded, forcing a smile, studying her own hands. She had inherited his fingers, but little else. Papa was tall, balding, and looked at the world through a pair of pince-nez. Mirelle had often watched him at work, his nose nearly touching the parchment as he carefully applied ink or paint.

Papa sighed, then looked around, impatient. "Your brother is late, as always."

Twelve-year-old Jacopo darted into the room. He was dressed in his brown school uniform, his black hair mussed like he'd just risen from bed, schoolbooks strapped together and dangling over one shoulder.

He winked at Mirelle. "I'll wager you and Dolce will spend the afternoon plotting to entrap worthy young men," he teased. "Who's the unlucky—er, lucky—man going to be, Mira?"

"Hush," their mother chided. "Your father and I will find your sister a suitable groom."

"Just think, it could be a man you've never met." Jacopo feigned an exaggerated shudder. "He could be fat like a frog, or speak with a lisp, or chew with his mouth open." He laughed aloud, then grew serious. "Don't think anyone will make *me* wed a girl I've never seen."

"Who would want to marry you, anyway?" Mirelle retorted.

"Me? The girls will fight over me." Jacopo spread his arms dramatically. "I'm heir to the famous d'Ancona ketubah workshop, which creates the most exquisite wedding contracts in all of Jewish Europe. *And* I'm a Torah scholar of distinction." Jacopo laughed. "Isn't that right, Mama?"

Mama glanced at Mirelle's clouded eyes and shot Jacopo a dark look, but said nothing.

"You flatter yourself," Mirelle said. "And you're wasting Papa's time." She stood on tiptoe to kiss her father's cheek, then turned and cuffed her brother's shoulder. "Have a good day, Papa. You behave yourself, *marmocchio*."

"Mirelle!" Mama shook her head. "Don't call your brother a brat."

"Come on, Jacopo," Papa said, already halfway out the door. "We're late."

Jacopo rolled his eyes at his sister. She looked away, smiling wryly despite herself.

After helping Mama with the morning chores, Mirelle busied herself with her music, practicing scales in their small drawing room where the family's pianoforte sat in a corner near the window. Mirelle loved listening to good music, discerning the intricate patterns of melody. She especially enjoyed when Dolce performed, for her friend was magnificent on both pianoforte and harp. Sometimes, though, Mirelle grew jealous of her friend's musical talent. Maybe now, she thought, with so much extra time, she might improve. Mama insisted that music was an accomplishment every young woman should possess. Mastering the keyboard was one way to keep her happy.

But as Mirelle played, her fingers kept sliding from the keys, her glance wandering out the window to the busy side street. The moment she heard the door slam, she jumped up and opened the piano bench to grab the exercise book secreted there.

Turning the pages of the book, she realized with a sharp pang that she had nearly completed the last of the equations Professor Ricci had left her.

Three years ago, Mirelle was visiting Dolce when Signor Morpurgo, her father, had informed her he'd paid a princely fee for a mathematics tutor.

"Mathematics!" Dolce had exclaimed, wrinkling her nose. "Why mathematics, of all absurdities?"

"I shouldn't have to explain," Signor Morpurgo had said brusquely. "You're my only child, heir to my businesses."

"Yes, but you don't expect me to *manage* them, do you? Isn't that my husband's job?"

"Of course." Signor Morpurgo laughed. "But you should understand the rudiments, sweetling. You know that I don't trust anyone, not completely. I'll select a husband for you with a good business head, but the wise woman—and I know you to be wise in all things, pet—should know just enough to make sure nothing goes awry."

Flattered by her father's praise, Dolce agreed to mathematics lessons. But she chafed under the rigors of the problems demanded of her. One day, she thrust the pages toward Mirelle, complaining, "No one could figure this out."

Mirelle found that the equations that stumped her friend came naturally to her, solutions arranging themselves in neat columns and tallies in her mind. The tutor—a professor who primarily taught struggling university students—quickly apprehended that someone else was solving Dolce's problems. Mirelle found his eyes upon her one day as she sat in a dark corner of the room, drinking in his lessons like a doe at a pond, absorbing every word. From then on, it became his delight to challenge her with more and more difficult calculations while Dolce looked on with a derisive smile.

After two years, Dolce, hiding her profound relief, bid her tutor a final farewell. Before he took his leave, he presented Mirelle with a thick book of exercises. "I hope you find these problems worthy of your attention, signorina," he said, bowing before her, a narrow hand pressing his heart. "You will enjoy solving them. So few of us share a deeper appreciation of the elegance and magic of numbers. And it is as rare as buried treasure to find a woman with a head for them."

*The magic of numbers.* The phrase stayed with Mirelle long after the professor had pocketed his wages and left Ancona. She had never heard something so plain, so artless, described in such a way. Numbers, magical? But the more she thought of it—the more time she spent with her nose in the book, scribbling out solutions—the more enchanted she became with the notion.

Something about numbers mesmerized her, made the world fade away. The bustle of the ketubah workshop, the messiness of the artists' desks, the fanciful decoration and sketch work she had no gift for were replaced by a world that seemed logical and fixed, firm around the edges. Opening the exercise book now, Mirelle told herself that she could always count on numbers. More than people, certainly. Math had a clear problem, a strategy, a solution. People? They were a mystery she couldn't always solve.

She seated herself in the window alcove to take advantage of the morning light and watched as her mother, straw basket tucked under her arm, halted in the middle of the road to greet some neighbors. Mirelle stared at the women, wondering if she might find the key to what puzzled her if she studied them long enough. They stood in a cluster, shadowed by the tall ghetto buildings, thick walls blocking the sun. The expression on her mother's full face made Mirelle shake her head. How could she be so happy? And why did the impossibly tedious daily rounds satisfy her—satisfy every other woman of the ghetto? She noticed Anna, their servant, leaning out of a window above her, sleeves turned up to her elbows, pinning laundry to the clothesline that stretched across the narrow street. She watched, wondering if Anna had ever wanted more from life than an endless round of cleaning and cooking. Where was the magic in that?

Around noon, Mirelle left the house and turned left into Via Astagna, the only true avenue in the ghetto. The Jews of Ancona had eked out a living up and down Via Astagna since the 1550s, when Pope Paul IV forced them to live on a single street behind closed gates. The street originated near the mouth of Ancona harbor and traversed the hillsides, cutting through the packed alleyways and half-paved culs-de-sac housing the overflow of Jewish families. Their population had grown, but the area where they were allowed to live had not.

Mirelle knew she was luckier than most ghetto dwellers. Her father's income from the workshop had provided her family a better home than many of their neighbors. But if she were a Christian, she'd live in a larger house still, filled with air and light, next to a park or in the mountains overlooking the harbor.

She found it difficult to reconcile her comfortable life with the nightly imprisonment to which she and her neighbors were subjected. Rabbi Fano often spoke of the covenant the Jews had with God, how the Almighty made them the chosen people out of all the nations. But why, then, she wondered, were they ridiculed, forced to wear ugly trappings, locked in at night?

Dolce's family lived in the first building inside the ghetto gates, and as Mirelle walked past the open stone archway, her mind drifted again, wondering what it would be like to walk where she wished at any hour, without Jewish insignia, like anyone else. To board one of the ships now at the harbor and set sail to those exotic addresses to which messengers carried her father's ketubot: the steppes of Russia, the sophisticated capitals of London and Vienna, the wilds of the New World.

She shrugged, dismissing her thoughts. What good would come of such dreams? Life in the ghetto was all she had ever known. And soon she would marry the man her parents chose and find a new home on these same streets, trapped within these crowded city blocks for the rest of her life.

*Not like Dolce*, she thought. *Dolce was born with the gift of making her own choices.*

The girls had been friends since they were five years old. Dolce's father was a substantial stockholder in Simone d'Ancona's business, and her mother, Sarella, had arranged for the girls to play together. Mirelle was nothing like the bold, vivacious girl she had met that day. Flamboyant as a peacock, Dolce's Austrian roots showed in her alabaster skin, glorious golden curls, and startling blue eyes, as well as the vivid flush that lit her cheeks when she was excited.

Dolce always laughed away questions about her looks. "My aunt was blond; so was her mother, and many of my cousins," she'd say. "All with blue eyes. Probably some Austrian nobleman found his way into my family tree."

Once, Mirelle had repeated Dolce's theory about her porcelain doll looks to her mother.

Mama set her lips in a thin line. "She talks too freely," she scolded.

Mirelle suspected that Mama only agreed to the girls' friendship because of David Morpurgo's continued investment in the workshop.

"Thinks her wealth allows her such liberties," Mama continued. "A girl her age, from a prominent household, shouldn't entertain such thoughts in decent conversation. We certainly raised you better than that."

But Dolce's outrageousness was exactly what Mirelle loved about her. Being with her gave Mirelle a sense of freedom and adventure, a liveliness lacking elsewhere in the ghetto. She would not trade

Dolce's friendship for a score of dull, modest girls, no matter what Mama wished.

Mirelle pulled the bell chain and a footman opened the door. The Morpurgo villa, where Dolce lived with her widowed father, was four times larger than any other Jewish home in Ancona, filled with beautiful paintings and statuary, floors and fireplaces of pink marble, and chandeliers that twinkled with crystal raindrops and took one of their many servants an entire day to dust.

The footman said Dolce was still in her bedroom. Mirelle climbed up a grand stairway and entered her friend's spacious room.

Dolce was lounging on a daybed, wearing a plum-colored silk bed jacket, reading a leather-bound volume.

"Not dressed yet?" Mirelle leaned over to kiss her friend on the cheek.

"Mirelle! Thank goodness you've come." Dolce dropped the tome on the floor. "I was longing for something to divert me from this dull book."

"Dull?" Mirelle seated herself on a low chair. "My own life's suddenly turned horribly dull."

Dolce's eyebrows rose. "What do you mean?"

"Rabbi Fano forbade me to work with Papa, and Mama agrees. Do you believe it?"

Dolce leaned back, resting her blond head against a bank of silk cushions. "Oh, Mira. To be honest, I never liked you working in that workshop. All those dusty desks, and that awful, cramped office, and the smell . . ." She shuddered delicately. "Your mother is right about that, at least. No man wants a woman like that as a bride."

"A woman like what?"

Dolce gave her a long, level look. "You know what I mean. Covered with ink and buried in numbers. Surrounded by other men all day long. People don't think it's decent."

Mirelle bristled. "You'll inherit your father's fortune, won't you? What's the difference?"

Dolce sighed. "The difference? I don't visit his office, don't tend to the details of his business concerns. I'm not friendly with the help. And I don't ever plan to be. My husband will take charge of my fortune when I marry, or I'll hire a manager. But you? You want to *be* the manager."

"So what? I'm better than any manager Papa could hire. And I care a lot more, too."

"Listen to yourself! You sound ridiculous. I realize you're angry, but the way I see it, the rabbi's done you a good turn."

Mirelle leapt to her feet. "You're like every other woman in the ghetto."

Dolce waved her back down. "Ha! Hardly. But you, you think that a woman working, when she has the choice not to, is acceptable. No one else thinks so. So it can't be right. Look. Papa promised to hire a dancing master. Take lessons with me. In a few weeks, we'll convince him to throw us a ball and we'll turn the heads of every young man in Ancona."

"Is that what I'm going to spend all day doing? Dancing?"

"Mira." Dolce sighed. "I know how you feel—really, I do. But it won't last. You'll fall in love and forget all about the workshop. You know what you need? You don't need to work, my dear. You need a *man*."

Mirelle rolled her eyes. "My mother plans to take care of that. She told Jacopo this morning that she and my father would find me the right husband."

"No, no, no." Dolce waggled a jeweled finger, rings sparkling in the afternoon sunlight. "Your mother? She'd find you someone stolid. Dreadful. Like Baruch, Menachem Goldsmith's firstborn, the most boring man in town. No, you need someone handsome. Dashing. With a hint of *adventure*. Haven't you always said you want more adventure in your life? We'll find him together."

Mirelle couldn't help laughing. "Now *you* sound ridiculous. Someone dashing? For me?"

"Of course someone dashing. You're prettier than you think, you know."

Mirelle, smiling at the compliment, knew no one would look twice at her when her friend was in the room. Dolce had been courted almost from the cradle. Jewish men desirous of a rich, beautiful wife—rabbis' sons and merchants, community leaders from Ancona and other cities—had lined up at her door, danced with her at balls, took her riding. She'd spurned them all. *Of course*, Mirelle thought, *Dolce has plenty of dashing suitors. But Mama and Papa want me to marry someone wealthy.*

Her parents often told her they hoped she would marry a man whose marriage settlement would allow her father to buy the ketubah manufactory outright. Since Dolce's father was their primary investor, this wasn't something Mirelle could admit aloud. But Dolce was smart enough to intuit the truth.

"You know," Dolce spoke up, interrupting her thoughts, "if you object to *dashing* so much, why don't you tell me what you *do* want? This man you'd like to marry. What's he like?"

"The man I'd *like* to marry?" Mirelle replied.

Dolce leaned forward, fixing her brilliant blue gaze on Mirelle's face. "Tell me."

Mirelle closed her eyes. She thought of her sweet father—so quick to surrender to the rabbi's demands. "If I could choose—and I know I can't—I'd want a man who knows his own mind, who acts, who doesn't care if people disapprove of him—not a scholar, not even a merchant." Her lips curled into a smile. "And handsome, of course."

Dolce chuckled. "He sounds marvelous. Be careful I don't steal him away from you."

Mirelle's lips twisted. "But most important, he should adore *me*, make *me* his reason for living. Put me first."

*Listen to me*, she thought, suddenly embarrassed. *What a thing to say out loud.*

"But that goes without saying!" Dolce exclaimed. "Oh, Mira. You'll find him—or he'll find you—and it will fix everything! You'll see."

*Will it fix everything?* Mirelle wondered. Could a mystery man—a handsome, confident suitor—really be the answer to her troubles? She wanted to believe it. Things always seemed to work out for Dolce; the universe bent to her will. But it never quite seemed to do the same for Mirelle. Maybe she would meet her perfect man, only to have Dolce snap him up. Maybe she would never meet him at all.

And maybe, she reflected, he didn't exist. Which meant the only way to deal with her problems was to solve them herself.

# 5

# April 4
# Ancona

"You have everything?" Francesca Marotti asked, placing a hand on the slight rise of her stomach. "You're sure, *caro mio*?"

"How could I not be?" grumbled her husband, Emilio, as he slung the last bundle onto the donkey cart. "You've asked me the same question twenty times." He tied rope around the bundles.

To Francesca's dismay, he'd backed the cart right up next to the outdoor altar to the Madonna, with no regard for the Lady's sanctity. But she knew better than to protest.

Barbara emerged from the henhouse, her skirt and black hair a mess of hay. Francesca bit her tongue at her daughter's beet-red face and disheveled appearance, but Emilio just grinned. The girl flung her arms about his neck, hugging him tightly. "What will you bring me, Papa?" she wheedled. "I want some Turkish delight and a string of glass beads from Venice. Promise me?"

"Don't tease your father," Francesca said, pulling her daughter back by the arm. "Nine is too old to be demanding sweets. And couldn't you have stayed tidy long enough to say a proper good-bye? He may be gone for two years or more."

Barbara groaned, rolling her eyes. "Papa, why can't you take me with you?"

Her father laughed, picking some of the hay from her hair. "I wish I could too, *bambina*. But a merchant vessel is no place for a young lady."

"She's no young lady." Francesca sniffed. "Don't encourage her."

Emilio put a hand on Francesca's stomach. "I want a boy this time," he told her, staring straight into her eyes. "I could take a boy with me."

Francesca saw her daughter's face droop. "I'm glad Barbara is staying here." She reached a hand out to the girl. "I'd miss her if she left."

Barbara evaded her touch and turned to hug her father a second time. "Turkish delight," she whispered loudly. "And Venetian beads. Yes, Papa?"

His arms wrapped around her and he looked over her shoulder, winking at his wife, who smiled despite herself. "And what should I bring for your *mammina*?" he murmured into Barbara's hair. "And for the new *bambino*?"

Barbara pulled away, glaring at her mother's midsection. "The baby won't want anything until it's older. And Mama will be happy with anything you bring."

"Mama will be happy just to have you back home again, safe and sound," Francesca said, stroking the arm of her husband's new uniform. The short blue serge jacket sat snugly on his broad shoulders, a dashing red sash cut across the blousy white shirt. He looked proud and tall in his striped quarter-length pants, his dark hair swept under his cap, his broad, swarthy face split in a rare grin. Just as handsome as on their wedding day. She remembered kneeling in the cathedral, full of gratitude that he had selected her—*her*—out of all the girls in Ancona. She'd trembled as he looked her over, the expression in his black eyes unreadable. She hoped not to be found wanting, but the mysteries of the wedding bed made her quake. Surely he would be gentle, she'd thought. And he had been, that first night, as tender as a frisky puppy, despite all the grappa he'd downed at the feast.

Unfortunately, his gentleness hadn't lasted beyond their first month of marriage.

"If only you didn't have to go." She wished the words unsaid the moment they escaped her mouth.

"This, again?" Emilio shook his head, frowning. "Just as I'm about to leave?"

"I'll miss you, that's all."

Francesca knew they had no choice. Russo had finally tracked Emilio down and threatened to break his fingers if he didn't pay him back. It had taken every penny secretly stored in the flour bin to satisfy him. And there were other debts, still unpaid.

"It's not like two years is forever," Emilio said, hugging his daughter again. "I'll earn enough in the merchant marine to take care of the debts and buy us a shop on the quay. No more stinking chickens or drooping fig trees or sunflowers wilting in the sun."

Francesca shut her eyes. Emilio's dream had always been to own a shop of his own. Just like the one his father had when he was a child, filled with fantastical objects of glass and copper and wood. Francesca remembered visiting it when she was young, a wonderland of cups and vases and glass animals all glinting in the beams that shone through the large plate window. But Emilio's father had borrowed money to pay for his own gambling debts, and had put the store up as collateral. He'd lost everything to Jewish moneylenders when Emilio was seventeen. Emilio's brothers and sisters had been parceled out to relatives far from Ancona like so many bundles, while she and Emilio, already married, had been forced to live off her meager inheritance.

Her husband despised farming, even though the patch of land at the foot of Monte Guasco, just outside Ancona, was the best part of her dowry. They kept chickens, selling their eggs, and grew sunflowers, figs, and whatever root vegetables they could raise to sustain themselves through the winter. But Emilio resented every moment he had to scratch in the sandy soil, blaming the Jews for the loss of his family's home and business.

Two years! Could she bear it? Francesca watched Emilio plod away, praying he'd be a happier man when he finally returned.

# 6

# MAY 2
# ANCONA

Mirelle's family always celebrated her father's birthday with a party at the workshop. Each year, the men's families, along with the Morpurgo family and other friends and neighbors, were bidden to an after-hours feast. Mama and Anna spent days in the kitchen, preparing goose sausage minced into a rich risotto, dredging artichokes with flour and frying them to a luscious crispness, and making a savory casserole of spinach, raisins, and pine nuts. The dessert was a rich fig pudding, Papa's favorite. Mama made marzipan treats for the children, too, cleverly shaped like the flowers and animals that adorned the ketubot.

This year, Mirelle had been pressed into kitchen duty, rolling and cutting. Her arms ached from shaking a burlap bag of pine cones to release the stubborn nuts; the sweetness of almond paste lingered on her fingers for hours after her work was done. Lines of the proverb Papa recited to Mama every Shabbat—*she tends to the affairs of her household and eats not the bread of idleness*—played in Mirelle's head as her mother bustled about the kitchen.

The day of the party dawned fair, small clouds chasing one another in the bright blue sky. Mirelle, a heavy apron protecting her lilac-colored muslin dress, packed baskets and sat in Mama's sewing room to finish her father's present. She'd braided a chain as a watch guard for his favorite pocket watch. Selecting the softest bits of burgundy, buff, and green-colored leather and delicate glass beads she'd bought from a Venetian trader, she'd woven the chain into a taut double loop. *He'll love it*, she thought as she sewed the loose ends tight, smiling at the image of her father always searching his pockets for his watch.

When they arrived, Anna directed four of the men to lay white cloths on the long tables in the back. Papa fussed that she didn't need so many helpers; Mirelle knew he wanted his men to keep working until the last minute. But he was fighting a losing battle. The rest of the men were already putting away their paintbrushes and inks and lounging in the doorway, watching for their wives and children.

Mirelle stood on the threshold, breathing in. The sharp, stinging smell of ink, paint, parchment, and glue, which had always made her eager to sit down to work, now served only to remind her of what she'd lost. But she forced a smile to her face, unwilling to ruin her father's celebration by sulking.

The men eagerly helped unload the cart, setting out the warm food. One of the tables was designated for gifts—so far, one shared present from the workmen; something from the Morpurgo family; and a package that had arrived several days earlier from Simone's widowed sister-in-law in Rome, Prudenzia Fermi.

Mirelle placed her gift in the center of the table, looking pointedly at her brother.

Jacopo winked at her. "I do so have a gift," he whispered, even though she hadn't asked.

"Where is it, then?"

He reached into his waistcoat, pulled out a parchment scroll with a crushed ribbon awkwardly tied around it, and tossed it on the table.

"I can retie that for you," Mirelle offered.

"Don't touch it. I don't want you peeking."

"It's messy. Let me."

But just as she reached a hand out, Mirelle heard a familiar voice call her name.

Dolce was at the door, arms full of sunflowers, her face as bright as the blooms. Dolce's father, aunt, and uncle crowded behind her.

Papa greeted them, welcoming them to the workshop as honored guests. *"B'ruchim ha'baim,"* he intoned in Hebrew. "Welcome, welcome!" He ushered them inside. "I know this isn't Sukkot, but you are my *ushpzin*, my sacred guests. As the Bible commands us: 'You shall rejoice on your festival.' I'm delighted you are here for mine."

"Blessings of the day, Simone," David Morpurgo said.

"Health and prosperity," his brother, Ezekiel, chimed in.

"That sounds like a toast," Simone said. "Come, help yourselves to some wine. Pinina bought a nice Sangiovese."

The men walked off. Dolce and her aunt turned to Mirelle's mother.

"What beautiful flowers, dear Dolce," Mama said. "I'll ask Anna to find a vase."

"No need," Dolce said. "My footman brought several. I thought we might divide them around the tables."

Quick annoyance rippled across Mama's forehead, but was swiftly wiped clean. Mama was always sweet to Dolce—at least, to her face.

As Mirelle glanced about the room, one of their neighbors, a widow, sidled over to Dolce's father, chattering, plying her fan coyly, putting a possessive hand on his arm. Mirelle bit back a chuckle. This wasn't the first time someone had tried to entrap Signor Morpurgo with feminine wiles. The moment Dolce's mother, Sarella, had died of a lingering illness when the girls were twelve, wealthy David Morpurgo had become the most eligible widower in the ghetto. But he was adroit at avoiding the snares of widows and mamas, and often told his daughter and her friend that he preferred the thrill of commerce and politics to a life hemmed in by a demanding wife. Besides, Mirelle suspected that he'd truly loved Dolce's mother, whose full-length portrait still hung in the villa entranceway. She remembered

Sarella's softness and gentleness—qualities that had clearly escaped her forceful, sharp-tongued daughter. For years, Mirelle had watched Dolce conspire against any woman who encroached too close.

"Why don't you want your father to marry again?" she had asked once.

"Why do you think?" Dolce replied, as if surprised by her friend's naivete. "If he marries again, who do you think will control our home and his fortune? And then, if there's a boy . . ." Dolce had dismissed at least two governesses, requesting male tutors instead. She was adept at unearthing nuggets of gossip that tarnished the most irreproachable maiden. When Mirelle chided her, wondering if her friend was standing in the way of her father's happiness, Dolce shrugged and replied, "We're fine as we are."

Eschewing matrimonial snares didn't prevent Dolce's father from enjoying the elegances of the fashionable world. A court Jew, given special privileges by the pope for his services to the Papal state, he was tolerated by Gentiles at public functions. He attended these affairs in a long-tailed coat and constricting pantaloons, shoes polished to a mirrored gloss, his salt-and-pepper hair pomaded and curled. He had to lace his portly figure into a corset of rigid whalebone to bundle himself into his stylish clothes.

Mama stepped forward briskly and took the sunflowers, rousing Mirelle from her reminiscences.

"Anna," Mama called, "fetch the vases Dolce's footman has for you."

Anna, her face damp with exertion, hurried over. Mama handed her the flowers and the maid bustled off.

"What a lovely gown!" Dolce said brightly, studying Mirelle from head to foot. "Turn around."

Smiling, Mirelle whirled. She was wearing one of the new high-waisted dresses in a soft lilac, tied with a moss-green ribbon under her chest. She turned back to return the compliment. Dolce, as always, was exquisitely arrayed in the latest fashion—a slim column dress of blue sprigged muslin, a tall hat tilted rakishly to one side, her feet encased in soft slippers of sapphire kid. Her blond curls were dressed high on her head, one falling delicately onto her shoulder.

"I wish I had your style," Mirelle said wistfully.

"You look charming." Dolce crooked her arm about her friend's waist.

In a few minutes, the narrow hall of the manufactory was full. The workers' children started a game of Speculation in the corner— Jacopo having snuck a pack of playing cards to the party in his pocket—and their giggling threaded through the earnest conversation of the grown-ups. Mirelle and Dolce circulated arm in arm through the crowded room before joining the large circle surrounding David Morpurgo.

"You're not worried that Bonaparte is going to rampage into Ancona?" Papa was asking. Mirelle's father was increasingly panicked about the French general's advances through Italy.

"What I don't understand," one of the workers said, "is what the French intend with us. The Austrians seem helpless to stop them. Will they free Ancona from the pope's control?"

"Bonaparte is only obeying orders from the Directory in France," Dolce's father replied. "Look at what happened in Mondovi. The people there cried out for a Republic as he marched through their streets. But did he give them one? No, he ignored them."

"Anyway, Italy's not the point," his brother, Ezekiel, argued. "The French are at war with Austria, not us. Italy's just a feint to force the Austrians to move troops from the Rhine to defend their territories in Lombardy. We don't have to worry about them."

"We don't?" Papa shook his head, disbelieving. "They may want to fight the Austrians, but they are on *our* soil. Heading in *our* direction."

"*Our* soil?" Narducci piped up. "Our homes are here, but I don't think anyone else in Italy would consider Ancona *our* soil. We're not citizens—"

"Because we're Jewish?" David Morpurgo said. "We may not be—but the Jews of France are. You have family in Paris, don't you, Simone?"

Papa nodded. "One of my cousin's sons is even serving in the French army." His face grew darker. "He could be marching against us even now."

"He's not marching against us," Ezekiel persisted. "Not against us Jews and not against the Italians. If you need proof, just consider Napoleon's address at Piedmont."

"What did he say?" asked one of the apprentices.

Ezekiel fished a newspaper out of his waistcoat pocket. "I'll read it out loud."

"Uncle!" Dolce protested. "You brought a newspaper to a party?"

"I thought people would be interested." Ezekiel shrugged his bony shoulders. "Why not?"

Mirelle hid a smile as Ezekiel read the proclamation: "Peoples of Italy, the French army comes to break your chains. The French people are the friends of all peoples, meet them with confidence. Your property, your religion, and your usages will be respected. We make war as generous enemies, and we have no quarrel save with the tyrants who enslave you."

"That's not true." Papa's face was set in grim lines. "Bonaparte is looting the country, taking any art and valuables he can lay his hands on. We may just be the road to Austria, but the French are certainly helping themselves to our treasures as they pass through."

*Always so afraid*, thought Mirelle. *Why is Papa always the first to suspect the worst?*

"*Our* art?" Narducci said, echoing the inflection he'd used when he'd asked, "*Our* soil?" He scowled. "Simone, do you really want to lay claim to paintings of crucifixions and Madonnas?"

"Besides, those are just rumors," scoffed Dolce's father. "Rumors circulated by the Austrians. The general will see that many of us want what the French have. A unified Italy ruled by the people, not by the pope, the Austrians, or any of our antiquated nobles."

"But if he does nothing but what the Directory tells him—as you say, David—what will it matter?" Papa shrugged.

David shook his head. "The French are still experimenting with their own republic. Right now they're struggling between the left and the right, the Jacobins and the Royalists, both trying to seize control. But eventually they will help us become a republic founded on the principles of the Enlightenment, no matter how long it takes. Isn't that right, Dolce?"

"*Viva la Repubblica*," Dolce said, giving a mock salute. "I hope so, Papa."

Mirelle smiled wistfully. Dolce always seemed to know what to say. She had a more enlightened education than most boys. The books she read—like Voltaire's *Candide* or Bacon's *The New Atlantis*, many of which she loaned to Mirelle—and the tutors hired to teach her gave her an astonishing range of interests. She could talk fashion, philosophy, poetry, and politics. She was a fearless horsewoman, adept on the harp and pianoforte, and spoke several languages. She even kept abreast of her father's wide-flung financial empire, which she would inherit. *And no rabbi will prevent it*, thought Mirelle, envy momentarily getting the better of her.

"Consider," Signor Morpurgo said, putting his arm around his daughter, "what the French have done for their Jews, giving them full citizenship. Imagine, being a citizen of Ancona—of all Italy!"

Mirelle's mother, who was hovering at the edge of the circle, coughed discreetly. "Simone, some of our guests are asking when you plan to open your gifts."

Mirelle bit her lip. As if Papa was five years old and this a child's party! But gift opening was a yearly tradition. Besides, Mirelle

realized Mama wanted to shift the conversation away from contro-
versial topics, especially the war. She disapproved of talking politics
in open company. You never knew who was listening, she'd say.

Obedient to their hostess's wishes, everyone trooped over to the
gift table.

There were polite exclamations as Simone unwrapped his presents.
His men had chipped in and bought him a fine ivory snuff box and a
jar of snuff. The Morpurgos gave him a magnifying loupe in a leather
case, which Papa passed around so every workman in the room
could look through it. "This will be helpful for close work," Papa said
gratefully, and the brothers smiled. Papa unwrapped a pair of gloves,
embroidered slippers, and linen handkerchiefs. He took his time
with each present, not noticing how the children fidgeted or whether
the grown-ups grew bored. He thanked each giver profusely, holding
up the gift and admiring it.

Finally, he reached for the family gifts that Mama had moved to
the bottom of the pile. Most of the guests had wandered off by now.
The children were playing hide-and-seek under the long worktables.
Their mothers and fathers huddled around the refreshment table,
talking quietly.

Papa opened Mirelle's gift and regarded it closely. "A watch guard!"
he exclaimed. "Clever girl! Did you make this yourself?"

"It's beautiful," Dolce said, reaching out a hand to touch it. "What
exquisite colors!"

The smile on Papa's face melted the frustration Mirelle had felt
toward him earlier. "I'm glad you like it."

"Like it? I love it!" He opened his arms and hugged her tightly. "I'm
going to put it on right now." He clipped the chain onto his watch,
fastening it to his pantaloons. He looked down for a long moment,
admiring it.

"My turn now, Papa." Jacopo reached for the scroll. "I made this
especially for you."

Papa took the proffered roll of parchment and smiled at his son. "You made it?" He slid the clumsy bow from the scroll. "I'm a lucky father to have children who care so much."

Jacopo shifted his weight from side to side as he watched their father unroll the parchment. Mirelle leaned forward to catch a glimpse, but Papa was holding it too close for her to see.

He stared at it, his face suddenly frozen. He glanced quickly toward his son, who couldn't hide his delight. Mirelle was surprised to see tears in her father's eyes.

"That's—remarkable," Papa whispered. "Simply remarkable." He held it up.

Jacopo had laboriously drawn a Jewish marriage license, etching an arch in black ink and decorating it with colorful Biblical characters, vines, and flowers in soft watercolors. Mirelle knew it was the brilliantly illuminated letters and the distinctive pointed upper border, called an ogee arch, which had led to the high demand for Ancona ketubot throughout Europe and beyond. At the top of the page was an enormous word in Hebrew, followed by a block of text that had been rendered in careful calligraphy. The effect was stunning.

"I had some help with the lettering," Jacopo admitted, "but the drawing is all my own."

"I knew you were talented," Papa said. "But I had no idea how much." He still looked astonished.

Mirelle bit her lip. "It's beautiful," she said, amid the chorus of wonder and congratulation.

Her father's eyes remained fixed on the splendid ketubah.

Mirelle swallowed hard, a lump of disappointment bitter in her mouth.

Were she only a boy . . .

She wandered away from the group, heading into her father's office. *I'm just going to take a quick look*, she thought. *No one will even notice that I've gone.*

Mirelle sat behind the desk and reached for her father's ledgers. Casting her eyes over the newly entered rows of numbers, smeared and uneven, she did a quick tally. She made a few small adjustments, but for the most part, everything added up. She felt almost disappointed as she started to close the book, wondering if anyone cared that she was no longer working there.

"Mirelle? What are you doing?"

She looked up. Narducci stood in the doorway. She felt a quick twinge of embarrassment at having been caught checking the books. Saying nothing, she shut the ledger and covered it with both hands.

Narducci gave her a sidelong look and chuckled. "Don't worry," he said. "Your secret is safe with me."

Mirelle smiled. "Thank you."

Narducci sighed. "I'm sorry that your father couldn't convince Rabbi Fano to let you stay on. All of us are. For a man of God and a preacher of peace, our beloved rabbi can be awfully vengeful.

"You know how much I admire your father," Narducci went on, "but we both know he has no head for numbers."

"He's looking for someone."

"I hope he finds him soon. Otherwise, there might be trouble."

Mirelle stared at him, surprised. "But everything's in order. I just checked."

"For now." The foreman looked at the ledger. "But I don't want to return to the days when your grandfather almost ruined us through his mismanagement."

Mirelle furrowed her brow. *What can he mean?* Her father's stories about her grandfather were full of his courage in leaving Alsace, his brilliance in founding the workshop. She had only the vaguest recollection of him, a stoop-shouldered old man with graying hair who would hold her lovingly on his lap and tell her bedtime tales in a thick accent. Jacopo—for whom he was named—had never even met him. "What are you talking about?"

Narducci sat on the other side of the desk and folded his hands in his lap. "My father told me. Your grandfather was a wonderful craftsman and scribe. He built this workshop from nothing, starting out as a solitary artist."

Mirelle nodded. This much she knew.

"But he ran into trouble when he brought in other workers. He promised to pay them lavishly, but to entice customers, he offered to do the work at a lower price than his competition. Then, like your father, he trusted in the quality of the men's work and let them spend as much time as they'd like. Too much time. They began to miss dates, to the embarrassment of the married couples. Never mind, he'd tell the men, we'll just use your work for someone else. But nothing spreads as quickly as a bad reputation. And no matter how beautiful the work, nobody wants a ketubah fashioned for someone else."

Mirelle glanced down. Her hands were still spread across the large leather-bound ledger. It felt warm to her touch, almost like a living thing. "But—ours is the most successful workshop in all of Italy."

"In all the world," Narducci agreed, his voice full of pride. "Now. But what saved us then was David Morpurgo's father."

"Dolce's grandfather?"

Narducci nodded. "Jacob went to him for a loan to save the business. He didn't want to let anyone go—I give him credit for that—but he couldn't pay them. Morpurgo looked at the books and agreed to become a partner in the business, but only if he managed it."

"I never knew that," Mirelle said.

"When the old man died, David took on the partnership. But in name only—he's involved in too many other businesses to keep such a close eye. You, on the other hand, young as you are—you have the head for it."

Mirelle flushed.

"Your father is brilliant," Narducci added. "He has the same gifts his father had before him, the same gifts Jacopo already shows—artistry, creativity, an ability to inspire his men. I'm honored to work for him. But this is a business, Mirelle, and you need more than a keen eye and a quick brush to run a business." He smiled at her. "There is more than one type of artistry, you know."

Mirelle felt dread crowding her throat. She slowly raised her hands from the ledger. "Papa's looking for someone."

Narducci nodded. "I hope he finds him. Soon."

Mirelle sat, silent, for a moment. "We should go back out there," she finally said, rising. "Mama will wonder where I am."

# 7

# MAY 10
# LODI

Daniel was suffering from painful water blisters as his company quick-marched along the shores of the Po River in hot pursuit of the enemy. To distract himself, he thought back over the last few weeks. It felt good to be a soldier under General Bonaparte's command. In the last month and a half, they'd vanquished city after city, celebrating victory at Montenotte, at Millesimo, at Dego—and, remarkably, later that same day, at Cosseria. Ceva followed, then Mondovi, where the residents had shouted "Long live the Republic!" as they massed on the streets, tossing flowers and fruit to the victors.

The general was already accomplishing the goals set out for him by the Directory when he began the Italian campaign: wresting control of Austrian-ruled lands in Lombardy and severing the Sardinian-Austrian alliance. The young Republic feared reprisals from the Austrians for executing the French royal family, especially their native daughter, Marie Antoinette. By sending Bonaparte into Italy, they'd created a second front, crippling Austria's hold on their Italian possessions. Napoleon was also charged with preventing the pope from supporting the Republic's enemies. The French rampaged through Italy's cities like wildfire, staging lightning attacks against the Austrians, Bonaparte's unconventional tactics utterly confounding them.

While the glory of victory stirred him, however, the bleeding and lifeless bodies on the battlefield turned Daniel's stomach. He recalled the Talmudic teaching, "Whomever destroys a soul, it is considered as if he destroyed an entire world." *Yet the Austrians would kill me without thinking twice.* He was a soldier, wasn't he? The first generation of Jewish soldiers since Roman times. If the Torah praised the victories of King David's warriors, the siege of Jericho—surely God would understand Daniel's defense of the French Republic.

The desperate Austrian retreat, the ranks whispered gleefully as they marched through the beautiful spring day, was trying to reach Milan with their forces still intact. Napoleon had cut off their river crossing at Piacenza. The retreating troops had left a force behind in Lodi, a half day's march south of Milan, to slow the French surge. So at Lodi, located on an Adda River swollen from springtime rains, its banks boggy and sprinkled with delicate wildflowers, Bonaparte now engaged General Sebottendorf.

As they dragged the cannons to the field, Daniel saw the enemy had taken positions on a narrow wooden bridge. He counted fourteen cannons pointed directly at them and estimated two or three battalions facing them. He'd gained enough battle experience not to tremble in the face of the enemy, but he couldn't help but feel a twinge of doubt.

"Want to cross?" one of the Austrians called. "You must pass us first!"

Behind the bridge stood the Austrian infantry, guns leveled at the approaching French.

"Ready, steady, boys!" cried Daniel's captain as they halted several yards away.

Daniel inhaled the clean, fresh air. The day was made for

picnicking under olive trees and taking a long nap after lunch, not for trading bullets and cannon shot. Red-throated birds chased one another in the blue sky, indifferent to the impending battle. Aristocratic Austrian officers, thinking themselves safe, mocked the ragtag French troops with elegant French taunts.

"Thus far and no farther," one called, pristine in his white uniform, sunlight catching fire on his gold epaulets. "How fares your country now? Are they still guillotining innocents?"

"Does the blood still flow in Paris?" another cried. "We don't forget what you did to our daughter of Austria, *fils de pute!*" He spat dramatically into the river flowing beneath him, to the raucous cheers of his men.

"Daughter of Austria?" Sebastian muttered to Daniel. "What are they . . . ?"

"They mean Marie Antoinette." Daniel rolled his eyes. Surely his comrade was teasing. "You remember? The woman who was once our queen?"

One end of Sebastian's mouth curled up. "Was she Austrian? Did I know that?"

Daniel shook his head. Sebastian, cool as ever facing the enemy, was quick to joke. But Daniel, remembering the horrors of the executions in Paris during his childhood, the terror of a knock at the door at midnight, didn't find him funny. He kept his tone light with an effort. "You're an ignorant old warrior, aren't you?"

"I was fighting the British in America during those years," Sebastian said with a chuckle, unashamed. "I kept my head down and hoped my cannon wouldn't backfire. No time for politics."

Daniel watched as a cavalry unit was dispatched upriver, his friend Christophe among them. Their orders were to ford the river half a league above Lodi and surround the enemy. Christophe was leaning forward in his saddle, spurring his stallion onward, moving swiftly to the front of the close-packed huddle of horses.

"Prepare to fight!" came the shout from a cavalry officer to their right. "Take the bridge!"

"You! You!" cried their sergeant, coming up from behind and slapping Daniel and Sebastian on the shoulder. "Deploy the cannon behind the cavalry."

Action kept Daniel's fright at bay. He and Sebastian ran to take the small bronze cannon, wheeling it behind the men on horseback into a small clearing of hard-packed earth. Pierre followed, leading a pony and the cart loaded with grapeshot and round shot—cannonballs.

"Hey," cried one of the men as he tried to keep his excited mount in check. "Move that cannon away!"

"We're ordered here." Daniel was sympathetic. The mere sight of a cannon made the troops nervous. A misfire killed or maimed more men than the enemy's barrage.

"Don't fret, boy," Sebastian told the horseman. "We won't fire until you're on your way downhill. You'll hear our helpful cannonballs whistling overhead and be glad we're clearing your path."

The rider, who looked perhaps sixteen, moved his skittish mare as far away as he could.

"*Allez! Allez!* Take the bridge," came the cry, and the grenadiers rushed forward. From his vantage point on a small rise above the scene, Daniel watched as they struggled at the foot of the narrow crossing, arranging themselves eight men abreast. Bullets whistled through the air as Austrian cannons demolished the head of the column. Spreading smoke befuddled the senses, while shouts and cries of pain rent the air.

Soldiers shrank as lead missiles assailed them. Two of Napoleon's commanders, Massena and Berthier, stood at the bridge's entrance with drawn swords, urging the men forward, pelting them with curses and cheers. A burst of military music rang forth from the riverbank. In a quick shift of emotion, Daniel's blood stirred with patriotic fervor.

From a distance, a party of sharpshooters pushed off in rowboats from the riverbanks, heading toward an islet just below the bridge. Reaching it, the sharpshooters spun their boats sideways, huddling behind as they took careful aim at the Austrians.

Daniel glimpsed Bonaparte astride a gray dappled roan, galloping toward them. His aides, a few paces behind, yelled at him to take cover.

But the general moved into the thickest part of the battle, where Daniel and his fellows were laying in the artillery, feeding grapeshot into the cannon's maw and exploding it over the heads of their troops. Their cannon fire just fell short of the enemy lines.

"Move up! Cannons to the right and farther up!" Napoleon cried, dismounting from his stallion and throwing the reins to one of his aides. "Come on, men, move the cannons right."

"General, you should retreat to higher ground," panted the red-faced officer who had seized the reins. Daniel recognized him as Major Junot, one of Bonaparte's staff officers.

"You won't reach the Austrians from back here." Napoleon, ignoring Junot, grabbed hold of one of the cannons, wheeled it forward several feet, and pointed it over to the right, where the enemy fire was heaviest. He turned his head, grinning, as he noticed his officers gaping at him. "Here, you sluggards, bring the rest here."

"But, General!" Junot protested, leading Napoleon's horse forward, blanching as bullets whirled past his commander's head.

Daniel and the others hastened to obey. Frightened as he was to move into the rain of fire, Daniel was astonished by Bonaparte's ice-cold calm.

"Here, hand me the round shot," Napoleon demanded, turning to Pierre. "I want to take out their artillery before they realize just how vulnerable we are."

He lay in the cannon shot like an expert. The heavy iron missiles boomed out of the red-hot mouth of the artillery and struck the Austrians squarely, taking out several cannons and a half-dozen men.

"Again! Again!" Napoleon urged, seizing another cannonball from the ammunition cart.

Realizing they couldn't budge him, his staff officers settled nearby, clearly unhappy that Bonaparte—and they—were so exposed. Runners from other companies rushed up, and Daniel saw on their faces how bewildered they were to find the general amid the cannons. Each time he stopped, impatient, scanned their missives at a glance, and shouted orders that sent them scrambling: "Tell Berthier to press forward!" or "Lannes needs to support Dallemagne! Have him fall back and head toward the Austrians' left flank!"

He worked beside the men as the battle waged on, loading and firing, seemingly unaffected by the volleys of gunfire and the grape-shot that landed perilously close. Screaming, Pierre suddenly fell, clutching his shoulder. Napoleon stepped over his writhing frame to take his place. A hideous, whinnying moan made Daniel peer over his shoulder. Napoleon's horse reared up on his hind legs, neighing wildly, blood rushing from his dappled flanks.

"Shoot him," Napoleon ordered Junot, white teeth set in a grimace, eyes bloodshot from smoke and dust.

Still mounted, Junot took a long-handled pistol from a holster at his hip. Transferring the reins into his left hand, pulling the horse toward him, he shot him in the head. The horse's legs gave out and he slipped to the ground. In an instant, a puddle of red surrounded his shattered head, blood gushing from his mouth. Daniel took several hurried steps backward.

"Look! Look! They are halfway across!" Napoleon cried exultantly. But a moment later, the Austrians rallied, and a torrent of gunfire made the French troops pause, then pull back.

"No, they mustn't!" Napoleon shouted. "Junot, give me your horse!"

The major slid down, tossing the reins to his commander. Napoleon swung into the saddle, riding furiously up the hill. "Keep up the cannon fire, boys!" he shouted over his shoulder, digging his heels into the reluctant mount, urging it into the midst of the retreating soldiers.

"Messana! Cervoni! Have your men ford that river!" he called out.

The two officers clambered down the shattered bridge joists into the river below, followed by their troops. They plunged into the waist-high water and moved swiftly toward the far bank. The Austrians, rattled by the determined French, shrank before their drawn bayonets. Daniel, wiping sweat and dirt from his eyes, saw the Austrians desert their guns and flee.

"Come on!" Bonaparte called to the soldiers on the bridge. "Let's cross!"

The French, steadied by the sight of their sooty-faced commander, surged across the bridge in one massive thrust, forcing the enemy forces back. They taunted the Austrians as they fled in disarray.

"The day is ours!" cried Pierre as he struggled to his feet, one hand clutching his bleeding and torn shoulder, face white under the smoke that darkened it. "*Vive la France!*"

That evening, Daniel and his mates visited Pierre in the makeshift camp infirmary. Heartened to learn that their friend would soon recover, the men talked about the extraordinary way in which Napoleon had fought beside them.

Screams and moans of the wounded rang out all around them. The air was redolent with the coppery smell of blood and the nauseating tang of infection. The little laudanum the doctors had received before the battle had quickly been depleted, and they were now offering rotgut to soothe the pain, saving their small supply of brandy for the officers. Every once in a while, the harsh grinding of a saw echoed through the tent, a sound that set Daniel's teeth on edge; he knew it meant someone was losing a limb. He was glad that Pierre, at least, had avoided anything worse than a few days confined to a hospital cot.

"He lay in cannon as well as any corporal I know," Sebastian said admiringly. "Like he was one of us."

"Our little corporal," Pierre said, propped against the wadded mass of his tunic. "To think we were worried when he first arrived in camp."

"Cool as a cucumber." Sebastian nodded. "His horse mortally wounded and all he said was, 'Shoot him, Junot.'"

Daniel reached for a roll of lint and took off his boots. A water blister had exploded; the open wound was red and angry. The pain had completely disappeared during the battle, but returned the second they won the day. He took a basin from a sleeping soldier, washed his foot as best he could, and tightly bandaged it. "Bonaparte's a marvel," he murmured, lips compressed as he wound the lint about his throbbing limb. "A truly great man."

# 8

# May 15
# Milan

The troops entered Milan, marching under a triumphal arch draped with flowers and twisting vines. Someone had raised the French flag just outside the arch. Soldiers and young boys stood on the city walls, waving hats and cheering, as company after company marched below them. Inside the city, the roar of the crowd was deafening.

Christophe cantered up on his ink-black stallion. "Do they truly love us, or is this just for show? Would they cheer just as loudly if the Austrians marched into the city?"

"Who cares?" Sebastian shrugged. "Look at that pretty wench over there. See? The one bending and showing us her . . ."

Daniel blushed. Despite his shorn hair and clean-shaven chin, his Orthodox Jewish upbringing still clung to him. He was accustomed to girls who were modest and covered their chests, not these lighthearted, light-skirted women who tossed roses and called bold invitations to the Frenchmen they thought most handsome.

Daniel realized as Christophe rode off that his friend was receiving a lot of this attention. During the two scant months of the campaign, his hair had brightened in the strong Italian sun to a brilliant gold, his face become bronzed, and he wore his blue cavalry uniform lightly, shoulders broad under its wide red lapels. Daniel grinned as he watched his friend rejoin the battalion, a red rose in his button-hole, blowing kisses to the prettiest of the signorinas. He wouldn't be surprised if Christophe found a warmer bunk tonight than his narrow soldier's bedroll.

The idea stirred Daniel's blood. You couldn't live in the army and ignore the lure of sex. Still, he intended to honor his religion, his family, and his bride by remaining a virgin until his wedding night.

The next morning, the men awoke to new orders—to rest, refurbish their equipment, and enjoy the delights of Milan. A great, heaving exhalation rose from the campfires as Daniel's fellows contemplated staying in one spot for a full eight days. Many a tin cup of the muddy mess that passed for coffee was raised in ardent relief.

"That's perfect," Christophe said, taking breakfast with Daniel. "Lissandra will be pleased."

"Ah, I wondered where you got to last night." Sebastian laughed. "Trust you to find a sweet little signorina to cuddle."

Daniel said nothing, but he couldn't help smiling. What would Christophe's mother think? He laughed inwardly as he imagined Odette's horror. Her beloved son, bedding a girl without the sacrament of marriage? Unthinkable.

# 9

## May 18
## Milan

Christophe stretched, his bare feet tickled by hay. Lissandra lay beside him, breathing rhythmically, breasts peeking over her tangled chemise, dark hair tousled. He leaned up on one elbow and looked down at her delicately flushed face, the long eyelashes brushing her high cheekbones. His desire grew.

"Lissandra, *cara mia*," he whispered, using the little bit of Italian he'd mastered. "Wake up."

Her eyes opened, and she smiled. He trailed his fingers under her skirts, and she sighed and turned onto her stomach to open her legs. He parted her thighs and moved between them.

"Yes," Lissandra moaned. "Christophe, my brave soldier, yes."

He could tell that she was ready for him. He plunged into her, feeling her tightness, groaning as she twisted her body and raised herself to her knees. He thrust deep. Her back rubbed up against his chest; she began to breathe in short gasps. He cupped one of her ample breasts from behind. She groaned. The nipple rose in his palm and as he rubbed it, he felt himself grow impossibly hard. He was close.

The girl was heaving beneath him now, panting, matching thrust for backward thrust. A gentleman, he knew, would wait until she found her own pleasure, but he was too far gone. With one strong push inside her, reaching as deep as he could, he expelled his seed, let it ripple out of him in wave after wave of shuddering ecstasy.

He lay there for a moment, panting against her, sweat pouring down his body and mixing with hers. Then he pulled out, turned her to face him, and gave her the first kiss of the day.

She eyed him, half-resentful, half-amused. "You are in a big rush," she complained in bad French.

"Sorry." He brushed her dark ringlets from her sweat-slicked breasts, leaned over and kissed first one, then the other. "You're irresistible, *chérie*."

She moaned again, and he decided to make amends for his impatience. He bent his head and kissed her exposed sex. He used his tongue and fingers to make her pant. Her legs curled around his head as he pleasured her. He could feel her tension rising and licked harder. After sleeping with so many girls throughout Italy, he knew exactly how to draw her over the precipice. Within minutes, she was gasping beside him on the straw, irritation transformed into deep satisfaction.

"Now we were both in a rush," he told her.

She just closed her eyes and snuggled close. He held her, thinking of his first woman. He'd been awkward then, but then the natural rhythms of the act had overtaken him. She'd had the grace to forgive him when he peaked too soon. He remembered how embarrassed he'd felt. And guilty, too, thinking of his mother and her preaching against the evils of fornication.

He'd been about to leave for the army when his uncle Alain gave him a packet. Opening it, he'd found a small pile of empty sheaths made from some rubbery material.

"*Capotes anglaises*," Alain explained. "English overcoats. You wear them"—he gestured toward Christophe's privates—"to protect yourself from pox."

"How dare you?" his mother burst out, snatching the condoms. "Encouraging him to sin!"

Alain shrugged. "Odette, it's only natural. The boy's a soldier now. A dalliance here and there will do him no harm."

But Odette threw the sheep gut sheaths into the fire, where they crackled and smoked. "He's a decent Catholic boy," she fumed. "No matter what this Republic of yours says. He'll keep himself pure for marriage."

"He's a healthy young man," Alain argued. "And he'll act like one. Better he be protected. Do you want him to be infected? Or worse?"

Odette had only turned away, shuddering.

Her first letters to him after he'd left had been full of warnings against the sin of fornication; every once in a while, she still returned to the subject. But with a new batch of (often-forgotten) condoms in his kitbag, Christophe found it easier and easier to ignore her.

"I have to report to camp." He disentangled himself from Lissandra. "I'll come back tonight."

She sat up, pouting. "What if my brothers find out what you've done to me?" she wailed. "Or if I'm with child?"

Christophe sighed. Why did they always ask this when it was too late? "Surely you're not," he said, buttoning his shirt. "And besides, be truthful. I wasn't your first, was I?"

"How dare you?" she retorted, snapping her legs shut. "I was a virgin, of course I was. You said you loved me. That was the only reason I agreed. And now"—her face puckered—"you're going to leave me!"

Christophe's annoyance turned to amusement. He'd lost count of how many Italian beauties had tried this game. They wanted money— money he didn't have. It could be months before he received his back pay. All he had was enough to cover the cost of the wine he bought before a night between the sheets. Or in the hay.

"I'm a soldier. I go where I'm commanded." He paused, noticing her quivering lips. Were those real tears? He shook off a twinge of guilt. "If it makes you feel better, go to church and confess your sins." He laughed, reaching for his breeches.

The lip trembling stopped. She stared at him, hurt shining in those beautiful dark eyes. "How dare you?"

He shrugged. Deep down, he knew he was really punishing his mother for her strict piety. The girl's hypocrisy simply made her a convenient target.

"Don't you come back tonight," she spat. "I'll tell my brothers what you made me do. They'll kill you!"

Christophe reached down, gathered her into his arms, and kissed her full lips. "Will you?" he whispered, stroking her hair gently. "Will you really?"

She stretched against him like a cat. "Come back tonight," she murmured, blinking up at him from under long eyelashes. "And find out."

"I will if I can, *bella* Lissandra," he said, releasing her and sitting down to pull on his boots. Then the impulse to tease her grew too strong. "Unless I find someone else to share my bed tonight."

She threw a handful of hay at him. "You do and I'll kill you both," she shrieked.

He laughed. How changeable women's moods could be. From purring to alley cat in an instant. "You? Nonsense, *chérie*." Boots laced, he rose and brushed the excess hay from his uniform. "Be a good girl and I'll return." He looked down at her body. "*Mon dieu*, you're beautiful!"

"Come back tonight," she urged him, thrusting her chest out enticingly. So much for protestations of virginity. "Promise me!"

With a careless wave, he turned on his heel and left the barn.

Back at the barracks, Christophe sank on his bedroll and sighed, exhausted. Daniel, who had wandered over to talk to him, shook his head but said nothing. Even so, Christophe could feel the waves of disapproval coming from his friend.

"Want me to introduce you to a friend of Lissandra's?" he asked, half in earnest and half-mocking. "You could do with a little loving."

Daniel studied his boots. "No, thanks. I'm fine as I am."

Christophe sat up. "Seriously, though, Daniel, why not? Your wife won't thank you for coming to the marriage bed a virgin. She'll want someone who knows how to pleasure her."

Daniel's lips thinned. "I wouldn't marry a woman like that."

"Like what?"

"Like . . . that." Daniel hesitated for a moment before adding, "We'll learn how to give one another pleasure."

"Two virgins together? You'll flounder around, not knowing what goes where."

Daniel turned away and Christophe realized he'd gone too far. "Or not," he said. "Don't mind me, Daniel. I'm tired."

"Did you get any sleep at all?"

"Not much." Christophe lay down again. "I should catch a little nap before maneuvers."

He closed his eyes and felt rather than saw Daniel wander off. He drifted, half-asleep, thinking about his friend's disapproval. Alain expected Christophe to sow his wild oats, and he wasn't disappointing his all-knowing uncle. This army adventure rewarded a young man's appetites: he could swoop in, charm a girl into bed, then march off the next day, forgetting her in the arms of another beauty.

But it was evident from his friend's thin-lipped stare that he thought Christophe was acting like a cad.

His half-conscious thoughts wandered. Was he wrong and Daniel right? Would he want Lissandra as his wife?

The idea made his eyes fly open. Definitely not.

He closed his eyes again, trying to picture his ideal wife. She would be pure in body and soul, he decided, a woman of integrity and virtue. A woman—he chuckled—that he had yet to meet. In the meantime, he would enjoy all the sweets Italy had to offer.

# 10

# JUNE 25
# ANCONA

"Barbara! Get dressed!" Francesca called as she stepped into the backyard. Beyond her henhouses and kitchen garden were fields of sunflowers and a small orchard of fig trees. She tied a black kerchief over her dark hair and loosened her apron. Her husband had been away for two months now and she'd grown used to deciding when to sow and weed, plant and pluck. In fact, she thought wryly, it was easier to get on with the work without Emilio's constant grousing, with just Barbara to chide into doing her chores.

"Is it already time?" Barbara was perched in the apple tree, where she often sat in the heat of the day, swinging her gangly legs and daydreaming.

"We said we'd meet at the harbor and walk to church together."

This was Father Candelabri's idea. "We don't know when the French will break through our defenses," he'd explained at a service a few days earlier. "Best none of you walk alone for now."

Sighing, her daughter jumped down and landed with a thud on the hard-packed earth. "Why are there all these extra services?" she asked, pumping the water spigot and sticking a hand under the tap.

Francesca grabbed her daughter by the nape of her neck and pushed her hair under the flowing water. "You're wearing a necklace of dirt," she scolded, "and there are spider webs in your hair."

Barbara sputtered, yanking her head away. "Church every day and clean every day, all because the French are marching on us," she muttered, rubbing her dripping head with a ratty towel. Eyes half-shut, she turned to her mother. "Fiona says that the soldiers take food from the farms. And . . . women, too."

Francesca, already in her sixth month of pregnancy, placed a protective hand over her bulging belly. "Rumors," she scoffed. "They won't want me, not in this condition. And you're still just a scrawny girl. Don't worry."

"But Fiona—"

"As if I have patience to listen to all the nonsense that girl spouts," Francesca said. "Go put on your church dress."

Barbara stalked inside. Francesca stopped at the little altar to the Virgin Mary in the corner of the yard. "Keep us safe, Blessed Mother," she whispered, touching the roughhewn statue's stone curls. "Keep the Corsican monster from our door. And bring my Emilio home from the sea, safe and sound."

Barbara came outside, wearing her faded green dress. The girl's skirt barely covered her scratched brown legs, and Francesca realized with a jolt that she'd grown a couple of inches again, seemingly overnight. With luck, Emilio would bring home enough soldi so they could afford new clothes.

The walk to the cathedral was steep; it made Francesca, burdened by her pregnancy, gasp for air. The women rounded a bend in the road and paused, looking over the panorama spread before them. The red, white, and pink stone buildings with their red-tiled roofs were bathed in a golden glow. In the harbor, multi-masted cargo ships with furled canvases were anchored in the bay.

"It looks so peaceful," said Francesca's friend Maria.

"And it will stay that way," asserted Bella Marscipona, a withered woman who'd looked old when Francesca was a child. Her age remained one of the city's deeply held mysteries. "The Virgin Mother will intercede. Something—or someone—will halt the Corsican in his tracks."

Francesca closed her eyes, half-scornful of the naïve statement but still hoping that old Bella was right. *Holy Mother, keep my husband safe*, she prayed silently. *And*, she added with a swallow, *help him become the man he should be.*

"Have you heard from Emilio?" Maria asked, as if reading Francesca's thoughts.

Francesca opened her eyes. "Not recently. He's not one for writing, my husband."

"It must feel strange with him gone. Quieter."

Francesca glanced quickly at Maria, who averted her face. *Does she mean what I think she means?* Francesca had never admitted to anyone how hot-tempered her husband could be, how his drinking and gambling woke the devil in him. Once or twice in the confessional, she'd been tempted to unburden herself. But she always ended up confiding only her own sins. If anyone in Ancona learned how her husband treated her, she'd be ashamed.

They made the final ascent to the cathedral.

As she entered, the coolness of the stone-vaulted cathedral washed over her. The church's familiar beauty soothed her. Even more than the small farm in the foothills below, this ancient building was home.

The women moved to the left transept, the Chapel of My Lady. Father Candelabri led a special mass for the women of the city every day, during which they prayed for Ancona to remain untouched by the war and destruction tearing through Italy.

Some women gathered below the altar of the Virgin Mary; others mounted the marble steps closer to the delicate portrait of the Madonna.

"Come up today," Maria said. "Seeing you there will touch the Holy Mother's heart and keep Emilio safe."

Francesca knew Mary favored those who kept her close in their hearts. *For Emilio*, she told herself, diffidently climbing the stairs.

Father Candelabri, his back to the devout, had just begun the antiphon: "*Introibo ad altare Dei, ad Deum qui lætificat iuventutem meam*—I shall go in to the altar of God, the God who gives joy to my youth."

Even with her eyes shut, Francesca felt her daughter at her side, breathing heavily, mouth open, arms slippery with sweat.

"Mama." Barbara tugged at her arm. "Look at the Madonna. Why is the painting doing that? Moving its eyes?"

The priest started the confession: "I confess to almighty God, to blessed Mary ever Virgin, to blessed Michael the archangel . . ."

Francesca opened her eyes. "Barbara," she muttered, "hush—"

"But Mama," the girl whined, her voice carrying through the high-ceilinged room. "Look!"

Unwillingly, Francesca turned her head toward the features of Our Lady Queen of All Saints, the image of the gold-crowned Mary, red dress peeking out of the folds of her blue mantle. This sweet face had graced Francesca's growing years, blessed her marriage to Emilio, witnessed the christening of their daughter, the girl who was once again tugging at her sleeve and whispering, "Do you see, Mama?"

"*Oremus*," pronounced the priest. "Let us pray."

And then she did see it. Her body throbbed with shock as the Virgin's downcast eyes looked directly at her and shed a single tear that fell from her right eye and trickled down her pale cheek.

"The Madonna!" cried Francesca, springing up from her kneeler and pointing at the portrait. "Mother Mary weeps! She weeps for us!"

A hush, then a cry, then a sudden roar as the congregation huddled around the altar, pushing and praying. Many of the women clasped their rosaries in their hands and sobbed as they murmured, "Hail Mary, full of grace . . ."

Francesca somehow found herself in front of the painting with a bewildered Father Candelabri. She knelt and reached up to grasp his arm. "She weeps—look how pale she looks, how she turns her head to watch us, Father."

The women fell to their knees. Father Candelabri raised a single finger and touched the wet mark the tear had left on the Virgin Mother's cheek.

"A miracle," he murmured, crossing himself. He whispered a line from the novena, Mary Help of Christians: "You are awe-inspiring as an army in battle array."

The women responded, "Defend me from the power of the enemy."

"What did I say?" Old Bella's voice rose above the hushed prayers and the sobs of the faithful, transfixed by the sweeping eyes of the weeping Madonna. "Our Lady will protect us from the Corsican monster! Napoleon will never enter our city now!"

# 11

# AUGUST 28
# ANCONA

Mirelle was playing the piano for her parents and a bored Jacopo one sultry evening when Anna poked her head into the parlor.

"Signor and Signorina Morpurgo," she announced.

Dolce and her father followed close on Anna's heels. Mirelle jumped up from the piano, grateful for the interruption. Mama and Papa rose more slowly.

"Come in." Papa welcomed them with a bow and a smile.

"Anna, fetch wine and biscotti for our guests," Mama added. "How lovely to see you, David. And you, Dolce."

Jacopo, having made his schoolboy's bow, looked around as if he wanted to escape. But a swift glance from his father made him sink back into his seat, while an even quicker glare from Mama, reminding him that Dolce was still standing, forced him to pop back up again.

"We're sorry to interrupt." Signor Morpurgo glanced at Mirelle. "That was a lovely tune we heard as we came in, *Piccola*. Won't you play it for us?"

Mirelle shook her head, smiling at his endearment. He had called her "little one" since she and Dolce were children. "I'm still practicing it."

"Another time, then." Dolce's father turned to Mama. "We are sorry to stop in so unexpectedly, Pinina. But she"—he nodded toward his daughter, his smile widening—"couldn't wait to share our news."

"Mirelle!" Dolce grabbed hold of her hands and sat down with her on the divan. "We're going to Venice!"

"We'll stay with Levi Balarin in the Ghetto Vecchio," Signor Morpurgo explained. "I'm going for business—and a ball at the Doge's Palace."

"Just think—a masked ball at the Doge's Palace!" Dolce sounded breathless. "The palace is exquisite, and just imagine the dresses the women will wear—the jewels . . ."

"You'll have a wonderful time," Mirelle said slowly.

"No, no, you don't understand!" Dolce cried. "You're coming, too!"

"I . . . ?"

Signor Morpurgo put up a hand. "If your parents permit, of course. We won't be there long—just a week. Balarin's wife will act as chaperone and look after the girls."

"That's very generous of you, David," Simone said.

"Mirelle, you'll love Venice! It's like living in a dream. Just think of the lovely young men we'll meet!"

Mama's smile faded slightly, as if she suspected Dolce's choice of suitors.

Anna entered, carrying a decanter of wine, crystal glasses, and a plate of almond biscotti. As she served the refreshments, Mirelle saw Jacopo was scowling. Noticing her eyes upon him, he hastily left the room.

Mirelle excused herself and followed him into the kitchen. "What's wrong?" she asked, grabbing his hand.

"It's not fair," he muttered. "Why do you get to leave?"

"Oh, Jacopo. It'll just be a lot of fancy lords and ladies."

"Yes, but you'll be *somewhere else*," he said bitterly.

Before Mirelle could answer, Mama entered the room, eyes

flashing. "Where did you go?" she demanded. "How rude! You espe-cially, Mirelle—after receiving such a marvelous invitation."

Mirelle, flushing, followed her mother back into the drawing room. When she looked around, her brother had disappeared.

The next few days were hectic, as both Mama and Dolce instructed Mirelle on how to behave in society. Mama harangued her on the importance of remaining modest, while Dolce explained how to flirt, walk in heels, and wave a fan.

"Men will throw themselves into the canals for your sake," Dolce said, laughing, as Mirelle practiced a coquettish look.

Mirelle shrugged, unconvinced. "For you, maybe. Not for me."

Mama fussed that there wasn't time to make Mirelle a new dress, that she didn't possess a ball gown rich enough for the Doge's Palace. "She'll look like a beggar compared to the noble ladies," she com-plained to Papa.

But the moment Signor Morpurgo caught a whiff of Mama's hesitation, he called on her. Mirelle never learned how he managed to convince her mother, but she was informed later that day that a dressmaker would be engaged in Venice to fashion a ball gown worthy of the event.

"He won't let us pay for it, either, Simone," Mama told Papa that evening. "He says Mirelle's doing him a favor, keeping Dolce com-pany while he conducts his business."

Papa's forehead wrinkled. "And you accept that? It's unlike you, Pinina."

Papa was right; Mama rarely accepted such grand favors. But she seemed willing to do so now. In fact, she stopped fussing altogether.

The day before they left, Mirelle walked by the kitchen and heard Jacopo talking in hushed tones inside with a group of his school friends. They were eating *bocconotti*—chocolate-frosted cream buns. As she hovered in the doorway, Moise said, "We should do it Saturday night, after Shabbat."

"What'll they do if they catch us?" Jacopo asked anxiously.

"What are you talking about?" Mirelle asked abruptly, entering the room. "Catch you doing what?"

"Moise, you and your big mouth!" Raffi hissed.

"It's just Mirelle," Jacopo said, glaring at her. "She won't tell."

"Tell what?" Mirelle demanded.

"There's a hole in the wall surrounding the ghetto—near the tanner's yard on the Christian side—and we're going to go through one night. So the Christians think they can keep us penned up?" Moise puffed his chest. "We're going to prove them wrong."

"Jacopo—you mustn't!" Mirelle turned to her brother, alarmed. "They'll flog you or throw you into prison!"

"It would be worth it," Jacopo replied grimly.

Mirelle knew better than to argue with him in front of his friends. But later that evening, she pulled him aside. "Promise you won't leave the ghetto at night," she said. "At least not until I'm back home."

"Why not? You get to leave—why can't I?"

"What if you got caught? Mama and Papa would be frantic with worry. Promise."

"I won't promise." He stared at the floor. "Don't ask that of me."

"You can't," she persisted. "Think how you'd frighten Mama and Papa."

He bit his lip. "They'll never know."

"I'll tell them if you won't promise." Even as she voiced the threat, she hesitated. She knew how much he longed to slip the bonds of the ghetto, just once. But he and his friends were too careless. What if they ran into the constable? It wasn't worth it.

Finally, she extracted a reluctant promise. He barely spoke to her the rest of the day, his face sulky and his voice curt. But before she left for Venice the next morning, he threw his arms around her and hugged her tightly.

They traveled up the coastline in a yacht Signor Morpurgo had borrowed from one of his wealthy business associates. The girls stood over the railing, pointing out sights along the way, and sat in deck chairs in the late afternoon, enjoying the gentle spray of the ocean.

"You've grown quiet," Dolce said, nibbling a pastry they'd been served with afternoon tea. "What are you thinking?"

"Just that it's been five months, now."

"Five months?"

"Since I was allowed to work for Papa."

"I thought you were past all that." Dolce sighed, looking at the horizon. "Venice will help. We won't be cooking or cleaning there, that's certain. Maybe we'll even find a beau to take your mind off that dreary workshop."

Mirelle shrugged. But as she watched the coastline slip by, a twinge of adventure tugged at her heart. Would she find a future in Dolce's dream of a city that Ancona could not provide?

"Look!" Dolce exclaimed, pointing.

Mirelle squinted to see. There, rising out of the haze of the water, was the faint outline of a city. She gasped as the yacht passed from the open sea into the Grand Canal. It was nearly twilight, but the waterway was crowded with smaller craft steered by red-capped men standing in their prows and melodiously calling to one another, long poles rippling through the water. Some of the narrow, curved-bottom gondolas had no awnings, while others concealed their passengers in small, curtain-draped cabins. Peering into one as they passed, Mirelle distinguished the shadowy outline of an embracing couple.

"Perfect for a romantic assignation," Dolce whispered.

The great white domed cathedral of the Santa Maria della Salute materialized from the mist as if by magic. As they moved out of the open waters and into the city's slender canals, Mirelle felt her excitement build. They drifted through watery streets banked by golden buildings, their stone and marble balconies crowded with bright flowers, green shutters opened wide. Even the laundry strung across the canal seemed to glimmer in the twilight.

People walked briskly across arched bridges, arms linked companionably. Gentlemen in figured waistcoats and tricorne hats, ladies in soft, flowing muslin and damask, flowers woven through their ornate curls. A cluster of boys in navy blue school uniforms yelled down greetings and waved from their perch on an ironwork railing. Every twist and turn opened a new vista, a new mystery.

They reached the dock and, after mooring the boat, disembarked. When her foot touched the ground, Mirelle was surprised to feel broken cobbles beneath her feet. All around her, narrow city blocks loomed, all twisting corridors and dirty, dilapidated building fronts. She and Dolce followed Signor Morpurgo onto a footbridge that curved over one of the canals, servants trailing behind with their luggage. Guards, their faces impassive, stood at a large stone archway. Mirelle's heart fell. Was this really the same city? The Venice they'd seen from the boat had seemed to float on air, but this . . .

The crumbling, crowded feel of the ghetto crept in on her. The sun slipped into the sea and Mirelle heard the familiar clang of a gate being slammed shut behind her.

# 12

# August 30
# Ancona

It was odd, Francesca thought as she brought another pitcher of water to her ailing husband, that her prayers to the Madonna could be answered in such a strange fashion.

Months had passed since she'd first witnessed the miracle of *La Madonna del Duomo*. Since then, thousands of worshippers had seen the Lady's eyes move, seen her smile or weep in despair. The townspeople had celebrated with candlelight processions full of cries of joy and adulation. Reports from Rome and other Italian cities claimed that the same prodigy had graced their congregations. Clearly, God was working through the much-loved portraits of Mary, the miracle of her mobile face keeping faith with her pilgrims.

Francesca was required, time and again, to tell her story—first to the priests, then to the city fathers, then to the skeptics and free-thinkers who tried to use logic and science to dissuade and discredit her. Barbara sat and watched, smirking, and Francesca couldn't decide what the child felt. Was she jealous of the attention being paid to her mother? Or had she absorbed her father's disdain for religion? Francesca reminded her early questioners that the child had witnessed the miracle first, but they swept that claim aside. Barbara simply hunched a shoulder whenever her mother testified, refusing to answer questions. In time, Francesca stopped dragging her to these sessions. Before long, she had almost forgotten the tug of the girl's hand on her arm that had made her turn. Francesca felt singled out by the Madonna's grace, almost as if she were herself a saint.

She remained steadfast in the face of the cynicism of nonbelievers, recalling Mother Mary's kind gaze blessing her. Even such well-known Jacobins as the lawyer Bertrando Bonaria could not refute the evidence of their own eyes. They came, sitting skeptically among the thousands of eager pilgrims, and left the cathedral pale-faced and openmouthed.

Bonaria, however, had sown a seed of doubt in Francesca's mind. Back in late July, he'd called her into his office and asked, "What exactly were you praying for when you first noticed the prodigy?"

"For our city's deliverance from the French general and my husband's safe return from the seas," Francesca replied, eyes fixed on the clasped hands in her lap.

"Your husband is . . ."

"A midshipman in the Venetian merchant marine."

"And you fear for his safety?"

"I'm his wife. Should I not fear for him?"

Bonaria scowled. "If he comes home wounded, I will take it as evidence that you and your fellow priests have concocted a fraud with your crying, smiling painting."

Father Candelabri spread his hands. "God forbid! Would you wish ill on the man just to prove your point?"

Bonaria laughed, clasping his ample midsection to keep it from juddering. "When you put it that way, Padre, it sounds dire indeed."

"Mary will protect him!" Francesca blurted, crossing herself several times.

But somehow, for reasons Francesca couldn't fathom, the Lady had failed her husband. Emilio had arrived home three weeks ago in excruciating pain, his arm cut almost to the bone. The wound had grown infected, running with black and green pus. The ship's medic had refused to treat him, grumbling that he couldn't spare the time to tend to the wound—unless Emilio wanted to lose the arm. So Emilio's captain had dispatched him on medical leave. Unpaid, of course.

"Come back in three months if they haven't taken the arm," he'd told Emilio, who had endured an agonizing donkey cart ride from the wharf to the farm before collapsing in Francesca's arms.

But the danger of death or amputation was past, Francesca reassured herself as she doused a clean linen rag with hot water. And perhaps Mary was testing her faith. If so, she would not find her wanting. Setting her lips in a straight line, she pressed the steaming compress on the wound as the doctor had instructed. Emilio cursed as she leaned against the wound with all her weight, trying to expel any lingering pus.

"You'll kill me," he muttered when she finally released him. The top of his lip was dotted with sweat.

"You can't abandon us so easily, *caro mio*." Francesca patted his arm dry and tied on a new bandage.

A week later, Emilio refused to stay in bed any longer. Francesca fashioned a sling and he made his way around the village. That evening, he brought his two favorite cousins home to drink grappa with him. They sat in the kitchen, elbows on the table, throwing back glass after glass.

Francesca, suckling her infant in the children's room, overheard their conversation with a rising sense of dread.

"Tell Roberto how you hurt your arm," said Desi, the town blacksmith.

"We were shipping some glass from Venice to Malta," Emilio said, his over-loud voice signaling that he had drunk too much. Francesca tried not to tense, knowing it would upset the baby, as she heard glasses clinking and more grappa being poured. "Some bastard Jew merchant was asking how many boxes we'd already loaded."

"How'd you know he was a Jew?" asked Roberto, the youngest of the cousins, an apprentice on the docks.

"Could anyone mistake that whiff of the devil? You know the type. Thick, bristling beard, beady eyes, salivating over how much the cargo would add to his coffers."

"Clearly a Jew," Desi agreed. "And?"

"So I said to myself, I can fool this Jew shit and maybe make a little money on the side. I brought back a couple of boxes we'd already loaded without anyone noticing. And they got counted again." Francesca heard Emilio take another slug of the grappa. "A good trick, no?"

"So then?"

Francesca pictured the scowl on her husband's face. "The Jew's helper saw me sneak out some other boxes. Rotten scoundrel gives a shout. I was about to hit him, to shut him up, when . . ."

Francesca moved the baby to the other nipple, willing him not to cry. She hadn't heard this story—not told this way, anyway.

"When what?"

"The Jew called this ruffian he'd hired to protect his goods. Big, gruesome-looking bruiser. He shoves me into a crate, the damn thing breaks open, and the glass shatters. One of the pieces cuts my arm, deep. Thought I'd never stop bleeding."

"How did they let those Jews get away with that?" asked Desi.

Another clatter of glass against glass. "Well, money talks, doesn't it?" Emilio said, slurring his words. "Why do you think we allow Jews to live here, in Ancona? When it's known they're supporting the French, piling up arms for them—"

"That's what they're saying down at the harbor," Roberto

interrupted. "Bloody traitors, the lot of them. Someone should teach them a lesson."

"Yes. Teach them a lesson—and soon," Emilio said.

Francesca shuddered. Not that she had any affection for the city's Jews—how could she, when she didn't know any beyond those she met in the marketplace?—but she hated the thought of Emilio wanting to hurt them. What would the blessed Madonna say? Surely her holy portrait would weep at the thought of violence.

Moving slowly but deliberately, Francesca took the now-sleeping infant off her breast and lay the boy in his cradle. "Sleep well, sweet Mario," she whispered. "Pleasant dreams." She said a silent prayer over him, listening to her husband's cruel laugh in the other room.

*Please, Blessed Virgin, do not let my babe grow up to brag and drink and hurt the women he loves.*

# 13

## SEPTEMBER 7
## VENICE

Daniel was lying on his bedroll, eyes shut, when his friend called, "Daniel!"

He opened his eyes. "What?"

Christophe grinned, waving a card, arms full of black silk. "Get up. We haven't a lot of time."

Daniel swung himself into a sitting position. It was late, twilight giving way to darkness. The lights of Venice twinkled across the water from their campsite in Mestre. Christophe held up domino capes and hoods. Two garish masquerade masks dangled from his wrist by gilt ribbons.

"We're going to a masquerade ball," Christophe said gaily, "hosted by the Doge of Venice's nephew, Lodovico Leonardo."

"*We're* going to a ball?" Daniel exclaimed. "Christophe, they'll throw us in prison! We're the enemy!"

"No, they won't." Christophe waved the card in the air. "We have an official invitation!"

Daniel shook his head. "And how did you wrangle that?" He started lacing up his boots.

"From my captain, won in a game of Hazard. He's an *aristo*, you know—barely made it out of the Terror with his head intact. But what does it matter? We have an *invitation*!"

Daniel nodded. Like Napoleon's wife, Christophe's captain wore a slender red ribbon around his throat during formal occasions to show the world how narrowly he'd escaped from *la guillotine*. He didn't speak of his blue blood often—Napoleon's Republican troops were less than sympathetic—but he did sometimes visit the Italian nobility that the French troops were busily subduing. He clearly didn't feel that attending their social events contradicted his military duty.

"We need to leave now—I've arranged for a dinghy to carry us across to Venice," Christophe said.

"Won't they know we're not the captain?" Daniel asked as he got to his feet. "Invitation or not?"

Christophe picked up the silk capes. "What do you think these are for?"

Daniel draped a domino over his shoulders. There was no gainsaying Christophe when he was in this mood.

Mirelle sat quietly as Signora Balarin's maid, Theresa, fixed her hair high on her head, letting some ringlets fall delicately onto her shoulders. Theresa powdered her face and applied the lightest touch of rouge to her lips and cheeks. Mirelle protested, remembering Mama's admonitions to remain modest, but Dolce waved away her objections.

Her ball gown—a rosebud confection of soft embroidered pink draped over a narrow white lace skirt—lay on the bed. Mama had given her a small sum to buy a new fan and some feathers for her hair. As she'd departed, Papa had also slipped her a purse filled with soldi. As they'd traveled down the coastline, Signor Morpurgo had overheard Mirelle marveling at her parents' generosity and suggested that he hold on to her funds for safekeeping.

"You can charge anything you buy in the shops to me, child, and

I'll handle the bills when they come in. That way, you won't have to worry."

Mirelle suspected he thought she'd lose track of how much she spent—and the treasures in Venice's stores might have tempted her, if she hadn't been more than capable of totaling up her bills. She purchased slippers, a new fan, and some pink ribbon to twine through her curls. Then she bought gifts to bring home—a lovely Murano glass pendant for Mama, some marbled paper for Papa, and a tooled leather case for Jacopo's drawing pencils.

After that, she just watched as Dolce indulged in a spending spree, buying Murano glass, exquisite pieces of Burano lace, and more gowns, slippers, fans, and jewelry than Mirelle thought her friend could wear in a year. When Dolce urged her to spend more, Mirelle shook her head. She wanted to keep a few coins to offer the servants as a thank-you at the end of the trip. It would be wonderful to spend so carelessly, she thought, but not everyone had Dolce's means.

Once word circulated that the wealthy Signorina Morpurgo had arrived in Venice, the Balarin home was besieged by young men. Mirelle enjoyed drinking coffee in Caffè Florian, the world's oldest coffee shop, and eating the plates of the Carnevale favorite, *chiacchiere*—fried dough dusted with sugar—Dolce's fawning swains brought them, and listening to music in the enormous plaza in front of the San Marco Basilica. They spent several afternoons floating down the Grand Canal in a gondola, a parasol tilted over their heads, Mirelle's hand languidly skimming the surface of the water. They even took a gay trip to the island of Murano with a party of other young people to watch the glass blowers.

Evenings, though, were spent in the ghetto. Signor Morpurgo would join them then, following a day filled with business negotiations. The Balarin household felt too small to contain all the suitors who came to woo the beautiful heiress. Yet while the rabbinical

scholars, bankers, shopkeepers, and businessmen were clearly courting Dolce, Mirelle also received a goodly share of flattering attention.

Dolce played fast and loose with her suitors—wearing flowers
sent by one, smiling sweetly upon another, forgetting her promise to
dance with a third. She flirted and preened and was almost insuffer-
able in her recounting of her conquests. Mirelle wondered if any man
would ever please her.

Tonight was the masquerade ball at the Palazzo Ducale. Tomorrow
they would pack and return home. While she was sorry to leave,
Venice didn't feel real. Mama might be disappointed that none of the
worthy young men had proposed, but Mirelle felt oddly relieved.

Theresa delicately slid the gown over her head. Glancing in the
mirror, Mirelle saw her eyes were sparkling, her cheeks delicately
flushed with pink. She threw her head up, laughing in excitement.

She hated covering her lovely gown with a domino and mask, but
there was no help for it. Dolce had bought herself a watered pale
green silk cape to match her new gown of ivory and seafoam green,
and she'd given her old dove-colored one to her friend. Mirelle's
mask was covered with tiny embroidered rosebuds, while Dolce's was
studded with sparkling jewels.

"Ready?" asked Signor Morpurgo, coming into the room with his
buff domino over his arm. He was dressed in clothing suitable for
a royal court: a cutaway coat over a fantastically embroidered vest,
knee-length breeches, and long, patterned socks. Lace decorated his
wrists and neck, while his waistcoat sported a heavy gold chain hung
with fobs, a quizzing glass, and an oversize watch. He held his gloves
and a mask in one hand; in the other, he clasped a slender case of
leather.

Mirelle nodded. "Shall I fetch Dolce?"

"In a moment, child. I have a token of the occasion for you." He
opened the leather case, revealing a necklace of pearls. "It will com-
plete your charming ensemble."

"Signor Morpurgo!" Mirelle, breathless, shook her head. "Mama would never allow me to accept such an expensive gift."

"She told me you'd say that." Dolce's father pulled a card from the box. "Read this."

It was written in Mama's handwriting. "My dear child," Mirelle read out loud, "I know your instinct will be to refuse this beautiful necklace. But I've agreed with Signor Morpurgo that you should set such scruples aside. Be a good girl and thank him prettily. Your loving mother."

Despite her misgivings, Mirelle allowed Signor Morpurgo to fasten the pearls around her neck. "Thank you," she murmured, forcing a smile.

After handing their invitation to a stiff footman standing at the waterfront entrance, Christophe and Daniel were swept inside. Already, throngs of masked, fashionably dressed people milled about the courtyard. Bowing and nodding as if he belonged, Christophe headed up a long marble staircase, stopping to salute the huge statues of Neptune and Mars as he ascended. Daniel followed close behind. Upstairs, they passed through several rooms, each one more ornately decorated than the one before, crowded with murals on walls and ceilings and hung with artwork that even Christophe, with his scant education, recognized as the work of great masters.

Before they could enter the great Sala del Maggior Consiglio, an immense room brilliant with candlelight that illuminated its magnificent artwork, a servant offered them a glass from a silver tray. Daniel downed his drink in a single gulp.

Christophe sipped more decorously and laughed. "You'll be drunk before the night begins if you keep that up. Let's find you some food and a lovely noblewoman to dance with."

Mirelle watched as Dolce's father slipped a purse to the guard at the ghetto gate. Hefting it, he opened the gate just wide enough for the three of them and a footman carrying a torch to slip through.

Mirelle felt the heaviness in her stomach lift as they left the cramped Jewish quarter. The Venetian ghetto was even more decrepit than her home in Ancona, with more people crowded into its narrow, tall apartments. Mirelle knew that medieval Venice was the birthplace of the first ghetto. She supposed it shouldn't surprise her how terrible it felt to live behind its gates.

They climbed into a gondola that would convey them to the Palazzo Ducale. For once, Mirelle was not wearing the yellow scarf required of Venetian Jewish women, though she'd tucked it in her reticule just in case, and Dolce had done the same. Signor Morpurgo hid his borrowed Venetian red Jew cap in his waistcoat pocket. In Ancona, the Jew bonnet was yellow, the same shade as Mirelle's scarf.

"I didn't know you could pay a guard to let us out after dark," she said, thinking of her brother's desire to escape the gates after nightfall. "Do you do it often, Signor Morpurgo?"

Dolce's father shook his head. "Not unless I'm forced to, *Piccola*. It's harder to do in Ancona, where I'm well known. If we're caught tonight, I can always show our invitation to the ball—most Venetian officials would accept that as a reasonable excuse. They certainly wouldn't want to flout the Doge's express wishes!"

"So we'll be the only Jews there?" Mirelle's heart fluttered at the thought.

Dolce sniffed. "Of course. From what I hear, the Venetians only love us when we make them rich. Which is why Papa was invited to this party. You certainly have assisted the Doge *and* his nephew to greater wealth, haven't you, Papa?"

Signor Morpurgo looked at the gondolier and footman, both of whom kept their faces expressionless. "Not a suitable topic of conversation, daughter," was all he said.

The girls quieted and Mirelle looked about her, enjoying the sway of the gondola and the sound of water splashing against its sides. The candles in the windows on either side of the canal were reflected in the ripples, and the stars and full moon above in the cloudless sky lent a certain enchantment to the night. *No wonder Jacopo wants to see this*, Mirelle thought, wishing her brother could be with them.

The splendor of the Doge's Palace left Mirelle breathless. She clutched Dolce's arm as they entered the Sala del Maggior Consiglio. Despite the room's vast size, it was packed with masked guests, their chatter almost drowning out the efforts of the musicians.

"I must find Lodovico Leonardo and have a word," Signor Morpurgo said. "Will you be all right?"

Dolce nodded. "Go, Papa." She took Mirelle's arm and the two of them walked slowly around the room. Mirelle was glad to be masked—it made it easier to be a stranger among all these glittering aristocrats. Several young men ogled them. One of them, in a silver domino and bird mask, detached himself from his friends and strode toward them.

"*Belle signore*," he said, bowing low. "We are consumed with admiration for your beauty and elegance. Might you grace us with your company?"

"The honor is ours." Dolce followed him toward the group.

"Alas," the bird mask said after exchanging bows, "we are not permitted to ask your names, *belle signore*. But it will be awkward not to be able to address you before the unmasking at midnight. How shall we call you?"

Dolce, bringing her fan into play, rapped his gloved knuckles. "You are forward, sir. But you raise an excellent conundrum. This being our first masquerade, we are innocent of the formalities. Certainly, no one can introduce us when we are all incognito."

"True," said the bird mask. "So you may call me Falco. I am, after all, a hawk searching for prey."

"How alarming," Dolce said, looking amused. "But in that case, I will be Sirena—a mermaid—which a hawk would not hunt. And my friend here—Bocciolo di rosa, or Rosa for short. A rose," she said, smiling, "just beginning to unfurl her petals."

"I'm Montagna," said a man who towered above the others.

*Mountain*, Mirelle thought. *The name suits him.*

"Leone," said the smallest of the group, puffing out his chest. He might not look like a lion, but he obviously thought he deserved the name.

"Segreto," whispered the last man, balancing on the back of a gilt chair. The man clearly had a secret, Mirelle thought, in addition to a pronounced slur. She wondered if he had been drinking too deep.

Guests were dancing in the center of the room; Falco extended an arm to Dolce, who took it, and they moved gracefully to the floor. Leone and Montagna both bowed toward Mirelle, making her giggle, while Segreto waved a servant over and plucked a drink from his tray.

An hour had passed, and Christophe and Daniel had danced with several lovely ladies. The beauty Christophe was leading to the floor now, a striking brunette whose clinging domino merely accented her curves, was fascinated to learn that he was a French soldier.

"French officer, actually," Christophe corrected, remembering who he was supposed to be. "A captain in the cavalry."

"And yet you are invited here, to the Doge's Palace?" she said wonderingly, batting her long eyelashes at him. "How is it possible?"

"If we were not instructed to keep our identities secret until the unmasking," Christophe told her, twirling her elegantly, "I could explain. Let me just say that my family tree extends across Italy, as well as France."

The brunette nestled in his arms. "Well, I will look for you at the unmasking," she told him. "For you intrigue me, Monsieur *le capitaine*."

Christophe bit back the correction that rose automatically to his lips—that he was no Monsieur, but rather Citizen *le capitaine*. Realizing that he and Daniel needed to take their leave before the midnight chimes announced the unmasking, he searched for his friend in the crush of bodies.

Mirelle was flushed and hot from dancing, first with Leone, then Montagna, and finally Falco. She waved her fan in a futile attempt to cool herself. The room was stifling, crowded with revelers, the windows latched tight against poisons the Doge thought lay in wait in the night air. Dolce was dancing with Montagna; Leone had wandered off. Segreto, slumped in a chair, looked as though he might at any second slip to the floor. If he were tipsy before, Mirelle thought, he had now drunk himself into a near stupor.

"You look hot and weary, little Rosa," Falco said, bending close to be heard over the noisy crowd. "And thirsty too, I'm certain."

"Very," she replied.

"I'll fetch some wine."

Mirelle glanced at his sprawling friend. "Wine—no, thank you. Perhaps some lemonade?"

"I'll bring some if I have to gather the lemons myself." The gallant bowed and turned into the mass of merrymakers.

Mirelle tipped her mask off her face to cool it. The movement roused Segreto, who hauled himself up and staggered before her, trying to bow and managing only to bump her. Mirelle's heart jumped as her mask clattered to the floor.

"You did that on purpose," he accused, staring at her exposed face.

"I didn't!" Mirelle bent to catch her mask by its ribbons.

"And you haven't danced with me. Am I so disgusting? I see you turning away!"

Mirelle stepped back, alarmed at his tone. Segreto grabbed her arm and pulled her close. "Give me a kiss," he muttered, so near Mirelle could smell the alcohol on his breath. "You coquette, dropping your mask. You know you want to."

"Let go!" Mirelle demanded, keeping her voice low. She yanked her arm from his grasp, but he reached out with both hands and grabbed her shoulders.

"One li'l kiss," he slurred.

"Unhand me," Mirelle cried, no longer caring if anyone heard her. His hands traveled from her shoulders up her neck to her chin. She slapped them away, hard enough that the sound echoed through the room. Heads turned, dozens of startled eyes widening.

"*Troia*," he swore. "I can pay, you know."

"You're calling me a whore?" Mirelle felt as though he'd punched her. Through a blur, she heard whispers, chuckles, saw fingers pointing. A flush heated her cheeks. "How dare you!"

She turned to flee; his hand grasped her elbow. With a gasp, she pulled away.

"My dear girl, isn't this our dance?" someone asked in French. A tall, broad-shouldered, black-dominoed stranger stood before Mirelle, extending a hand.

"What?" Segreto whirled toward him. "Who the hell are you?"

Mirelle stared at the stranger. A slow smile grew on his face. Was he laughing at her?

He nodded encouragingly. "Come, the music won't wait."

"Of course," Mirelle replied, taking his hand.

He ushered her swiftly away from Segreto, who stood cursing behind them. Still in a daze, Mirelle replaced her mask and allowed him to lead her onto the dance floor.

"Sir, thank you." Mirelle looked into the stranger's face. She admired his strong jaw, though the amused twist of his mouth made her hesitate. Since he'd spoken in French, she did the same. "I appreciate your kindness, though it was unnecessary."

Through the mask, green eyes twinkled at her. "What would you have done?" he asked. "Run him through? I'd happily lend you my sword if you want to engage him in a duel."

"I don't intend to fight him," Mirelle said, biting back a chuckle.

"Oh, too bad," he joked. "I'm certain you would have bested him."

She wondered how a Frenchman could be present at this event. Perhaps, she thought, he was an aristocrat escaping the Revolution. Many had fled to London, others to cities throughout the Continent. Yes, she concluded, he must be a noble émigré. But then she grew confused again when, as he twirled her, she caught sight of an army uniform beneath the domino. If he was a French soldier, was he not an enemy of the Doge, his host?

She decided it didn't matter. Whoever he was, he had helped her when the rest of the ballroom merely gawked and laughed. As the dance ended, Mirelle found she was reluctant to leave him.

"I'm happy to have served you," the man murmured in her ear as he escorted her off the floor. "I'll consider myself amply rewarded if you tell me a secret."

"A secret?"

"Tell me something of yourself," he murmured.

"Sir!" Mirelle unfurled her fan and touched him lightly on the wrist. "Spare my blushes."

"But you forget, lovely lady—I won't see your blushes beneath your mask."

"Even so, you are too forward." Mirelle wished Dolce could see her flirting so expertly.

"It's a small enough boon to ask, is it not—one small secret?"

Mirelle thought for a moment. What in the world could she tell him? She recalled that glimpse of his uniform under his domino and smiled. "All right." She looked up at his mask, at his glinting green eyes. "My secret? I don't belong here, any more than you."

"Daniel," Christophe said, pulling his friend away from the refreshment table, "we need to head back to camp. Before it's time to unmask."

Daniel popped a pastry into his mouth. "Agreed," he replied. "Though I'm surprised you don't want to dance more with the little beauty you so gallantly rescued."

Christophe laughed. "You saw that?"

"The whole room saw it," Daniel said. "The lady I was dancing with was impressed by your courtesy." He rolled his eyes. "When she learned we were friends, she demanded an introduction. There she is, over there." He nodded toward a lady in a blue cloak, who was fanning herself and smiling invitingly at them.

"Really?" Christophe asked, intrigued. He glanced at a gold-chased clock on the mantlepiece. "Well, there's still time."

Mirelle refused all other offers to dance. Flushed and unsettled, she decided to find somewhere to cool down.

She stepped close to a doorway someone had propped open and breathed in the sea air, fanning herself. Just beyond was a balcony where couples flirted, some embracing openly, in the moonlight. For a moment, she imagined herself in that romantic setting with the French soldier, then shook her head, annoyed. She would never see him again.

As she chided herself into composure, she watched two of the Doge's guards approaching, hands resting in obvious menace on their sword hilts.

One of the servants stepped up to them. "What is it?" he asked in a low voice.

"Where is Lodovico Leonardo?" the shorter of the two asked. "There are some French soldiers—imposters—here tonight."

French soldiers? Were they speaking of her rescuer? Mirelle's heart thudded.

"We have orders to start the unmasking early, at eleven rather than midnight," the taller guard said brusquely. "Once everyone removes their masks and cloaks, we'll arrest the imposters."

The servant led them off.

Alarmed, Mirelle searched the room for the black domino. She thought she saw him dancing with a blue-caped woman across the room, but by the time the music stopped, he had vanished.

*Perhaps he's already left*, she told herself. He wouldn't be so foolish to stay until the unmasking, not if he were an imposter. An enemy.

But despite telling herself that it was none of her concern, Mirelle kept an eye out for him until she caught sight of him again, talking to a dark-haired man wearing another black domino.

Lodovico Leonardo, the Doge's nephew, stood on a small dais at the front of the room. The guards flanked him, their swords half drawn from their scabbards. "Friends," the party's host called out genially, "your attention, please?"

The merrymakers ignored him, chattering and laughing. Mirelle moved swiftly through the crowd as people began shushing one another. She elbowed aside the noble guests until she reached the two men. Panting slightly, she touched her dance partner's arm.

He turned, startled. "Yes, lovely lady?" he exclaimed, his surprise at her gesture causing his voice to carry above the hubbub.

A few people turned to stare.

Mirelle bit her lip. How could she tell him it was imperative that he leave—now—without attracting the attention of either the guards or nobles—whom, she realized, would turn on these men in an instant?

"It's hot," she muttered, clutching his arm and digging her nails through the silk. "I feel faint."

"I'll take you outside," the soldier said gallantly.

He started to lead her away, but Mirelle realized that he was leaving his friend behind. Thinking quickly, she dropped her fan and, as if overcome by the heat, tottered forward a few steps. "Oh, no!" she called out, leaning heavily on his arm. "Sir, perhaps your friend could . . ."

"Daniel," cried the soldier. "Would you fetch this lady's fan, please?"

The second man scooped it up, brought it forward, and handed it to her with a bow.

Mirelle leaned in. "Both of you need to leave," she hissed. "Now."

They looked at one another blankly. Mirelle's rescuer shrugged, looking amused. "Is it a game?" he asked. "Another secret, perhaps?"

"You must hurry!" Mirelle muttered.

Just then they heard the Doge's nephew proclaim, "Time for the unmasking, friends! Please, everyone, stay where you are."

"Christophe," the friend asked anxiously, "It's not midnight already, is it?"

Mirelle pretended to gasp, closed her eyes, and sagged against Christophe.

"Daniel, help," he cried. "She's fainted. Let's carry her outside, into the fresh air."

They half hefted Mirelle through the crowds, down the wide staircase, and onto the dock. As soon as they were out of sight of the guards, Mirelle straightened.

"Quick," she said to them, "go now. They'll arrest you if they discover you during the unmasking."

The two soldiers stared, openmouthed.

"How—" the one named Daniel started to ask.

"No time to explain," Mirelle urged them. "Go."

Christophe took her fingers and kissed them. "Our most sincere thanks, lovely one," he said, then climbed into a gondola.

Mirelle watched as the gondolier pushed out of the dock and away, putting the fingers the soldier had kissed against her hot cheek. Would she ever meet him again? Had he even been real to begin with?

Surely not, she told herself. He was just part of the dream that was Venice.

# 14

## SEPTEMBER 11
## ANCONA

Emilio's arm was healing, though he wondered if he would ever regain his strength. He couldn't even pick up the crates of vegetables Francesca sold in the marketplace. When she'd gathered the crop into baskets and asked for help earlier, he'd lifted one only halfway to the donkey cart before, feeling a sharp twinge, he'd let it drop, scattering produce on the sunbaked dirt.

Barbara had laughed at him, so he'd slammed into her with his good arm, knocking the brat on her back. Scrambling to her feet, eyes blazing, she'd screamed for her mother. Of course, Francesca came scurrying out to see what he'd done.

Before she could try to solve everything with some wretched prayer, he'd turned on his heel. "I'm going to town," he'd said before hurrying from the house, her accusing eyes scorching his back.

He hadn't told her the bad news yet. He'd received official notice two weeks earlier, delivered when the merchant marine had put into port. Emilio had struggled through the letter—he'd never learned to read fluently—then crushed the paper in his hand.

*Due to complaints about you from a Venetian merchant of influence*—a Jew bastard, they meant—*we hereby discharge you from service. As a potential thief, you are not entitled to any back pay.*

*We will look upon any attempt to join another ship with extreme prejudice.*

In other words, Emilio thought now, stalking down the dusty road toward town, they had it in for him. All because of a harmless trick that bearded crook deserved!

His arm throbbed. Would it always be useless—he forever forced to depend on his pious nag of a wife? He winced, thinking of Barbara's childish pout after he'd struck her. He loved her—of course he did—but she shouldn't have laughed. He wasn't sorry he'd hit her, not one bit.

Entering the cool, shadowed tavern, he reached into his pockets for the few baiocchi he had left. Having returned to Ancona still unable to pay back his gambling debts, no one would let him try his luck, not at dice and not at cards. He had to depend on Francesca's scarce egg and vegetable money, which was barely enough for a drink. Emilio looked around, hoping someone might stand him a few. But it wasn't yet midday. Most of Ancona was hard at work. Just as he should be, setting up Francesca's produce stand in the marketplace. He glowered at the idea. Emilio Marotti was no farmer or huckster. Let her do it.

The sun blinded him, and he flung his good arm up to shield his eyes. Maybe someone would buy him a coffee at the café near the harbor. He kicked moodily at rocks on the roadway, not realizing that Cardinal Ranuzzi was on the footpath until they bumped into one another.

"Emilio!" The cardinal raised his hands to grasp Emilio's elbows. "Are you still home? I thought you'd be back at sea."

Emilio pulled away, hunching his shoulders. "I'm not completely healed yet, Your Excellency. And I've decided the merchant marine isn't for me."

"Really?" The cardinal peered into Emilio's disgruntled face. "How strange. Unless . . . is there a tale behind that decision?"

Emilio squirmed. In the common way of things, the cardinal would not have bothered with him. But Desi had told Emilio about his latest sermons, rants about how the unfaithful were poisoning the pure air of their Catholic harbor town. The priest, Emilio knew, was more welcoming of late to the farmers and fishermen who sat in the cathedral's back pews, downwind from the wealthier merchants and nobles.

But what could Ranuzzi want from him?

"Excuse me, Excellency, I'm on my way . . ."

The cardinal laughed genially. "I won't scold you for not coming to church, if that's what concerns you, my son. I leave that to your conscience. After all, your wife . . ." He spread his hands expressively.

Emilio laughed. "She attends enough for us both, doesn't she?"

"One can never be too devout, of course." The cardinal shrugged. "But she's not my concern right now. You are. Tell me why you're not going back to the marine."

Emilio wanted to say it was none of his business, but this was a man of the cloth. You couldn't just tell a priest to bugger off. "Well— the person who hurt my arm, a Jew, accused me of theft."

Ranuzzi nodded, heavy jowls swinging. "A Jew, eh? Then it's true what Roberto told me. Let me buy you a coffee and you can tell me all about it."

His reluctance fading, Emilio let himself be led back toward the harborside café. Why turn down a free coffee? It would be a relief to tell someone—even this nosy priest—how badly he'd been used.

"That's the whole story," Emilio said an hour later, pushing his chair back. The café table was covered in coffee cups and glasses of water, crumbs of sandwiches and pastry.

"Wait." Cardinal Ranuzzi leaned forward. "What will you do now?"

Emilio shrugged. "Help Francesca with the farm, I suppose, until something better comes along."

"That tiny farm won't get your father's shop back. I'd be surprised if you can do more than live hand to mouth. No wonder you're bitter."

Emilio glared. Was Ranuzzi mocking him? "What's it to you?" he grunted.

"I can help you overcome your ill fortune." The cardinal straightened, concern written on his face. But then his expression turned blank. He moved back, murmuring, "Wait," under his breath.

"Cardinal!" A fashionably dressed, portly man stepped forward, a tricorne hat tilted rakishly over his forehead. "Well met, Excellency!"

"Bertrando Bonaria." The priest inclined his head. "Good morning, *avvocato*."

The lawyer bowed, then looked inquisitively at Emilio.

"This is Signor Marotti, Francesca Marotti's husband." The cardinal suddenly looked amused. "You interviewed Signora Marotti while investigating the prodigious portrait, did you not? Father Candelabri told me you wished poor winds and ill favor upon this good man here, as proof against the Madonna's authenticity." He paused, staring suggestively at Emilio's face, which blackened as he made sense of the cardinal's ornate words. "As you can see, however, he landed without mishap."

"You're Marotti?" Bonaria rumbled.

"You wished me ill?" Emilio half rose from his seat, fists clenched.

Ranuzzi put a hand out, stopping Emilio. "Gently, my friend," he said. "It was a philosophical discussion, nothing more. Bonaria bears you no actual ill will. Do you, *avvocato*?"

"Of course not, Excellency," Bonaria hastened to agree. "I wish you both good day—and especially good fortune to you, signore." He scuttled away as quickly as his heavy body allowed.

The cardinal laughed quietly, templing his fingers. "Well, that proves what I suspected. You're a man swift to act, are you not, Emilio?"

"I won't put up with slurs against me, if that's what you mean. Or against my family."

"And what about your city? Do you care as much for Ancona as you do about your wife and children—about yourself?"

Emilio couldn't understand what the priest was getting at. Tired of whatever game he was playing, he started to stand once more. "Whatever you say, Excellency. I'm off."

"Wait!" The cardinal raised a hand. "Listen for a moment. I need men who'll rise quickly to a challenge. You could be one of them."

Emilio's brow furrowed. "What's it pay?"

"Not a salary—but in time, I promise you reward."

"What kind of reward?"

"I can't explain. You'd need to trust me. But enough to buy that shop you want."

Emilio tilted his head, considering. What could this priest have in mind? It sounded like loot of some kind. Emilio knew the church was riddled with crooked clergymen. But for a priest to openly sanction theft? Impossible. "Tell me more," he finally said.

Ranuzzi nodded, cautiously noting who was in the other café seats before continuing. "You know that the miracle of the Madonna brought many Christians back to the fold—not just here, but throughout Italy."

"So?" Emilio kept his face expressionless. Hell's teeth, the priest wasn't trying to drive him back to the faith after all, was he? He had more than enough of that at home.

"The pope is reluctant to interpret the signs. But several of us realize the truth and aren't afraid to act. The Madonna has signaled us to take up arms against the godless French—to do what we can to harass and harm them." The cardinal leaned forward. "And not just the French. Also the Jews, who curry favor with the invaders by stockpiling arms to attack the honest Catholics of Ancona."

The cardinal kept his voice low. "You hate the Jews as much as I do. I remember when they refused your father more time on his loan. He lost his shop and your family never recovered. Now another Jew hurt your arm and had you thrown out of the merchant marine. No wonder you've no love for them. Join us and you'll be well cared for."

"Join you? Who are you?"

"We call ourselves the Catholic Fellowship, the guardians of the one true faith in Italy. We recognize that if we don't protect ourselves, the French won't hesitate to endanger our immortal souls by denying us our faith, just as they've imperiled their own Catholics."

"Guardians of the one true faith." Emilio snorted. "And how are you guarding this faith?"

The cardinal shifted even closer to him. "By being patriots. By troubling the enemy wherever we can."

Emilio pursed his lips. He might not be a devout Catholic—he left that to his eternally praying wife—but he certainly would like to chase the damn French from the country. And he wouldn't mind getting even with the Jews, too.

"The trick you tried to pull off against that Jew merchant—that's just the type of thinking we need. Join us, Emilio, and I promise you won't regret it. What do you say?"

Emilio met the cardinal's extended grasp and shook firmly. "I'll join you. And I won't let you down."

# 15

# FEBRUARY 1, 1797
# ANCONA

Papa argued with Mama about wasting time, but in the end Mama prevailed, and the entire family went to the tailor for new spring clothes. The shop was a dark, quiet refuge in the middle of the busiest part of the ghetto. The tiny room at the front of the store couldn't accommodate them all, so Jacopo and Mirelle mounted the steep wooden staircase to the second floor, where Balsamo the tailor lived with his wife, her sister, and his three young children. It was hard to imagine so many people fitting in the cramped room, yet it served Balsamo's family as living, eating, and sleeping quarters.

When Mama called for Jacopo, Mirelle came halfway down the stairs with him. Papa was standing in his shirtsleeves while the tailor took some final measurements.

"Can you hurry?" Papa asked, fidgeting. "If I'm away too long, my men might slack off—and it's our busiest season. You know what they say in Proverbs: 'Slothfulness casts into a deep sleep and the idle soul shall suffer hunger.'"

"Stay still, then. 'A man cannot spin and reel at the same time,'" Balsamo countered. "That's from Proverbs, too."

Smiling, Mirelle tucked that saying away for another time. "Say good-bye to me before you leave, Papa," she called.

Balsamo's sister-in-law, Fresca, sat upstairs with them, carefully stitching a sleeve. Not wanting to disturb her, Mirelle wandered to the high window that looked out on Via Astagna. Kneeling on a window seat, she watched as dozens of people passed by—apprentices hurrying on errands, housewives with their shopping baskets, children rolling hoops on the cobbles. Two shopkeepers lounged in their shop doorways, laughing and talking. As she perched there, Mirelle drifted back into yet another daydream of her dance with the Frenchman in Venice. She'd tucked the memory away, like the secret he'd requested. She hadn't wanted to share its sweetness with Dolce, but of course her friend had pried every detail out of her, sighing over its romance.

The sound of footsteps running up the stairs made her turn and stand. Papa came into the room. "Mirelle, come give me a kiss good—"

A burst of noise interrupted him. Shouting. A scream. Then another, piercing the morning air.

They froze, confused, as the shouting grew louder.

" . . . all the Jews' fault!"

"Bonaparte will kill us all!"

"The Jews brought the French here!"

"Find the weapons they've hidden!"

"Kill them! Kill the Jews!"

Simone reached the window with three long strides. Heart pounding in her throat, Mirelle followed close behind.

She gasped, horrified. On the pavement, where the young children had been playing, bodies sprawled flat in pools of blood. One boy cried for his mother, clutching a maimed hand. Fallen groceries rolled over the roadway into the gutters. A woman bent over a child, shielding him, as men beat her from behind with cudgels. One of the storekeepers slumped in his doorway, his hand holding a torn chest, a bloody knife on the doorstep beside him. The other was gone.

"Kill the Jews!" The shout was clear now. "French lovers! Bonaparte sympathizers!"

A piercing shriek rose from the floor below. Mirelle, transfixed and dizzy, recognized her mother's scream.

Papa jerked both her and Fresca away from the window. "A hiding place, signorina! Hurry!"

Fresca flung open a tall cabinet in the back of the room, which held a large clothing press. Papa pushed Mirelle, face first, beneath it. She could just fit in the space between its elevated legs.

"Stay there!" Papa demanded. "Don't move!"

The press stood directly on the floor. Mirelle put an eye to a knot-hole in the wooden slats and the room below swam into view. Her heart thumped with fear. Men on the first floor, three of them, beat Jacopo with staves, the thudding blows echoing. The tailor sagged against the wall, a trickle of blood running from mouth to chin, the top of his skull bashed in. Mama, dress torn, kneeled in a corner of the room, begging with the rioters to spare her son's life.

Mirelle heard a rushing in her ears. The scene beneath her blurred, growing distant.

Her vision sharpened as her father burst into the room, wildly waving a fire iron. She gulped back a scream. Papa barely made it through the door before someone plunged a dagger in his stomach. Groaning, he staggered over to Jacopo, who was lying flat on the floor. Mama screamed again.

One of the attackers grabbed her from behind. "Shut your Jew mouth!"

The rasping of her own breath was loud in Mirelle's ears. She tried to stifle the noise. Covering her mouth didn't help. Time slowed; the dreadful world beneath her swerved out of focus. She bit her lip, tasting blood, hoping the pain would stop her from fainting. Jacopo and Papa lay lifeless on the floor. A hulking man pulled at Mama's skirts. A shout from outside distracted him; he stopped what he was doing, pushed Mama to her knees, pulled a knife from his stocking top, and held it to her throat. She spat at him. He knocked her on her back and straddled her waist. One of Mama's hands frantically pinned her skirts together, the other grabbed at the man's blade. Blood ran from her palm down her arm. Mirelle willed herself not to cry out.

"Let's go!" someone called. "There are more Jews to kill!"

The man on top of Mama jumped off, nicking her cheek with his knife. He slammed her ribs with his boot and she rolled into a ball, groaning. Then he and the other rioters stampeded from the tailor's shop, knocking bolts of cloth to the floor as they went. One draped itself over Jacopo's mutilated body.

Mirelle, heart pounding, watched them leave. The cries from the street battered her ears. Should she go down? But Papa told her to stay.

Then he was moving, groaning. Mama crawled to him and collapsed against his side. With a backward kick, Mirelle flung open the cabinet door and ran downstairs to them both.

Hours later, after the rioters cleared the streets and the sounds of horror had changed to wails of pain and mourning, the Morpurgos' servants appeared at the tailor's shop with a cart. As they carried Mirelle's father and mother out to it, Mama screamed at them, hysterically insisting that they take Jacopo's body—but Mirelle's dead brother was left behind.

Mirelle stumbled alongside the cart. The walk was a blur. They passed the ghetto gates. They were closed, unusual for the middle of the day. A large chain and padlock were thrust through the iron-work. Dazed, Mirelle fixed her gaze on the heavy chains, staring as they passed. A chill stole up her back; something was wrong with the gate. Try as she did through her shock and fear, however, she couldn't make herself understand what.

A night later she sat up, thoughts of her brother assailing her. Her father lay in his bed, groaning in pain. Mirelle knew Mama sat next to him, her own injuries stubbornly untended. The night was pitch black, the air still thick with smoke from the fires that had been set throughout the ghetto—fires that rekindled in one corner even as they were extinguished in another.

Mirelle, her eyes wide, was haunted by the vision of the lock and chain at the gate. She shook her head. What was different? Then she realized it. The padlock had been dangling on the ghetto side. The Jews had locked themselves behind the gates of the ghetto, preferring its imprisonment to the violent embrace of their Gentile neighbors.

# PART TWO

## FEBRUARY 1797

# 16

## February 1, 1797

They brought him home to Francesca with a gaping wound in his side.

"What in the world happened?" she cried as the men placed him gingerly on the bed. "Emilio, what happened?"

He grunted in pain, not answering.

Desi, sooty forearms covered with blood, cried, "Send the girl for the doctor!"

"Barbara!" Francesca screeched, wringing her hands. "Barbara, come here!"

The girl peered in the doorway. "What happened?"

"Run!" Francesca shouted. "Get Doctor Poratti!"

Her husband's open wound was seeping blood onto the sheets and floor. "I'll get some linen," she said, voice trembling. "Roberto, can you haul some water up from the well?"

She pulled a sheet from the clothespress at the bottom of the bed and started tearing it into strips. Roberto, whose face was splashed with blood and tears, hurried from the room. She heard him grunting as he turned the stubborn handle, winching up a bucket of water.

As he hefted it inside, she seized the bucket, poured it into her soup cauldron, and swung the cauldron onto the fire. When it was hot, she dipped several of the fresh bandages in the water and brought them, still dripping, into the bedroom.

Emilio tossed and turned, muttering with pain. Francesca bit her lip and began praying the first words that came to mind: "We bless You, Lord, who has heard our prayer and commanded deliverances for our friend and Your servant, who has been under Your afflicting hand . . . "

She took one of the soaking cloths and pressed it against the wound to stem the bleeding. The moment she grazed his skin, Emilio roared out.

"May he not only live," Francesca continued loudly, "but declare the works of the Lord!"

"Shut up!" Emilio screamed, edging away from the compress. "Francesca, leave me be!"

She reared back as though he had struck her. "Emilio, you need the Lord's help to heal your wounds!"

She held the cloth against his side again. He groaned as it blossomed with deep red stains. She let it drop in a wet heap on the floor, took up another, and pressed it tighter against the wound. He tried to push her away, but his hands were feeble. His lack of strength frightened her more than the bleeding gash.

"Desi," she said to the blacksmith, who leaned weakly against the wall. "Tell me what happened!"

"It was the cursed Jews," he started, but just then Barbara panted into the room, the doctor close behind.

"Please step aside, Signora Marotti," the doctor said, opening his black physician's case. "Someone—Roberto—take her outside."

Emilio's cousin seized her arm to lead her to the yard.

"There's water boiling on the fire, *Dottore*," she said over her shoulder.

"You're a good wife, my dear. Take the girl, too, would you, Roberto? Desi, you stay. I may need you to hold him down."

The baby began to wail. Francesca slipped from Roberto's grasp and went into the children's room. She sat down on the rocking chair and put him on her breast. "Help me, Lady," she whispered, thinking of the peace she'd felt every time the Madonna rested her gaze upon her in the cathedral.

"Mama?" Barbara stood at the foot of the chair. "What happened?"

*Calm, calm,* Francesca told herself. "I don't know, Barbara. We'll find out soon."

Emilio's free-flowing curses in the next room made her stiffen. She took another deep breath.

Little Mario's cries rose to meet his father's. Francesca gathered the baby up and took him out into the cold air, rocking him against her. He settled down, whimpering.

Roberto was slumped on the bench under the magnolia tree. Francesca sat beside him. "Roberto, if someone doesn't tell me what happened, I'll go mad."

The boy—he was still a boy, even if he'd recently sprouted dark hair on his chin and under his nose—looked at her with wide, tragic eyes. "It was horrible," he muttered. "Horrible."

"Horrible? What was horrible?"

Another earth-shattering cry came from the cottage, followed by a whimper of such pitiful intensity that Francesca half rose.

Desi emerged, face white under the dirt. "The doctor is giving him syrup of poppies now that he's tended to the wound."

A moment later, the doctor came out. "Don't disturb him," he instructed Francesca. "Sleep is his best remedy right now. I'll return in the morning to change the bandage. Don't touch it! It may seep a little, but unless you see a river of blood, he's fine. I know you, Francesca, you won't panic at some red spotting. Don't send for me unless he spikes a fever. I can't tell who else was foolish enough to get hurt in this idiotic brawl. I've already been called for in a dozen places."

"You might want to stop at the cathedral first, *Dottore,*" Desi said. "The cardinal . . . "

"Of course our blessed man of peace is the first to strike a blow." The doctor shook his head. "Fools, all of you—you and your so-called Catholic Fellowship." With that, he stuck his hat on his head and strode away.

For two full days, Emilio slept, waking only fitfully to sip barley water and swallow a few mouthfuls of food. Francesca was too busy to pay attention to the gossip that floated up from the harbor and marketplace.

On the third day, he'd recovered enough to tell her his side of the story.

"They're saying people were killed in the riots," she said. She didn't want to ask, but she needed to know. Breathing deeply, she added, "Children, too. Tell me you didn't kill anyone."

Emilio shrugged. "The cardinal planned it, told us where to go. He sent me and the boys to the tailor's shop. Gave us absolution beforehand, said whatever we did was for Christ's sake."

Francesca cringed.

He put a hand on his wound and grimaced. "It still hurts. Fucking hell. The cardinal told us what to do. So what if we hurried a few Jews to burn in hellfire forever? They were heading there anyway." He scowled. "After the tailor's, we moved on. I knew where I wanted to go: the house of the richest Jew in the ghetto. You should see this villa!" He stopped and cleared his throat. "Are you sure the doctor said I can't have anything to drink? Not even some wine in water?"

"He said no. You risk infection."

"Damned doctor. Hurt me worse than the bastard who stabbed me. Worse even than when I cut my hand in Venice. Bring me some of that disgusting barley water, then."

Francesca hurried to the kitchen and came out with a pitcher and a cup. She poured him the drink, then sat back down. She had to hear the rest, had to know.

"Go on," she said.

"Like I said, you should have seen this place. How a Jew is allowed to live this way . . ." He shook his head in disbelief. "It was like a noble's house, crammed with statues and paintings. Rich trinkets scattered about. No sign of the family, so I started scooping up my share when a man suddenly burst in yelling. A whole gang of servants were right behind, all armed. The cardinal told us the Jews were hoarding arms to help the invading Frenchies, and when they came in waving those swords, I knew he was right. They're traitors, I tell you. They deserved everything we gave them." He took another swig of barley water. "Every single one of them had a sword. But had no idea how to use them. I couldn't help myself. Laughed. Shouldn't have. The first man—the rich Jew himself, I wager, he was certainly dressed rich enough—slashed my side. I fell. If the others hadn't crowded around me, pushed him back, he would have killed me. Worse luck, I had to leave all the loot—and so did Desi and Roberto, to help me home. Bastards." He cursed. "The Fellowship will make it up to us, though."

"The Fellowship?" Francesca twisted her hands in her lap. "Is this what you've been up to, all those nights I thought you were doing good works? Planning an attack on the Jews?"

"On the Jews and the French. The French are almost here, Francesca. Someone must stop them. Your Mary painting hasn't kept them from conquering city after city, has it? They're on their way here—with the Jews in league, plotting to help them seize Ancona."

"How dare you say anything about Our Lady?" she burst out. "How do we know why she looks down upon us? Who are you to say she has failed?"

Emilio's eyes were alight with malice. "Cardinal Ranuzzi says she's encouraging us to take up arms. That's why he organized the Catholic Fellowship. Not to sit around and fret, not to cower behind the walls of our church—but to do good works, *real* good works, the kind they erect statues for, write songs about. Patriotic works. Don't forget, Francesca, we have a cardinal on our side. He must know better what your Lady wants than you do. He's a prince of the Church, isn't he? And you're just some peasant woman."

Francesca turned away, body shaking. Throwing a shawl over her shoulders, she left the house and went out to her small backyard altar. There, she lowered herself to her knees, hands clasped before her in prayer, and burst into tears.

# 17

# FEBRUARY 3

The attack changed everything. The ball in Venice seemed to have happened in another lifetime; its dreamlike quality and Mirelle's subsequent romantic fantasies were tainted by the nightmare she was now living. For the past two days, she'd sat on a wooden box in the middle of her parents' drawing room, mirrors concealed by black velvet, a sideboard covered with loaves of bread and cake, olives and oranges. Mama wouldn't leave her wounded husband, so Mirelle welcomed the parade of well-wishers alone. She pushed away the memories of violence that threatened to overwhelm her, accepting the pats and kisses and whispered prayers that were all the Jewish community of Ancona had to offer.

Everyone paid their respects: the rabbi, her neighbors, the two Morpurgo brothers. Dolce came early and left late each day. The men from the workshop stood awkwardly, pushing their wives forward to say what they could not. Mirelle endured the prayers for mourning in her mother's old black silk dress, which was now ripped open at the neck—a tear inflicted upon her by the rabbi's wife as a symbol of grief while they lowered her brother into the ground. Mama refused to stir from Papa's side, even for the funeral. So Mirelle stood solitary, feeling alone in the world, convinced that nothing would ever feel whole again.

As she sat shiva—the week-long observance of mourning—she

was flooded by memories of her brother. She remembered him as a baby, taking his first steps from Mama's arms to hers. How his face had lit up when she'd kissed his chubby cheeks. How Papa had given him a bundle of candy the first day of school, telling him that his study of Torah should always be sweet. How proud both parents had been of his talent for art and his progress in the ketubah workshop. How she'd miss his off-key singing at the Shabbat table, their tussle over the largest piece of Mama's pastry, his teasing about the still-unknown man she'd eventually call husband.

During the second day of shiva, Signor Morpurgo explained how he and his servants had defended his home. "They were taking what they could, destroying the rest," he told a rapt audience. "But we scared them off. It's amazing what you can do when forced to it. Imagine me, wielding a sword!"

Rabbi Fano grunted, his thin mouth pursed disapprovingly. "I hear you actually wounded one. If he had threatened your life, perhaps you would have been justified. But in defense of mere property?"

Morpurgo glared. "And after they took my property? Do you think they'd have hesitated to kill us? Are we not here, mourning one of our own?"

"What would you have us do, Rabbi, if they attack again?" asked a neighbor. "Cower and hide, rather than fight?"

The rabbi grimaced. "In a moment, you'll quote 'an eye for an eye,' or some other Biblical verse endorsing violence. But have not generations of scholarship taught us better? I ask again: Should we not abstain from killing for mere property?"

Dolce, sitting up stiffly, retorted, "With all due respect, Rabbi, my father works very hard for that 'mere property.'"

Rabbi Fano shook his head, his long gray hair brushing his narrow shoulders. "Surely, David, your daughter doesn't mean to be so bold, so unmaidenly. She should remember her place."

Mirelle stared at her friend. How did Dolce feel, being called unmaidenly by the rabbi before everyone? Did it sting her the way Mirelle's banishment from the workshop still stung her?

Dolce took a long, shuddering breath before replying, "No wonder adherents of the Enlightenment abhor religion, Rabbi. Why should I curb my tongue when I disagree with you?"

"Dolce," her father cautioned her. "Show some respect."

"Am I entitled to less respect than he?" she flashed. "I will be happy to show the same level of respect I'm shown."

Affronted, the rabbi bowed. Though she agreed with Dolce, Mirelle wished her friend had kept her opinions to herself. Her brother's shiva was not the place for such disagreements. She put a hand up to her throbbing temples.

Signor Morpurgo was watching her closely. "Let's change the subject," he said quietly.

"What will happen when the French get here?" someone asked, and conversation shifted to General Bonaparte's campaign. Half-admiring, half-fearful, they spoke of how he'd cut a swath through Italy before arriving at the gates of Mantua and forcing the city to surrender. The French were heading inexorably toward Ancona, and it seemed only a matter of time before the city fell.

For the past two nights she'd sat up, propping her eyelids open, afraid to sleep. Fearing the dreams that visited when her hands dropped and her heavy lids fell shut. Nightmares suffused with the copper taste of blood, the suffocating smell of fire and smoke, the terrifying touch of men's hands crawling over her skin. Her parents dead. Via Astagna deserted, buried in fog. Even during the day she kept her breathing shallow, fearful that her sorrow might burst forth from her tightly laced corset.

On Saturday morning, Mirelle woke to the sound of cannon fire outside the city gates. Despite her anxiety that the French could strike Ancona any moment, she realized she needed a respite. The urge to escape the ghetto that held the Jews fast, like unwitting flies in a spider's web, was too strong to resist. Today she was prohibited from sitting shiva, mourning superseded by the holy Shabbat. No one would be surprised if they stepped through the half-open door and found her away from home.

When she'd returned from Venice, she'd made Jacopo show her the gap in the walled street he and his friends had talked about. Then she'd kept on finding ways to delay him from sneaking out.

Her heart ached, remembering how she'd stopped him. Eventually he would have overruled her; his desire to escape had been too strong. It was one of many life's ambitions he'd never realize now.

You had to be young and slender to fit through the fissure. Christians avoided the alleyway because of the tanner's shop that sat at one end. A permanent stench—of urine and dung and rotting animal hides— sat in the alleyway, and when the wind blew from the east, it crept into the ghetto, causing the Jews on that poorest of side streets to flinch behind their handkerchiefs.

Drawing near the gap, Mirelle looked to all sides. She heard the faint chanting of Shabbat services in the synagogue up the street— the rising sound of the pious, a sound that drifted off in the wind as she strode toward the crack in the wall.

She wrapped the ends of a black shawl around her, the damp February wind whipping at her dark dress. Her curls threatened to tumble from the cloth hat tied tightly beneath her chin. She took the ends of her ribbons, tied them over the brim of her hat, and folded her body nearly double. Heavy stones scratched her shoulders as she squeezed through, but in a moment, she was outside the gates.

Heart pounding, she made her way out of the city toward the promontory where the Jewish cemetery sat. Without her Star of David armband and yellow kerchief, both deliberately left behind, no one would ever be able to tell she was Jewish.

Within minutes, she had climbed the steep hill and was standing just outside the graveyard, on a shallow rock that commanded a view of the gleaming turquoise harbor far below. She entered and made her way to the new burial plots dug in the attack's aftermath. Staring at her brother's grave, she hoped the wind would sweep away the heaviness in her heart.

She knew she should not be here. Not on the Shabbat, when shiva was forbidden. Not outside the still-locked gates of the ghetto, which were all that stood between her and the mob that had killed her brother. Especially not now, when the French troops were rumored to be camped just beyond the city, fresh from their victory at Mantua. Not when any moment could bring more terror and blood.

But something drew her to this little patch of earth overlooking the city, begrudgingly given to the Jewish community generations ago when it became clear that the narrow ghetto alleyways could not house the dead along with the living.

The white pillar gravestones with their curved tops glowed in the thin winter gloom. Pelted by light rain, Mirelle fixed her eyes on the fresh mound of dirt that contained her brother's remains.

"Jacopo . . . *marmocchio*," she whispered, somehow hoping the familiar taunt would restore him to life. It was unimaginable that she would never see him again.

The enormity of what her family had lost assailed her. The family legacy, the next generation of artists, the very workshop itself—all slaughtered together with her young brother. A knot tightened in her chest. The air seemed too thin to breathe.

She thought of her parents—how her mother had doted on Jacopo, the light in her eyes as she'd watched her only son study his lessons or peered down at him from the synagogue balcony every Shabbat. She thought of her father's pride in the boy's work—how he'd been growing into the best artist in the workshop, how Papa's talents had reflected themselves in him. How happy he'd made the both of them. Tears streamed from her eyes.

Jacopo was dead, and the workshop would die with him.

*No.* She rested a hand on the grave. She was no artist, it was true— no craftsman. She had none of her father's talents. And she was not a man—not a suitable heir to the family business. But it was still her family business, her heritage. She recalled Narducci's tale of her grandfather nearly bankrupting the manufactory, and the whisper of a smile came to her lips. A whisper of defiance.

She could preserve her family's legacy—and she would.

Tears rose, and she swore a vow to the mound of earth before her: "I'll take care of everything, Jacopo—Mama, Papa, the workshop. I promise."

She stood for a few more minutes, waiting for some peace to descend on her soul. Instead, tears spilled down her cheeks, her breath caught in her throat. She cried until she could barely breathe. Nothing helped. Her well-wishers had all told her that time would heal the wound, but she couldn't imagine a time when she wouldn't grieve.

Just as she was about to succumb again to her despair, she remembered her parents at home. Had they noticed that she was away? Were they frightened for her safety?

"I'll take care of them, Jacopo," she repeated. Then, not bothering to wipe away her tears, she headed home.

# 18

# February 6
# Ancona

The weather turned rainy and a perpetual pall hung over the camp. Daniel couldn't dry his socks or his trouser legs, which stuck to his ankles and legs like seaweed. *Even the dustiest of mountain trails is better than this*, he thought, peeling the clammy cloth off his thighs.

A year in the Army of Italy had hardened him. His once-slender arms and chest were now crisscrossed with muscles that flexed as he effortlessly carried a heavy pack and musket over miles of rocky terrain. His legs, too, were thick as cables, testing the seams of his narrow trouser legs.

The troops had camped outside Ancona for nearly a week. A rumor had threaded its way through the ranks: the general preferred to wait out any resistance rather than engage insurgents who'd stockpiled arms inside the city gates. It reminded Daniel of the early months of the campaign, when all they'd done was wait. The only difference now was that Christophe was obsessed with the young woman who'd saved them in Venice.

"We need to go back," he told Daniel. "I was a fool, not asking her name. How will I ever find her again?"

"Perhaps you won't." Daniel smiled, waiting for his friend's inevitable outburst.

"I must! This was fate, Daniel. I can't stop thinking about her—about her lovely face, the way she was so brave, helping us escape!"

In the months since Milan, the French forces had struck the Austrians again and again like lightning. Daniel couldn't help but admire Bonaparte's sheer nerve and rock-solid resolve. Napoleon spread his armies thin and marched them hard—thirty, forty miles a day. Then he brought them back together, always attacking the Austrian lines where least expected.

Despite this string of victories, it was said that Bonaparte was now miserable. Whispers circulated through the men's tents that the great man had written his wife, telling her that he'd never been so bored as by this sorry campaign. Daniel and the others caught his mood. They snapped at one another, at the foul weather, at the long wait. Their food supplies were running low and they would have to take the city to replenish them.

"It'll be soon," Sebastian consoled them after their meager dinner that evening, lighting his pipe.

"Not soon enough." Pierre touched his aching shoulder. His wound always troubled him in damp weather.

Daniel said nothing, looking over the bay at the harbor. Something about the city glowing white against the hillside stirred a childhood memory. "I just remembered—I have cousins in Ancona," he said. "Perhaps I'll meet them."

"Cousins in Ancona?" Christophe picked his head up and stared at him. "In the army?"

Daniel smiled and shrugged. "Doubtful. The boy's too young and the father too old. And I don't think the pope's army accepts Jewish soldiers in its ranks."

The next morning, their orders remained unchanged. Daniel's lieutenant poked his head into his tent early in the afternoon.

"I'm rounding up volunteers to go foraging," he said. "Christophe and Sebastian are coming. You too, no?"

It was drizzling again, and Daniel felt cold and damp. But he was hungry, too. He stared at the mud at his feet. "What do you think you're going to find?"

The lieutenant, Adrien, who was just a few years older than Daniel, looked thoughtful. "There are farms outside the city. Maybe the farmers will treat us to a hen. Or some cheese. I'd be happier with a pig, but I know you—"

"No pigs," Daniel said. "It's bad enough I can't keep kosher. What my brother Salomon would say . . ."

Christophe, entering the tent just then, laughed. "He'd tell you you're going to hell—that is, if you Jews believed in hell. Look, my stomach can't take this. From what I hear, it's going to be a few more days before we attack the city. Let's go, shall we?"

Daniel laced up his boots and followed. Sebastian was waiting outside the tent. As they left camp, Adrien rounded up a few more men, who grumbled but acquiesced.

They tramped through brackish lanes, the ground squishing beneath their feet. The rain was gentle, but it soaked every inch of their uniforms.

Noticing Daniel's drawn face, Sebastian laughed. "You need to learn how to be a soldier, *mon ami*. If I told you what it was like in America, fighting the British . . ."

"No one's complaining," Daniel snapped. "Just where are these farms, anyway?"

"Around that bend—about half a hectare away." Sebastian motioned down the road. They passed a grove of almond trees, their leaves just unfurling.

"Not so bad, then," Christophe said. "I can just about taste—"

A shout cut his words short. Daniel's breath caught as a mass of men ran toward them from all sides, surrounding them, shrieking, waving cudgels and daggers. His mind whirled. *Ambush!* He snatched his saber from its sheath and was comforted by the twang of metal against metal. His fellows formed a tight knot, back to back, ready to fight.

"*Cani francese!*" one of the Italians cried. "*Arrenditi oti uccido!*"

"What's he saying?" Christophe muttered. "Daniel?"

"Surrender or be killed, I think." War-hardened as Daniel was, his heart skipped a beat. After all those terrifying battles, was this how he was going to die? At the hands of Italian thugs?

"We're not going to surrender, and I for one would rather not die here," Sebastian said coolly. "Sir, shouldn't we charge them?"

Adrien often took his lead from Sebastian, since he was the unit's most experienced soldier. So Daniel wasn't surprised when Adrien cried, "Charge them, men!" And he was even less surprised when Christophe was first to leap into the fray, sword arm flashing.

Overwhelmed by the direct assault, the Italians raced away down the roadway, screaming curses as they fled. One man, a swarthy ruffian already sporting a bandage from an earlier injury, was left behind. He lay in the dirt, howling in pain.

"What should we do with him?" Christophe looked down scornfully.

"Just leave him." Sebastian kicked the Italian in the ribs and laughed as he curled into a tight ball.

"No." Daniel was aghast. "We should bring him to camp, get him a doctor."

"They'll return for him," Sebastian argued.

Adrien stood apart, face drawn tight in concentration. "This was an ambush—not a well-planned one, but an ambush all the same." He glared at the Italian. "What's your name?" he demanded. "*Nome?*"

"Emilio Marotti," the Italian groaned.

"Daniel, Christophe—take him back to camp to be interrogated," Adrien ordered. "The rest of us will head to those farmhouses. I'm hungrier than ever."

Daniel watched as the men marched down the road, then turned to his friend. "Should we carry him between us?"

Christophe shook his head. "I'm not carrying the bastard. He can walk. Tell him so."

"But he's hurt."

Christophe started down the road, looking over his shoulder, face hard. "Let's go."

Daniel dug deep, trying to remember the right words. "*Alzati e cammina*," he said, grabbing Marotti by the elbow and forcing him to his feet. "*Muoviti!*"

# 19

## February 7

After a week, the period of mourning officially ended. Even though Mirelle felt that the heavy stone on her heart would never lift, she slipped from the house early that morning and made her way to the ketubah workshop.

Sabato Narducci was in her father's office, sifting through some letters, though not using Papa's desk, which might have upset the workers. It certainly would have upset Mirelle. He stared as she entered.

"I came to work," she said in answer to his unasked question. "Papa is still in bed. I know he's worried—"

"No, no, Mirelle. You've been through so much already. You should be at home with your family."

"Thank you—but I want to be able to tell Papa all is well."

"We're making do. Truly, child, go home."

Mirelle studied his face. She couldn't let him brush her off. The workshop was her family's responsibility, and she was the only one who could tend to it right now. "That's kind, Signor Narducci, but I'm certain you're shorthanded. Weren't Baruch and Tonio wounded in the attack?"

"We're doing our best," Signor Narducci said heavily, sitting down. "Yes, we're shorthanded. But we're managing."

"Can't I do something for you? Has anyone checked this morning's schedule of deliveries? Or the accounts?"

Narducci looked down. "Not yet."

Mirelle picked up the heavy ledger and turned the pages. For the first time since her brother had died, a kind of peace settled over her. But the feeling was short-lived. She frowned to see heavy lines striking through obvious errors. One entire page of figures was scrawled out, as though the bookkeeper had surrendered to confusion. She flipped to the page where she had made her last calculations and moved forward slowly; her face blackened as she turned the leaves of the big book.

"Oh, my," she whispered under her breath. "What a—"

"Mess?" Signor Narducci shrugged. "Your father isn't happy with Arturo. He's spoken with David Morpurgo and they're looking for someone else."

"Putting this to rights will take days," Mirelle said unhappily. A quick visit, under the circumstances, might be excused, but what would Rabbi Fano say if she stayed on? She thought of Jacopo and her parents. She set her mouth in a firm, determined line, picked up a pen, and started to work.

Narducci, watching her, seemed to intuit what she was thinking. He paused for a long moment before asking, "Do you know what will happen now that your brother . . . ?"

Mirelle shook her head. "Papa should explain all that." She picked up the delivery schedule. "Well, here, at least, we're in good shape," she said, running a practiced eye down the list. "We haven't missed any of our dates yet. But"—she pointed to the top date—"this commission for London is coming up fast. Who's working on it?"

Narducci looked at the notation. "Leo. I'll check in with him this morning, make sure he's aware of the date."

❈

After returning home, Mirelle walked resolutely into her parents' bedroom. The shiva was over and it was time to resume their lives, hard though that would be.

Her mother slumped in a chair by the bed, asleep, her face still crusted with blood, a dried trace of saliva in one corner of her mouth. One was not supposed to wash or comb one's hair during shiva, and Mama looked unclean and unkempt. Her father lay in bed, his body tense, his hand at his side where the stab wound was slowly healing. He opened his eyes as she entered the room and stared blearily, barely able to lift a hand in greeting.

"My darling girl," he murmured before letting his eyelids fall shut again.

She could feel the pain radiating from her parents; she had to take a deep breath to stop from bursting into tears. Turning on her heel, she went into the kitchen and poured warm water from the kettle into a basin, then collected her ivory comb from her room.

Kneeling by her mother's side, Mirelle wrung out a flannel and gently began to clean the blood and dirt from her face. Mama's eyes fluttered open. She reached down and touched the top of Mirelle's head.

"Mira'la," she whispered, her voice thick. "What . . . ?"

Mirelle took her hand and kissed it softly. "It's been a week."

Mama's eyes flooded with tears. "My Jacopo. My baby."

"Shhh," Mirelle said, putting down the cloth. She began loosening her mother's hair from its pins. It tumbled down her back, snarled and filthy. She gently tugged at the tangles.

Mama was sobbing quietly now. Mirelle looked at her father. He was lying in bed, open eyes fixed on his wife and child. A tear ran down the side of his face, wetting the bank of pillows supporting him.

"How are you feeling, Papa?" Mirelle asked, voice hushed.

"Fine, child. Healing quickly." But his waxy face and eyes, deep pools of dark pain, belied his assertion.

"I stopped into the workshop this morning," Mirelle told him.

He and her mother shared a swift look.

"You know you're not supposed to—" Mama began.

"Things have changed, Mama. I needed to go—and the men needed to see me. It was important to make sure that everything was all right."

"Is it?" Papa asked, scouring her face anxiously.

Mirelle nodded. "Signor Narducci has the deliveries well in hand. I can't say the same for the accounts, though I did start to put them right."

Papa sighed wearily.

Mirelle waited for him to say something more. When he didn't, she said, "After I've cleaned Mama up, I'll fetch the barber."

Her father smiled with obvious effort. "A sweet thought, child."

"Dolce's father suggested it, Papa. They've been here every day. Everyone came to condole with us—all the neighbors and the boys from . . . from school . . ."

Mama began to wail loudly. Mirelle stopped combing her hair and hugged her tightly.

"Thank you for greeting them." Papa's voice was a mere thread, hard to hear over Mama's sobs. "It's been a week? The medicine makes me so sleepy."

Mama sat up and wiped her face with her grimy apron. "Time for your next draught." She rose from the chair and stepped over to the table, where a reddish liquid sat in a small vial. She carefully measured a few drops of the opiate into a cup of water, stirred it, and brought it to him, reaching behind his back to support him.

"Must I?" Papa complained. "Can we not wait for the doctor? It's long past time for me to leave my bed. To return to work."

Mama shook her head. "I'll ask him when he comes, but I want you to take this now. I insist, Simone."

He opened his mouth—like an obedient child, thought Mirelle—and swallowed.

"Please tell everyone how grateful we are," he said to Mirelle, settling back against his pillows. His eyes closed.

Mama sat down in the chair, looking limply out the window.

"Mama, you must let me help nurse Papa. You need sleep. Use my bed."

But her mother shook her head, struggling against tears. "I can't leave him, Mira'la. I can't lose him, not like I lost . . ."

Mirelle nodded softly. "Can I bring you anything? Anna tells me you've barely eaten since . . . for a week now. Let me bring you some food. Everyone's brought a dish."

Mama sighed. "All right. Something small." She stopped suddenly, wincing. "I haven't asked, but you must know by now who else was killed. How many?"

Mirelle's shoulders sank. "More wounded than killed, thank the Lord. But at least ten dead. I'll fetch you some food and we can talk."

When the doctor finally arrived, later than expected, Papa was awake again. Mama tried to shoo Mirelle from the room, but she refused to leave, concealing herself modestly behind a screen instead.

"The site of the stab wound is healing nicely," the doctor said after examining Papa and applying some camphor to his stomach and side. "Another few days—perhaps a week—and you can return to work on a very limited basis. Not until then, however."

Papa nodded. "I'd like to talk with my foreman. Can he pay a visit?"

"A short one. Your best medicine is sleep. And plenty of tea or water—no coffee, no spirits." The doctor started to put his instruments away. "But just because the immediate danger is past doesn't mean you're completely healed."

The air in the room grew still.

"The dagger thrust compromised several of your internal organs, Simone. You'll have difficulty making your water for a long time. Perhaps forever. And should you become sick—with even a trifling illness, such as a cold—you'll find your resources are depleted. Sickness will drag on for long periods or may carry you off unexpectedly."

Mirelle covered her mouth with a hand.

"So you're saying," Papa said, his voice ragged, "I'm living on borrowed time?"

The doctor cleared his throat. "Medicine is not an exact science, my friend. But there are accounts of patients who never fully recovered from such wounds. I would suggest hoping for the best—a long life ahead—but preparing for the worst."

"The worst has already happened," Mama murmured. "Our Jacopo . . ."

"I know," said the doctor softly. "I understand your daughter is of age to become betrothed. Perhaps her husband might take over the ketubah works when—*if* necessary?"

Mirelle's other hand rose to clasp the first. Was this possible? Could they find her a husband who could manage the factory with her help? Then she felt ashamed. How could she think of taking over the workshop when what it really meant was taking what had once been Jacopo's? Yet her visit that morning had proved how important it was for her to return. She would have to convince Papa that her continued presence was the best thing right now, rabbi or no rabbi.

"No, no," Papa said. "My nephew, Beniamino, will inherit."

"We should send for him," Mama said. "To train him."

The doctor's bag snapped shut. "Don't wait too long," he said. "Merely as a precaution."

# 20

## FEBRUARY 9

In the end, Ancona fell into the general's hands like a wet, bruised plum.

He rode into the city with a squadron of cavalry, Christophe two rows back from the officers. The French negotiated a cease-fire with the pope before a single shot was fired. The rains had stopped, and high, puffy clouds chased one other in a brilliant blue sky. Craning his neck, Christophe enjoyed the sight of the red-tile-roofed buildings rising from the edges of the sea, elbowing one another in their climb up the sheer cliffside, surrounding the bay like an amphitheater of rose-tinted stone. People lined the streets—some cheering the French soldiers, waving handkerchiefs and small, handmade flags, others sullen and withdrawn.

"I want to see the harbor," Napoleon called to Junot, smiling and waving from his saddle. "That's why we took the city, after all."

"I can show you, Cittadino Generale," said a small, dapper man who'd maneuvered his way beside the general's mount. He had joined them at the gates of the city as they entered, introducing himself with an elegant bow as Fedele Bianchi, leader of the city's Jacobin Club.

"Is it true that a ship that sails from your port is just ten days' distance from Constantinople?" Bonaparte asked. He shot a glance over his shoulder. "Lucien, think of it: the riches of Constantinople. We could set sail tomorrow and arrive next week. What a treasure to lay before the Directory! And the man who takes Turkey—what power he would yield!"

"Careful, brother," laughed the boy-faced Lucien Bonaparte, who served as one of the general's aides. His sleepy blue eyes gleamed. "Your ambition is showing."

"Pah!" The general waved a hand. "Whatever I achieve is for the glory of the Republic."

Christophe's chest swelled. *Silly hero worship*, he chided himself. As if he were a boy instead of a war-weary soldier. But even so, it was an honor to serve Bonaparte. Christophe repeated the general's words in his head, to recall them for Daniel later that evening: *For the glory of the Republic . . .*

The ranks of onlookers thinned. Some dirty-faced boys tried to mix in with the orderly rows of the grenadiers, but they were shooed away.

Bianchi regaled Bonaparte's staff with facts about the city as they rode toward the port. "Ancona was named by the Greeks, Generale. They called it an 'elbow,' and the name 'Ancona' derives from the Greek word."

"I was told Trajan built an arch here," Bonaparte said. "We must arrange a parade so our soldiers can march under it."

"Consider it done." Bianchi clasped his right hand to his chest. "I will make the arrangements. Tomorrow? The next day? What a glorious day for Ancona!"

"Tomorrow, perhaps," Bonaparte said. "But I interrupted your history lesson, signore."

"Please, honor me with the title of Cittadino." Bianchi stopped short. "We are such admirers of the French, of your revolution, of your tender embrace of liberty!" Bianchi moved his fingers to his mouth, kissed them extravagantly, and flourished them in the air. "We seek—no, we demand!—your assistance in helping us throw off the shackles of il Papa."

Both Junot and Lucien Bonaparte cast a worried glance toward Bonaparte. Everyone knew he was frustrated by the Directory, which kept dispatching contradictory orders on how to treat local progressive movements. Christophe recalled the victory at Mondovi, where citizens had cried "Long live the Republic!" and soldiers had helped them plant Arbres de la Liberté, the Liberty Trees of the Revolution. Yet in Milan—under orders—Bonaparte had rebuffed the political clubs of Milan, and he would probably do the same here.

But Bonaparte did not seem to mind the little Italian's enthusiasm. "We shall see," the general replied, looking around.

"Here," Bianchi said, "is the port. We approach the Arch of Trajan, Generale."

Bonaparte dismounted and threw his reins to his groom. The rest of the men followed suit, tying their horses to a railing near the harbor and forming ranks.

"I have long admired Emperor Trajan." Bonaparte surveyed the high expanse of sparkling white marble.

The archway was an impressive monument, Christophe thought, towering above the harbor wall, supported by two pairs of fluted columns, a steep marble staircase leading up to it. It was twice as high as it was wide, and the white stone gleamed brightly against the blue sky.

Bonaparte stood beneath the arch with the Italian, his back to his troops, gazing out upon the turquoise waters. The ocean lapped the shoreline; a few seagulls flew languidly overhead.

"Trajan was a commoner, like me," Bonaparte said, his voice echoing through the archway. "Yet he was one of Rome's most beloved Caesars. We have much in common, he and I—both generals fighting beyond our country's borders to secure peace. Under Trajan, the Roman Empire expanded to its fullest extent. He conquered Germany, the Near East—what, Lucien?"

Bonaparte's brother, who had dismounted and followed him up

the steps, whispered in his ear. Christophe noticed how much alike they looked, with their beaky noses and flushed cheekbones.

Bonaparte laughed and shrugged. "A great leader, as I said." He came down the worn marble stairway, the wind whipping at his bonnet. "And yet—I say it again, brother, and fear not to do so—by birth, nothing but a commoner."

# 21

Mirelle sat with Dolce in the smallest sitting room in the Morpurgo mansion, a room Dolce favored for its street view. The sky-blue walls and a sentimental frieze of white swans, necks intertwined as they floated close to the ceiling, made the room feel airy and spacious. The furniture was upholstered in peach silk, and inlaid tables and elegant knickknacks were scattered about. Seated in that tranquil oasis, trying to set her mourning aside, Mirelle found it difficult to remember that a conqueror now commanded their city.

But it was so. The ghetto was still locked and barred against Gentiles, whose threats had grown dire during French diplomatic negotiations with the pope. The Christians circulated rumors, Signor Morpurgo told the girls, that the Jews planned to supply the French from a cache of weapons concealed somewhere in the ghetto. But they were not to worry, he hastened to reassure them: Bonaparte's troops would counter any fresh attacks.

Mirelle wished she were back at home. She felt heartsick; her loss was still an ever-present bruise. But Mama had insisted that the two girls spend the afternoon together at the Morpurgo mansion.

Mirelle and Dolce sat sewing. At least, that was what they'd intended to do. But Dolce threw aside her organdy shirtwaist after setting a few untidy stitches. Mirelle's own needle moved slowly and steadily. She concentrated on her embroidery, trying to forget the heartbreak of the outside world. Her sewing was not as effective a distraction as her nervous friend, however. Dolce roamed the room, fidgeting with the curtains, adjusting them so they could view the street, yet remained unseen.

"Should you not ring for a footman to attend to that?" Mirelle asked, watching Dolce struggle with the heavy silk drapes.

"Look up, Mirelle," Dolce demanded. "Is anything happening at the gate?"

Mirelle craned her neck. "The guardhouse is empty, the street deserted. It's been deserted for days."

"You'd think Bonaparte was the bogeyman, scaring everyone into hiding. He needs to come to the ghetto and reassure the people. What's keeping him?" Dolce walked back to her seat, irritably shifting her skirts.

Mirelle tucked her embroidery into her workbasket and held out a hand. "Give me your blouse."

Dolce shook her head, her face bright with mischief. "Mirelle, forget the blouse. Don't you want to see the French troops? I hear they are charming."

Mirelle sighed. As if she could think of flirting with soldiers at a time like this. "Dolce! If your father heard you . . ."

Dolce rose, lifted her arms high over her head, and paced in a tight circle. *She looks like a blond tiger*, Mirelle thought, half-admiring, half-disapproving. *A tiger trapped behind bars.*

Imprisoned, just like every other girl on the cusp of womanhood. Mirelle's thoughts drifted back to the argument she'd had with her parents that morning. She'd once again left the house early and gone to the workshop for a few hours of work. For the past two mornings she'd sat at her father's desk, concentrating on the accounts, helping Signor Narducci make decisions about some of the newer commissions. It soothed her bruised soul to be there; it was a brief escape from the pain of her brother's murder. This morning the numbers had once again woven their spell on her, and it had been nearly midday before she'd made her way back home.

Mama was standing at the front door when she walked in. "Where have you been?" she asked accusingly.

"At the workshop," Mirelle responded, trying to make light of it. "I'm not late for luncheon, am I?"

"Mirelle," her father called from his bedroom, his voice still weak. "Come here, please." He was propped up in bed, his face sallow, pain etched into his forehead, long fingers fidgeting over the coverlet that was drawn to his chest. Mirelle saw disapproval mixed with the suffering on his face.

"Are you feeling any better this morning?" she asked.

"How likely is that," Mama sniffed from behind her, "when the rabbi paid us a visit this morning?"

"Rabbi Fano?"

"Is there another rabbi in Ancona?" Mama asked sourly.

"Pinina, hush," Papa said. "Mirelle, where were you?"

"I told Mama—at the workshop. The men appreciate it, Papa. And it's good to know that everything is going smoothly, isn't it? With you sick and Jacopo . . ."

Mama gasped.

Mirelle cast her a pleading glance. "Mama, I'm sorry, but it's important to have someone from the family there." She looked at her father's pained expression. "Papa, aren't you pleased to know the men are managing? That I'm helping them manage?"

Papa closed his eyes.

"Mirelle, didn't you hear what your mother said? The rabbi paid us a visit today." Papa opened his eyes again. "And it wasn't a condolence call."

Rage bubbled up inside Mirelle. Weren't rabbis supposed to be compassionate, especially in the face of such tragedy? "What did he want?" she asked, voice shaking.

"People are talking about your visits to the workshop. He demanded assurances that this would not be a permanent arrangement. It's not that he was unsympathetic."

"He doesn't sound sympathetic." Mirelle sat in her mother's chair with a thud.

Papa took her hand and stroked it lightly. "I know you thought you were doing a good thing, child. I appreciate your intentions. But you mustn't go back. Promise me?"

"But, Papa—"

"Mirelle," Mama snapped. "Are you going to argue with your father? Now?"

Mirelle opened her mouth, then shut it again. She wanted to ask what the rabbi had said, if he had threatened them with sanctions once more. But her father's fingers trembled in her grasp. She couldn't upset him, not just then.

But now, watching Dolce pace restlessly through the room, she felt her own prison bars—the ones formed from society's expectations—close tightly around her. *I must find a way to break them down,* she told herself, sewing Dolce's discarded shirt. *Rabbi or no rabbi, Papa and the workshop need me.*

# 22

Christophe watched as Bonaparte walked the length of the quay. The rest of the cavalry tied their mounts to a long fence rail near the water and followed him on foot to the center of the harbor, where the Via Astagna ran upward through the steep hillside. A huge stone and iron gateway blocked the street entrance, a deserted guardhouse standing beside it. The gate was padlocked from the inside, secured by an enormous metal chain.

"What is the meaning of this?" Bonaparte demanded. "Do your citizens believe they can keep out my troops with a mere lock, Signor Bianchi?"

"I . . . I'm not certain . . ."

Before the Italian could stammer out the rest of his reply, a man emerged from a villa near the gate. The elaborate home seemed out of place on the crowded Via Astagna, whose close-packed houses created puddled shadows despite the noontime sun.

Christophe watched the man draw nearer. A look of confusion crossed the general's face.

"Lucien! What is that man wearing?" Bonaparte demanded.

Lucien didn't respond. Instead, Major Junot stepped up and said, "He is a Jew, General. This must be one of the cities where they enforce what Jews must wear on the streets."

The man drew closer. Christophe could see that he was richly dressed, his clothes tailored to his portly proportions. Only his arm-band and ridiculous yellow bonnet set him apart from other Italians. He came up to the barred gate and, looking through its ironwork curlicues, doffed his cap and bowed deeply.

"General Bonaparte? I am David Morpurgo. Welcome to Ancona's Jewish Quarter."

"If you are Jewish," Bonaparte told him, "you must know you have nothing to fear from us. Why are these gates locked?"

"Not against you, General. Against this city's Catholics, who recently led a riot here, killing and maiming our people. They've threatened to harm us again if we support the French cause."

Bonaparte's eyes narrowed. "How did they think you planned to support us?" the general demanded. "And why did no one tell me you were living under threat?"

Morpurgo shrugged. "I speak of the Gentiles' suspicions, not actual facts, General. They insist we've concealed a cache of weapons within the walls of the ghetto to fight on your behalf. I only wish it were true."

Bonaparte raised an eyebrow. "So you will open this gate?"

The Jew shook his head. "My people are afraid. Blood still stains our streets. Please understand, General, this is not a sign of disrespect."

Bonaparte thought for a moment, lips pursed. Then he turned to Junot. "We have some Jewish soldiers in our ranks, do we not?"

The major shrugged. "I'm not sure."

"General?" Christophe called out, standing stiffly at attention. "You have a unit of artillerymen formed of almost all Jews."

Bonaparte turned, his face flushed with quick anger. "Who gave you permission to speak, soldier?"

"No one, sir. Sorry, sir." Christophe looked directly into the general's hooded eyes, his heart thudding in his chest.

"The men need to understand military discipline," Bonaparte snapped, looking at Junot.

"Yes, sir." Junot's light gray eyes turned hard as slate as he surveyed Christophe head to toe.

"Approach, soldier," Bonaparte told Christophe.

Christophe stepped out of the ranks and took three steps forward. He snapped again to attention, swallowing hard as he pushed out his chest.

"What is your name? I see you are a corporal."

"Christophe Lefevre, General."

"Not from a military family?"

"No, General. My father died at the Bastille. My uncle, who raised me, is a printer."

"And now you are a corporal in III Corps. But one clearly without a proper understanding of the usages of military rank. How long have you been serving?"

"Since I turned seventeen. A little over a year now."

"All with the Army of Italy?"

"Yes, General."

Bonaparte turned to Junot, his stern face lightening. "Can you imagine being eighteen again, my friend?"

Junot smiled. "That was before we met, General. I find it hard to remember my life before we met."

Bonaparte laughed. "Flatterer." He turned back to contemplate Christophe, seemingly mollified by his trim appearance. "At ease, Corporal."

Christophe relaxed a fraction, keeping his shoulders stiff.

Morpurgo cleared his throat. "General, if I may . . ."

Bonaparte looked over his shoulder impatiently. "Wait a minute." He turned back to Christophe. "Corporal, you were saying—about a unit of Jewish soldiers?"

"Yes, sir. Many of them enlisted when I did. One is a friend of mine from childhood."

"You are friends with a Jew? Isn't that unusual?"

Christophe allowed himself a small smile. "He apprenticed with me in my uncle's printshop. That was unusual, too."

Bonaparte looked at Morpurgo. "Would you wait a moment?"

Morpurgo nodded.

Bonaparte turned his gaze back to Christophe. "Walk down to the beach with me so I can give you some orders," he said, and moved toward the water's edge.

Christophe followed, breath caught in his throat. *Given orders directly by the general. Wait until Daniel hears this!*

# 23

The sudden din of clanging metal brought both girls to the window.

Several soldiers stood at the ghetto's entrance, swinging hammers and axes. The clash of iron against iron reverberated through the narrow streets.

"What are they doing?" Dolce's voice rose uneasily.

Mirelle yanked the curtain aside. "It looks like . . . they're breaking down the ghetto gate!"

Up and down the Via Astagna, shutters flung open and heads poked from the buildings. Fingers pointed at the gates. A wave of shouts, excited and terrified, echoed along the street.

"Where's Father?" Dolce rang a small crystal bell imperiously.

A footman appeared, his face flushed.

"Where is my father, Antonio?" Dolce demanded.

"He left the house about an hour ago, mistress, and has not returned. Shall I ask if anyone knows where he has gone?"

Dolce shook her head. "Where is Uncle?"

"He has headed in the direction of the ghetto gates to investigate the commotion."

Dolce dismissed Antonio with a wave of her hand, then returned to the window, elbowing Mirelle aside. "What do you think is happening?"

Before Mirelle could answer, the room shuddered with the shock of an enormous crash. The floor trembled beneath them. The clamor rocked both girls back from the window. Mirelle involuntarily clapped her palms over her ears. Dolce whirled around and snatched up her shawl and kerchief.

"I'm going to see," she shouted over the racket.

"Dolce! Is it safe?"

"You do what you like," her friend snapped. "But I'm going." She strode from the room, narrow skirts swirling about her ankles.

Mirelle ran after her.

"Shalom," Daniel called as the men in his unit stepped over the ruins of the smashed gate and entered the main street of the ghetto. *"Yehudim! Ain l' fached!"*

"What are you saying?" Christophe asked curiously.

"I'm telling the Jews not to be afraid of us," Daniel responded. "Where are they all? *Yehudim! Bo hena! Kumm hier!* Come here! *Venite qui!"*

An old man approached, his dangling sideburns and dark clothes marking him as a pious Jew. "Why have you broken down our gate?" he asked querulously. "What will the Gentiles say?"

"You are under the protection of the French Republic," Daniel told him. "There is no reason to fear."

The man fingered his armband. "You talk as though you were the Messiah himself," he quavered.

Daniel noticed a small knot of people gathering in the street. Where the men wore yellow bonnets, the women covered their hair with yellow kerchiefs. He gritted his teeth. In other Italian cities they had conquered, he recalled, the whores wore similar kerchiefs.

Thinking quickly, he unpinned his tricolor rosette from his jacket lapel. "Come here, old man," he said, as gently as he could.

The man took a reluctant step forward. "What do you want?"

Daniel reached out. With a quick twist, he pulled the man's armband off his forearm and then plucked the hat from his head. He dropped both into the gutter.

"What have you done?" the man cried, stooping to pick up the discarded clothing.

But Daniel gripped his arm and pulled him upright. "Here," he said, pinning the tricolor onto his jacket. "Wear this instead."

The other soldiers followed his lead, tearing off yellow armbands and head coverings, replacing them with the tricolor. Some of the crowd grabbed the cockade with glee; others accepted it fearfully. A few even slipped their armbands into their pockets, too scared to fully accept the change.

"You speak to us in Hebrew and Yiddish," a tall, painfully skinny man said, "but you are a soldier."

"I am Jewish. Almost every Frenchman here is Jewish," Daniel said. "And we are all soldiers—an artillery unit. We've fought alongside Bonaparte himself."

"Jewish soldiers." The man shook his head in disbelief. "Perhaps Jehudah is right and you are the Messiah in disguise."

Daniel laughed. "I am merely a French soldier and citizen of the Republic."

"Uncle!" A young blond woman in a rich red gown, her arms draped with a fine silk shawl, grasped the skinny man's elbow. She had to shout above the sound of clanging metal; some of the soldiers were still hammering the iron gates. "What is happening?"

"The end of times, perhaps," the man shouted back. "These soldiers are tearing down the ghetto gates and say we can discard our armbands and hats."

"Truly? How wonderful!" The woman slid her armband off her arm and removed her head covering, holding them at arm's length for a dramatic moment before dropping them into the gutter.

Daniel looked at her in surprise, taken by her beauty. He bowed. "Signore. Signorina. I am pleased to make your acquaintance. I am Daniel ben Isidore of Paris." He had to shout to be heard over the noise.

"I am Ezekiel Morpurgo, and this is my niece, Dolce." Ezekiel looked at the girl disapprovingly. "Dolce, did you really come here all alone?"

Dolce looked around. "I thought Mirelle might follow me but—oh, there she is!" She waved, and a slender, brown-haired woman stepped forward. She had already been intercepted by one of the other soldiers and relieved of her Jewish insignia.

"This is Mirelle," Ezekiel said. "Her brother was killed in the riots that caused us to lock the ghetto gates."

Daniel bowed again as Christophe joined them, elbowing him in the ribs.

"There is great beauty in Ancona, I see," Christophe commented, looking at Dolce with appreciation.

Daniel smiled at his friend's stylish slouch. He didn't think Christophe's flirtatious manner would do him any good in a Jewish ghetto, but it was amusing to watch him try.

"They are all Jewish, these soldiers," Ezekiel told the two girls.

"Really?" Dolce's eyes widened as she looked the two soldiers up and down.

Christophe grinned. Daniel opened his mouth to correct the old man, but the hammering and sawing of metal grew even louder, making conversation impossible.

Several soldiers carried driftwood from the beach. Daniel stepped back to let them through. The earsplitting clatter of the iron gates being chopped to pieces stopped. The soldiers piled the iron onto the large stack of beach wood.

"Are your men mad?" Ezekiel asked Daniel. "Those gates are iron. They won't burn."

"But if we set fire to them, everyone will know we're in earnest," Daniel replied. "We'll collect the pieces of iron after we extinguish the flames."

Someone splashed oil from a container on the pile, while another soldier dropped a fiery torch on the logs. With a whoosh, the bonfire caught hold and flames rose. A cry of wonder sprang from everyone's throats, followed by the Shehecheyanu blessing. Daniel joined the Morpurgos and Mirelle in chanting, "Blessed art thou, Lord our God, King of the Universe, who has granted us life, sustained us, and enabled us to reach this occasion."

Christophe waited until they had finished the Hebrew prayer before nudging Daniel again. "Won't you introduce me to your new friends?"

Daniel performed the introductions and Christophe bent his head over Dolce's hand. "Signorina. We are delighted to present you with this token of our great esteem." He fished a couple of cockades out of his jacket pocket and pinned one to Dolce's shawl with a flourish.

Mirelle's eyes were fixed on the bonfire. "Is this really happening?"

The blond French soldier turned to her, smiling. But then the smile froze. Mirelle stared at him, the back of her neck tingling.

"Do you remember me, signorina?" Christophe asked in a hoarse whisper, as if he could barely utter the question.

"Remember you? Why would I remember you?" It was hard, suddenly, to breathe.

"We have met." Christophe's voice was insistent. "You must remember."

"What a strange thing to say." Dolce tossed her head. "You've never been in Ancona before, have you? Mirelle has only left Ancona once in her life."

"Only once?" Daniel looked from one to the other curiously. "Where did you go?"

Mirelle, her eyes locked with Christophe's, suddenly paled. "Venice," she whispered.

"Christophe!" Daniel cried out. "It can't be. Is this the young lady from the ball?"

"Yes!" Christophe cried exultantly. "I knew you could not forget me, lovely lady." He bowed low, flourishing his cap. "I knew we would meet again—I told you so, Daniel, didn't I?"

"You're *that* Frenchman?" Dolce studied first Christophe, then Mirelle. "But how romantic!"

"The very same," Christophe said, handing Mirelle the second cockade.

Dazed, as if struck by a lightning bolt, she stared at him, clutching the Revolutionary badge in ice-cold fingers. "I'm glad you got away," she said, heart hammering.

"We were grateful to you," Daniel replied, bowing low.

"And now you are here, Jewish soldiers tearing down the ghetto gates." Mirelle couldn't believe it. She had almost convinced herself that the blond Frenchman was a figment of her imagination. Not real. He couldn't be. And yet there he stood, the ghetto gates burning behind him.

Christophe shook his head. "I'm not . . ."

Daniel interceded. "He's not Jewish, though I am, as are most of the men here."

Mirelle felt a sharp pang of disappointment. For the briefest of moments, she had dared to hope. *I knew it couldn't be*, she thought. But she still felt drawn to him. Wanting to conceal her tumultuous thoughts, she tore her gaze away from the blond stranger and stared again at the blaze. "My brother would have rejoiced in this day," she whispered, fingers trembling as she pinned the emblem to her shirt-waist collar. "He always longed to be free of the ghetto."

"I am sorry for your loss," Daniel said. "If I may ask, signorina, who is your family?"

"My father is Simone d'Ancona," Mirelle said, shaking off her sorrow and drawing herself up proudly. "Proprietor of the best ketubah workshop in all of Italy—in all the world."

"Simone d'Ancona?" Daniel asked, an amazed look on his face. "Does he have relatives in Paris? And in Bischheim?"

"He does," Mirelle replied, staring at him in astonishment. She struggled to control her voice. "How can you possibly know that?"

Daniel's laugh rang out over the hubbub of the crowd and the crackling of the bonfire. "We are cousins, you and I," he said. "That's how I know."

# 24

# FEBRUARY 12

Mirelle was playing piano when she heard a knock at the front door. Anna was elbow-deep in bread dough, so Mirelle went to answer.

Dolce stood there with Daniel and Christophe.

"They wanted to pay the family a condolence call," Dolce said, the twinkle in her eye belying her solemn face, "and I said there was no time like the present."

Mirelle stepped aside to let them enter. "Show them into the parlor, would you? I'll let Mama and Papa know that they're here."

As Mirelle headed toward her parents' room, she felt Christophe's piercing green eyes fixed on her retreating back.

Papa, who'd risen from bed the previous day for the first time since the attack, was sitting in an armchair by his bedroom window, looking out at the street, while Mama tidied his bedside table. Mirelle told them of their visitors.

"I must go see them," Papa said, rising with difficulty.

Wife and daughter ran to take either arm.

"Is that wise, Simone?" Mama asked.

"It's three steps and I'll lie on the divan in the parlor. You can suffocate me with all the blankets you want. But how often does a cousin from Paris pay us a call?"

Arm in arm, they helped him to the room. The moment they

entered, both young men jumped up and hurried over. Between them, they settled Simone on the cherry-red divan and tucked a warm robe over his lap. Mirelle slipped from the room to ask Anna to bring some wine and sesame biscuits. When the refreshments arrived, Mirelle poured the wine, watering it for her father, then handed the tray around. She stood, head bowed, as Papa recited the blessing over the wine, trying to ignore the Gentile's eyes on her face.

But as they drank, she watched him curiously from behind the shield of her wineglass. He sat in a rare beam of sunlight, his golden hair gleaming in its rays. He leaned forward, sipping the drink. His eyes flickered back to her and lingered on her face. Her breath grew ragged as she met his gaze. Not daring to hold his glance any longer, she turned away to study her cousin.

When she looked at Christophe, it was his penetrating green eyes and quick, easy smile that made her heart beat faster. He was the epitome of a fairy tale hero—tall and broad, with a glint of mischief about him. But with Daniel, the first thing she noticed was the worn, patched French uniform. Were the patches the result of battle scars? A Jewish soldier—who would have thought such a thing possible? Looking more closely, Mirelle noted with approval his taut, wiry frame, the tiny sun wrinkles around his dark eyes, the close-shaven olive complexion, the black curly hair. He was a handsome man, her cousin.

"So you are Isidore's son," Simone was saying to Daniel in flawless French.

Mirelle's grasp of the language was nearly as good as her father's, having had the advantage of Dolce's tutors. Only Pinina struggled to understand. Every once in a while, Simone or Mirelle stopped to translate.

After condolences had been extended and a brief conversation about the French conquest of the city had concluded, the subject turned to family history and how they were related. It appeared that Isidore and Simone were either third or fourth cousins on their fathers' side.

"I haven't seen the French branch of the family since I lived in Bischheim," Mirelle's father said. "I was a small child when my father moved to Ancona to start the ketubah works."

"I understand that your workshop is the most illustrious in all of Europe," Daniel said. "You are to be congratulated."

"That's very kind." Simone smiled, clearly gratified.

"Not at all," Daniel said. "I hope to see it while we're stationed here. You know that Christophe and I were apprenticed in his uncle's printshop? I'm interested to compare the two."

"That reminds me," Christophe said, a mischievous expression lighting up his face, "we have a delivery for you, Signor d'Ancona."

"For me?" Simone's eyebrows rose.

Christophe pulled a missive embossed with a heavy seal from his coat pocket and handed it to Simone with a flourish. The thick paper crackled as Simone slipped a finger under the seal, unfolded it, and read.

"Your general wants to visit my ketubah manufactory?" he cried. "Tomorrow?"

"What?" Mirelle jumped up to look over her father's shoulder. She translated the note for her mother, who sat twisting her apron in her lap.

"It's a tremendous honor," Dolce said, her face glowing. "My father arranged it when he paid the general a visit. General Bonaparte wanted to know what was worth visiting in the ghetto. He's going to commission a ketubah for his wife, Josephine."

"But Dolce," Pinina said in rapid Italian, "how will it look when the general arrives, and Simone cannot be there to meet him? He's not well enough."

"Not be there to meet him? Are you joking, wife? Of course I'll be there. Thank your father for us, Dolce. An honor, indeed!"

"Mama, from what Cousin Daniel and Corporal Lefevre tell us, it will only be a quick visit. The general is going to tour the ghetto in the morning and head to the cathedral in the afternoon."

"My father, uncle, and I will accompany him during his visit to the ghetto," Dolce said. "May Mirelle join us? Papa specifically asked that I invite her."

"Oh, no, Dolce—I'll help Mama and Papa in the workshop, of course, but I couldn't possibly spend the entire morning with you," Mirelle protested. "Not on such a gala occasion—in my current state—"

"Ah, but signorina, you must!" Christophe chimed in. "After Venice, I thought I'd never see you again. I insist you accompany your friend."

Mama might not have understood Christophe's words, but she clearly grasped his meaning from his tone. Mirelle flinched as her mother scowled at the French soldier.

"You can't refuse the general's request," Daniel said gently. "He is wearied by politicians and wants to be shown the ghetto by someone with no hidden motives. Signor Morpurgo told him you were the ideal choice."

"Besides, Mira," Dolce added, "my father feels that seeing the French in possession of the city after all you've suffered will be healing for you."

"Dolce—"

"There is no more to be said, daughter," her mother said, a strange, knowing look on her face. "If Signor Morpurgo wishes it, you must represent the ghetto as best you can."

# 25

## FEBRUARY 13

"She's my angel!" Christophe told his friend, stretching one long leg before him as he perched on a fallen log. "I never stopped thinking about her, knew I'd see her again. It's fate."

Daniel was shaving, his eyes focused on the sliver of glass he had propped up on a branch. It had turned temperate suddenly, as though Bonaparte's troops had brought the spring with them. His heart pounded oddly at the thought of his cousin—the warmth of her smile, the unhappiness lurking deep in her eyes. He bit his lip, resentment bubbling inside him. Christophe would never fully understand Mirelle's tragedy, the hollow emptiness of her brother's death. How could any Gentile know what it meant to be hated simply because you were born Jewish? Daniel thought of his childhood, of the days before the Revolution when he'd heard slurs on the street and in the printshop—even from Christophe himself, before his friend learned better. And now he thought he loved a Jewess?

"I don't understand you," Daniel said slowly. "It doesn't seem like you, this sudden infatuation."

Christophe laced his fingers in his close-cropped hair. "I never knew true love before."

"True love?" Daniel couldn't believe what he was hearing.

"You don't believe me?"

"With this girl? I'll wager she's been strictly raised. You can't flirt with a modest Jewish maiden. Her parents would never consider you a suitor. Do us both a favor and forget her."

Christophe rose. "You're right—you *don't* know her, even less so than I do. I'm the one who danced with her in Venice, remember? There's more to her than her upbringing. She has spirit, fire. Remember how she saved us?" He paced, avoiding the gnarled tree roots breaking through the thin soil that, a few yards distant, gave way to shoreline.

Daniel shook his head. "She's not like those freethinking girls in Paris. And certainly not an Italian light-skirt. She's a modest Jewish girl, raised to be a virtuous wife and mother. She celebrates the festivals, keeps herself pure." Daniel glanced up, groaning. "Oh lord, I'm just making this worse! That's what you want, isn't it? To be knight-errant to some untouched maiden."

Christophe bit his lip. "I want . . . I want something different. When I think of the girls back home, the girls I've met here, and especially the ones I slept with, I feel queasy. You know who I mean. Girls who flirt from behind their fans, dampen their muslins, part their legs—"

"The ones who flirted with you, you mean," Daniel interrupted, a twinge of lust lancing through his body. "And you flirted back!"

"I admit it. But they left me feeling empty inside, wanting something more than their kisses, their bodies." He looked at the sandy soil. "I thought fair maidens only lived in fairy tales or medieval romances. I never thought I'd actually encounter one."

"You don't know that you have," Daniel retorted. "You know nothing about her. I'm shocked, actually, that if you had to fall for a Jewish girl, her friend isn't more to your taste."

Christophe shrugged. "Her friend has none of the sweetness I see in Mirelle's eyes."

"Oh, please. You just want something you can't have." Daniel used the towel around his shoulders to wipe away the rest of the shaving cream, then ran a hand down the planes of his cheekbones to his chin. "Mirelle was raised chastely, like me. She's something you'll never have. You like the challenge more than the girl."

Christophe laughed. "You don't believe in love at first sight?"

"Oh, please. Love at first sight? You two are strangers. Meeting her exactly three times can't have changed that."

"So today I will learn more about her," Christophe said. "She is going to show General Bonaparte her father's workshop, and we've been seconded to his escort. What better place for me to get to know her than the place where her father works?"

Daniel plucked his looking glass from the tree branch and dropped it into his kitbag. He pulled his braces up over his shirt and buttoned it. "You promise you'll behave? You won't hurt her?"

"I won't." Christophe's face lit up. "I would never hurt her."

Daniel watched his friend's retreating back. His lips twitched, thinking how horrified Christophe's mother would be if she knew her son was infatuated with a Jewess. His smile faded, however, when he reflected that Odette, once again, would blame him. Any excuse to blame a Jew.

Later that morning, they arrived at the steps of Villa Morpurgo, traversing the narrow streets carefully. The mood of the ghetto had changed dramatically since the day they'd dismantled the gates. Children played outside in the streets; mothers hung laundry from their rooftops, calling to one another. The shopkeepers called out their wares confidently; the young Torah students sang a song as they strolled down the street, arms draped over each other's shoulders.

Christophe's attention turned to a young Italian woman, a woven basket tucked against her hip, which was swaying seductively. "I remember back in Paris when you told me not to stare at Jewish girls because of their modesty," he mused. "That one must not have listened."

Daniel glanced at her, grinning. "She must not have."

"Well"—Christophe clapped his friend on the shoulder—"let's go see your cousin, who *is* a modest Jewess."

Once seated on a plush, straw-colored couch, Christophe pounded a cushion to soften it. He placed it between his head and the top edge of the sofa.

"What are you doing?" Daniel snapped, amused and appalled.

"I haven't felt this comfortable in months." Christophe settled in, tilting his head back, eyes drifting shut. "Women always take an infernal amount of time to get ready."

"Some of us don't take that long," came a voice from the doorway.

Christophe's eyes flew open and he flung himself upright. "Signorina d'Ancona! Good morning," he said, bowing low.

Daniel felt the atmosphere in the room shift as Mirelle stared back at Christophe. The air seemed charged, as if vibrating in the aftermath of a cannon blast.

"Why is he here?" she demanded bluntly in Hebrew, turning to her cousin.

"The general asked us to escort you and Signorina Morpurgo this morning," Daniel answered in the same language, frowning at Christophe's suddenly rapt face. "But my friend is sincere in wishing to further your acquaintance, cousin."

"He isn't Jewish," Mirelle replied. "What can he gain from getting to know me better?"

Christophe stared from one to the other, clearly annoyed at the language barrier. With a shrug, he sank down on the sofa and leaned back again. "If you're going to ignore me, I might as well take a nap," he said, looking up under hooded eyelids at Mirelle's astonished face.

"I am a guest in this house, monsieur," Mirelle told him in fluent French. "Please, you'll embarrass me if you fall asleep."

Christophe swung his feet back down and stood. Once again, he bowed low. "Citizen Corporal, if you please, signorina, not 'monsieur.' We no longer use such titles in France."

"Citizen Corporal," Mirelle said, her hands on her hips, eyes flashing with amusement. "Where were you raised that you think it's proper to take a nap in a stranger's home?"

"Ah, my childhood home was a strict one, sweet scold," replied Christophe, eyes twinkling. "But I have spent months outside, sleeping under the stars in a bedroll—sometimes in the shelter of a tent, but mostly not. So I take comfort where I find it."

"Much like the rest of Bonaparte's army," said a sultry voice from the doorway. "His troops have ravaged our farms, pillaged our towns and villages."

Daniel turned toward Dolce, who was leaning against the door-frame. If Mirelle was demure in black muslin, Dolce looked magnificent in green velvet. Both soldiers bowed as she swept them a deep curtsy. Despite Dolce's beauty, Daniel found his eyes drawn to Mirelle. Was it Dolce's wealth that made her seem unattainable? She reminded him of the noble ladies he'd seen in Venice, the ones who'd peered over their fans, looking past him for more eligible suitors.

"Our commander is known for saying, 'The war must feed the war,'" said Christophe. "It is a harsh reality we simple soldiers regret."

Dolce swept an arm grandly about her. "I shall send you back to your quarters with ample supplies. Perhaps then you will leave this neighborhood in peace."

"I think you underestimate the sheer volume of food it takes to feed the army," Christophe retorted.

Daniel was surprised at his friend's impatience. He would usually flirt with a woman as captivating as Dolce. But he, too, seemed interested only in Mirelle.

"And you underestimate just how wealthy I am." Dolce laughed gently. "We can keep the troops fed for a day or so, at least."

"It would be a great mitzvah," Daniel said. "It's been a while since we've eaten well."

"A mitzvah." Christophe paused, head tilted to one side. "I've heard that word before, but I don't remember . . ."

"A good deed," Dolce said. "We Jews believe they serve us better than gaining absolution in a little wooden box."

Christophe laughed. "I gave up confession and communion many years ago. Many French citizens have stopped practicing Catholicism."

Mirelle looked perplexed. "How can any nation give up on religion?"

Daniel felt reassured. No, a Gentile would never win his cousin's heart.

Christophe was surprised when the girls didn't ring for a carriage. He thought they would drive, and that he and Daniel would ride behind them.

"The ghetto streets are too narrow," Mirelle explained, seeing his glance toward the mounts.

"My servants will bring your horses back to camp," Dolce added.

Because of his friendship with Daniel, Christophe had often been in Le Marais in Paris, but even those crowded and dirty streets seemed luxurious compared to Ancona's ghetto alleyways. The houses rose straight up from the gutters, hiding the sun. There was no space between the apartments, pink stucco nestling next to gray stone and peeling yellow walls. Dozens of sallow-faced children stared out from inside doorways and windows. Mirelle and Dolce, evidently used to the muck of the streets, held their skirts high and kept their eyes on the ground beneath their slippers. The cobbles of the streets felt loose underfoot, as though the ground was still boggy from the recent rains.

Christophe took Mirelle's arm. "The street is only wide enough for two," he said. "You and I will lead the way."

Mirelle looked at his hand on her arm as if she wanted to pull away, but she didn't. Her modesty excited him. He longed to make her blush.

"I have met many beautiful ladies in Italy," he told her, "but none quite like you, signorina."

"I'm certain you say something similar to those ladies," Mirelle countered, the color in her cheeks steady. "You strike me as someone who enjoys flattering—or perhaps flirting with?—every woman you meet. The mark of the conquering soldier, perhaps."

"So you don't think I'm serious?" Christophe placed a hand on his chest, striving to look hurt despite the twinkle in his eye. "I will have to work to gain your trust."

"You may not succeed," Mirelle said.

Christophe chuckled. "Nevertheless, it's the truth. Something about you touches me deeply." He smiled to see a blush finally decorate Mirelle's cheeks.

"Why should it?" she replied. "You're a Christian, a soldier, from another world entirely. You don't know anything about me."

"Ah, but I do!" Christophe squeezed her arm. "After all, we shared a secret, didn't we? An adventure? Shall I tell you about yourself?"

"You'll be wrong."

"Let me try. Your eyes seem demure until mischief flashes in them. I think some part of you yearns for a different life than the one you have here in the ghetto. The type of adventure, perhaps, to be found at a masquerade ball."

A shadow crossed Mirelle's face.

"No? Am I so very wrong?"

Mirelle shook her head. "Very wrong. Don't you know I've been raised to be obedient? Dutiful? Those are the qualities my people prize."

Christophe stifled a smile. "Nonsense. They've taught you to believe these things from childhood. I know what they're like, those chains with which your family and religion so gently and lovingly bind you. But my chains shattered the day my father died at the Bastille. The Revolution taught us Frenchmen—and women—to cast aside religion and replace its misguided restrictions with the light of reason. What if I could show you a different world—a world outside the confines of your ghetto and your family?"

He heard something catch in her throat. She averted her face, lips tight. They walked on in silence, but Christophe kept his hand on her arm, all the while wondering why he was, in fact, attracted to her. She was right about her quiet modesty. Yet she had helped him and Daniel escape detection at the ball. There was a suppressed quality in her, a kind of longing that excited him. Daniel was right—she was unlike the loose women of Italy, the ones all too willing to be seduced. Mirelle would not give herself easily to a man's keeping. But once she did, he thought, she would be loyal forever. He wanted her to be loyal only to him. The thought made him close his eyes, longing to do more than touch her arm.

Bonaparte was already at the workshop when the foursome arrived, being guided from workbench to workbench by Mirelle's and Dolce's fathers. Mirelle's mother hovered in the background, at a table laid with a snowy white cloth and covered by delicacies. The workmen bent over tall tables, standing cheek by jowl or sitting perched on high stools. The bustle of the room and the smell of ink reminded

Christophe of his uncle's printshop in Paris. The only thing missing was the clatter and clang of machinery.

Dolce and Mirelle curtsied deeply to the general, who was leaning over a ketubah.

"Ladies." Bonaparte bowed, a warm smile creasing his face. "I am pleased that you'll accompany us during our visit to the ghetto today."

"We're honored to have been asked," Dolce said.

Bonaparte looked both girls over, head to foot, nodding approvingly. Then he turned to Mirelle. "I was admiring your father's beautiful artwork, signorina, and was just giving some instructions for a marriage contract to be created for my own bride. Perhaps you have heard of her? Her beauty is spoken of not just in France but throughout all of Europe."

"Yes, indeed, Citizen General, we have heard much of your wife's charm and beauty," Mirelle said. "Fortune certainly smiles upon you."

Bonaparte's chest swelled. He beamed at Mirelle, who returned his regard with twinkling eyes.

"I understand you help here at the workshop," Bonaparte said. "Your father tells me you know the business as well as he does. Come assist me."

"Of course, Citizen General," Mirelle said. She moved closer to the samples that her father had spread before the general. "Which of these pleases you?"

Christophe had noticed, bemused, how Mirelle began to glow with an inner light the instant she entered the workshop, as if she were a jewel and this her natural setting. The general, known for his gallantry to women, seemed to have discerned it, too. He leaned in, took Mirelle's arm, and tucked it into his. Christophe felt color rush to his face; ducking his head, he moved aside.

Dolce led him to another table, where a workman was tracing an arch with gold paint.

"Signorina, tell me about these documents," Christophe said, hoping his interest would conceal his sudden flare of jealousy. "My friend tells me they are Jewish marriage certificates."

"The most beautiful in all of Europe," Dolce replied. "Jews as far away as the Russian steppes and even the Americas commission work by the ketubah makers of Ancona."

"And what does it say?" Christophe pointed at the ornate, neatly painted words.

"It is a contract assuring the woman of clothing, food, and"—Dolce smiled—"happiness in the marital bed. If the husband fails to uphold his side of the bargain, the woman can collect the sum designated here, which is"—Dolce leaned closer, careful not to disrupt the crafts-man—"three hundred scudi. Cheap at the price."

"You would command more, I take it?"

"Without a doubt. I am not some poor girl who would wed at any price. Or wed any man who comes along. I'll wait for the right one."

"And Signorina d'Ancona? She is not betrothed, is she? She is free to marry whomever she likes?"

Dolce lay cool fingers on Christophe's arm and ushered him aside. She put up her fan and whispered behind it, "Today she is. But who knows what tomorrow brings? Since the death of her brother, her fortune is uncertain. Her father's health is frail, and he may die at any moment. If he does, she and her mother will be forced to depend on relatives from Rome. And what if they refuse to provide for them? My father has nothing good to say of Mirelle's aunt. Will her French family take her in if she needs it?"

"Daniel's family?" Christophe asked, bewildered by the sudden flow of confidences. "They are poor people themselves, but I'm sure if she needed it . . ."

"Of course, if worse comes to worse, she can stay with me, as my companion," Dolce said smoothly, her eyes on Christophe's face. "But she is far too proud for that."

Christophe glanced at Mirelle, who was showing the general another ketubah scroll.

"But no matter what, she is not for you." Dolce's pretty lips curled in a smile. "Mirelle would never consider marriage outside her religion."

"You might be surprised. Who knows?" Christophe's green eyes challenged Dolce's blue ones. "The liberty we French bring to Italy may teach her to think differently."

# 26

"This way, Citizen General," Signor Morpurgo said, ushering Bonaparte out of the ketubah workshop. Mirelle nodded farewell to her parents and followed the contingent along the narrow streets to a tiny courtyard where a small garden plot had been dug and fenced off. A quiet crowd was gathered there.

"We have heard of Liberty Trees being planted throughout Italy—a symbol of the Revolution, honoring your liberation of our country," Signor Morpurgo said. "We Jews have a tradition of planting trees on our own Arbor Day, a holiday called Tu B'shvat—which, by lucky chance, was just two days ago, on our Sabbath. We decided to combine these celebrations this year and plant our Liberty Tree to honor Helek Tov!"

Bonaparte looked confused. "Helek Tov?" he asked. "Who is that?"

The crowd chuckled and Signor Morpurgo smiled. "It is a Hebrew rendering of your last name, General: Bonaparte—which we translate as "a good part." We are honored to have you play a 'good part' in the latest episode of our history."

Dolce's uncle, who had hovered in the background during the workshop tour, now stepped forward. "Our history has not always been a happy one, Citizen General. We are indebted to you for breaking down the ancient gates that held us fast. For liberating and protecting us. Your actions have made our lives lighter."

Bonaparte nodded. "I see. Helek Tov—Bonaparte. A good omen." He thought for a moment. "I was going to announce this later today, but this seems like an opportune time. Your city has lived under the boot of the pope for far too long. The treaty I negotiated allows me to declare that Ancona is now Republic Anconitana, and to replace the papal governor of Ancona with a municipal council. This council includes three members from the Jewish community: Samson Costantini, David Morpurgo, and Ezekiel Morpurgo!"

A resounding cheer rose from the assembled. Mirelle, standing next to the general, glanced toward Dolce. Her friend did not look surprised. Of course, Bonaparte would have informed the Morpurgo brothers about their appointment before this announcement. No wonder, Mirelle thought, Dolce's father had been so eager to encourage Papa to give Bonaparte a ketubah scroll as a gift.

Boys from the yeshiva began digging the hole for the sapling designated as the ghetto's Liberty Tree. A group of singers sang the beautiful lines from the Song of Songs to a tune generally sung on Tu B'shvat:

*See! The winter is past; the rains are over and gone.*
*Flowers appear on the earth; the season of songbirds has come.*

Women passed through the crowd, offering platters of dried fruit and nuts and glasses of wine. Bonaparte raised his eyebrows as a plate was presented to him.

"What's this?" he asked, turning to Mirelle.

"The foods we traditionally eat on our holiday," she said. "Please take some."

The general helped himself to a handful, then reached for a glass of wine, which he downed in one swift gulp. "A charming ceremony, but we must move on," he said to Dolce's father. "It's time for us to head to the cathedral. I'm curious to see this miracle portrait that caused so much uproar—and we have other business there as well."

"We will part ways with you here," Signor Morpurgo said, smiling genially. "You understand, Citizen General, that Jews cannot enter a Catholic sanctuary. Do you still plan to attend my daughter's salon tomorrow night?"

"I hope to," Bonaparte said. "But one never knows. A general's life is not his own to command."

"Of course," said Signor Morpurgo. "We hope you will honor us with your presence. If not, I will see you at the municipality before you leave Ancona."

The two men bowed. Bonaparte signaled to his soldiers and they followed him up the steep hill toward the cathedral. Mirelle watched as her cousin and his friend marched off.

The celebration continued after the general left. Mirelle tried to slip away, but Signor Morpurgo stopped her.

"I will walk you home myself," he said. "And we will see you tomorrow."

"There's no need," Mirelle protested. "It's only a few steps away. And I'm afraid I won't be able to attend the salon. My mourning . . ."

"Nonsense," he said. "We're not Christians, who mourn a full year. Jacopo would want you to enjoy yourself, my child. *I* want you to enjoy yourself."

Suddenly, Mirelle felt the older man was standing too close. He breathed fumes of spiced wine on her neck. She edged back.

"You are too busy to escort me," she tried again. "Oh, and congratulations on being appointed to the council."

"I want to talk to you about that," he said.

Before he could say anything further, Dolce was at her side. "Papa, I'm ready to go home."

"Your uncle will take you. I'll escort Mirelle. I need to run a few errands that take me past her house anyway." He looped an arm around Mirelle's waist.

Mirelle was suddenly tired of being pushed and pulled by one man or another. The general had not let her arm go the entire time they were together. Had she imagined him casting a measuring glance at her figure? She would have expected that Dolce, so like his wife in temperament and beauty, would be more to his taste. Then there was Christophe, who thought he knew her better than she knew herself. It flustered her. And now Dolce's father, a man she had known all her life, taking command of her in such a possessive manner . . .

She pulled away. "I don't need an escort," she said, suddenly realizing how loud her voice sounded. People turned to stare. She spoke more softly. "I just want to go home and make sure my father has not taken ill as a result of this morning's excitement."

Signor Morpurgo's eyebrows rose. "I understand, child. But I'm walking your way. You won't object to my walking with you, will you?"

Dolce's eyebrows rose and her face hardened. "I need you at home, Papa," she snapped. "Uncle can take her."

"I'm walking that way anyway. I have business to attend to." Signor Morpurgo sounded annoyed.

Dolce looked from one to the other, finally fixing her eyes on her friend. "Very well. Mira, I'll see you tomorrow." Then, not waiting for Mirelle to protest, she turned away.

The walk home was only a few minutes. Mirelle felt ashamed of having made a fuss. Dolce's father led her through the narrow streets, adjusting his quick stride to her slower gait.

"I've been honored by the general's confidence in me," he told her. "It's been a whirlwind, has it not?"

Mirelle nodded. "So much has happened since the riots. One moment everything is ordinary, the way it always was. And the next . . ." Her voice broke.

Signor Morpurgo took her arm in his. "This is the first sorrow ever to come into your young life. I wish I could tell you that it would be the last. Unfortunately, I can't make that promise, though I'd give my heart's blood to be able to do so."

Mirelle glanced at him from under her eyelashes. The tenderness in his tones made her uncomfortable. But she told herself she was being ridiculous. He was her friend's father, that was all. "You're too kind," she murmured. "You've suffered yourself, I know. I was only a child, but I still remember how upset you were when Dolce's mother died."

Signor Morpurgo squeezed her arm. "Thank you, my dear. Missing her as I did, I never wanted to marry again. Dolce certainly did her best to dissuade me when there was even the remotest chance. But now, with this political appointment—and with Dolce being your dearest friend, and you both nearing marriage age . . ."

Mirelle's heart skipped a beat. "I hope you find someone who will make you as happy as Dolce's mother," she stammered.

Was she imagining the lingering caress on her arm? "You're a dear, dear girl," he said, his voice throaty. "A dear girl. I must tell you . . ."

They turned the corner and stood in front of her house. Mirelle stopped in surprise. A pile of chests and suitcases was lined up at the doorway. "Someone's here," she said. "My aunt and cousin must have arrived from Rome."

Morpurgo's lips thinned. "So it seems. But if you could give me just one more moment."

Mirelle looked at the baggage, glad to change the subject from whatever it might have become. "They're certainly here for a long stay."

"So it seems. I can't tell you how sorry I am that the religious nature of the work means you can't inherit yourself. You, *Piccola*, would certainly have been worthy."

Mirelle couldn't help but smile at the compliment, futile though it was. Unlike his daughter or her mother, Signor Morpurgo didn't just dismiss how she felt. How rare to have someone understand her! "Thank you," she murmured. Then, with another glance at the crowded porch, she added, "I'd better go help Anna."

Signor Morpurgo nodded. "I'm sorry, child, it doesn't look like we'll have time to talk more. Not today, anyway."

Mirelle slipped her arm out of his. "Thank you for your escort, Signor Morpurgo, and for bringing the general to visit the ketubah manufactory." Without waiting for a response, she mounted the stairs, stepping between the boxes and chests piled high on the stone steps, and headed inside.

# 27

Mirelle followed the sound of voices in the parlor. There, sitting with her parents, was a fashionable older woman, her traveling gown a deep lilac, her velvet hat swathed in black net. Black gloves lay on her lap. Next to her, sprawled on the sofa, was a boy who looked younger than his eight years. He was dressed in rich clothing, but nothing seemed to fit; his pantaloons were too full, his jacket too short.

"Ah, Mirelle," Papa said, rising with some difficulty from his chair, "your aunt Prudenzia and cousin Beniamino have just arrived from Rome. My dear sister-in-law, this is our daughter, the joy of our house."

Mirelle curtsied. Prudenzia smiled serenely, extending two fingers in greeting. Then she seemed to think better of it and brushed Mirelle's cheek with her lips, a butterfly kiss Mirelle barely felt. Not bothering to rise, Beniamino nodded.

"She's lovely, Pinina," Prudenzia said. "You say you've found her a good match?"

As Mirelle's head spun from her aunt toward her mother, she noticed the shocked look on her father's face.

Mama flushed, shaking her head at her sister-in-law. "Nothing is certain yet," she said. Then she turned to her daughter. "Is Dolce's father outside? Does he wish to speak with your father?"

"Dolce's father?" Mirelle heard her voice rise in surprise. Or was it trepidation?

"He did accompany you home, didn't he?" Mama persisted. "He said he would."

"Yes, but he saw we had company and left me at the doorstep."

"I see you're right, Pinina. Nothing *is* certain." Prudenzia's laugh was like tinkling crystal.

Simone looked from his wife to his sister-in-law, forehead furrowing. "I don't understand."

"Later," Mama said.

Heat crept up Mirelle's cheeks.

"Mirelle, perhaps you should show your cousin his room." Mama gestured toward the boy still lounging on the divan. "He looks tired. He will sleep in . . . in . . ."

"In poor Cousin Jacopo's room, yes, Aunt?" Beniamino chimed in, his round face fixed on hers. "Mama says she'll share Mirelle's room."

Mirelle looked at her mother's flustered face. "Of course, Mama," she said carefully. The boy couldn't possibly understand how his thoughtlessness hurt her parents. "Come with me, Beniamino. What do they call you at home? Ben? Or Mino?"

"Beniamino," her aunt said sharply.

A flicker of annoyance crossed the boy's face. He kept his silence until they were halfway up the stairs, then blurted, "You can call me Mino if you'd like. And I'll call you Elle. They can be our secret names for one another."

Mirelle laughed. "All right. Do you have lots of secrets from your mama?"

Mino blinked at Mirelle and she noticed that his eyes were large, dark, and nearly lashless. *Like a doll's marble eyes*, she thought. Something about them disquieted her.

"Oh, I do," he said, laughing. "Lots and lots of secrets."

# 28

An agitated crowd stood grumbling outside the cathedral, clustered in the stone courtyard beyond the narrow flight of steps to the portico. A pair of red marble lions guarded the entranceway, powerless in the face of the French troops. Daniel knew the citizens of Ancona were desperate to block the looting of the church. He had seen this in every other Italian city they had occupied: a mob of angry Catholics surrounding the steps of the church, shouting in bitter protest. Once again he brushed away the commandment that always perturbed him when pillaging the Italians: *Thou shalt not steal.*

Bonaparte had anticipated the demonstration. A squad of artillerymen lined up outside the cathedral, ready to fire upon the crowd. Foot soldiers loaded carts with gold and silver chalices, ivory and gem-encrusted crosses, and exquisite works of holy art. Bonaparte's catalogers, Monge and Berthollet, stood by making notes in their memorandum books, attributing a value to every piece. The men, by now well-practiced in the art of confiscation, passed valuables hand to hand from deep inside the sanctuary. The precious metals twinkled and gleamed in the bright sunshine, their lustrous beauty infuriating the faithful.

A clergyman, his purple sash marking him as cardinal, stood at the church entrance ineffectively blocking the soldiers, arms clutched across his chest. The moment Bonaparte arrived, he stalked down the steps. "I protest," he cried. "This is an outrage!"

Bonaparte smiled tightly, not bothering to bow. "You are Cardinal . . . ?"

"Ranuzzi," the portly, red-faced man spat out. "I've served as spiritual leader of the San Ciriaco Cathedral for many years. And what you do here—I repeat—is an outrage!"

One of Bonaparte's aides whispered in his ear. A look of astonishment flickered across his face, followed by a withering glare. "From what I am told," he said in Italian between clenched teeth, "you are leader of more than this sumptuously adorned cathedral. You are the head of an insurgency called the Catholic Fellowship—the group that led a deadly attack against the Jews of this city, as well as ambushed a contingent of my men. We are holding one of your rogues—"

"*Mio marito!*" cried a woman, darting out of the crowd. She kneeled before Bonaparte, her forehead on his boots, hands gripping them as she wept.

He stared down at her from over his aquiline nose. "What does she want?" he growled.

One of his officers stepped forward and saluted briskly. "It's her husband you are holding, sir."

"Get her off my feet," Bonaparte snapped. "Woman!" he barked in Italian. "If I have imprisoned your husband, he deserves his fate."

An impassioned flurry of words from both the cardinal and the woman followed. Daniel, though his Italian was improving daily, couldn't follow what they were saying after the first few sentences. But Bonaparte, who was born on the island of Corsica and whose mother tongue was Italian, had no such difficulty.

He finally kicked out, flinging the woman off his boots. "I'm going inside," he said, ignoring the pleas from both woman and cardinal. He turned to his aide. "Send some men in with me as a bodyguard."

"You, you, and you," said the aide, pointing at Daniel, Sebastian, and one other artilleryman. "Accompany the general."

They walked up the cathedral's worn stone steps, passing a deep portal formed of four columned arches. The air grew musty and cool as they entered the sanctuary.

The cardinal followed on their heels, still protesting. "It is a crime, an injustice against the faithful of Ancona, a—"

Bonaparte turned and glowered at him, stopping him mid-sentence. "Shut your mouth or I'll have you shot," he snapped.

Ranuzzi, turning white, subsided. But he still kept pace, dark eyes flashing in frustration. Daniel reluctantly admired the man, who, unlike many of his fellow countrymen, did not cower at the general's bullying.

The church was nearly empty except for the looting soldiers. In a side chapel not yet touched by the French, a cluster of women knelt, praying and crying, before a portrait. Daniel had had little contact with Catholics before coming to Italy, aside from Christophe and his mother, and had only once set foot in the famous Notre Dame Cathedral. But there was no escaping the images of the Virgin Mother and her son, even when they had been forced underground in Revolutionary France—and here in Italy, their likenesses dotted every street corner and crowded every church.

The portrait was small and glowed in the dim light of the cathedral. Under its heavy, gold-painted frame, Mary looked pale and weary, her eyes downcast. Her gown, a delicate red, draped at the neck, and a blue-gray headdress was thrown over her head and shoulders. Her mantle was topped by a magnificent gold crown that was studded with painted gemstones and had an elaborate cross at its peak. Around her neck she wore a string of actual pearls and other rare jewels.

Bonaparte whirled, turning on the cardinal. "Is that the portrait that's caused so much fuss?" he asked. "The one that's supposed to prevent me from conquering Ancona?"

The cardinal swallowed hard. "You've heard about that, then?"

"The whole of Italy has heard about it—and about the other Madonna portraits in Rome, Ascoli, and Frascati that are reportedly repeating the miracle, much to the delight of you Catholics. Doesn't seem to have worked, though, does it?"

"The ways of the Lord and His blessed mother are not given to us to understand fully," the cardinal said, folding his hands piously. "And who can say that we know what the future holds—for you, General, or for Italy? But yes, that is indeed the miraculous portrait."

Sebastian, cupping a hand, murmured to Daniel, "Some of the men want to burn the damned thing."

His whisper carried through the chapel. The women sank to their knees, praying to Mary to smite the unfaithful.

Bonaparte looked from his soldiers to the women, lips curling in sardonic amusement. "No one's burning it," he declared, first in French and then in Italian. He stepped into the chapel, scattering the kneeling women. They retreated to the back of the room, muttering angrily. Their murmurs reverberated around the chamber, echoing off the stone walls. "Quiet!" Bonaparte bellowed. "*Silenzio!*"

Reluctantly, the women quieted. Bonaparte turned to address them.

"You have been prey to a massive fraud," he said, taking the portrait off the wall and holding it in his hands, disregarding their cries of horror. "Your clergymen have manufactured this miracle to convince you that I am your enemy. I am not your enemy, and I will prove this foolishness wrong by staring down this Mother Mary. You will see: the painting will not respond."

He stared at the portrait. The tension in the chamber mounted as the seconds ticked past. Something about the silence unnerved Daniel; he reached for his saber and lightly curled his fingers about its hilt.

Finally, Bonaparte looked up. "There! No moving eyes, no tears, no smiles—nothing but canvas and paint. I've given your Madonna a chance to confront her enemy, but she has not engaged me." He placed the portrait on the lectern, nodding at the huddled women in the chapel corner. "You have been told that we are despoiling your churches. But these valuables should serve the people, not lie here useless while your countrymen hunger for a simple crust of bread."

The cardinal, who had remained silent for a time, now seemed unable to stop himself. "Everything you are seizing—and sending back to enrich France's coffers—is dedicated to God's glory," he announced. "These women know that these artifacts serve God's Holy Church!"

Bonaparte looked at him, amused. "Good cardinal, I have nothing but respect for the Catholic Church. My own uncle was a priest before the Revolution. But why should you pile up riches here in God's house when so many people starve in your streets?"

He stepped toward the portrait. The women drew in an audible breath; Ranuzzi hissed in protest. Sebastian moved between him and the general, his saber half drawn from its scabbard.

"Your Lady wears a veritable treasure about her neck," Bonaparte said. "While most of what we take is destined for France as war booty, I've heard of a local hospice in urgent need of funds. These gemstones can supply that." He touched the necklace. "Think of the men and women who, nearing their final reward, will bless the residents of Ancona for giving up these precious—"

He stopped mid-sentence, his face drained of color. He drew in a deep breath and let the string of gems fall back against the Madonna's chest. He grabbed an embroidered gold cloth from the lectern and dropped it so it completely hid the portrait.

"Everyone out! Now!" he cried, gripping the lectern with both hands, his knuckles white.

Daniel and Sebastian jumped into action, waving their sabers and pushing the women out the door. The cardinal was about to follow them when Bonaparte bellowed, "Not him! He stays!"

"You! Tell me more about this portrait," Bonaparte demanded, grabbing the cardinal's hassock, pulling him so they faced one another.

"What do you want to know, Cittadino General?" Ranuzzi asked.

"Who first saw it? When did it happen? How did it first appear?"

The cardinal's face crinkled. "The woman hanging on your boots outside? The one you nearly kicked in the face? She saw the miracle first. Francesca Marotti."

Bonaparte turned to Daniel. "Go," he barked. "Bring her here."

Daniel saluted and headed out of the cathedral, wondering as the sound of his boots reverberated through the near-empty church what the general had seen that upset him so. Had the miracle portrait really stared back at him? Cried? Smiled?

He hoped he'd recognize the Marotti woman from the others in the crowd. They were all dressed alike, in black dresses and modest head coverings. Daniel realized that his own mother would fit in well with these women. The thought made his stomach twist.

"Francesca Marotti!" he called, standing on the steps. "*Lei dov'è?*"

"Who wants her?" someone demanded. An older woman stepped out of the huddle of women and stood with fists at her waist.

Daniel thought quickly. "The cardinal wants her. Is she here?"

"I'm here," came a low-pitched voice. Francesca Marotti moved toward the steps, gently patting the older woman's shoulder as she passed by.

Daniel regarded her. The woman looked worn: her eyes were shadowed, her lips pale in a sallow face. Her dark hair was bound in a bun at the nape of her neck, covered by a kerchief. Daniel put out a hand and she grasped it, fingers rough and knotted against his palm. He led her up the stairs.

They walked through the cathedral, footsteps echoing. Francesca looked pained to see the soldiers dispersed throughout the church. They entered the chapel, where Bonaparte stood at the podium, eyes fixed upon the gold cloth draped over the portrait, frowning blackly. Ranuzzi leaned against the stone wall in a corner, hands folded in prayer. Francesca started toward him.

"You wanted me, Excellency?" she asked.

Before he could answer, Bonaparte bellowed, "Over here, woman!"

Startled, she turned around. "But I thought . . . ?" Her eyes sought Daniel's.

"The general wishes to speak with you," he told her.

The cardinal nodded. "General Bonaparte has questions for you, Signora Marotti."

Francesca thought for a moment before shaking her head. "I will not answer unless he releases my husband."

The general's face turned to stone. "I won't be blackmailed!" he shouted. "If you don't tell me what I want to know, I'll execute your husband for the conspirator he is!"

Francesca blanched but stood firm. "Then I will go silent to my grave."

"I assure you, woman, I can arrange that as well," Bonaparte snapped back.

She turned to the wall where the portrait usually hung. Seeing it removed, her gaze skirted the chapel before finally recognizing the frame lying under the gold cloth. "My Lady will not let harm come to me," she said calmly. "And if she does, it's God's will."

Daniel had never before seen Bonaparte so agitated. His face purpled and veins stood out on his forehead.

Cardinal Ranuzzi stepped forward. "May I suggest, General? Free Marotti and imprison me in his place. As you have said, I lead the Catholic Fellowship. I gladly surrender myself, so this woman's husband can be returned to her."

Bonaparte drew a deep breath, quieting his rage through sheer force of will, scowling at the clergyman. "You'd like that, wouldn't you, Ranuzzi? I make you a martyr for the Catholic cause throughout Italy, and suddenly conspirators pop up out of nowhere to harass my troops. No, Cardinal, I think not."

"Then we seem to be at an impasse." Ranuzzi's eyes glinted with malice.

Bonaparte walked over to Francesca and took her by both hands. She tried to pull away, but he held her fast. "If you tell me what I need to know—simply what you have already told others—I'll consider freeing your husband. What I saw . . ." He shook his head as if to clear it. "Never mind." He stared into her eyes, and for a moment she seemed mesmerized. "You were first to see this so-called miracle, but you were not its only witness. I am giving you a chance, signora. I want to hear your story, but if you force my hand, I will seek out others. You don't want that."

"I don't want that." Francesca spoke as if in a trance. "But you must free Emilio first."

Bonaparte shook his head. "No, Madame. I will not." He turned to Daniel. "I will give her time to consider. You—what's your name?"

"Daniel Isidore, sir," Daniel said, standing to attention.

"Corporal Isidore. Stay with her. Don't let her speak with anyone— not the cardinal, not any of her other countrymen. Bring her to the Palazzo Triumph this evening. I will speak with her again directly after supper."

"Yes, sir," Daniel said, saluting. He turned to Francesca. "Come with me, signora."

Francesca's calm ruptured. She looked toward the cardinal, her face distraught. "If you hadn't brought Emilio into the Catholic Fellowship . . ."

"He was more than willing," Ranuzzi replied coldly, folding his hands across his chest. "It's in God's hands now."

# 29

Francesca marched out of the chapel and past the crowds, Corporal Isidore's presence preventing her from speaking to the people who crowded around her. Father Candelabri tried to block their path, but the French soldier put a hand to the hilt of his saber in obvious threat.

"*Non parlarle*," he said. "Don't speak to her. She's a prisoner of the French army."

Father Candelabri crossed himself and moved out of the way.

Bella Marscipona, however, tried to grab the soldier's arm. "What do you mean, she's a prisoner? Isn't it enough you've taken her husband? She has a baby and a child to care for. Let her go!"

"Where are you taking me?" Francesca asked, suddenly panicked. "I have to go home."

"Let her go!" Several other women crowded around them. The old woman's gnarled hand grasped the Frenchman's forearm tightly, her fingers curling into his uniform sleeve.

The young soldier stood for a moment, as if undecided about how to handle this. Finally, he yanked his arm free. "Get away, old woman," he yelled, looking shamefaced. "I'll take her home to her baby and child. No harm will come to her—unless you provoke me!"

"It's all right," Francesca said, hurrying to assure her neighbor.

The thought of little Mario let down her milk; she put a hand to her breasts as her blouse grew damp.

They left the commotion of the cathedral behind, and Francesca led the boy down the steep hill toward home. *I could take him anywhere in Ancona*, she thought wildly, *and he wouldn't know the difference. If it weren't for the baby . . .* She had to think of something other than her hungry child, otherwise she wouldn't have enough milk to feed him. She hurried, making the soldier stumble over the rocky path.

"You speak Italian," she said over her shoulder to distract herself from her thoughts. "Where did you learn it?" With his thick, curly hair and dark eyes, the soldier might pass as an Italian—until his accent betrayed him.

"Here—in Italy. It's not very good."

"It's better than most soldiers. Most just know *dammi* when they want to take something. And *cibo* for food."

They reached the farm. Francesca heard Mario wailing from inside the small house. Not caring if the soldier followed her or not, she picked up her skirts and ran inside.

Barbara sat at the kitchen table, trying to make Mario take goat's milk from a sopping rag. She looked up, furious. "Where were you? He's been screaming for an hour! I didn't know . . ."

Francesca plopped into a chair, grabbed the baby, and thrust up her blouse so he could latch on. He was almost purple with fury, reminding her unexpectedly of the French general.

"Shh, little one, Mama's here," she crooned.

The baby lunged at her breast. She flinched as his newest tooth sunk into her nipple.

The soldier, who stood in the doorway, flushed brick red and turned away.

"He's hungry," Francesca said.

"I see that." The boy kept his face averted.

"Who is he?" Barbara demanded. "Why is he here?"

The baby's frenzied nursing slowed down, and Francesca let out her pent-up breath. "He's a French soldier, sent to guard me."

"Guard you?" Fear entered Barbara's face. "Why? What did you do?"

The soldier glanced around the kitchen, eyes lighting on every-thing but the nursing baby. Francesca, covering herself with her shawl, wondered what he made of her home. Craning her neck, she inspected her gleaming pots and pans hanging around the red stone hearth, cane-back chairs, and the polished wood table, sullied only by the heap of wet cloth Barbara had used to feed the baby.

"What's your name, soldier?" she asked him.

"Daniel Isidore," he said, looking at Barbara. "She's your daughter?"

Francesca nodded. "Barbara. And the baby is Mario."

"Mama! What did you do?" Barbara repeated impatiently.

"I refused to tell General Bonaparte about the Mary portrait unless he let your papa go."

"Really?" Barbara's face lit up. "Good for you!"

Francesca deftly pulled the baby from one nipple and put him over her shoulder, rubbing his back. He let out an enormous burp from deep in his belly, making the soldier's lips twitch.

"Do you have brothers and sisters at home, Daniel?" she asked.

"I'm the youngest," he replied. "But we have lots of little ones in the neighborhood."

Barbara sat at the table, looking calmer. "Where do you live?"

"Paris." He smiled at her. "It's very different from Ancona."

"Paris!" Barbara breathed out in wonder. "Is it as splendid as they say?"

The boy's face grew somber. "It's the most beautiful city in the world. But life there isn't easy right now."

Francesca put the baby onto the second breast, pulling the shawl securely. She, too, was curious about France. "Because of the revolu-tion? What was that like?"

"I was very young, signora," Daniel said. "But the man I was apprenticed to was at the Bastille the day it fell."

Mario had fallen asleep at Francesca's breast. She gently disengaged him and left the room to put him down. "What I don't understand," she said when she returned to the table, "is how any nation can turn away from the Lord God. Don't you know it's a sin?"

Daniel laughed gently. "I'm not a Christian, signora—I'm Jewish."

"Jewish!" Barbara leapt from the table in shock.

Daniel looked pained. Francesca studied him. *A Jew*, she thought wildly. She would never have guessed! She trembled slightly, looking him over from head to foot. She had seen so few Jews up close.

"No horns, I'm afraid," Daniel said dryly. "Really, I'm no different than you."

"Except you are damned for all eternity," Francesca blurted.

He sat silent for a moment. Francesca was surprised to see a smile flit across his face.

"What's so funny?" Barbara scraped the chair back and sat.

"I forgot you Christians truly believe that. A woman I knew in Paris—a Catholic, like you—would tell me the exact same thing almost every day. You made me think of her, that's all."

Francesca didn't know what to say. He looked like any other young stripling—not more than eighteen, perhaps even younger. He was polite and soft-spoken. And handsome, with his short, curly dark hair and expressive eyes. His skin was tanned, and he was slender yet strong. His nose wasn't even that long—certainly not the hooked, deformed beak she'd seen in pictures.

"But you *are* damned," Barbara said, looking to her mother for support. "How can you laugh when you're going to burn in hellfire forever?"

Daniel frowned and said nothing. Francesca rose. "I'll make us something to eat," she said. "Can you eat at my table?"

"I'm a soldier, signora. I can eat anywhere." Daniel raised his eyebrows. "As long as it isn't pork or seafood."

Francesca fought the urge to laugh. "Pork or seafood? Do you think it's a holiday? I left some bean stew to simmer this morning. Can you eat that?"

"With pleasure," Daniel said. "Can I help you?"

"Help me? No. I may be your prisoner, but you're my guest."

Daniel suddenly looked tired. "You're quite calm. I've never seen anyone stand up to the general like that."

"He's formidable," Francesca admitted. She moved about the kitchen, bringing out bowls for the stew and a jug of wine, cutting some brown bread and putting it in a straw basket. "I was frightened, but the Madonna told me what I must do." She placed the food on the table, then sat.

Daniel lowered his head for a moment and whispered under his breath in a strange language. It didn't sound like French.

"What are you saying?" asked Barbara, already gnawing the heel of the loaf of bread.

"I'm saying thanks for the food," Daniel told her. "Don't you do that too?"

"We do," Francesca said, eyeing her daughter balefully. She extended a hand to Barbara. "Bless us, Oh Lord, and these thy gifts, which we are about to receive from thy bounty, through Christ Our Lord. Amen."

"Amen," said Barbara around a full mouth.

"Amen," echoed Daniel, dipping a spoon into his bowl.

They ate quietly for a few minutes. Francesca was surprised that, rather than an awkward silence, the mood felt companionable. It was her duty as an Italian and a Catholic to despise this young soldier, but for some reason she couldn't do it. *Why not?* she wondered. Not only was he French, an enemy, and her captor but he was also, of all things, a Jew. She never thought she'd eat a meal with a Jew. She winced, thinking how furious Emilio would be when he found out. Daniel poured some wine and said something else under his breath. Again, it clearly wasn't French.

"What language is that?" Barbara asked.

"Hebrew," Daniel said. "It's the language we Jews use to pray."

Francesca shook her head. "I don't understand. The priests say they outlawed religion in France. Didn't they? Or just Christianity?"

"All religion," Daniel replied. "Though they started allowing priests back just last year. But we Jews have lost our Shabbat—our Sabbath, the holiest day of our week—just as most Christians no longer go to church on Sundays. Many of my traditions—how I used to dress and keep my hair, for instance—aren't permitted. But it is difficult to completely lose touch with your faith. I still follow the rituals I can, praying before meals and drinking wine." Daniel finished his bean stew and pushed the plate away. "The woman who used to tell me I was damned—Citizeness Odette—still prays to your Holy Family, even if she hides her rosary in her pocket. Many French Catholics keep their faith."

"So they have not fully forsaken the Lord, then," Francesca mused.

Daniel shook his head. "Officially, we're free to believe as we choose."

Francesca felt queasy. It was wrong to allow such a conversation before Barbara, but she wanted to hear more. "They say your government has sold churches off to the highest bidders, stolen the bells and silver from French churches just as your army has from ours. That priests aren't allowed to celebrate mass on Sundays and must swear allegiance to your Republic rather than the pope."

Daniel sighed. "All true, signora—though most of this happened during the Terror. It's not so bad, now, honest."

"We've heard about the Terror," Francesca said. "Weren't you frightened?"

"It's like my master used to say: revolutions are fed on blood," Daniel said. "Our lives are better than when the king and queen stole bread out of our mouths. They will be even better when our borders are secure."

Francesca eyed him, incredulous. "You believe that? What has Ancona to do with France's borders? What gives you the right to come here and take the treasures from our city and imprison our people? My husband? Me?"

Daniel sighed. "You're casualties of war, signora. We're fighting the Austrians and the pope, both of whom threaten the Republic's survival. Nothing is more important than that."

The baby started to wail. Francesca rose to get him.

"Mama's right," she heard Barbara say, voice dripping with malice. "You shouldn't be here. You *are* going to hell when you die, all you Jews and Frenchmen. I only wish my father had killed more of you."

# 30

After Barbara hissed her malediction at the French soldier, the afternoon dragged uncomfortably. A few neighbors stopped by to check on Francesca, but Daniel chased them off. Barbara whined that he wouldn't let her go play. Sensing the tension, Mario whimpered and fussed. Francesca felt wretched—frightened at the thought of provoking the general once more, terrified that she might be imprisoned along with Emilio in the French camp. If they did not allow her to return home, who would care for the children?

When Daniel, his eyes on the sun setting in the horizon, told her it was time to head to the Palazzo Triumph, she stooped to pick up Mario.

"You can't bring him." His mouth was pulled tight. "The girl can watch him."

Francesca, ignoring him, put the baby on her shoulder. "He's fussed all afternoon. Barbara can come too and hold the baby outside the Palazzo. Please? I can't leave them home alone again."

Daniel looked like he was about to back down when Barbara came dancing into the room and crooked two fingers at him, maliciously invoking the evil eye. "*Malocchio!*" she whispered.

Francesca took two steps in her direction and slapped her. Barbara started to cry, Mario to wail. Daniel's eyes turned hard as obsidian. He grabbed the baby from Francesca's arms, thrust him at Barbara, then seized Francesca's elbow and dragged her away. "She can get a neighbor if she can't manage herself," he hissed. "Let's go!"

Out on the road, they stumbled a few paces before Daniel stopped. "Where do we go?" he snapped. "Where is the Palazzo?"

Francesca wanted to scream back at him, but his dark expression stopped her. "It's this way," she said, pointing, trying to remain calm. "In the hills overlooking the harbor."

They walked in silence. Francesca told herself that Mario would be fine, that Barbara would take care of him. She stole another glance at Daniel. His shoulders were slumped, his mouth set, the look in his eyes still black and angry. He must dislike having to be so rough, she thought. He was so young, so far away from home. Had he ever been forced to manhandle women and children before?

As they rounded a curve in the road, she gathered her courage. "Daniel? I'm sorry for what Barbara said. I thought what my husband and the Catholic Fellowship did in the ghetto was terrible."

Daniel glared at her. "They killed my cousin, you know. A schoolboy. What could he have possibly done to deserve that?"

"You have cousins in Ancona?"

"What difference does that make? Your Catholic Fellowship killed so many. And why? What did my people ever do to them? Lend them money? Refuse to pray to Jesus?"

"They thought the Jews were on your side—the French side."

"So your daughter hates me for being both French—and Jewish? What a loving, compassionate Christian you're raising, signora. My congratulations."

Francesca opened her mouth to respond, then thought better of it.

"We must hurry," Daniel said. "The general does not tolerate tardiness."

As they ascended the steep road toward the magnificent palace looming before them, Francesca felt a creeping sense of intimidation. The mansion was hewn from the same rose-colored stone as most of Ancona's buildings. Two of its four stories were punctuated with double arched windows, each window divided by a slender white column. Francesca found it hard to believe that the pope's representative resided alone in the Palazzo; it could easily house ten or more of Ancona's poorer families, with room to spare.

They walked through the magnificent stone archway leading to the front portico and toward the marble stairway of an immense entranceway. Francesca's ragged black dress and straw bonnet made her shrink back inside herself. She had lived in Ancona all her life, yet this was the closest she had ever come to this edifice. If not for the French invasion, she would probably have died before seeing its interior.

The vast marble expanse of the entrance hall made her gasp. Towering naked statues leaned in seductive poses against black marble columns. A stunning, ornate ceiling mural led the eye inexorably upward to a scene of shockingly half-draped maidens, breasts bare, being chased through sunlit clouds by nude satyrs and dimpled cherubs.

Francesca and Daniel both ducked modestly at the same time. She felt a maternal throb of feeling for the boy. "We don't have to look, do we?" she whispered.

"No, we don't," he said, the tips of his ears glowing red.

Daniel said something in French to a guard stationed at the end of the foyer where two doors opened left and right. The guard nodded toward a door down the hall. There, Daniel gave their names to another guard standing at stiff attention. He flung the door open and announced, "Signora Francesca Marotti and Corporal Isidore, as commanded."

Francesca breathed a little easier entering the room. Its mint-green walls were striking, but, aside from a plaster relief on the ceiling, decorated with grapes and leaves, the room was modest after the scandalous foyer. The general stood to one side, poring over a large, detailed map. With him were several other officers—his aides, Francesca guessed from their elegant uniforms. They were much more finely dressed than Daniel. Bonaparte himself was by far the most inconspicuous, his coat simply buttoned to the top, lank hair skimming his epaulets.

"Signora Marotti!" he greeted her. "Welcome to my temporary home!"

Francesca ducked in an awkward curtsy.

Bonaparte clucked his tongue. Of the five men who were gathered around the table with him, three saluted and left.

"Madame, may I present my brother, Lucien Bonaparte, and my longtime friend and secretary, Lucien Bourrienne? Bourrienne will take notes as you describe when you first witnessed the so-called prodigy of the San Ciriaco Madonna."

Francesca felt ice tingling throughout her body. She struggled to maintain her composure. "I will be happy to speak about this, General, for it is a joy to relate how the Blessed Lady honored me. But she has instructed me to relate her story only after my husband is released."

Bourrienne gulped. One of Lucien's eyebrows lifted. Bonaparte strode over to Francesca, seized her shoulders, and stared into her face. His eyes blazed in fury. She tried to step out of his grasp, but he held her fast.

"Do you mean to tell me," he yelled straight at her, blasting her with his hot breath, "that you remain obdurate? Madame, do you not know that I can have your husband killed—and you as well?"

Trembling, Francesca could not tear her eyes away from the general's fulminating glare. His fingers sank cruelly into her shoulders.

"You hold me in your power," she said, in such a soft whisper that Bonaparte had to lean in to catch her words, "but still, I will not yield. You may end my life, but my soul is in far greater jeopardy. If I do not heed Our Lady when she commands me to be a loyal wife, to honor my wedding vows, I will burn in hell forever."

"Bah!" The general let her go, pushing her so that she nearly fell backward. He strode about the room, hands clasped behind his back. His mouth was thinned, his eyes narrowed. "Lucien," he said, turning to his brother, "what should we do with these Italian fools? How do we teach them that the Church is nothing but superstitious nonsense? How do we bring them to the joy of reason, of enlightenment?"

Bonaparte's brother looked thoughtful. "Robespierre showed us how. I'd hoped other countries, seeing our revolution and the joy it's brought the people, would not need to experience a similar Terror. But it appears that every nation must undergo its own crucible of blood."

Francesca's eyes widened in horror. Lucien's face was softer than his brother's, his eyes wider. Anyone would have thought him the gentler of the two. But the callousness of his words filled her with dread. As if the people he spoke of were not real, not people with hopes and dreams and lives of living, breathing Faith.

"You may be right." Bonaparte nodded. "Yet these superstitions have a genuine hold on the people. Why even I, for a moment . . ." His voice trailed off. He turned to Daniel, who was standing stiffly to attention at a post near the door. "Corporal, tell the guard to bring in the prisoner."

Daniel saluted and left the room. Francesca felt her knees grow weak. *Emilio. I'll see Emilio soon.*

"I am not freeing him, you understand, Madame," Bonaparte told her, his eyes cold. "But he may convince you to speak."

Francesca willed herself to stand upright; she was finding it difficult to breathe. The men returned to their study of the map, ignoring her.

Minutes ticked by. The men were arguing now, their French flowing over Francesca like a torrent. She looked at the lovely room's soothing green walls, trying to derive some comfort from their calm beauty.

"Ah!" Bonaparte said, looking up when Daniel finally returned, holding Emilio by the arm.

Francesca burst with joy to see him, but after another look, the happiness died in her throat.

"Emilio!" Francesca could barely say his name. "What have they done to you?"

Her husband was bruised and battered, lips swollen and crimson, right eye blackened. When Daniel released his arm, he staggered slightly, then pulled himself upright.

"Emilio Marotti, as requested, sir," Daniel said, saluting, his eyes snapping with—was it anger? Contempt?

"Francesca, what are you doing here?" Emilio asked. His voice was hoarse and gritty; his swollen mouth garbled his words.

"Not a word, madame," the general commanded. "Marotti, the men questioning you have informed me that you were responsible for killing at least two people during the attack on the Jewish ghetto, wounding many others. For that alone, you should be executed. You were also party to the ambush on my soldiers before we entered Ancona. You wanted to kill them all, didn't you?"

"We never had a chance," Emilio said, putting up a hand to his lips. "The men with me were cowards."

"But you would have killed my men?"

Emilio hawked loudly. He looked like he was about to spit on the parquet floor, but Daniel stepped forward and shoved his musket in the prisoner's face.

"Show the general some respect," he barked.

"Stand down, Corporal," Bonaparte said, looking amused. "You can't teach a peasant how to behave in a palace. We learned that at Versailles."

Daniel edged back, his face wiped blank.

"Again, man—you would have killed my soldiers?"

"It's war, isn't it?" Emilio growled. "Your men are here to rape our women and rob our land. Why shouldn't we defend ourselves?"

Lucien Bonaparte tilted his head to one side. "The man makes a good point, Napoleone," he said with a laugh.

Francesca blinked, momentarily distracted by the Italian form of the general's given name.

"Bah!" Bonaparte put his hands behind his back and paced again. "Listen here, Marotti. You deserve to be hanged for your crimes. But I am a merciful man and will let you go free for a simple bargain. If you instruct your wife to tell me about witnessing the miracle of the Madonna portrait, you may walk out of this palace tonight."

"Is that why she's here?" Emilio looked astonished. "You'll let me go if she tells you that? Francesca, for Christ's sake, tell the man what he wants to know. It's not as if you haven't repeated the damned story to every passerby in Ancona."

Lucien and the general exchanged glances.

"Our guest does not seem to be the believer his wife is," Lucien murmured.

Francesca's cheeks grew warm at the younger Bonaparte's amused comment. "Our Lady told me to make sure you were free before I said anything," she muttered, head ducked low.

"*Porca miseria*, you risked my life because of your crazy notions? Mary is talking to you now? Have you gone mad?" Emilio staggered toward his wife, fist upraised. "Tell the general what he wants to know!" he cried between clenched teeth. "Do it this minute! And when we get home, I promise you . . ."

Francesca quailed under his threats. She reminded herself that he had been beaten, held at the mercy of the French for a week now. She cast an appealing glance toward Daniel, but he was looking away, shoulders hunched.

The general turned to her, his face twisted in a grimace. "Your husband commands you to tell me what you know, signora. You've said yourself you will honor your wedding vows. That is what your mother of God has demanded, is it not? And the most important of a woman's vows is to obey. So?"

Francesca felt deflated. She took a deep breath, filling her lungs with air. "I will tell you everything you wish to know."

# 31

When Signora Marotti finished her story—and for a tale that had provoked so much drama, it was remarkably brief—Daniel was surprised by how much pity he felt for her. Her faith was clearly genuine. It was a shame she was married to a bully who did not deserve her.

Before dismissing the couple, the general told Marotti sternly that if he were detected in any new anti-French activities, he would be hanged without trial or recourse. He bade the guard at the door to usher them out.

Daniel turned to follow them.

"Hold on, Corporal Isidore," Bonaparte said.

So Daniel remained at attention as the Marottis left the room. He exchanged a final glance with Signora Marotti as she passed. Moved by the kindness and sincerity beneath her piety, he felt sorry they would never meet again.

After the Marottis exited, a door in the opposite wall opened. Daniel was surprised when Christophe entered with two strangers in civilian dress. Bonaparte was bent over the map again, and it was Bourrienne who addressed them.

"Corporal Isidore, you know Corporal Lefevre, of course," Bourrienne said. "I'd like to introduce you to Marc-Antoine Jullien and de Saint-Jean d'Angély, both writers of repute."

The four men exchanged bows. Daniel glanced at Christophe quizzically, but his friend simply shrugged.

"Corporals Lefevre and Isidore have been with the Army of Italy since before General Bonaparte took command," Bourrienne continued. "Their background may be of interest. Both came to the army having served as apprentices in a Parisian printshop owned by . . . your uncle, yes, Lefevre?"

"Yes, sir," Christophe said. "Lefevre Printers. On the rue des Prêtres Saint-Germain-l'Auxerrois."

"And how long did you work there?"

"We were both apprenticed after the fall of the Bastille," Christophe said. "That makes it—seven, no, eight years before we joined the army."

Bourrienne nodded knowingly. "So is it safe to assume that you can manage a press?"

Daniel and Christophe exchanged glances. Neither had expected this.

"Yes, sir," Christophe replied.

"Excellent. Jullien here studied in London before joining the Jacobins and working with Robespierre. He has written our *Courrier de l'Armee d'Italie* for several months now, which General Bonaparte subsidizes. D'Angély, a lawyer, has been writing a second paper for the troops, *La France vue de l'Armee d'Italie.*"

"Also subsidized by General Bonaparte," d'Angély murmured.

"Indeed. Perhaps you are familiar with these papers?"

"I've read both," said Daniel. "They're quite different from one another, aren't they? The *Courrier* is more radical, while *La France vue* is more conservative." From his years in the printshop, Daniel knew how much influence the press could have on the thoughts and minds of the public. Clearly, Bonaparte had learned that lesson as well.

"That was our intent." Bourrienne nodded. "To appeal to both extremes. Now tell me, as professionals, what do you think of the quality?"

Taking a quarto sheet of newsprint, Christophe scanned the page quickly. "It's sloppy work, sir. Letters dropped, ink smudged. Not left long enough to dry."

"Several misspellings," Daniel added. "No one proofing the plates."

Bonaparte left the map and bounded over. "See, Bourrienne? Wasn't I correct?"

"They can spot a fault, general," Bourrienne said, not looking totally convinced. "But can they make it right?"

"The men working the presses now make excuses, saying it is impossible to print when they have to keep moving with the army," d'Angély said. "But they were not trained as printers."

"They're not wrong, though," Daniel mused. "Such a large print run—distributing to the entire Army of Italy while keeping up with the troops . . ."

"They also say that the press we're using—a small one, so it can be transported easily—is not adequate to the volume they have to print," Bourrienne added.

"Could you not centralize the printing in one city—Venice, perhaps, or Milan?" Daniel asked. "Have runners bring fresh news to the printshop? Then you could use a more substantial press—or even two or three. It would help, too, in maintaining the supplies—ink and newsprint, neither of which improve when transported through storms or heat. Or on the backs of mules, for that matter." Daniel handed the pages back to Bourrienne.

"I told you, didn't I?" Bonaparte crowed. "These are the men."

Daniel and Christophe looked at one another again.

"Begging your pardon, sir, but neither of us joined the Army of Italy to work as printers," Christophe said, standing at attention.

Bonaparte's countenance darkened. "May I remind you, *Corporal*, that you are a soldier and will do as you are commanded? This is the second time I have spoken to you about insubordination. I warn you—do not let there be a third."

"Yes, sir," Christophe said, straightening his back even more. "I beg your pardon, sir."

Bonaparte's face softened. "Never mind, soldier. Had someone tried to remove me from active service and put me on the back lines, I would have felt the same. But this task is much more instrumental to the morale of the Army than your strong arm and brave heart."

"We appreciate your confidence in us, sir," Daniel spoke up, throwing Christophe a cautionary glance. "We won't disappoint you."

The general nodded. "I think centralizing the press is a worthy plan. Once we've taken Rome, we may relocate you there—but in the meantime, you'll set up shop here in Ancona."

"Here, sir? A fine thought, sir." Christophe grinned from ear to ear. "In fact, sir, Ancona would be an excellent permanent location for the press. It is nearly in the center of Italy, is it not?" He looked at the map spread out on the table.

"We will start here, as I said." Bonaparte nodded decisively. "Give Bourrienne a list of your requirements. As commanders of our printing staff, I'll promote you both to the rank of regimental sergeant-major. With the appropriate raise in pay, of course."

Daniel couldn't believe it. Jumping to the second-highest non-commissioned rank in the French army would typically take years to achieve—but then, the Revolutionary army was rife with stories of generals who'd leaped from obscurity to prominence in an astoundingly short time. The enlisted men often discussed the youth of their officers—Bonaparte himself, all of twenty-seven years old; Junot, twenty-six; Joubert, twenty-eight. The troops' admiration of these men knew no bounds. Every one of them thought they, too, could become a Bonaparte or a Bernadotte, who had attained his general's insignia a mere four years after joining as a volunteer. Perhaps, Daniel thought dizzily, this was just the first step.

Of course, not everyone could reach so high. Sebastian, a soldier since before the Revolution, was still only a sergeant. And now Daniel outranked him. He couldn't help but grin, picturing Sebastian's face when he learned the news.

Of course, Daniel realized, he would miss his comrades. They would be leaving the day after tomorrow for the march on Rome, while he and Christophe would be stuck here in Ancona.

He tried to convince himself of the good in this change. His parents would be pleased that he was out of immediate danger. And it would give him a chance to know his Italian cousins better.

And, he thought darkly, casting a glimpse at his grinning friend, it would give Christophe a chance to shake off his infatuation for Mirelle.

# 32

Mirelle couldn't sleep. Too much had happened that day: the general's visit to the ghetto, the walk home with David Morpurgo— did he really want to marry her?—and her aunt and cousin's arrival. And then there was that maddening green-eyed friend of Cousin Daniel's. Why did her pulse flutter and an uncontrollable warmth radiate through her whenever she stole a glance at him? And how had he known that she longed to escape the ghetto, for life to offer more than just being a wife and mother?

She wasn't the only one feeling strain. Papa was curt at dinner, a sure sign he was exhausted. At Mama's insistence, they all retired early. But now Mirelle, head and heart full, tossed restlessly beneath her down coverlet on the cot Anna had set up in her room. Her aunt, of course, slept in the more comfortable bed.

Desperate to rest and unsure how to quench the unruly emotions that plagued her, her thoughts landed on her brother. What would Jacopo have done, had he lived to see the French occupation of Ancona? She closed her eyes and pictured her brother's thrill at witnessing the knocking down of the ghetto gates. How he'd hated being penned up every sundown! A sudden thought forced her eyes wide. She sat up, hearing Jacopo's voice in her head: *I'd leave the ghetto at night*, he told her. *See those stars over the open harbor. Why haven't you?*

*Of course.* She lay down, but now the covers suffocated her. She pushed them off, trying to move as quietly as possible, and sat up. Her aunt didn't stir.

She heard her father's snuffling snore, then waited for the deep draw of breath that told her Mama was also fast asleep. Her black dress was draped over the chair where she'd left it. She slipped off her nightdress and pulled the gown over her slender body in the dark, not bothering with corset or stays. Her heavy cloak would cover her. All she intended was to step past where the gates used to stand and into Catholic Ancona, to honor her brother's wish. Then she'd return to bed.

Mirelle let herself out of the house into the dark and mist. Treading carefully, she turned toward Via Astagna. The ghetto was deserted, candles doused, shutters closed. Her thin shoes scuffled along the cobblestones, bare echoes in the silence that hung heavy all around her.

It wasn't until she reached the old gateway that she realized she was violating the recently imposed French curfew. All residents of Ancona were to be indoors by ten o'clock. She'd paid scant heed to the curfew announcement. She'd never planned to be out this late.

She was too far gone to turn back now. *Just let me get through the gates and close to the harbor,* she thought. *One good look at the sky and the stars, then I'll go right back home. For you, Jacopo.* She crept past the open stone archway.

Her body trembled as she left the ghetto. She remembered the mixed fear and exhilaration of stealing through the gates with Dolce and her father in Venice. Now, taking a few steps into Gentile Ancona, she wasn't sure what she felt.

A moment later, she heard heavy boots on the cobbles. Three soldiers patrolled just ahead on the Via Astagna, muskets slung over their shoulders. One carried a lantern, the second a bottle of wine. A third lagged behind. Mirelle glanced about. The street was too narrow to avoid them, unless she knocked on a door and begged to be taken inside. Should she? No, not unless she wanted Mama to know what she'd done.

*What's the worst they can do?* she asked herself, heart pounding, as she waited for them to approach. *They're French soldiers, like my cousin Daniel. Not like the Christians of Ancona, or even that drunk Venetian nobleman. They'll just escort me home.*

"Halt!" one of them called, his cry echoing off the high walls of the ghetto.

She didn't move.

"What are you doing out at this hour?" the second asked, shining the lantern in her face.

She started to answer, but the first soldier flung up a hand. "*Tais-toi*," he said rudely. "Jacques, what a stupid question. What type of woman would be out this late unaccompanied? Only whores."

"You're right, Pierre." Jacques, licking his lips, moved the lantern down her body.

"Please. I was just walking home." Fear crawled up Mirelle's spine.

Pierre laughed thickly, taking a drink from the bottle. "She's a pretty piece."

"I haven't had a woman since Milan." Jacques reached out and grabbed Mirelle's arm. "Give us a kiss, girl. We won't report you if you do."

"Let me go!" Mirelle cried, struggling in his grasp. She readied her fist to strike him, but realized that this man, unlike the drunk noble in Venice, wouldn't be deterred by a mere blow.

The third soldier came up to them. "What's going on?"

Mirelle's eyes flew open. Christophe Lefevre stood before her, holding a lantern aloft.

"It's nothing, Sergeant," Jacques said.

"We just wanted a kiss," Pierre added.

Mirelle pulled out of Jacques's suddenly slackened grasp. "Corporal Lefevre! Thank heavens. Tell these men to leave me alone!"

"Signorina d'Ancona!" The soldier peered at her under the hood of her cape, then turned on the men, mouth pinched. "Let her go this instant! How dare you harass an innocent woman?"

"She was walking the streets alone at this hour. What were we to think?" Jacques protested.

Christophe put a protective arm around Mirelle's shoulders. "I'll bring you home," he said. "On your way," he added brusquely to the men.

"Oh, so she's your doxy," Pierre sniggered. "Sorry, Sergeant-Major."

Mirelle froze, hands clenched in indignation.

Christophe turned on him in unmistakable fury. "*Tais-toi!* This is a decent woman."

"If you say so." Jacques shrugged. "We'll leave you to it."

"Be off," Christophe growled.

Looking relieved that he wouldn't press the matter further, the two men hurried down the street. Mirelle and Christophe watched as they turned toward the quay.

"Are you all right?" Christophe asked gently. "What are you doing out at this hour?"

She felt her heart turn over in her chest at his tenderness. Instead of replying, she burst into tears. *Why am I crying?* she thought, appalled. But the French soldier's kindness had triggered emotions buried deep within her.

Christophe led her to the front steps of one of the houses, helped her sit, and handed her a handkerchief. He sat silent, waiting, as she carefully dabbed at her cheeks.

It took what seemed like an eternity, but Mirelle finally stopped weeping. "It was for my brother," she said, her breath catching in hiccups. "He always wanted to leave the ghetto at night. I stopped him when he was still alive. So he told me to do it for him now."

"He . . . told you?" Christophe raised an eyebrow.

Mirelle nodded. "Yes. He wanted to see the stars over the harbor.

It was as if he whispered to me." She broke off. "Listen to me," she muttered, "talking like a madwoman. It was stupid. I should never have left the house."

Christophe reached out to touch her shoulder. "No. I understand."

Mirelle bit her lip. "You do? Because I don't. Here I am, outside the ghetto at night, nearly freezing."

Her body was trembling uncontrollably. Christophe took off his jacket and draped it over her shoulders. His trapped body warmth seeped into her shaking frame and quieted it.

"Did you forget the curfew?" he asked gently.

Mirelle nodded.

"Did you do what your brother asked you to do?"

Mirelle stared, suspecting he might be mocking her. But his face was solemn.

"Do you need me to walk you to the harbor so you can honor your brother's wish?"

Mirelle gazed at him, then nodded. *How strange*, she thought. *He was here at exactly the right moment. Just like in Venice.*

They walked silently down to the waterfront, close enough that she could reach out and brush against him, if only she dared. She wished, more than anything, that he would touch her. As they stood under the stars that Jacopo had longed to see, she realized with a start that she was not thinking of her brother.

"They are beautiful, aren't they?" Christophe pointed to the heavens. "Do you believe your brother is up there, looking down? Do Jews believe in heaven?"

Mirelle shook her head. "Not in that way. But perhaps his spirit does know."

"I'm certain of it. Just as I know my father watches me." He lapsed into silence.

The moment stretched between them and she grew afraid of what she was feeling. "I should go home. Someone will see me."

"I'll take you."

"I'm so grateful. If you hadn't come along just then—"

"But I did." Christophe's voice was thick. *"Dieu merci."*

Mirelle gazed back at him. *Dieu merci*, she thought. "Please, don't mention this to anyone. Especially not my cousin. Please. Promise me."

Christophe nodded, his face softening.

*What can he possibly think of me?* she wondered.

As they started back, Christophe said, "My father died at the start of the Revolution, at the Bastille. I was only nine years old. But even so, I know what it's like to lose someone you love."

In a few short sentences, Christophe told her how his uncle and father had gone with the National Guard to the Bastille, demanding gunpowder for the muskets they'd been given. When the governor refused, two guardsmen clambered over the prison walls and cut through the chains securing the drawbridge, starting the famous assault. But Christophe's father, Noel, stood too close. The heavy bridge toppled directly on his head, killing him instantly.

"Uncle Alain raised me, gave me a profession," Christophe said. "But there's no replacing your own father."

"Or your brother," Mirelle agreed.

They arrived at her door, and Mirelle removed his jacket. She paused halfway up the stairs. "Thank you for helping me," she whispered. "Yet again."

# 33

## February 14

The next morning, Mirelle tried to find a moment to ask her mother about Signor Morpurgo. But Mama was bustling around the house, making sure their houseguests were comfortable.

Seeing her mother fully occupied with household tasks, Mirelle decided to speak with her father. Still exhausted from the previous day's events, he had stayed in bed.

She slipped into his room and sat on Mama's chair. "Am I disturbing you?"

Papa smiled tiredly at her. "Not at all, child. I'm happy for your company."

"There's something we need to discuss."

After arriving back to bed the previous night, she had decided on a foolproof plan. At least, she hoped it was foolproof.

"Is there?" Papa settled himself against his bank of pillows.

"When you bring Beniamino into the workshop, I want to come too."

Papa sighed. "Mirelle—"

"No, listen, Papa. You're going to be occupied in teaching my cousin about the business. That's going to be difficult enough without having to manage the men and the accounts—especially after what I've seen in the books. It doesn't have to be every day—just two or three times a week, to keep everything running smoothly."

Papa shook his head. "You heard what we said about the rabbi."

Mirelle knew this would be the most difficult hurdle. She picked up his hand and kissed it. "He asked if this would be permanent, didn't he? If he reproaches you, tell him it's just temporary. Just until you have Beniamino trained."

"Your mother won't like it."

Realizing she'd convinced him, Mirelle was careful not to smile. "Probably not. But she'll agree if I tell her I'm there to make sure you're not overexerting yourself. She's worried about your health, Papa. I am, too."

Papa sighed. "I don't want you to worry."

"Then let me do this."

He closed his eyes. "If you can persuade your Mama, I would be grateful."

It wasn't until late afternoon, when Prudenzia had retired to rest, that Mirelle finally managed to corner her mother. She was sitting at her desk, writing a note.

Before Mirelle could open her mouth, Mama jumped in with a question of her own. "What are you wearing tonight?"

"Tonight? To the salon? But I thought—"

"I didn't want you to attend, but now you must. To take your aunt."

Mirelle stared at her mother. "Won't she feel uncomfortable? She won't know anyone and wasn't invited."

Mama folded her note and heated the wax to seal it. "Dolce invited her. Her father must have said something. And your aunt is accustomed to much more glittering social functions than this. From what she says, she spends half her life attending parties and making calls. We can't usually offer her such events in Ancona." She dripped wax on the note and applied her seal. "So let's take advantage of this one, yes?" She looked straight at Mirelle. "We need to amuse your aunt so she doesn't go running back to Rome with Beniamino. The boy must learn his responsibilities if he is going to inherit your father's workshop, and that will take time. Months, maybe years."

Should she broach the subject of the workshop? No, Mirelle decided. The time wasn't right.

Mama rang a bell for Anna, who appeared in the doorway, wiping her hands on her apron. "Take this to the Morpurgo house, please," Mama said, "and hurry back to prepare dinner. We'll eat early so Mirelle and Prudenzia have time to dress."

Anna made a face. "I've already started dinner."

"Let me go, Mama," Mirelle said. "I can deliver the note and be back in ten minutes."

"Just don't tire yourself, child. You have a big night ahead."

Mirelle left her mother's missive with a servant at the Morpurgos'. She turned to head back down their marble stairway—and was startled to see Christophe Lefevre on the bottom step. A flutter danced in the pit of her stomach.

"Signorina d'Ancona," he said, his face lighting up as though the mere sight of her brightened his day. No one had ever looked at her like that before. "Give me a moment and I'll escort you home."

"There's no need, Sergeant. It is 'Sergeant' now, isn't it? That's what those men said last night. Are congratulations in order?"

The soldier grinned at her. "I'm still not used to it. Anyway, I'd much prefer you call me Christophe"—his voice dropped to a whisper as he leaned close—"because I'd like nothing better than to call you Mirelle. Did you know that it is French for 'admired one'? Which suits you, my lovely lady. So if you please, admired Mirelle, may I call you by your charming name?"

His soft voice thrilled her. "I shouldn't allow it, but I owe you a debt of gratitude. So yes, you may—in private, at least."

She waited as he rang the bell and delivered his note. "From the general," he said, rejoining her and extending his arm. "He leaves for Rome tomorrow, so he sent apologies to your friends. He'll drop by the salon if he can but doubts he'll have time."

"You're heading to Rome?" Mirelle rested her fingers lightly on the crook of his arm. He reached down and tucked her hand more securely. "My relatives have just arrived from there. I'm bringing my aunt to the salon this evening. She'll be sorry to miss the general."

"Actually, I'm not leaving," Christophe said. "Daniel and I have been stationed here. Which means we can get better acquainted."

"Not leaving?"

"Not leaving. And can I say how pleased I am to be—"

Mirelle half pulled her hand out of his arm. She needed to remember he was a Gentile, no matter how attractive he was. "Please don't," she told him sternly, raising her chin. "I am indebted to you for your kindness last night, and in Venice, but it's not proper for you to flirt with me."

"And why not?" Christophe asked. "And who's to say it's flirting? I know you feel something."

Mirelle bit her lip. "And if I do? What does it matter? We come from different worlds, you and I."

"Do we? Did we not break down the gates that stood between us?"

Mirelle had to smile at that, but then she turned pensive. "More than mere gates separate us. I have a duty to my family. Now that my brother is dead, their future depends on me."

Christophe mulled this over. His voice grew serious. "Signorina d'Ancona—Mirelle—a few months ago, I was part of an army that was mocked throughout Europe. A fledgling army that everyone said could never vanquish the mighty Austrians, never make their way into the heart of Italy. Yet here we are. A mere few days ago, your people were penned inside the ghetto. That's no longer true either. Can't you see how times have changed for us both? How can you talk about family and duty and the things that separate us, when fate has so clearly brought us together?"

Mirelle stared at him. Could he be right? She drew a deep breath, a sudden rush of freedom entering her chest—a feeling close to giddiness.

"You are all I think of," Christophe continued, "from the moment I wake until I sleep at night. Even then, you wind like smoke through my dreams. I've fallen in love with you."

Mirelle felt her breath catch in her throat. "If that's true, I'm sorry for you."

"*If* it's true!" Christophe stopped short and shifted to face her. He stood above her, his jaw tight. "Do you think I've said this before? Oh, I've had my dalliances. I won't deny that. But never before have I met a woman who is the embodiment of all I desire in life. I may not deserve you, admired one—but no one could ever love you as I do."

Christophe's protestations overwhelmed her. In Venice, perhaps, such avowals might have been part of a romantic dream that one would remember fondly once awoken. But this was Ancona, and this handsome soldier was making this declaration to *her*. "I'm sorry," she repeated, not quite sure what else to say. "The distance between us is too great."

"Am I alone in my feelings?" Christophe asked, his voice cracking. His sudden vulnerability touched her heart. "If that's true . . ."

Mirelle looked around. They were just a few paces from her house. Thankfully, the street was, for once, nearly deserted.

She tried to convince herself that she didn't care for him. *He's a Gentile*, she reminded herself. *A foreigner, a soldier.* And yet when she opened her mouth to tell him that she would never love him, that such an idea was impossible, the words refused to leave it.

*Fate somehow keeps bringing us together,* she thought. *And he says he loves me.*

Then she remembered what Dolce had said back when the rabbi had first exiled her—that a man would chase all thoughts of the ketubah manufactory from her mind. She felt ashamed to admit that her friend might be right. Especially now, when Papa needed her more than ever.

The silence between them lengthened. Christophe stepped forward. She moved back, putting up her hands to stop him.

"I'm not leaving tomorrow," Christophe said. "But a soldier's life is subject to command. I may be ordered to ride away next week. Next month. Would you leave my question unanswered?"

Mirelle tried to speak, but she couldn't.

Christophe bent his head, looking into her eyes. She wondered if he could sense her confusion, the jumble of thoughts and emotion. He nodded, as if her eyes had answered him. She felt like a large stone rested on her chest, stifling her. And yet some part of her rejoiced. She might not fully understand how she felt, but she was pleased that he was staying in Ancona.

"If I call on you, will you be glad?" he asked. "Can we get to know one another better?"

"My parents would not allow it. You're not Jewish."

He turned to leave.

She reached out and touched his elbow. "But they'll admit you if you come with Daniel."

He looked back, eyes hopeful.

"Come with Daniel," she whispered, her cheeks hot.

# 34

Mirelle led her aunt toward Dolce's salon, both women carefully negotiating the cobbles. Light splashed into the narrow ghetto streets from every window in the Morpurgo villa. Linkboys, holding torches high to illuminate the dark streets, ushered sedan chairs, while curious children pointed at the arriving guests. Merriment resounded from the open doorway.

Prudenzia looked approvingly at the mansion as they entered. "Clearly a wealthy family, niece," she said. "You've chosen your bosom friend well."

Mirelle bit her lip. Did her aunt think she was friends with Dolce just because the Morpurgos were rich?

"Signora Prudenzia Fermi and Signorina Mirelle d'Ancona." The footman's voice announcing them carried over the chatter of the crowd.

Mirelle recognized only a few faces. At her father's behest, Dolce had invited not only the town's Gentile and Jewish freethinkers but also a more aristocratic crowd than usual. They must have come, Mirelle thought, to pander to David and Ezekiel, given their new roles on the municipal council. And, of course, to meet the great general, who—Mirelle looked about her—did not seem to be in attendance. In fact, no one from the French forces was there.

"D'Ancona?" came the question from a few steps away. A gentleman raised a quizzing glass and leveled it at Mirelle. "Surely not a member of your family, Marchesa Arianna?"

The bejeweled woman standing next to him languidly turned her head to look. Mirelle had worn her best dress, a low-waisted ivory gown embroidered with flowers around the hemline and sleeves. As fashionable as it was, it looked shabby compared to the marchesa's exquisite raiment, a wide brocade black silk gown.

"A member of *my* family, Barone Confidati? Surely you jest. She's a Jewess, yes?"

The baron shook his head. "Ever since the French removed their insignia, it's impossible to tell. Well, nearly impossible." He laughed, tapping his nose.

The marchesa rapped his knuckles with her fan. She pretended to whisper, but her deep voice carried. "I can always count on you to be droll—or naughty. What a dreadful affair this is!"

Her cheeks burning, Mirelle turned away and searched the room for Dolce. But her aunt touched her shoulder, whispering, "Is that the Marchesa Donna Arianna Alonzo di Ancona?"

"I don't know. I've never met the woman before. Nor do I care to."

Prudenzia sniffed. "Nonsense, child. In Rome, I rub elbows with nobility all the time. You must learn to introduce yourself to them."

To Mirelle's horror, her aunt stepped forward and curtsied. Holding the pose, she said, "Marchesa, I bring you greetings from the Duchessa di Torlonia. I saw Teresa last week in Rome."

The older woman raised her chin. "What a treat for you," she finally said, slowly, as if every word were coated in honeyed poison.

Prudenzia rose gracefully, ignoring the snub. "I attended one of her receptions, raising funds for the wounded. Her husband, the Duca di Torlonia, honored us by speaking of the preparations for the local hospitals."

"A charity event?" Barone Confidati glanced at the marchesa. "I understand now."

Prudenzia seemed unperturbed, but Mirelle frowned. "What exactly do you understand, sir?" she asked.

The baron looked down his long nose at her, but she refused to quail. She put up her own chin, deliberately imitating the marchesa.

"Generally, the duchesa is the most discerning of women," the baron explained. "But she does extend hospitality more widely when she issues invitations for charity."

"Come, Aunt," Mirelle said abruptly, drawing her away. "Our hostess is waving at us."

Prudenzia lingered long enough to curtsy again, collecting the barest of nods from both marchioness and baron, before catching up with her niece, who was striding swiftly through the room.

"Slow down," Prudenzia hissed in her ear. "You look like you're running a race. And why were you so rude to the baron?"

"Rude to the baron? Don't you understand? He was mocking you!"

Prudenzia shook her head, smiling. Mirelle stopped short and stared at her.

"You need to ignore the small affronts, child," Prudenzia said. "They learn to tolerate you soon enough. When you are elevated in Jewish society . . ."

Mirelle flushed. Was her aunt hinting that Dolce's father wanted to marry her? Mirelle was sorry now she hadn't pressed her mother for the truth.

"My dearest Mirelle! I am so happy to welcome you and your aunt to my home!" David Morpurgo stood before them. His stocky body was bundled into a well-cut coat, his fingers thick with rings, his hair pomaded until it shone. "Signora Fermi, I feel we are already acquainted." He bowed over Prudenzia's extended fingertips.

"My dear, dear Signor Morpurgo!" Prudenzia practically burbled with delight. "Such a pleasure to be included in such a distinguished event, among such company. Why, Mirelle and I were just chatting with the Marchesa Donna Alonzo di Ancona!"

*The next thing you know*, Mirelle thought, *she'll tell everyone she and the marchesa are the best of friends.*

"How delightful!" Morpurgo said. He threw Mirelle a quick wink and she raised her fan to cover a giggle. "Let me extend your circle even further. May I introduce you to my sister-in-law, Speranza Morpurgo? I feel certain you two have much in common."

Frankly, Mirelle could think of no more unlikely pair, but she watched in relief as Dolce's father led her aunt away.

She found Dolce in the center of a small group that was avidly discussing General Bonaparte's ransacking of Italy.

"It is said," Bertrando Bonaria was saying, "that he is in negotiations with the pope and the terms are no less than thirty-three million francs to leave the pope in office!"

"What is that in scudi?" someone asked. When the currency was translated, he whistled.

"I don't mind the money," Dolce said. Mirelle admired her poise. "The pope has plenty of that. But I do mind the art treasures he's sending back to France, filling their coffers while emptying our own."

"And the church artifacts," said a man Dolce introduced as Conte Annibale Ranuzzi, cousin to Cardinal Ranuzzi. Mirelle was shocked to see the cardinal himself standing to one side. She knew of his importance in Ancona as the foremost clergyman at the Cathedral San Ciriaco. She assumed David Morpurgo had invited him because of his standing in the city, and that the clergyman felt it politically expedient to attend. There could be no love lost between them—not if the rumors of the cardinal's role in the ghetto riots were true.

"At least he didn't take the Madonna," said another, more modestly arrayed churchman. "You said he grew white as he stared at her blessed countenance, did you not, Cardinal?"

"Indeed, Father Candelabri," the cardinal said, joining the group. "He was certainly moved by her. Would that she had made him return the rest of our treasures!"

"You'll never see those back," the count said, shaking his head.

Just then, there was a commotion by the main door. Everyone turned, and all conversation abruptly ceased as Bonaparte strolled in, accompanied by his aides. Signor Morpurgo moved smoothly over to him just as the general said to someone, "In my youth I had illusions. I got rid of them fast."

Bonaparte's aides exploded in laughter. Mirelle watched as Dolce's father bowed, then led the general over to their group. Dolce deftly handled the introductions. Bonaparte's eyes lit up as he saw Mirelle in their midst.

"My dear Signorina d'Ancona! Tell me what everyone has been talking about." He moved next to her and put a hand on her arm.

Mirelle thought quickly. She certainly couldn't tell him that they were complaining of his looting of Italy. But she was curious what he might have seen in the Mary painting. "We were wondering, Citizen General, if the painting of Mary smiled upon you. I hope she did!"

Bonaparte suddenly grew silent, his jaw tight. Mirelle realized she'd made a terrible mistake. She blushed fiery red.

After a long pause, the general softened. "No, not a smile, my dear young lady," he said, forcing a laugh. "But you don't believe in Mother Mary anyway, do you?"

Mirelle, still flustered, shook her head.

Cardinal Ranuzzi stepped in to interject, "Do *you* believe, General? We are told that much of France is godless now. Is that true?"

Bonaparte glared for a moment at the cardinal, then grew thoughtful. "I'm used to salons in France," he said slowly, "where guests freely consider philosophy and politics. I assume the same latitude of expression prevails here. That being so, I will confide in you, Cardinal." The general bowed stiffly. "These are unofficial thoughts, you understand. There was a time when the ideals of the Enlightenment forbade religion. Perhaps that was a mistake." He paused to take a wineglass from a servant. "No society can survive without a code of morals, and there can be no proper code of morals without religion." He took a sip of wine and glanced toward Dolce approvingly. "Excellent vintage, Signorina Morpurgo. Yes, I agree that people need religion."

The Catholic clergy stared at him in shocked approval. Bonaparte smiled benignly upon them before concluding, "I still believe, however, that religion must be controlled by the government. Which is why our priests take oaths of loyalty to the Republic, rather than professing sole allegiance to the pope. And that means the current state of affairs here in Italy and elsewhere in Europe is far from satisfactory."

The cardinal's smiling face turned dark. "That is nothing less than blasphemy, General."

"I know you think so, Cardinal. How could you not?" He paused, his hand tightening involuntarily around Mirelle's arm. "In a recent letter, I bade General Rusca to explain to the magistrates, the heads of monasteries, and the parish priests that I offer ministers of religion—all religions—whose principles are exemplars of their faith nothing but the utmost respect."

He loosened his grasp, allowing Mirelle to slip out of his hold. She moved to one side, hoping he would not take offense. He didn't seem to notice. "But where clergy become instruments of civil war and discord," he said, his voice deep with threat, "I will destroy their monasteries and personally punish every parish priest. Is that clear, Cardinal?"

Ranuzzi bowed. "Of course, General. We preach nothing but heavenly peace."

"Then practice what you preach," Bonaparte said, scowling. "And there will be peace on earth as well."

"But, General," said a civilian who had arrived with the French contingent. "You can't mean you are in favor of returning Catholicism—or any other religion—to France, can you?"

Bonaparte laughed. "I'd forgotten you were here, Jullien. My friends, this man was Robespierre's righthand man for several years and is no friend of any of the established religions—Christian, Jewish, or Moslem."

"You haven't answered me," Jullien said, piercing gray eyes fixed on the general's face.

A tense silence fell over the gathering. A couple of the general's aides put their hands on their sword hilts. Lucien Bonaparte took a step toward Jullien, as if to shield his brother.

"I will tell you how I feel about religion," Bonaparte said slowly. "Though I'm not certain I like your tone. Back when I was in school, aged eleven or twelve, I heard a Catholic sermon. The priest declared that Cato, Caesar, and other great figures of antiquity were damned. Can you imagine? The most virtuous men of antiquity would burn in perpetuity because they did not adhere to a religion that did not exist in their time!"

Dolce's uncle Ezekiel let the general laughter subside before saying, "And yet, General, you are as a savior to my people—truly, as we named you, our Helek Tov."

Bonaparte's brother translated the term for the Gentiles in the audience. The general patted Ezekiel on the shoulder. "I cannot speak for the precepts of your faith," he said. "For all I know, you too condemn the great Greek and Roman thinkers—but how could I do otherwise than feel for your condition?" He hesitated, as if uncertain he should continue. Then, swallowing, he said, "My family was expelled from our birthplace, the island of Corsica. We were like any other exiles—shivering, poor, not certain whom to trust or where we'd find our next meal."

Bonaparte looked at his empty wineglass and Dolce motioned to one of the servants, who took it and handed him a full one. The general downed it and took another from the tray.

"Our flight was short-lived, and we found a home in mainland

France," he said. "Your people, on the other hand, Signor Morpurgo, have been exiles for generations. Having lived that life myself, however briefly, your people's plight moves me."

Another silence followed, which Ezekiel broke. "We are honored by your confidences."

Bonaparte nodded. "Well! We have been solemn and philosophical long enough. I have an early-morning departure to prepare for. A pleasure, Signorina Morpurgo."

"Mirelle and I will walk you out, General," Dolce said.

Bonaparte extended an arm to each. As they walked through the salon, the general's aides trailing behind them, Mirelle saw her aunt try to extricate herself from her conversation with Speranza so that she could be introduced. With some relief, Mirelle saw that Speranza had a firm grip on Prudenzia's forearm and was not letting go.

Just as they neared the door, Dolce was called away by one of the guests. Excusing herself with a brief curtsy, she hurried off.

As soon as Mirelle was left alone with Bonaparte, he motioned to his aides to walk on and leaned toward her, whispering into her ear, "You asked what I saw in the portrait. I have not confessed the truth to anyone until now. You are an unbeliever, like me, yet you thought she might have smiled upon me." His face darkened.

Mirelle's breath suddenly constricted in her throat.

He shook his head as if to clear it. "If I confide in you, will you keep my secret? You realize that if you tell anyone, anyone at all, I'll know."

"I'll keep your secret, General," she murmured, shaken by the sudden menace clouding his expression. "I promise."

He peered at her for a long moment. Then, seemingly satisfied, he spat, "She glared at me."

"Glared?"

"It felt like my own mother had struck me. Like my entire body was plunged into icy water. A terrible shock."

"I'm . . . " Mirelle couldn't think of what to say, but the general didn't wait for her reply. He clicked his heels together and stalked off into the night, hands clasped behind his back.

When Mirelle didn't return to the gathering right away, Dolce came looking for her. As they walked back to the salon together, Mirelle deliberately dismissed Bonaparte's words from her mind and touched her friend's arm.

"I'm amazed all this nobility decided to attend," she whispered.

Dolce laughed. "They've no love for the French. Most are certain the Austrians will return, and everything go back to normal. But for now, they're bowing to the new order."

Mirelle related her conversation with the marchesa and baron. "Clearly they don't like the new order much," she concluded. "Oh, and my aunt is the biggest social climber you've ever met. She'll want to befriend you instantly."

Dolce nodded. "Papa told me. She won't impose upon me."

The girls stepped back into the salon and Signor Morpurgo, waiting by the door, took Mirelle's arm. "Come with me," he said. "I want to say something to you."

Morpurgo led her to the front of the room, where he clapped his hands. The room quieted.

"My dear friends—both old and new," he said. "I am beside myself with happiness—happiness at the Jewish people's liberation from ghetto shackles, the free air of enlightenment making its way through Italy in the train of the French, and by the new political appointments my brother and I have accepted." A smattering of applause followed. Signor Morpurgo looked at one of the servants, who pushed open a side door with a gloved hand. Several footmen carrying trays with champagne glasses entered, exchanging full glasses for guests' half-empty ones.

"I'd like you all to join me in a toast," Signor Morpurgo said, raising his glass.

Everyone followed suit.

"To our beloved Ancona, a city looking forward to a spring of hope. Her future has never seemed so bright!"

"To Ancona!" chorused the crowd, drinking deeply. But not all. Mirelle, sipping from her glass, noticed that some of the nobility and clergy pointedly refrained from joining them.

"I have one more toast to make," Signor Morpurgo said as the servants bustled around once more. "As you know, I have been a bachelor for many years, since my beloved wife Sarella died. I am not above feminine wiles"—at this, the room laughed—"but I never thought a woman could take my dear departed wife's place. That is, until recently." He raised his glass in Mirelle's direction.

She stared at him, her heart beating so fast that it was difficult to hear past its pounding.

A sudden wave in her direction distracted her. Mirelle saw her cousin and his friend enter the room from the corner of one eye.

"My dear Mirelle," Signor Morpurgo said, and her breath froze in her throat. "Of course, I mean you. Having already secured your parents' permission, I would like to take this moment, surrounded by our friends and loved ones, to ask you to consider my proposal. No," he said as she opened her lips, wildly trying to think of what to say, "don't answer now. You must have time to consider. But I do want to propose a toast—to Mirelle d'Ancona, who someday soon, I hope, will be my wife!"

He drank, then threw his glass into the roaring fireplace. A cheer rose from the room, and Mirelle's aunt cried out, "To Mirelle! My dearest, most darling niece!"

Mirelle's eyes sought Dolce's. Her friend was not smiling.

Mirelle was appalled. *How could he? To propose so publicly, without discovering how she felt beforehand? Without talking to his own daughter?*

She swiveled toward Daniel and Christophe. Daniel stood at the entrance, a startled look on his face. Christophe, however, had turned on his heel and was already halfway out the door.

# PART THREE

## March–June 1797

# 35

# MARCH 1

The day after the French took possession of Rome, Cardinal Ranuzzi convened a meeting of the Catholic Fellowship. They looked a sorry bunch to Emilio—moping about the darkened cathedral dining hall, a single candle flickering on the long oak board. He saw many fewer faces than before the French occupation.

Desi sat next to Emilio, shirtsleeves rolled up, looking like he was itching for a fight. But nothing had convinced Roberto to come.

"I'm done," he'd told Emilio wearily, sitting at a coffeehouse table on the dock, watching the enemy march. "The French aren't leaving any time soon. And you, cousin, you're endangering your life just by attending this meeting. What did Bonaparte say? That you'd be hanged if they caught you? Be smart. Think of Francesca and the children."

"Be smart?" Emilio raged. "Do you think the French can threaten me? This is our country and they've no right here. Easy for them to talk about liberty! What liberty have they given us? We'll only have liberty when we take it back!"

But Roberto merely shook his head, like the coward Emilio called him, and refused to come.

Most of the men at the meeting seemed unwilling to act as well. The cardinal led them in prayer and they bowed their heads meekly.

Emilio waited for all the God talk to end before speaking. "We need to show them!" he burst out. "They can't keep us penned in like this, their soldiers parading our streets! And you all looking like death warmed over, like frightened little girls!"

"Emilio," the cardinal said, "calm down."

"Calm down? We're too calm! We need to hit them—hit them hard!" Emilio's breathing grew ragged. "Look here! I stood up to the general, spat in his face. I face a sentence of death just for being here. Think that stops me?"

"Did you really spit in the general's face, Emilio?" asked one of the dockhands. "Wouldn't Bonaparte have strung you up for that?"

"The general's not a patient man." Ranuzzi quickly put up a hand to stop Emilio from replying. "And he's a parvenu, sensitive of his dignity. Let's assume Emilio's spit was more gesture than real. But he is right about one thing: we should show them that they haven't cowed us."

"But how?" asked Desi. "We tried an ambush—that didn't work."

"Let's just wait them out," said another man, servant to Barone Confidati. "My master said the French won't be here forever. Maybe just months. Then everything will return to normal."

The cardinal shook his head. "I wish that were true." He shifted in his seat. "But I've read the terms of the Treaty of Tolentino. In addition to paying the French, the pope permitted a French garrison to remain in Ancona. Permanently. Even if they leave the rest of Italy, the French are in our city to stay."

"Then the pope is a traitor!" Emilio cried, fists clenched. "He's betrayed us."

Ranuzzi shook his head. "It seems simple when you're one man in one city. The pope holds the entire spiritual world in his hands. We can't know."

"That's rot!" Emilio spat on the ground. "Mere excuses. All you churchmen stick together. What has your precious Fellowship done, anyway—except almost get me hanged?"

Ranuzzi crossed his arms across his chest. "Shut up, Marotti. If you don't like how I run things—"

"I don't!" Emilio sprang to his feet. "Why I ever thought a priest could lead a group of brigands. . ."

"Brigands?" Ranuzzi's face turned sheet white. "We're patriots—don't you forget it!"

Emilio sniggered, reclining in his chair and stretching his legs. "Of course, we are. When we win, we're patriots. Right now, to the French and their lackeys, we're nothing but cutthroats and bandits."

"Don't be ridiculous!" Ranuzzi thrust his face into Emilio's so their noses were almost touching. "We're patriots and Catholics, on a holy mission."

"Fine by me." Emilio snorted. "But if we're on a holy mission, we need to *have* a holy mission. So what is our mission, Cardinal?"

An uncomfortable silence fell over the men. Ranuzzi slumped in his chair, face wrinkled in concentration. Emilio noticed the expression with satisfaction. *So I shook up that snooty priest,* he thought. *Now, if I can only light a fire under the rest of these custard-hearts.*

"Why did Bonaparte let you go, anyway?" the baron's servant asked. Emilio remembered that his name was Nino. "Doesn't seem like him."

"He wanted Emilio's wife to tell him about seeing the Madonna portrait," Ranuzzi answered. "Because she was first to see the miracle."

"Still doesn't explain why he let you go," Nino persisted.

"She was smart—unlike all of you—and refused to talk until he released me," Emilio answered. "Seems the portrait spooked him in some way. *Buffone.*"

"Marotti, try to speak of our Lord and His Blessed Mother with respect," Ranuzzi hissed. "I was there when the general saw the prodigy. Our Lady affected him in some deep, spiritual way. This is no deception we're practicing on him."

"Isn't it?" Emilio shrugged. "I don't believe the portrait actually moved its eyes. Or cried. Or smiled."

"Are you calling your own wife a liar?" Desi asked.

"*Uffa!*" Emilio ran the fingers of both hands through his dark hair. "I know she believes it. My wife can't lie, pious misery that she is. But couldn't this just be a clever sham that you, Cardinal, or someone in the cathedral arranged? Bah!"

The cardinal flushed almost purple. "It's not a sham," he said, locking eyes again with Emilio. "Perhaps I was wrong in asking you to join us."

"And stop calling Francesca names," Desi protested. "*Porco Diavolo*, what is the matter with you? You should be down on your knees, praising Christ and all his saints for a wife like that, instead of insulting her."

As the men around the table nodded, Emilio felt the mood of the room shifting. He looked around at their gutless faces. "Listen," he said more quietly, "if I talk rough, it's because I'm upset. Embarrassed. What have we really done since the cardinal pulled us together? Sure, we dispatched a few Jews to an eternity of hellfire—but what else? It keeps me awake at night, the thought of the French and the Jews ruling us. I lie down feeling sick to my stomach, and wake wanting to puke them out. I'm less of a man because the French are here. Aren't you?"

Ranuzzi spoke up. "You know, the portrait rallied the people before. The general really was rattled by her. But he refuses to admit the truth of our Faith, calls it superstition. He's a slave to the godforsaken Enlightenment of the French."

The men turned toward him. Ranuzzi looked at the ceiling, as if seeing visions in the air. "We should take the painting, display it secretly. Bring people to our cause." He paused, thinking. "The general left it in the cathedral, with orders that no one remove the cloth covering or move the painting. He's stationed a soldier to guard it. But it would be simple enough to get past him."

Emilio thought for a few moments. Then it came to him.

"Display it?" he said, his voice echoing in the chamber. "I think we should burn it."

# 36

# MARCH 5

"What do you mean, you don't want to marry him?"

Mirelle stared at her mother, hands clenched beneath the breakfast table. It was nearly three weeks after the salon and every morning started with the same question. "I didn't say that," Mirelle replied. "All I said was, I'm not sure what to respond."

Mama reached for the toast. "Just tell him yes. Sweetly."

"Pinina," Papa warned. "Let the girl make up her own mind."

Mirelle knew her father was annoyed because Mama had kept Signor Morpurgo's interest a secret for so long. Nor was he pleased at the prospect of marrying his only child to a man older than he. Mama and her aunt, however, badgered her day and night. Everyone in the ghetto told her what an excellent match it was, what a wonderful thing for the ketubah works and for her parents.

Mirelle was working at the ketubah manufactory again—just two mornings a week, which was all Mama would allow. Mirelle had made the same argument to her that had won over her father, but Signor Morpurgo's proposal had added one more weapon to her arsenal: she'd threatened Mama that she would refuse him outright if she were not permitted to help Papa, at least until Beniamino was settled. Mama had caved under the pressure but insisted that Mirelle be home by noon every day.

Whenever she walked through the ghetto streets and past Dolce's home, Mirelle reflected on how her life had changed because of Signor Morpurgo's shocking proposal. The entire Jewish Quarter treated her differently, as if the Morpurgo fortune was already in her purse. But not Dolce.

The day following the salon, Mirelle had decided against visiting Dolce, afraid of meeting her friend's father. So she'd dispatched a note, asking Dolce to come to her. Dolce hadn't responded for two days. When she did, her letter was not what Mirelle expected.

> *I think it is best if we don't see one another.*
> *I'm shocked that my father would consider marrying you. I'm being honest about this—unlike you, who clearly set your cap at him for some time. I know your parents always wanted to find you a wealthy husband, but I didn't think you'd stoop so low to entice my father—my father!—into marriage. Know that I will do everything I can to convince him against the match. It's disgraceful, frankly, to think of you becoming his wife, replacing my beloved mother. I don't want to see you until the matter is settled, one way or another.*
> *From someone who once thought herself your friend,*
> *Dolce Morpurgo*

Mirelle had stood in the hallway, crumpling the letter in her fist. She'd stalked to her desk, intending to write a furious letter in response, but instead only stared off into space. Until she made up her mind whether to accept Signor Morpurgo or not, she had no idea what to say.

Rising from her desk, she'd gone in search of her mother and handed her the note so she could see Dolce's displeasure for herself.

Mama just shrugged. "She's been spoiled all her life," she said. "She'll be fine once she realizes the marriage is inevitable."

"But it's not inevitable. I haven't said yes yet."

Mama shook her head. "What are you waiting for, Mira? Do you think you'll find someone kinder? Someone better equipped to support you—and help your father?"

"But—he's *old!*"

Mama reached up and stroked Mirelle's hair. "Yes, he's old," she said softly. "But some girls do better with older husbands. You might, I think." She pushed Mirelle's hair off her forehead and smiled brightly. "He'll certainly always care for you."

"You think I might do better with an older husband?" Mirelle was aghast. How could Mama think that?

Of course, Mirelle couldn't explain her other reason for hesitating. Mama and Papa would die of shock if they knew she was considering a Gentile as a husband. That is, if Christophe still wanted her. Since the salon, he had disappeared utterly from view.

Mirelle might long to see the French soldier again, but she was too proud to summon him. She wrote him a letter and tore it to shreds, scattering the pieces in the fireplace. Several times she set out to walk by the French barracks, but always turned back before reaching it. Daniel often visited the family. Mirelle suspected it made him feel less lonely in a foreign land. But when she opened her mouth to speak of his friend, that same pride stopped her.

She spent her days and nights thinking of Christophe, conjuring up his slow smile when she'd catch him staring at her. She replayed their conversations, sometimes changing the words to convince herself that she did, in fact, love him. Other times, she felt guilty about her obsession, but she couldn't stop herself. Secretly, she imagined dire scenes—a runaway horse, a burning building, even standing under the wedding canopy with Signor Morpurgo—just so Christophe could rescue her. He would throw her over his saddle and they would ride off together. He'd already rescued her twice. Surely, he'd do so again.

She put off answering Signor Morpurgo, inventing one excuse

after another. She tried to reason with herself, convince herself she was afflicted by infatuation, a feeling built on nothing. Her common sense had never failed her before this. But her feelings persisted.

The thought of Dolce was like a bruise. Christophe was an ache, a longing buried deep. Mama and Prudenzia were gnats, which Papa helped her swat away. And David Morpurgo? Surprisingly, he was more like a balm, a soothing presence in the sudden upheaval of her life. But, still, she felt nothing more for him than she'd feel for a loving uncle.

He visited constantly, appearing mornings and evenings, always ready with an excuse for Dolce. Mirelle's lips thinned to hear that her friend was suffering sneezing fits as the flowers bloomed, her eyes red and head aching. Mama, privy to Dolce's letter, knew that the girls weren't speaking, but Aunt Prudenzia didn't.

"Mirelle, you're not a good friend to poor little Dolce," Prudenzia scolded one morning as the ladies sat with Signor Morpurgo over coffee and biscotti. "You haven't been to visit her in days! And with her feeling so poorly."

Signor Morpurgo interrupted the strained silence. "Mirelle is right to stay away," he said, calmly dipping his cookie in the coffee. "These are delicious, Pinina. When Dolce suffers, she makes everyone miserable. Right, Mirelle?" He turned to her, smiling benignly.

"Yes," Mirelle murmured, her voice low.

"Well, I suppose you have some excuse," Prudenzia tittered. "A wedding to prepare for."

"Aunt!" Mirelle kept seated with an effort. "Please don't."

"Mirelle, really!" Mama sounded impatient. "Your aunt only means to be helpful."

At that, Mirelle jumped out of her chair. "I know what she means," she exclaimed. "I know what everyone means! But shouldn't this be my decision? Not yours, not Aunt's, not . . ." She waved a hand toward Signor Morpurgo, whose face creased in concern. Mirelle flung her hands in the air, then dashed from the room, up the stairs, and into her room. She slammed her door behind her.

Mino would tell her what happened next—Mino, who should have been at work but was pretending his stomach ached. He crept into her room about an hour later while she lay limply on her bed, staring at the ceiling, wishing Christophe loved her enough to rescue her.

"They're going to leave you alone," Mino whispered in her ear.

She sat up. "Who's going to leave me alone?"

"Your mama and mine. Signor Morpurgo insisted."

"He did what?"

Mino winked slyly. "What will you give me if I tell you?"

"Give you?"

"Dessert tonight. Anna says it's your favorite. *Bocconotti.*"

Mirelle looked at him, perched on the end of her bed, swinging a foot idly. "I thought your stomach hurt."

Mino ignored her. "Agreed?"

Mirelle hadn't tasted cream puffs since surprising her brother and his friends, when Jacopo was still alive. She didn't care if she never ate another again. "Fine, agreed."

"I was hiding under the table. You didn't see me, did you?"

Mirelle shook her head. She'd grown used to Mino secreting himself in odd places, slinking in and out of rooms like a cat. What he'd said that first day was true. He had plenty of secrets.

"Well, after you left, the old man told your mama and mine to let you be." He paused, eyes glinting. "He said that if they kept it up, you'd be an unwilling wife. That you'd be much more biddable if they left you alone."

"He said 'biddable'?" Indignation burned inside her.

"That means you'll do what they want, doesn't it?"

Mirelle detected malice in the boy's smile. *Careful,* she warned herself. *This one tells tales.* "Something like that," she replied, controlling her temper. "Did he say anything else?"

"Just that you were a sweet, docile girl and didn't need to be badgered into accepting his offer. 'She'll see the sense of it soon,' he said. 'But not if you put up her back'."

Mirelle worked hard to keep her emotions in check. "And your mama and mine agreed?"

Mino laughed. "Well, yours did. Mine said she would, but I'll wager she'll still nag you. Mama isn't very good at leaving things alone."

Mirelle wanted to shake him. "If you're feeling better, shouldn't you go to work?"

Mino jumped from the bed. He clutched his stomach and winked at her. "Oww," he groaned comically, not even trying to sound genuine. He started from the room, then turned back. "Don't forget. You owe me your *bocconotti* tonight."

# 37

## MARCH 7

"Hurry up! The men are waiting!"

Mirelle lifted her head from the accounts when she heard Signor Narducci chiding Beniamino. Papa was out, visiting a prospective customer. Mirelle watched as Mino dragged through the workroom, dropping a brush on one man's table, a fresh sheet of parchment on another. His arms were loaded down with supplies, and he moved slowly, awkwardly.

"Never mind," one of the men said, handing him back the brush. "I needed this an hour ago. I used something else."

"So why have me fetch it?" whined Mino. "You're making extra work for me."

"Extra work?" The man muttered to his neighbor. "As if the boy actually did any work in the first place."

Mino whirled, dropping the other items. "I'm not your blackamoor!" he cried. "You just wait! When I inherit the workshop, you'll be out on the streets!"

"Beniamino . . ." Sabato started.

But Mirelle rose from her seat and came into the workroom. "Mino, let's go outside for a few minutes," she said, taking his arm and ushering him toward the door.

"They hate me," Mino said, pulling away and stalking out.

"Shhh." Mirelle followed him, glancing apologetically at the men.

Mino sat on the stoop next to the workshop, kicking his heels against the low stone wall. "They hate me," he repeated. "I'm sick of it! I hate this place. I want to go home!"

Mirelle wasn't sure what to say. He complained, day in and day out, often pretending to be ill to get out of work. It was a rare day that he didn't have a headache, a backache, a sore throat.

"Never mind, darling," Prudenzia would say, soothingly brushing his hair behind his ears. "Go to bed and Anna will bring you some breakfast. I'll come up presently to read to you."

As she sat next to him on the stoop, Mirelle recalled a conversation between Papa and Signor Morpurgo a couple of nights ago. The older man had counseled Papa to set aside a sum for Mirelle and Mama in case of his death.

"But why should I?" Papa asked. "When you plan to marry the girl."

Mirelle kept sewing, head lowered.

"She hasn't said yes yet. And even when we wed, that doesn't absolve you of your responsibility to your family."

"You're right." Papa sighed. "I will. But not yet."

Mirelle wondered why not, but Signor Morpurgo seemed to understand. "The pain of Jacopo's death will subside," he said. "Even if it doesn't feel like it now. It took me years to remember Sarella without sadness. But don't delay too long. That boy is undependable. You should ride him harder, Simone."

But as much as Papa tried to teach the boy, Mino was obstinate and, Mirelle feared, inherently lazy. Papa asked him to do no more than fetch supplies and observe the workings of the manufactory. It was a gentle enough form of apprenticeship. But when Mirelle questioned Mino to gauge what he had learned, he shrugged and turned away. And his whining grated on everyone's nerves.

Right now, Mirelle wanted to slap him. How could anyone think he'd be a better owner of the workshop than she? She'd accepted that she'd never be allowed to manage it on her own, or even with a husband, but the thought of this horrid brat assuming Papa's legacy appalled her. Why couldn't she—or even her mother—inherit it? Why must it go to a man? Especially this spoiled monster? Fury bubbled up inside her.

"What is wrong with you?" She reached over, shaking him by the shoulders. "You should be proud of this place. It's a family legacy—something my father and grandfather built from nothing into the most illustrious of its kind in the world. Aren't you ashamed, complaining and dragging like a slug?"

Mino looked like he'd swallowed an untreated olive, the drupe twisting his mouth. "I don't care!" He kicked at her shins. "Go away! I hate you!"

He jumped off the stoop and ran down the street. Mirelle sat limply, watching him go, wishing with a sharp pain that life could return to a time when her brother was alive, when everything was as it should be.

An hour later, her father returned. When he realized Mino wasn't there, his face darkened. "Where is he this time?"

Mirelle explained what had happened.

Papa shook his head. "That's all I need," he muttered. "Now your aunt will yell at me this evening that we're mistreating her beloved son again. That no one ever treated them like this in Rome." He threw the sample copies of the ketubot on his desk and sat down with a thud. His face was flushed; he laid a hand gingerly on his injured side.

"What's wrong, Papa? Are you in pain?"

"When don't I have pain?" he grumbled. "But the doctor says he's done what he can and only in time will I fully heal. If I ever do."

"But becoming upset just makes things worse," Mirelle said, rising and kissing his forehead. "Relax a moment. I'll get you something to drink."

"No, no, I'm fine." Papa stared at the samples on his desk.

Sabato stuck his head into the office. "When will young Meyer come talk with us about his ketubah?" he asked. "Which did he like best? I'd like Yosef to work on this one—he hasn't had a commission for a while and he's growing tired of simply coloring in the other artists' illuminations."

"Meyer won't be paying us a visit." Papa frowned at the pile on his desk.

"But—the wedding is in a month! Did you explain how long we need to do the work?"

Papa sighed. "He's not ordering his ketubah from us. He's going to a shop in Rome."

Mirelle stared at her father. It was almost unheard of that someone from Ancona would commission a ketubah anywhere but from her father. With a sinking feeling, she asked, "Is it the rabbi, Papa?"

Papa's fingers fidgeted with the stack of documents.

"It is, isn't it?" Mirelle asked. Her hands started to shake. "We've been losing work for a while now. All because of me."

Signor Narducci backed away. "I'll be here if you need me, Simone."

Papa waited until his foreman left before lifting his head. "It's been a slow few weeks, yes."

"It's not fair!" Mirelle burst out. "That wretched rabbi! Can't he wait until you have Mino trained? All I'm trying to do is help while you do that."

Papa sighed again. "And how long will that take? When the boy acts the way he does?" He cradled his face in his hands.

Tears crowded Mirelle's throat but she pushed them back. "I can't do this to the workshop. To the men. They don't deserve this."

"Mirelle—"

"I'll leave if you want me to," she said slowly.

Papa turned away, his hand back at his side. Mirelle wrapped her cloak around her and started toward the door. She felt the men staring at her as she walked through the long row of worktables and wondered if they blamed her for the lost work. Sabato Narducci stood by the door and patted her on the shoulder as she stepped past. She bit back tears.

Standing in the shadowy ghetto street, Mirelle couldn't decide what to do. She didn't want to go home, to face her mother and aunt and her nasty brat of a cousin. If Dolce weren't angry at her, she would seek refuge there. But as it was . . .

The thought of Dolce put another idea into her head. She turned toward the remnants of the ghetto gates and the Morpurgo mansion.

One of the footmen opened the door when Mirelle rang. "The mistress is out riding," he told her.

Mirelle felt relieved that her erstwhile friend wasn't there. "Is the master home?"

The servant didn't blink. Everyone in the mansion knew that David Morpurgo had proposed to her. Perhaps the man thought she was here to accept him. Would Signor Morpurgo think the same? A flush rose to Mirelle's cheeks. *It doesn't matter*, she told herself. *As long as he helps me.*

Signor Morpurgo came rushing out of his office to greet her. "Mirelle, my dear! What an unexpected pleasure!"

Mirelle saw the hope in the man's face and bit her lip. "Good morning, Signor Morpurgo," she said. "Might I speak with you? I won't keep you more than a few minutes."

"You can keep me for an eternity, child, you know that," Morpurgo replied gaily.

Mirelle said nothing, just followed his outstretched arm into his office. It was a large room, cluttered with desks, chairs, and paper-filled cubbyholes. As she entered, Dolce's uncle rose from behind one of the desks.

"A pleasure to see you this morning," he said, looking at her curiously.

"Zeke, can you give us a few minutes?" Signor Morpurgo asked.

"Certainly," he replied, bowing himself out of the room.

"Sit down, child." Dolce's father indicated a low sofa covered in silk brocade. "May I call for some refreshments?"

"No, thank you," Mirelle faltered. "Truly, I won't impose on you that long."

David Morpurgo sat down opposite her and waited.

Mirelle wondered how to start. She stared at the man for a few minutes, thinking of all the times he had indulged both her and Dolce with fatherly treats—toys and sweets when they were children, dancing and music lessons, flowers, and books as they grew older. If only he'd remained the uncle she still thought him. She remembered how uncomfortable she'd felt when he'd presented her with her pearl necklace in Venice. Maybe this was a mistake.

But she was there, and he was waiting. She cleared her throat. "I have a favor to ask."

"If I can grant it, consider it yours." He reached out and stroked her hand.

She stopped herself from pulling away. "You know I've returned to work, just until Papa feels Beniamino is ready to take—to take Jacopo's place." She felt a pang, saying her brother's name aloud, but forced herself to continue. "You were once kind enough to ask the rabbi to allow me to stay in the manufactory. He still opposes it, despite the changed circumstances. He threatened us back then with sanctions—now he's encouraging grooms in our city to commission their ketubot elsewhere. Papa lost another customer just this morning because of his threats."

"Indeed." He didn't sound surprised.

"You knew?"

Signor Morpurgo nodded. "It's no secret that the rabbi opposes your working, *Piccola*. He visited me just this week, asked me why I permitted my betrothed—"

"But we're not betrothed!" Mirelle blurted.

Signor Morpurgo smiled wryly. "No, not yet, anyway. And so I told him."

Mirelle drew herself up. "I'm honored by your proposal, truly. But right now, all I can think about is helping my father, my family, through this difficult time. You tried to help me once—to no avail. Would you try again? Convince the rabbi to let me keep working— just until my cousin is ready to take . . . to take my brother's place?"

Signor Morpurgo's face creased with a benevolent smile. "And if I do, child, how long will you need to work? For the rabbi is right about one thing: it would not be fitting for my betrothed."

Mirelle shook her head. "Please don't misunderstand. Granting me this favor does not mean that I'll accept your hand. I—I'm still thinking that over."

Signor Morpurgo laughed. "I see. Well, I hope that it will, at least, make you think of me more kindly. Let me see what I can do."

# 38

# MARCH 10

Daniel and Christophe had put the press to bed around midnight. They'd printed Bonaparte's military newspapers for a month now, reporting on the general's actions throughout Italy and political events in Paris. Daniel marveled at how Bonaparte used the papers to make himself the hero of France. As both commander and ruler of Italy, he seemed unstoppable.

Daniel and Christophe had worked out a plan with Bourrienne the night before Bonaparte left for Rome. They'd requisitioned rooms in the town's municipality and procured three machines, along with a tall cabinet for lead slugs and quads, two tables to load the chases, and stacks of newsprint. They used one room to dry the newly printed pages, replicating Alain's arrangement of laundry lines in Paris. The soldiers working under them loaded paper, translated written copy into headlines and text, and pulled the levers. With so much help, and just one or two papers to print nightly, the work was more than manageable.

So Daniel, rising at noon, looked forward to an afternoon free of duty. He and Christophe had moved into barracks hastily erected by the harbor to house the garrison. It was pleasant to sleep under a roof again; Daniel's army cot, lumpy though it was, was softer than a bedroll on the ground.

At the mess, he found Christophe sitting over the remains of his meal.

"I'm going to visit my cousins," he said. "Do you want to come?"

Christophe kept his face carefully neutral. "No. I'm not inclined to court another man's fiancée."

"No one said anything about courting her." Daniel took a bite of his pasta. "And she's not betrothed yet. She's still making up her mind." The sudden flash in Christophe's eyes made Daniel narrow his. "But if her mother has anything to say about it, she will accept him," he continued. "So maybe you're right to stay away."

Christophe grimaced. "You don't want me to come."

Daniel realized with a start that his friend was right. He didn't want him to come. "Your choice." Daniel sopped his bread in the sauce on his plate. "We should have another edition from d'Angély later this afternoon. If I'm not back, you set it."

"All right." Christophe rose and walked away.

Mirelle met Daniel at the door when he arrived, ready in her walking dress, a parasol in one hand. "I saw you from the upstairs window," she said. "Are you ready for our walk?"

He nodded. "Yes, but I'd like to say hello to your parents first."

Mirelle reached back and shut the door behind her. "Papa is at work. He'll be home when we return. Mama invites you to stay for dinner."

"That's kind, but I need to get back to the presses this evening."

"We'll dine early." Mirelle put a hand on Daniel's arm. "Shall we go?"

The day was warm for early March, despite the brisk wind. As they strolled along the harbor, Daniel smelled the salt rising off the churning water. The sun shone brightly, glistening on the waves, and

Mirelle put up her parasol. Soldiers from the French garrison were drilling near the quay. Olive-skinned men off-loading a ship eyed the couple suspiciously. Mirelle appeared indifferent to their glares. Still, Daniel pulled her hand more tightly through his arm.

"They don't like us much, your countrymen," he said.

Mirelle nodded. "They never liked us Jews, either. If they had their way, I'd still be wearing a yellow kerchief and an armband."

"In my case, it doesn't matter—they'd hate me for being French or for being Jewish," Daniel mused. "Or both. Of course, if your father were here, they'd still know him for a Jew—by his earlocks."

"But not either of the Morpurgo brothers," Mirelle said. "They've been dressing like Gentiles for years. Dolce's father is encouraging my father to cut his earlocks and beard."

Daniel smiled. "Because of the laws in France, all of my family is clean shaven, even Salomon. If you knew my brother, you'd realize how astonishing that is."

"My father won't do it," Mirelle said. "Not because he's so religious—he never asked Jacopo to grow earlocks—but his own father was devout, so it feels natural to him." She hesitated a moment. "Sometimes I wonder if we've lost something in our rush to be like the Gentiles."

"I suppose only our children and grandchildren will be able to judge." Daniel thought back to his cousin Ethan's essays, written before French Jews were given citizenship. Ethan had urged Jews to become more like their Gentile counterparts, to fit in better. Daniel had been swayed by those arguments, and doing so had made things easier for him in the army. But his parents and brother, like Mirelle's father, still clung to tradition.

They strolled along the waterfront. Daniel smiled at the touch of Mirelle's hand on his arm. He might miss the excitement of marching and fighting with his company, but there was something sweet about this quieter life. Mirelle was like the girls he'd grown up with—only better, somehow. If only he had been the one to rescue her in Venice, to catch her eye at the ghetto gates. But Christophe had beaten him to it, as always. Funny, Daniel thought, that had never bothered him before. And if she didn't choose Christophe? Then it would be Morpurgo, the man her parents wanted her to marry for his wealth. Too slow and too poor—was it any wonder she'd never even considered him a suitor?

"Speaking of the Morpurgos," he finally asked, to stop his thoughts from drifting into forbidden areas—after all, he could never double-cross his best friend, even if Mirelle were free—"what have you decided?"

Mirelle's face fell. "My mother so clearly wants me to accept," she muttered. "Now that my brother is dead, she says it's my duty to the family to marry a rich man, to finance the workshop and provide for her. Signor Morpurgo is the richest man in our community. But he's so old. I've known him my entire life, he's like an uncle. The thought of it . . ." Her tone was bitter. "Dolce hasn't spoken to me in weeks. Neither has your friend."

"Christophe knows he can't give you the life that Signor Morpurgo can."

Mirelle stared. "But I thought—he told me—he loves me."

The confession seemed forced from her lips. It stabbed at Daniel's heart, and he searched for something comforting to say. "Doesn't his leaving you alone prove that he does?"

Mirelle shook her head. "Did he think about asking me? Shouldn't it be my choice?" Her footsteps dragged. "My aunt keeps needling me, saying I'll have fine clothes, be able to travel, even move to Rome." Mirelle sighed. "She's desperate to return to Rome herself, but Papa says Mino must stay here. They argue about it all the time. I wish . . ."

Daniel desperately wanted to smooth away the sorrow from her face. "You can't turn back time. Signor Morpurgo and I often cross paths in the early evenings at the municipality. He seems kind. He'd always treat you well, wouldn't he?"

"I suppose. And Dolce would grow accustomed. But I can't pretend to love him. If I'm in love at all . . . But that's just foolishness."

"Christophe?" Daniel hoped he was wrong.

Mirelle pulled her arm from his. "Yes. Christophe." She looked at the ground. "It's crazy. He's a Gentile. But I can't stop thinking about him."

"He's a good fellow, but he's a charmer." Daniel was betraying his friend, but he couldn't stop from blurting the truth. *After all*, he told himself uncomfortably, *a match between them could only end in unhappiness.* "He's been with one Italian beauty or another in every town in Italy. He says he feels something different for you than the others, but that doesn't stop him from flirting."

"Doesn't it?" Mirelle closed her parasol and dug at the ground with its point. "I see."

Daniel bit his lip. "He says he feels something different for you," he repeated, to assuage his pang of guilt.

"How could he?" She dug deeper into the sandy soil. "He doesn't know me, not really. And I don't know him."

He stared at her, his discomfort growing. *If Christophe knew how she felt!*

She put her hand back on his arm and they continued their stroll. Within a few turns, they were at the marketplace. Mirelle pointed out the best stalls, telling Daniel where to buy fruit, cheese, and vegetables. He bought some dates and olives, as well as a loaf of bread. Mirelle bought some early spring flowers.

"They'll brighten our table tonight," she said as the flower seller wrapped them in paper.

They turned once again. Daniel felt someone bang into his side.

"*Scusi!*" came a high-pitched voice.

Dropping Mirelle's arm, Daniel reached out to grab the child who'd bumped into them. It was Barbara, Francesca Marotti's daughter. The young girl was breathing hard. A boy skittered to a stop before them. Recognizing Daniel, Barbara made the horned sign of the evil eye. "*Ebreo*," she panted to the boy in explanation. "*Diavolo*."

Mirelle stiffened. "*Comportatevi bene*," she told them. "Behave yourselves."

Barbara stuck out her tongue. "She's probably a Jew devil herself," she told the boy. "Let's get out of here before they cast a spell on us."

They scurried off.

"How in the world does she know you?" Mirelle asked.

"It's a long story." Daniel looked around the stalls until he located Francesca. "Here, come meet Signora Marotti. She's the girl's mother."

Mirelle followed him to the stall.

"Signora Marotti," Daniel said. "It's good to see you again."

Francesca looked up in surprise. Her baby was asleep, wrapped in a shawl tied at her chest. "Daniel! I thought you were long gone, with the French troops."

"I'm stationed in Ancona," Daniel explained. "Signora Marotti, let me introduce a neighbor of yours and a cousin of mine. Mirelle d'Ancona."

"I bought eggs from you once," Mirelle said. "And some artichokes."

"I remember," Signora Marotti said. "I was grateful for your help that day."

Daniel wondered what they meant, but he sensed neither of them wanted to say more. "Signora Marotti was the first to see the miracle of the Mary portrait," Daniel explained to his cousin. "General Bonaparte wanted to question her, and I was commanded to bring her to him."

Just then, a squat, swarthy man pushed past them. Emilio Marotti.

"I need money, wife," he growled, paying no attention to Daniel and Mirelle.

Mirelle's fingers trembled on Daniel's arm. He glanced at her, alarmed at her sudden pallor.

"More money?" Francesca sounded weary.

"Just give it to me," her husband demanded, hand extended.

"Good-bye," Daniel muttered as Signora Marotti fumbled in her pockets and dropped a handful of coins into her husband's out-stretched palm. He ushered Mirelle swiftly back to the quay, where he settled her onto a bench near the water, beside the lapping waves.

"Are you all right?" he asked. Her cheeks were still pale as milk.

"That man killed Jacopo," she whispered faintly. "I watched through the knothole in the floor. He struck him with a cudgel. And he stabbed Papa."

Daniel froze, the hair on the back of his neck rising. He took her fan from her limp grasp and waved her face with it, tense fingers nearly splintering the wood. *I could have protected her*, he thought angrily. *If I had been there, I could have stopped this tragedy from happening*. With fury in his heart, he remembered Marotti stretched out on the roadway after he'd tried to ambush his fellows. Daniel should have left him there to rot—or, better yet, executed him on the spot.

"Can I fetch you some water?" he said, wanting to comfort her even while he cursed his weakness. "Do you have smelling salts?"

Mirelle shook her head. "Let's just go home," she murmured. He leaned in to catch her words. "Back to the ghetto, where it's safe."

# 39

## MARCH 15

Emilio stood in the shaded archway of Ancona's municipality, waiting for the councilmen to finish their morning meeting. The sun shone brightly on the street, crowded with horses, carts, and carriages. This open spot was almost too public for what he had in mind. *But on the other hand*, he thought, *who would suspect me here?*

He was dressed in a French uniform stolen from the barracks by the harbor. The French spent so much time parading or flirting with Italian women that they forgot to post a guard on their own quarters. Or else, Emilio thought with a smirk, they believed they were invulnerable in the city they had conquered. Well, he was about to show them different.

He was still bitter over the Madonna portrait. The moment he proposed burning the painting, the cardinal had forbidden him to return to the Catholic Fellowship. Ever. And no one—not even Desi—had defended him. He remembered the horror on their faces, the black condemnation. Well, he'd show them, too! What had they done, after all, since attacking the Jews? Not a damned thing. Yet they refused to consider the one good idea anyone had come up with. They were all cowards! Yellow-bellied cowards!

The uniform was too big on him. He'd brought it home to Francesca to fix. He remembered the fear in her eyes when he'd thrown it at her.

"Where did you get this?" she asked in a horrified whisper, looking toward the children's room.

"Never mind where I got it. I have to wear it." He didn't need her annoying him right now. He had enough of that outside his home. "And don't tell anyone about it. *Capisci?*"

"Believe me," she muttered, spreading the uniform out on her legs, "I won't tell a soul."

It had taken longer than he liked for her to fix the uniform. She'd refused to work on it during the day, refused to work on it until the children slept at night. And as he'd watched her sew by candlelight, she had driven him mad with questions: *What are you going to do with it? What if they catch you? Who else knows? Is this a plot of the Catholic Fellowship? Don't you care about us? Don't you care about yourself?*

"Shut up and sew," had been his answer every time. Or, on the nights when she was particularly exasperating: "What are you looking for—a belt in the eye? Just get on with it."

But Francesca had done a good job, he thought now as he stood in the puddles of darkness made by the city hall's arched entrance. He kept the French soldier's shako cap low over his forehead. No one walking in or out of the building gave him a second glance.

He wished he'd been able to steal a French saber or a musket, but the dagger tucked in his boot, with its comforting bite, would have to do.

Echoing footfalls grew nearer. He'd watched the same spot for a week now, so he knew the council left for their midday meal just as the church bell chimed twelve. He moved deeper into the shadows of the long hallway.

Someone pushed open the doors and they emerged, mouths flapping, arms waving in emphasis. Emilio knew his target: the Jew who'd slashed him with his sword, the wealthy one whose home they'd tried to ransack. And there he was—at the back of the group, talking with a tall, skeletal man.

Emilio slipped his stiletto from his boot. He waited, holding his breath. Then, when the Jew was two steps away, he rushed up and plunged the dagger in his side.

The Jew screamed. The skinny man shouted. The others whirled, shock on all their faces. Rather than running past them, Emilio moved swiftly backward through the heavy doors into the municipal building. He'd practiced how to escape—through the hallways and out through a door to a secluded garden. From there he could head to the hills.

He'd already left food and bedding in a cave a few miles south of the city. He would be safe there for the night while they looked for the murderer. Since the man was just a damned Jew, he told himself, no one would really care. And since Emilio was wearing a French uniform, no one would connect him to the murder. But best to be out of the way for a day or two, just in case. Emilio grinned as he thought how the resulting uproar would drive a wedge between the cursed Jews and the French. He'd wreck their damned alliance.

He sped through the corridors, the shouting receding as he ran.

Emilio came home a day later to a frantic Francesca. She was kneeling in their backyard shrine to Mary, rosary beads sliding through her fingers in time with her moving lips. Barbara and the baby were with her.

"Papa!" Barbara jumped up, running into his outstretched arms.

Francesca rose slowly to her feet. "Where have you been?"

He pushed his daughter away and thrust the baby at her. "Take him for a walk," he ordered. He pulled a few coins from his pocket. "Buy some sweets. Don't come home for a while."

"But why? What are you going to do?" Barbara stepped out of reach of his fists.

"Take the money and go," he repeated, more harshly this time.

She snatched the coins, put the baby on her hip, and disappeared.

Emilio grabbed Francesca by the arm and pulled her into the house. He'd been waiting for this moment ever since his blade hit bone in the Jew's body. After the riots in the ghetto, he'd been too injured to enjoy his blood lust, but not this time.

"Take off your clothes," he barked, his voice rasping in his throat. "Get on the bed. Now."

"He's not dead, you know." Francesca sat up as soon as she judged it safe, slid out of bed, pulled on her clothes, and picked the sheets off the floor. Emilio still lay prone, breathing heavily, the whorls of dark hair matting his chest slick with sweat.

"He's not dead? Who's not dead?" He opened one eye and glared at her.

Francesca flinched, sheets and blankets cradled in her arms. Had he decided to pretend he'd had nothing to do with the near-murder of the Jew from the ghetto? "David Morpurgo, the city councilman," she said. "The Jew."

"He's not dead?" Emilio looked at her blankly. "Of course he's dead. I thrust the stiletto deep, felt bone. How can he still be alive?"

She threw the bedclothes down at his feet and stood before him, arms crossed over her chest. It was worth chancing a few bruises to know the truth. "You admit it?"

Emilio swung his legs onto the floor, reaching for his breeches. "What if I do?"

Francesca drew in a shallow breath, quelling the desire to rip his face apart with her fingernails. She knew he felt wronged by everything he claimed the Jews had done to him, to his father—but how could he be so vicious? Her piety slipped away as she contemplated his smug smile. Putting a hand on her chest to slow the dangerous thudding of her heart, she was swept with guilt at her disloyalty, her fury. She forced herself to speak softly, deliberately. "If you care about us, our safety, you should leave. You endanger us all."

"You'd like that, wouldn't you?" Emilio, still shirtless, a grimy bandage wrapped around his old wound, strode barefoot across the floor and out the bedroom door. Francesca heard him rustling in the kitchen, doubtless looking for a bottle of grappa. She heard the rub of a cork being pulled, the splash of liquid in a cup. She winced at his loud "aaah" as he drank deep.

She followed him, leaned against the doorjamb. "Lamb of God," she whispered, keeping the prayer low, "who takes away the sins of the world, have mercy on us."

"Praying, are you?" He drank again and glowered dangerously. "Make me something to eat. How are you so sure the godforsaken Jew isn't dead?"

She moved swiftly past him and took a skillet out of the cabinet. "I can fry some eggs."

He nodded, pouring another drink. "The Jew?"

"Alive. And they know it wasn't a Frenchman who tried to kill him."

Emilio frowned. She imagined him thinking, *So that part of the plan didn't work.*

As she cooked, she reminded herself of her wedding vows. She was stuck with this man, no matter what he did—and God and the priests instructed her to be a helpmeet to him. "They haven't come looking for you yet," she told him, "but your name is definitely being mentioned. Desi said you should probably leave Ancona for a while."

She put the plate of food on the table, along with some slices of day-old bread and a crock of soft cheese. He took the bottle and cup with him, sat down, and tore the bread into two pieces with a grunt. She leaned against the doorjamb again. *Go,* she willed him. *You do none of us any good here.* She chastised herself for wishing him dead rather than simply gone, but the thought kept resurfacing, no matter how hard she tried to suppress it. She wasn't willing to hand him over to the French or the city council, but if they took him without it being her doing . . .

She stopped herself, lips moving as she mouthed the prayer she had memorized as a child: *Most loving God, regard my prayer and free my heart from the temptation of evil thoughts.*

He wolfed down the food and gulped his third cup of grappa. His face was scrunched in concentration, eyes moodily fixed on the glass.

"Are you going to go?" her fear prodded her to ask. "They'll hang you if they find you. Remember what General Bonaparte said."

"Where would you have me go?" he asked, his face surly. "Why do they care about that Jew bastard, anyway? And why in the name of Satan is he still alive?"

Francesca shuddered. *How is it that the Lord God and all his angels saddled me with such a creature?* "I don't know how he survived," she told him. "But you won't, if you don't leave."

That was when his face changed. All the bravado left it and it caved, crumpled. She watched, horrified, as he dissolved into tears.

"Why didn't it work?" he asked, looking up at her piteously. "It was the perfect plan. The Jew would be dead, the French blamed. Why didn't it work?"

Her anger toward him melted. She sat next to him and put a hand on his knee. In an instant, he was on the floor at her feet, his head in her lap. She rubbed his thick black hair as if he were a naughty child. But he was no child.

After a few moments, she pushed his head up and stood. "I'll pack your things," she said. "Sleep in the mountains for a while. I'll get word to you when it's safe to come home."

# 40

# MARCH 16

"Ring the bell," Christophe said, stepping back from the ornately carved villa entrance.

Daniel pulled the cord. The ringing sounded deep within the mansion, making Christophe remember the last time he was there: the evening of the salon, when Morpurgo had proposed to Mirelle. Christophe knew Mirelle had not accepted the wealthy man yet, but surely she would soon. Especially now that he had survived this attempt on his life. If Christophe hadn't been ordered by the garrison captain to make this visit of condolence . . .

A servant led them to a room where other well-wishers were gathered. Dolce flitted in and out, greeting newcomers and ushering small groups into her father's chambers. The moment she stepped into the room, she was surrounded by fawning young men, one after another whispering words of comfort and support into her inclined ear. Christophe glowered. It felt like being summoned to a royal audience, something no patriotic Frenchman would warm to. Refreshments were set out on a sideboard—pastries and fruit. Dolce's face lit up upon seeing Daniel. She stood for several minutes, talking earnestly to him. She truly seemed to favor him. Why couldn't Daniel see it?

Just last week, Christophe had chided his friend as they worked together in the printshop. "You'll never have such a chance again.

She's the most beautiful Jewess in town, isn't she? Not to mention the wealthiest."

"She's not serious," Daniel retorted. "I'm just new here, a foreigner and a soldier, a shiny new toy. She'll tire of me in a month."

Christophe wondered if his friend were right. He admired Daniel's resilience in the face of such temptation. Would he have had the same fortitude? He thought not. But perhaps, he mused, watching Dolce lightly rap his friend's knuckles with her fan, she *was* just amusing herself.

He helped himself to a custard tart and a glass of Madeira. Just as he swallowed the last morsel, Dolce disengaged herself from Daniel and approached him.

"I'm surprised to see you," she said softly. "Would you spare me a moment?"

"Of course, signorina." He put down the plate and glass and followed her.

She led him into a smaller salon, one with sky-blue walls and a frieze of plaster swans.

"This is my favorite sitting room," she told him. She settled herself on a peach-colored divan, gracefully straightening her skirts.

"Your father is well?"

"He will be," Dolce said. "The wound would have been deeper if he hadn't been wearing a corset. The knife struck one of the whalebone struts. I trust you won't mention that, however. He would not like it known that his vanity saved his life."

Christophe couldn't help but snort. "A corset?"

Dolce laughed. "I should not have told you. But you'll keep his secret, won't you?"

Christophe half bowed. "As my lady commands," he said gallantly.

"Good." Dolce shifted on the divan, leaning forward. "Now, tell me. What's happening between you and Mirelle? Are you the reason she still hasn't accepted my father's proposal?"

Christophe tried to hide his surprise. "I haven't spoken to her since your salon. It's clear that we're not a good match, no matter what we feel."

"But you love her." Dolce clasped her hands in her lap. "Don't you?"

Christophe stared. What had Mirelle confided? Why was Dolce asking? "And if I do?"

"It's wonderful." Dolce's white teeth shone like ivory against pink lips as she beamed at him. "The chance meeting in Venice—reuniting here. So romantic!"

He frowned. "But your father wants to marry her." It was a statement, not a question. Christophe studied her beautiful face, trying to gauge if she were sincere.

Dolce shrugged. "Think about it this way. Your mother is a widow, correct? Would you want her to marry your friend Daniel?"

Christophe sputtered with laughter. "Daniel—and my mother? My mother thinks he's the devil incarnate—a cursed Jew. Besides, it's different for a man."

"Oh, of course." Dolce waved a careless hand. "But if you truly love her—and she loves you—what do you care about my father's feelings?"

Christophe's eyebrows rose. "You surprise me. Don't you want your father to be happy? And can't he do more for her than I can? He's rich and I'm a penniless soldier."

Dolce rose, paced to the window, and gazed out at the street beyond. "I love my father, but I love Mirelle, too. And my father won't make her happy."

Christophe's heart skipped a beat. "What are you saying?"

"He's rich, but do you really think Mirelle cares for wealth? That she wants to be an old man's pet? Doesn't she deserve better? But perhaps you don't know her that well after all."

Christophe studied her silently. She swiveled back, her stare searing him.

"Her duty—"

"Ah, yes, her duty. You really aren't the man I took you for, are you?" She sighed. "I should return to my guests."

Christophe jumped up, extending a hand to stop her. His head was whirling. He had been trying to forget Mirelle—a difficult task when at any moment he might stumble across her path. And now . . . what was Dolce implying?

She stood, watching him. Then she said, almost as if the words were dragged from her, "I keep thinking of the wedding night, you see."

Christophe felt himself turn to stone. That old man and his beautiful Mirelle . . .

He closed his mind to the image. "But he's your father. Don't you want him happy?"

"My father?" Dolce shrugged. "Do you think Mirelle is the first young thing he's pursued? He wants someone like my mother—someone sweet, obedient, kind. Everything I'm not." Her voice cracked slightly. "Besides, shouldn't you think of her happiness rather than his? Perhaps she's right to fear the worst—that your love isn't true."

Christophe's mouth gaped. "She's afraid I don't love her? Signorina, assure her that I do!"

"I'll do what I can," Dolce said, breaking into a smile, "but it's you who must convince her, by deeds as well as words. If you care for her, show it! You have to *fight* to win her." She paused, eyes raking Christophe's face. "But remember this: she is my dearest friend. If this is just a game to you—if you really don't care—you must be honest with me."

"This is no game!" Christophe blurted.

"I certainly hope not. For you're right—Papa is wealthy." Dolce raised her fan, eyes lowered modestly. "Think, Sergeant, of everything she'd give up for you. Wealth, leisure, a position in our society. Her religion. You must be certain you are not offering her false coin. And if I'm to help you, I must be sure as well."

"Be sure," Christophe said. "Be very sure!"

Dolce smiled serenely. "Then I will help you."

The chime of a carriage clock on the mantle made them both jump. Dolce moved from the window. "I must go back to the drawing room."

A twinge of doubt crossed Christophe's mind. "Before you go," he said slowly, "I need to understand. You once told me that she'd never marry a man who was not Jewish."

Dolce threw up a hand, her long fingers sparkling with gems. "Do you want to marry her or not? Yes or no?"

Christophe took a deep breath. "Yes."

Dolce nodded briskly. "Good. Leave it to me."

# 41

## MARCH 17

Mirelle stared at the note.

"Who's it from?" Prudenzia asked. She and Mama were in the small parlor, working on their embroidery.

Mirelle thought her aunt rude for prying, but she bit her tongue and replied, "From Dolce. She wants me to come see her today."

Mama looked up from her sewing. "Well, of course you will. You should have come with us yesterday, to see her father. Even if you won't—"

"And you should," her aunt interrupted. "You owe the family the duty of marrying well."

Mirelle threw an annoyed glance at her mother.

"Never mind that now," Mama said hastily. "You have known Signor Morpurgo your entire life. It is unkind not to pay him a visit, to wish him a speedy recovery."

What her mother said was true. But Mirelle felt awkward visiting him. Even were she and Dolce still on speaking terms, it would have been difficult. But any attempt to bridge the yawning chasm between them had been rebuffed. Until now.

Mirelle read the letter again:

*I realize how badly I've behaved. It's clear to me now that you did nothing to attract my father's affections. And why*

*shouldn't he hold you in affection? You are a dear and true
friend to my entire family. I am determined to return to the
way things were before, when we saw one another daily. Since
I cannot stir a step with my father still in his sickbed, I beseech
you to come to me. Will you? Today?*

Part of Mirelle welcomed the olive branch her friend was extending.
Another part remained angry. *I really did nothing—how did she put it?—
to attract his affection. How could she think I was on the catch for him?*

"Would you like me to come with you?" her aunt asked eagerly,
already folding up her embroidery.

"Mirelle should make this visit on her own," Mama said firmly.
"Besides, we are promised to Signora Narducci's at-home this
afternoon."

"Signora Narducci." Prudenzia's lips tightened. "She gives herself
airs, hosting at-homes when her husband is simply a worker. Really,
Pinina, you should stick to your own class of people and not bolster
her pretensions by attending."

"Abrianna Narducci is a good friend," Mama said, eyes flashing.
"She was here every day when Simone was wounded. And her husband is not just a worker—he is the most skilled scribe at the workshop. It's a privilege to have him work for us."

"Still." Prudenzia ignored her sister-in-law's spurt of anger. "You
can't compare the Narduccis with the Morpurgos. You can send your
friend a note of apology. Or you go, Pinina, and offer my regrets in
person. Tell her I have a sick headache. Then I'll go with Mirelle."

"I'm not going to lie to Abrianna," Mama said indignantly, shaking her head emphatically. "If you pretend to have a headache, you
must stay home."

"And really, Aunt, I don't want company," Mirelle said. "Dolce and
I haven't spoken for weeks. We have so much to catch up on. *In private*." She stressed the last words.

"Very well." Her mouth screwed tight, Prudenzia picked up her embroidery hoop and began to add stitches, her needle plucking angrily through the taut material. "I must say, though, that Ancona is very different from Rome. Very different indeed."

"We know that, Aunt," Mirelle said. "You've told us so. Many times."

Dolce came down the stairs as soon as Mirelle arrived. "Mira!" she exclaimed, wrapping her arms around her friend, hugging her tightly.

"It's good to be here." Mirelle stepped out of Dolce's embrace. "I've missed you."

"I know." Dolce hung her head. "I've been stupid. How could I be upset with you? But anyway," she picked her head up quickly, before Mirelle could speak, "that's all in the past and we won't talk about it ever again. Will we?" She looked straight into Mirelle's eyes, almost daring her to contradict.

Mirelle wanted to tell Dolce how hurt she'd felt. But she let it go. After all, she told herself, Dolce had been through a lot lately. Better to make peace and move on.

"Papa is napping," Dolce said. "But he'll want to see you when he wakes." She studied Mirelle's face, as if looking for any sign of embarrassment or discomfiture.

Mirelle, feeling both, kept her chin raised with an effort. "Let's not disturb him. I hear you've been a wonderful nurse, in constant attendance. You must need some fresh air. Why don't we take a stroll in the garden?"

"A quick stroll would be most welcome. I haven't set foot outside since it happened."

Mirelle nodded. "Wrap up, then. It's not cold, but there's a stiff breeze."

Dolce threw a shawl over her shoulders and they stepped out the back door. The limited space of the ghetto didn't allow for much of a garden, but Dolce's father had built a tall wall behind his house and hired a gardener to cover it with ivy. A single orange tree grew next to a narrow gravel walk, and rose bushes were laid out in a square around a small bench. The girls could span the garden in six steps, but by ambling slowly along the gravel walkway, they were able to enjoy the sun and breeze.

After a few turns, a distant church bell chimed three o'clock. "I need to make sure Papa takes his medicine," Dolce said. "Why don't you wait out here? It's quite pleasant. I'll send someone with some chocolate."

*Is she trying to keep me from seeing her father?* Mirelle sat on the bench, wrapping her shawl about her shoulders. "Some chocolate would be lovely."

Dolce slipped back into the house. Mirelle sat looking at the still-flowerless rose bushes. Soon, she thought, they would bloom, filling the little slip of a garden with their scent. If she married David Morpurgo, she'd sit here every afternoon. It felt very far from the cramped ghetto streets just beyond the garden walls. Mirelle had heard talk, though, that some of her neighbors might leave the ghetto. Their new freedom allowed them to live wherever they wanted in Ancona. Their children even attended school with the Gentile children now. Signor Morpurgo, wealthier than everyone, might well decide to move. Delighted as she was at the thought of more space and light, Mirelle wondered how Christian neighbors would react to living next door to Jews.

She owed Signor Morpurgo an answer to his proposal of marriage. He would give her everything she'd ever thought she'd wanted as a child—dresses and comfort and kindness. Did it matter that she'd outgrown those desires? That she wanted a life outside the ghetto, a life where she'd be free to do what she did best? If she couldn't have

her heart's desire in Ancona—to keep working at the workshop—
perhaps she could find a place where her talents would be welcome.

She shook herself out of the pleasant daydream. She had to think of
her family. Signor Morpurgo would ensure the future of the ketubah
works, no matter how terribly Mino might mismanage them.

Marrying him, however, meant duties that alarmed her. The wife of
a wealthy politician needed to speak up at the dinner table, keep abreast
of the events of the day. Like Dolce. Dolce was a wonderful hostess,
Mirelle thought wistfully. Of course, she'd had years of practice.

But even more important, Signor Morpurgo stirred nothing inside
her but affection and respect. Like her father, he seemed to understand her better than her mother or even Dolce. But the thought of
surrendering to him—under the wedding canopy, in the marriage
bed—made her feel queasy.

What did she want, really, from a husband? An image of
Christophe swam before her—young, handsome, with that bit of a
swagger that drew her eyes whenever he appeared. She had no idea if
he were rich or poor, if he even had a home to give her. By marrying
him she would have to surrender her entire past, including the love
of her parents and the religion she was born into. But part of her
yearned for the adventure they would have—for a young soldier just
starting out in life rather than an old man whom she regarded as a
second father.

The thought of hurting her parents stopped her cold. They'd
suffered so much since the riots. Not just Jacopo's death—a wound
that ached every day—but her father's injuries, which still showed no
sign of healing. How could she make their lives harder? Breaking the
promise sworn solemnly on her brother's grave?

And yet part of her rebelled against her mother's wish that she
marry David. She felt she was being sold, body and soul, to the highest bidder. Why should she consider her parents' feelings when they
were so willing to ignore hers?

It seemed like an impossible dilemma, but she knew which way her duty lay. And she'd been raised to do her duty.

"Your chocolate, signorina."

Her head jerked up. Christophe stood there, his smile broad, holding a silver tray with a tall chocolate pot, two small china cups, and a plate of cake. Her mouth opened in shock, but anything she might have said was silenced by the appearance of a servant with a small table. Christophe stood aside to let the servant put the table down, then placed the tray on it.

"Shall I pour?" the servant asked.

At Mirelle's nod, Christophe sat next to her. The bench was small, and she felt the heat of his thigh against her skirts. The servant poured two cups of chocolate and left.

"This is a surprise." Mirelle strove for calm, hoping he couldn't hear the tremor rattling her voice. "I thought you decided to cut my acquaintance."

"I did." Christophe shifted on the bench so he could watch her face. "But I was wrong. It was just . . ."

"That I received a proposal from a worthy—and wealthy—man?" Mirelle's bitterness made her sound sharper than she wished. "So you concluded that I would accept him?"

"I would not have blamed you. Why wouldn't you choose a rich man over a penniless soldier?"

*Penniless. Well, that answers one question.*

"But if I loved you and not him?"

Christophe's eyes never left her face. "Do you?"

Mirelle took a deep breath, lacing her hands together in her lap. "You're asking me—"

"To love me. Me, not him."

She fixed her eyes on the ground. "Do you realize what you're asking?" Her uncertainty turned the question into a pointed barb.

"Do you think my parents will permit me to marry you? A Christian? And penniless besides?"

"If we truly love one another, what does that matter?" Christophe put a hand to her cheek, and she closed her eyes at his touch. "I would send you to Paris, to my mother and uncle. I will inherit his print-shop one day. We could be happy there, Mirelle."

*Not quite penniless, then. He has a future to offer me. But Paris! Yes, I want to travel, but not live so far away!*

"I need to give Signor Morpurgo my answer soon," Mirelle said, her chest hammering. Giving in to her heart made no sense. She'd lose a rich future, the chance to support her parents, to help the ketubah workshop. To honor her promise to her dead brother. But the throbbing pulse deep within her made her want this man who watched her solemnly, love alight in his eyes. She took a deep breath. "But I won't give him an answer today."

The servant who had poured their chocolate returned and eyed their untouched cups. "Signorina, the master is awake and asks that you visit."

"Of course." Mirelle stood, fingers trembling as she straightened her skirt.

Christophe rose, took her hand, turned it over, and kissed her palm softly. "I will visit you tomorrow, signorina. Will you be at home?"

"I will," Mirelle said before pulling away. The imprint of his lips burned.

The servant led Mirelle to the sick room. Signor Morpurgo, sitting on a daybed, was dressed in a thick robe, his feet in cloth slippers, a striped afghan covering his lap and pooling at his feet. He looked recently shaven. Dolce was nowhere to be found.

"*Piccola*," he greeted her. "I was delighted to hear that you had come to visit me. I apologize for not rising to greet you."

"How are you feeling?" Mirelle asked.

"Sit, child." He motioned to a chair. "I can't complain. The doctor tells me I was lucky. Luckier than your father, in fact. The ruffian's blade missed any vital organs. I should be up and around in about a week."

"I'm glad." Mirelle shifted in her seat. "Have they discovered who attacked you?"

"Not yet, although everything points to a man named Emilio Marotti."

At the name, the blood rushed from Mirelle's cheeks. "Marotti? That's the man who killed my brother and wounded my father."

"Is it?" Signor Morpurgo turned serious. "We will bring him to justice. I'm told he's hiding in the mountains. He can't stay there forever."

Mirelle wondered if the man's capture would make her feel better about Jacopo's death. She thought not.

Morpurgo watched her for a few seconds before saying, "I owe you an apology."

"An apology?"

"I made a mistake, proposing to you in such a public setting. I didn't mean to embarrass you. I was just swept up in the day's excitement."

Mirelle's cheeks felt hot. "Don't apologize. I was—am—honored by your offer of marriage. I certainly don't deserve it."

"Don't say that!" Morpurgo shook his head vehemently. "My girl, if you only knew how much more you deserve! Your modesty is one reason I fell in love with you. Your kindness. Your calm, capable soul. You are beautiful—inside and out."

"Beautiful? Me? Compared to Dolce, to my aunt, to other women in the ghetto, the ones who have thrown themselves at you . . . Why me, Signor Morpurgo?"

He smiled. "David. Please call me David. Why you? I've asked myself that question many times. I know I'm too old for you, Mirelle. You have been friends with my daughter since childhood. In fact, that was one reason I thought of you—because Dolce loves you. I know she reacted badly at first, but she invited you here today. So clearly she's coming around to the idea. She's always resisted the idea of someone taking her mother's place. But you'll have your own place here, in both our hearts."

Mirelle wondered if Dolce would ever really accept her as her father's wife. Or if she could ever accept David as anything more than her friend's father.

"I'm older than your father," David continued, watching her closely, "but men older than me have married young girls and the couple has been happy. Especially if the marriage is blessed with children—with sons."

Mirelle blushed.

David's smile deepened. "And consider this. Without boasting, women *have* thrown themselves at me—and not one of them tempted me. Not one. Not until I saw the young woman you've grown into, like a spring blossom unfurling before me. My darling, you may not love me now, not as I love you. But I promise you will never lack for anything. And perhaps you will, in time, grow to love me, too."

"You must be the kindest, most generous man in the world," she said, wishing she didn't have to hurt him. "But I simply can't—"

David raised a hand. "Don't say no, not yet. All I ask is that you think about it."

Mirelle blinked back tears. He looked at her with such tenderness that her heart went out to him. It would be so easy to say yes, to give in to a life of ease and comfort. She'd been fond of him her entire life. But there was Christophe. She needed to think. Needed time.

Leaning forward, she picked up his hand and raised it to her lips.

"All right," she replied. "I'll consider it. You've been so patient with me that I dare ask for just a little more patience."

"How much more, exactly?"

She was relieved to hear amusement in his voice rather than indignation or anger. When she looked up, his eyes were twinkling. "Tell me how long I must endure waiting."

She drew a deep breath. Did she dare? "My birthday is the nineteenth day of June," she said. "I will be eighteen years old, a perfect date to contemplate marriage. Give me until then."

David's eyebrows rose. He looked less amused. "June nineteenth?" he asked. "You really want me to wait more than three months for your answer?"

Mirelle stood, her breath constricted in her throat. "I do," she said, barely able to believe her own audacity. "I'll give you my answer then."

# 42

## APRIL 8

The weather was unpredictable that early spring. Glorious days would turn overcast in seconds, torrents of rain pelting the streets and harbor. Mirelle's father was caught in a downpour one morning late in March while supervising the unloading of a new shipment of vellum. The calfskin parchment, imported from Tuscany, was reserved for the finest of ketubot, and Papa trusted no one but himself to check it off the boat.

He returned home that evening, clothes still damp.

"You'll catch your death," Mama scolded him.

He shrugged. "I had no time to change during the day."

"You shouldn't be this careless, Simone! You'll be ill!"

He laughed. "Nonsense! It was an excellent day. A beautiful shipment of vellum came in, and we completed three major commissions this afternoon. And two of those were completed three days before expected. Everything is just fine, Pinina. You worry too much."

But the next morning Mirelle found him hunched over a cup of beef tea at the breakfast table. "Papa, what's wrong?" she asked. He never drank beef tea unless he was feeling ill.

"I have a headache," he confided. "And my bones ache."

"Mama was right," Mirelle said. "I'll get her."

"No—don't!"

She turned, surprised.

"Don't tell your mother," he cautioned. "You know how she worries. She'll have me back in bed in an instant. And there's too much work to do."

"But Papa," Mirelle protested. "If you're sick, you must take care of yourself. You know what the doctor said."

"Pah!" Simone stared moodily into his cup. "What does he know?"

Mirelle wanted to argue, but just then Mino came gamboling into the room, whining about the workday ahead. Frowning, Papa hustled the boy off to work, and Mirelle lost her chance.

She pushed the thought out of her mind. Today, one of the days she didn't go to work, she would entertain both her suitors—Christophe in the late morning and David in the early evening. Mirelle kept considering what life as a soldier's wife would be like. Would she regret giving up the rich and comfortable life David offered, possibly resenting Christophe for it? And yet—how could she marry her friend's father? Every time she pictured her wedding night, only one man came to mind. And it wasn't David Morpurgo.

Christophe appeared almost every day she didn't go to the workshop, with an increasingly uncomfortable Daniel in tow. Sometimes Dolce joined them and flirted with Daniel, freeing Christophe and Mirelle to talk. Mirelle found it odd, watching Dolce pursue her cousin, like a cat stalking a mouse. So many men had tried to woo and win her friend. But Daniel just shied away from her advances.

But Mirelle had little time to contemplate the mystery—not when Christophe's mere presence sweetened the atmosphere like champagne bubbles.

Christophe was taking Mirelle's desire to know him better seriously. Today he spoke again of how his father died at the Bastille, how his uncle Alain had arrived with the news late that evening, his clothes torn and face bloodied. Mirelle was shocked to learn that his mother had once wished him to become a priest.

"I was a child," he explained as they walked along the harborside. "My mother said the priesthood was my destiny—and being young, I believed her."

"A priest?" Mirelle pulled away from him.

"Uncle Alain took me under his wing after Papa died, taught me my trade. I met Daniel there, and learned that Jews were not the monsters my mother and the priests claimed them to be."

Mirelle's mouth grew dry. "You thought we were monsters?"

Christophe stopped short and, tightening his grasp on her elbow, swiveled her to face him. "I won't lie to you. It's what I was taught from the cradle: how you killed Christ and were condemned for it, how God punished you with misshapen features, forced you to wander the earth forever cursed. Ask Daniel and he'll tell you what a brat I used to be, making his life a misery. But I've changed."

Later that morning, the four of them sat in the parlor, discussing the movements of Bonaparte's men. When Daniel mentioned deploying cannon in battle, Mirelle asked about his calculations. Christophe sat across from her, eyes shifting from one enthusiastic face to the other.

"I didn't realize you were so fond of mathematics," he finally said when Daniel's explanation wound to a close.

Mirelle flushed. "You know I keep the accounts for my father, help him manage the workshop."

"Well, you won't have to work once we're wed," Christophe said gaily.

Mirelle stared at him. "But your mother works in the printshop, doesn't she? I'm curious to see how the business is run." She paused thoughtfully. "Probably much the same as our workshop."

Christophe looked taken aback. "I assure you, *chérie*, my uncle's printshop needs no assistance, especially not from my wife. My

mother felt obligated to work there, to pay Uncle Alain back for housing us and apprenticing me. But I wouldn't want the same for you."

"Not even if I wanted to?"

Christophe laughed. "You'll be too busy making me happy."

*I can do both*, Mirelle thought bitterly.

"*Do* you want to?" Daniel chimed in. "Work at Alain's printshop,
that is?"

"Perhaps," she said.

Christophe's expression soured.

Dolce often praised Christophe's handsome manners and face. In
contrast, she spoke about her father's age, his vanities of dress, his
annoying habits born of years of living as a widower. Mirelle knew
her friend was trying to sway her. She learned to distrust Dolce, in
this at least.

David Morpurgo came less often than Christophe—perhaps two
or three times a week, generally for dinner or to squire her to an evening's entertainment. When he did, he was made joyfully welcome
by her mother and aunt. Prudenzia was always happy to chaperone
Mirelle. Ancona's society was nothing compared to Rome, she often
commented scornfully, but at least David had entrée into the few
fashionable houses that existed in this backwater. Mirelle disliked
how much of an upstart her aunt was, but she was a far better guide
than Mama when it came to dress and social graces.

David didn't overwhelm her with attention, but he showered her
with small gifts: ingenious bouquets and sweets, expensive, out-of-
season fruit. Under her mother's approving eye, Mirelle accepted
them all. But she wished she could refuse them.

Over the next few days, Mirelle noticed Papa doctoring himself—in small ways, so that Mama wouldn't realize. He'd ask Anna to prepare a tisane and sip it surreptitiously or force himself to swallow spoonfuls of restorative lamb jelly. In the office, he worked more slowly than usual, sometimes putting his head down on the desk to rest. At mealtimes, he pushed the food around on his plate. Mama clucked at that, but he always managed to devise some excuse—he was tired from the long day, excited about a new commission. Busy with the annual spring cleaning before Passover, she remained none the wiser, and Mirelle kept forgetting to mention it to her.

One afternoon Mirelle and Mino sat outside while her cousin droned on with his usual refrain, complaining about work in the ketubah workshop. She paid scant attention. But when Mino mentioned her father, her ears perked up.

"Your father used to be out in the shop much more often," he observed. "The men wouldn't dare insult me then. But when you're not there, he spends the day in his office, sleeping or dosing himself. So they feel free to torment me."

"Papa's doing what?" Mirelle was startled.

The boy looked at her with his big, innocent eyes. "He's been sick for nearly two weeks now. Surely you knew?"

*Did I?* Mirelle felt a wave of shame. She should have pieced all the clues together. Gone to Mama with them, even if Papa said not to. She scrambled to her feet. "I'm going to find Mama."

Her parents were in the dining room, Mama listing all the tasks yet to be accomplished before the first night of the holiday. Papa's eyes were glassy, his cheeks sallow and drawn. How could Mama be so oblivious?

Mirelle interrupted her mother mid-sentence. "You should be in bed, Papa."

"Mirelle!" Papa's lips tightened.

Mama stared at him, alarmed. "Bed? Why?"

"Ask him," Mirelle said, pointing.

Simone sighed, his look of betrayal softening under his wife's scrutiny. "I've been feeling under the weather since the rainstorm," he admitted. "But I just need rest."

"Mino says he's been spending his days in his office, sleeping," Mirelle persisted.

Mama rose. "Simone, get into bed this instant. I'll send for the doctor. We're not taking any chances."

Papa glared at Mirelle. "You see? Now you've worried your Mama. Pinina, please. The last thing I need is more time in bed."

But Mama wouldn't take no for an answer, and she bundled her husband under the covers for the rest of the day. Perhaps, Mirelle thought later, this enforced rest was the final straw, because as soon as he sank into the feather bed, Papa's fever spiked. By midnight he was delirious.

By dawn he was dead.

# 43

# APRIL 13

"Mama, that soldier's out there again," said Barbara, peering through the window into the front yard.

"Again?" Francesca's hands were deep in bread dough. The baby was playing peacefully on a mat in the kitchen. The little house was as serene as Francesca could remember it. Punching down the dough, she suppressed the wish that Emilio would stay away forever. *How differently I felt when he first left to join the merchant marine. When all I had to worry about were his gambling debts and temper.*

Before he had shown his true nature, before he'd killed or hurt anyone. And taken such pleasure in it.

"What does he want?" Barbara asked. "Why won't he leave us alone?"

Drying her hands on a scrap of towel, Francesca walked over and glanced out the window. "He wants to find your father."

"When will Papa come home?" Barbara's face was scrunched, holding back tears.

Francesca felt a pang of pity for her daughter. No matter how badly Emilio treated the child, she still adored him. *Just as I did once.*

"I'll throw rocks at him," Barbara said. "Chase him away."

"No, don't," Francesca said quickly. She reached out and smoothed her daughter's hair.

Barbara pulled away. Francesca wondered why the child couldn't accept her caresses gracefully.

"Just ignore him."

"But Mama—"

Francesca boxed the child's ears. Barbara stomped off to her room and slammed the door.

Francesca looked out the window again. There he was, sitting on the large rock in the front, keeping a close eye on the house. She glanced toward little Mario, shoving his tiny fist into his mouth, his chin and blouse wet. He was teething again. She walked over and wiped his tiny face with her towel. He laughed at her, then started babbling. She leaned close and tickled his stomach. He gurgled a laugh, making the world feel right for a small slice of time.

"Who's the sweetest baby boy in the world?" Her singsong voice rang out. "Who? Who?"

He reached chubby arms toward her and she lifted him, his sweet heft nestling against her neck. She closed her eyes, breathing in his warm, milky smell. When had Barbara lost her baby sweetness? When had she turned into a whining, gangly girl? Would this baby do the same?

She tried to put him down, but he grabbed hold of her shirt and fussed, so she propped him against her hip and finished kneading the dough. After plopping it into a bowl and throwing a damp towel over it, she swayed around the kitchen, rocking from foot to foot to lull the baby to sleep. Barbara was unusually quiet. Francesca hoped she'd wept herself to sleep. It wouldn't be the first time.

The baby sagged against her. He was quiescent enough to lay in his crib. Creeping softly, Francesca opened the door to the children's room. Barbara was nowhere to be seen. The window was wide open, curtains blowing inward with the breeze.

Careful not to tense, Francesca slipped Mario into his crib and covered him with a warm blanket, humming a wordless lullaby when he started to stir. He settled down, one thumb jammed deep into his mouth. She pressed a butterfly kiss on the soft fuzz atop his head, quietly closed the window, and tiptoed from the room.

She opened the front door to find Daniel, gripping a squirming Barbara, standing before her, his fist raised.

"Shush!" Francesca hissed. "The baby's asleep."

"Take your brat," Daniel thrust Barbara forward, "and tell her not to throw olives at me."

"Barbara, what did I say?" Francesca caught her daughter's elbow and shook her slightly.

"You said not to throw rocks. I didn't throw rocks." The girl yanked her arm free.

"Barbara!" Francesca chastised her.

"If he's going to skulk on our land, he can't complain if he gets hit with an olive or two," Barbara snapped.

"For Heaven's sake! Go play with Fiona. And don't hit Daniel with anything ever again. You hear?"

Barbara scampered off, not bothering to reply.

"You're not going to punish her?" Daniel pushed his tall shako cap off his head and tucked it under one arm.

Fists tight at her side, Francesca's stomach clenched. "What are you doing here, Daniel?" she asked. "I've seen you lurking in my yard for days. What do you want?"

"What do you think I want?" Daniel's eyebrows rose. "I want your husband. Where is he, Signora Marotti?"

"You expect me to tell you?"

Daniel moved the cap from one arm to the other. "Why do you defend him? Hide him? He's a murderer, signora. A coward. I thought you a devoutly religious woman. *Thou shalt not murder*, says the Ten Commandments."

"He's my husband." The words stuck in Francesca's throat. "'For better or worse' were my marriage vows."

"This much worse? He killed my cousins. Not just the boy, but his father, too, who died last week. The doctor said his death was due to complications from your husband's attack, that his body was too weak to protect itself against illness. Your *husband*, madame, left *his* wife a widow and both her and his daughter paupers."

Francesca felt weak in the knees. She walked past Daniel, went to the small bench in the yard, and collapsed onto it.

Daniel hovered behind her like a malevolent spirit, breathing hard on her neck. "Where is he, Signora Marotti? Tell me. He deserves to be hanged for his crimes."

"So you would make *me* a widow, Daniel?" she cried. "It's not enough that your own family has suffered—you want to harm me and my children, too?"

"I'm not the one who's harmed you." Daniel moved to stand in front of her. "He has. You're an honest woman, a good woman. You know what I'm saying is true. Yet you continue to shelter him."

Francesca closed her eyes. She brought Emilio clothes and food three times a week. It would be an easy matter to show this young soldier his hiding spot, to give him up. Could anyone blame her? Would anyone even have to know? She thought of the portrait of the Madonna, still covered by gold cloth in the cathedral. What would the Lady do in her place? If only she could see the Madonna's blessed face, gain peace from a smile or tear. But Francesca knew: the Lady wouldn't betray her Son. Just as Francesca wouldn't betray her husband.

"Go away," she told Daniel, her eyes still shut. "And leave us alone."

# 44

# APRIL 14

They buried Papa next to his son, Mama weeping on Mirelle's shoulder, somber black dresses and bonnet ribbons fluttering in the stiff April wind. Mirelle couldn't help but compare this shiva to the one held for Jacopo. They sat on the same hard boxes, mirrors covered, sideboard full of funeral offerings from kind neighbors. But everything else had changed.

Prudenzia and Mino now owned the house as well as the manufactory. David Morpurgo explained it to Mama one afternoon while Mirelle listened, their faces drained of color.

"The house was entailed as part of the workshop property," he said. "It was necessary back when Simone's father needed collateral for a loan to keep the business running. Simone should have altered the will, but he never found the time. Had he not died so suddenly . . ."

"We're homeless? We don't even own the furniture? Everything belongs to Prudenzia?" Mama wiped her eyes. "What are we to do?"

Morpurgo pursed his lips, glancing sidelong at Mirelle. A pang struck her heart. She knew what he meant. *I am still in mourning*, she thought, shrinking away. *He cannot make me choose now. Not yet.*

Once Prudenzia learned she was mistress of the house as well as the workshop, her manner turned from barely polite to openly hostile. The day after the shiva was over, while they sat at breakfast, she turned to Mama.

"I should have the best bedroom," she proclaimed. "Anna and Mirelle will move you into Mirelle's room by nightfall."

Mama sobbed into her handkerchief, but Mirelle raised her chin and looked straight into her aunt's flinty eyes. "We'll make the necessary arrangements, Aunt."

"Excellent. And Mirelle, tell that Christian soldier to stop visiting. He's not welcome."

Mirelle closed her eyes. "I'll tell him."

Prudenzia poured herself a fresh cup of coffee. "I assume your mother will live with you once you marry David Morpurgo."

Mirelle's throat clenched. "Yes. *If* I marry him."

Prudenzia snorted, her upper lip curling. *She knows*, Mirelle thought, *I've no alternative now*.

That afternoon, she sat down to write a note to Christophe—the hardest letter she'd ever had to write, too painful even for tears.

*My aunt refuses you entrance to what is now her house. Though I wish things were otherwise, I recognize that this is necessary. When my father was still alive, I had some choice in whom to marry, but no longer. Even then, our marriage would have betrayed my faith and my duty to my family. I believe my head would have eventually prevailed against my heart. For you know where my heart lies.*

*For my widowed mother's sake, I must marry David Morpurgo. He may be old, as you constantly remind me. But he has never been anything but good to me. He leads our Jewish community with compassion and generosity. And he will give both my mother and me a fine home, free of want.*

*We must no longer meet. Any future we might have shared was always just a figment of our imaginations. In time, dearest, you will come to accept that, as I have.*

Mirelle sanded and sealed the letter like an automaton she'd seen once displayed in the port—her movements precise, her sorrow tucked deep, where it couldn't burst forth.

The next day, Daniel found Mirelle crying in the sitting room, face buried in her hands.

"Cousin," he said, his heart twisting, "what can I do? How can I help?"

Mirelle straightened, startled, and dabbed at her wet cheeks with an already moist wisp of lace. A polite smile quivered on her lips. "I'm fine."

Without asking permission, Daniel sat next to her and took her hand. "Mirelle, you can talk to me."

It was as if a dam burst. Mirelle pulled away, hands rising to hide her tears. She wept for several minutes, shoulders shaking. Daniel sat unmoving, wishing there was something he could do or say. As her tears turned to gasps, he pulled out a square of fresh linen from a pocket and placed it between her fingers.

She resolutely wiped her eyes and cheeks and then, with an apologetic glance, blew her nose thoroughly.

His mouth twitched.

"I'll wash it before I return it," she murmured, tucking the handkerchief into the depths of her skirt.

They sat in silence for a minute while her breathing evened out. Finally, she swiveled toward him. "Christophe. The letter. How did he . . . ?"

Daniel had known the question was coming but dreaded it all the same. "He's upset," he said slowly. "But he knows how difficult your situation is—and will do nothing to worsen it."

That wasn't strictly true. That morning, he'd practically had to tie his friend to a chair to prevent him from besieging Mirelle's home.

"Get out of my way!" Christophe had raged, trying to shove Daniel aside.

"You read the letter," Daniel argued. "Don't you understand? You'll only make things worse."

"Why?" Christophe demanded, prowling their narrow sleeping quarters, his riding whip angrily slashing the air. "She needs me now. More than ever."

Daniel leaned against the door, refusing to stir.

"She doesn't want to marry that old man," Christophe fumed. "It's *me* she loves."

"And you love her?"

"Have you not been listening? With all my heart!"

"Then prove it," Daniel said. "Respect her wishes and walk away. Allow her to do what's right for her family. It's all you can do now."

Eventually, Daniel had managed to calm him long enough that he'd felt it was safe to leave the barracks. Christophe had still been pacing and flicking his whip when he left, however, and Daniel didn't know how long his impulsive, impetuous friend would stay away. He glanced at Mirelle's miserable face.

"I wish I had another choice," she muttered.

"I know," he said, placing his hands over hers. "I'm sorry."

They sat, silent, while the clock on the mantle ticked. He felt drawn toward her, almost against his will. Inching closer, he placed an arm around her shoulder and tipped her head into the crook of his neck. Mirelle clasped his free hand with both of hers. He felt her soft hair and sweet breath against his skin and shut his eyes, trying not to think of how close her lips were.

"Well," came a familiar voice from the doorway, stripped of its usual rich amusement.

Mirelle pulled out of Daniel's embrace to greet her friend. "Dolce. Hello."

"What's going on?"

Mirelle smiled wanly. "Daniel came by to pay his respects."

"Is that *all*?" Dolce slanted a searching glance toward him.

He hated the warmth that crept up from his neck into his face. Rising, he bowed toward Dolce. "I'd best be off."

Dolce moved forward and lay her long fingers lightly on his arm. "Don't leave on my account."

"Duty calls," Daniel responded brusquely, and with a nod at Mirelle, he left the room.

Dolce frowned, staring at the empty doorway. Mirelle gestured toward a chair. "Won't you sit?"

Her friend seated herself, her eyes still slightly narrowed as she studied Mirelle's face. "You've been crying."

Mirelle nodded.

"Well, maybe I can help. I've come here to invite both you and your mother for an extended visit. It will give you time to settle your affairs without feeling pressured by that witch of an aunt."

"Dolce! Do you mean it?" Mirelle felt a burden lifting. Then a thought struck her. "Was this your father's idea?"

"No," Dolce said. "But he'll welcome you both, of course."

Mama entered the room, still bearing the weight of Papa's death in her eyes. Her face looked sallow, her shoulders hunched. Mirelle jumped up and hugged her. "Mama! Dolce has invited us to stay with them."

Mama looked from one girl to the other. A slight smile—the first one Mirelle remembered seeing since her father had died—flickered across her face. Then it vanished.

"But child, if we leave, we'll never be able to come back home again. Prudenzia won't let us."

"I know," Mirelle said. "But we can't stay here. Once we're at Dolce's, we'll be able to think of a plan."

# 45

# APRIL 24

Nine days into the visit, Mirelle woke, her heart heavy with grief. She felt awkward living under the Morpurgo roof but tried to set those feelings aside for her mother's sake. Mama needed to be away from her memories and the home she had lost. *If only we could leave Ancona altogether.* But at least they no longer lived under Prudenzia's roof.

Mama was still deeply mired in her mourning. Her husband's death had revived all the anguish of her son's murder. She never left her room, and drew the shades closed day and night.

As for herself, Mirelle knew where her future lay. David Morpurgo, wise diplomat that he was, kept a respectful distance, never once alluding to his desire for her in her presence. But as she'd left the dining room the first evening, she'd glanced back and seen his face. He'd regarded her like a prize already won, his gaze warm on her slender body. She'd kept her expression blank as she exited but hadn't been able to help the shudder that overtook her in the hallway. *What is the matter with me?* she thought. *Why do I feel dead inside when he looks at me?*

She reminded herself that she still had a month of freedom left. Her thoughts centering again on her mother, she rose, dressed, and headed downstairs, where she asked the butler for Dolce. She was out for her morning ride, so Mirelle sat in the blue salon and waited.

When a thud at the front door announced Dolce's return, Mirelle followed her friend upstairs to her bedroom and waited as she removed her velvet habit behind a screen.

"I'm worried about Mama," Mirelle said finally when Dolce emerged and sat at her dressing table. "All she does all day is sit in her room. It's not healthy."

"I know," Dolce said, bidding her maid to pin up her long blond curls. "Do you think she'd agree to help with my reception next week? Address some envelopes? I want to have a party to celebrate Papa's recovery."

"She won't attend."

"Perhaps not. But if she's working alongside me, she'll have to leave her room. Is she awake? I'll go ask her." Dolce swept from the room.

Mirelle let her go, thinking Dolce might be more successful alone.

Mirelle came downstairs thirty minutes later, and was pleased to find Mama seated at a small writing desk, Dolce perched on a chair beside her. The two had their heads bent together, talking refreshments.

"Coffee cream pastries? They sound wonderful, child—but it wouldn't be a party in Ancona without orange cake. I have a recipe I can give your cook."

Dolce nodded. "And your cream puffs. Would you share that recipe?"

"That one?" Mama sounded reluctant, but she was smiling. "That's a family secret."

Mirelle laughed. "And it needs to stay in the family. But Mama, if Dolce's cook doesn't object, why don't you bake them yourself for the party?"

"Dolce?" Mama looked more cheerful than she had since Papa passed away. Mirelle silently blessed her friend. "What do you think?"

"Wonderful." Dolce tossed a bright curl behind her shoulder. "Thank you, Signora d'Ancona."

Mama took Dolce's hand. "Child, why don't you call me Pinina? I'm a guest in your home and Signora d'Ancona feels too formal. After all"—Mama glanced at Mirelle and looked quickly away—"Mirelle has been invited to call your father David."

Mirelle noticed a flicker of a frown cross her friend's face, quickly masked. "Thank you, Pinina," Dolce said. "We are family, aren't we—related by blood or not?"

"Is there something you'd like me to do?" Mirelle asked them both. "Because otherwise, I'll go for my morning walk."

"Is Daniel calling for you?" Mama asked.

Mirelle noticed the swift, suspicious glance Dolce shot in her direction. Her friend couldn't be jealous of her cousin's affection for her, could she? "Not this morning."

"Take one of the maids, Mirelle," Dolce said. "I'd come myself, but . . ."

"No need." Mirelle left before they insisted on a chaperone.

Since her father had died, Mirelle was visited by daily waves of remorse. And searing, relentless guilt for not paying more attention to Papa's illness. As penance, the only thing that felt right was working at the ketubah workshop daily, if only for a few hours. Though she'd prefer to spend all day there, she was still cautious of the rabbi's censure. And she had to time her visits to avoid encountering Prudenzia.

The second day after the shiva, Mirelle had arrived at the workshop early.

"We are sorry for your loss," said Narducci, speaking for the men. "We feel bereft, all of us."

Looking around, Mirelle knew it was true. She also saw expressions of relief on nearly all the men's faces—relief that she hadn't totally deserted them.

"I don't know what the future holds," she told them. "But I know what Papa would have wished. And that was for us to keep the workshop thriving."

The men nodded and headed to their desks. Mirelle checked the work that had been done during the week of mourning, swallowing hard when she encountered one of her father's decisions—and even harder when she had to make a decision in his stead.

Then the door burst open and Mirelle's head whipped up. Her stomach fluttered as Prudenzia strolled in. She ducked behind the open door and stood, nerves alight, as Prudenzia made her way from table to table, dressing down the men.

"Why are you using gold paint?" she demanded, pointing at Abraham with an imperious finger. "Didn't I tell you yesterday the yellow would be just as good—and far less costly?"

"Yes, but . . ." Abraham stopped himself.

Mirelle's throat clenched. It had been her decision to use a touch of gold in the design, expensive though it was. Bless Abraham for not exposing her.

"And what's this?" Prudenzia snapped, fingering the parchment on another table. "This is too heavy." She glared. "I said to use the heaviest vellum only for important commissions. I thought I made that clear." She turned toward the office. "Narducci!"

Narducci walked calmly into the room. "Every one of our commissions is important, Signora Fermi."

"Nonsense! This is a ketubah for a clerk, not a merchant or a banker."

Mirelle couldn't contain her anger any longer. "It's *our* work," she said, stepping out from behind the door. "The work of the d'Ancona Ketubah Manufactory, the best in the world. We take pride in our high standards, Aunt, and the men need to know we'll maintain them."

"*We?*" Prudenzia's lips thinned. "*We're* not going to do any such thing. This is my workshop now."

"Your son's workshop," Narducci corrected gently.

"Which I manage," Prudenzia snapped.

"Your workshop?" Mirelle retorted. "Just as my house is now your house, and you'd like to put me and my mother out on the street?" The words felt like daggers in her mouth. "You could barely wait until the shiva was over to take my mother's room away from her, could you?"

An audible gasp rose from the men.

Prudenzia, falling back a step under their glares, colored brick red. "How dare you?" she exclaimed. "That's a private matter."

"Private? Ha! You think my mother and I are too polite to tell everyone how you treat us." Mirelle's fists clenched.

"I've done nothing wrong," Prudenzia said, clasping a hand to her chest. "Go home, Mirelle. You're sick with grief—you don't know what you're saying. I'm sure it's no wonder."

Mirelle held back a wave of tears with effort. "No wonder? Of course it isn't—when you are destroying everything my father, my mother, my"—her voice broke—"brother held dear. Everything I hold dear!"

"Now, now, child," Prudenzia said, reaching out to touch Mirelle's shoulder.

Mirelle flinched. "Don't you dare. We both know what you are."

Prudenzia looked around. At the sharp condemnation on the men's faces, she gave up her pretense of sympathy. "You need to leave, Mirelle. You're not welcome here."

Narducci moved between them. "Signorina Mirelle is always welcome," he said calmly. "She understands what cutting corners and making bad decisions would do to us."

"How dare you tell me who is welcome and who is not?" Prudenzia snapped through gritted teeth. "You'll learn your place soon enough! All of you!"

At that, she whirled and slammed out of the workshop. And since then, Mirelle had avoided her.

*Truly*, Mirelle thought now, walking through the ghetto streets, shading her face with a parasol, *Papa should have found a way to leave me the manufactory, entailment or not, Jewish law or not. I'd manage it better than Mino, and certainly better than his mother.*

She let herself in by a side door. Narducci stood in the stockroom, examining different types of parchment.

"Good morning," he greeted her. "We're happy to see you, but be wary. Your aunt has not yet arrived today."

"After I check the books, is there anything else I should do?" Mirelle asked. "If not, I'll be back tomorrow."

"No, we're fine. It's a calm day, at least so far."

Mirelle went into the office and opened the book of accounts. She quickly tallied up the newest numbers, then returned to the stockroom.

"Everything is in order," she told Narducci.

"You're a good girl, Mirelle," he said. "Leave now before your aunt arrives."

"Wish the others well for me." Mirelle started toward the door. But a sudden roar of voices stopped her.

She and Narducci peered into the main room. Mirelle could see her aunt, looking out of place in her fashionable puce walking dress, standing before the men. Beside her was a swarthy man with broad shoulders.

"Turko," Narducci breathed, his face wrinkled in distress. "Oh, Lord, no."

"Turko? Who's Turko?"

"A monster. He was foreman of the Simon Tov Ketubah Works

in Rome. This is bad. I need to hear what's going on. Go home now." Without waiting for a response, he pushed past her and made his way to the front of the room.

Mirelle stood by the open door, not sure if she should stay or not. She was helpless to help the men. But surely Papa would have wanted her to discover what was happening. She slipped into the back of the room, careful to stay out of her aunt's line of sight.

The man was speaking. "We'll open our doors at six in the morning, close them at three a.m. I'll divide you in three shifts so we can work through the night. If necessary, I'll hire new men to fill out your ranks."

"New men from where?" someone called. "Every skilled man in Ancona already works here."

"Who says they have to be skilled?" Turko countered.

The men gasped in unison, then began shouting.

"What? Would you ruin us?"

"Don't you know it takes years to train someone?"

"How dare you come here and change how we work! If Simone were still alive . . ."

The last shout made Mirelle's face pucker. She took a deep breath. The men's anger was plain, but there was deep despair lying underneath it. She recalled an evening about six months ago when one of Papa's young workers, Gabriele Levi, had visited. Because of a death in his family, he wanted to move to Milan to care for his brother's widow and children.

Jacopo had looked confused as Papa and Gabriele argued back and forth. After Gabriele left, Papa had explained that his workers were all committed to him for a period of years. They couldn't leave his employ unless they paid enough money to compensate him for their loss. After all, he had invested in their training. If someone left, he lost not only their skills but also all the time and effort put into their education. So Papa had laid out a payment plan for Gabriele, which both men had agreed was fair.

That was why, Mirelle realized, the men looked aghast. Even if it became unbearable at the manufactory, they were not free to leave. Their articles bound them to the shop, to Prudenzia, and now to Turko.

"*Cazzo!*" Turko's voice boomed. "I don't give a fig how you used to work, and I won't stomach insubordination. Signora Fermi wishes me to manage this shop, and manage it I will. If that means the lash, my arm is strong and my aim sure. And here"—he waved a piece of paper in air—"this list goes on the office door. If you're late, if you don't deliver your work on schedule, if you mouth off—you pay a fine. First fine is five scudi. Second is ten. Break the rules a third time . . . Well. Break the rules a third time, lads, and your life won't be worth living."

Mirelle cringed as the men groaned. Several of them looked to Narducci, as if expecting him to say something. He swallowed hard and stepped forward.

"Signora Fermi," he said, keeping his eyes fixed on her face. "You cannot have considered what bringing this man here will mean. We know what he did to our fellow workers, our friends in Rome. His cruelty didn't produce better work, just more of it. Sales fell off and many were dismissed. Turko's fines meant their families suffered too—his whippings and other punishments scarred many of them for life. I've even heard of some brought to the brink of death—"

"That's enough." Prudenzia's voice dripped acid. "I won't stay in this backwater any longer. Someone must manage the shop and make sure there is no malingering. With Turko in charge, I'll be able to return to Rome."

"If a manager is all you need, why not appoint the man who knows how we do our best work?" The question came from deep inside the pack of men. "Narducci speaks for us. Let him manage us."

"Yes, Narducci!" The cry rose from all corners of the room.

"Silence!" Prudenzia shouted. She looked at Turko, who was surveying Narducci with a toothy grimace.

But the men would not be quieted. They continued to shout Narducci's name. Finally, Turko reached behind him, pulled a bull-whip from his belt, and flicked it toward the ceiling with an enormous crack. An immediate silence fell.

"The next man who speaks out of turn," Turko said, "will feel my answer on his backside."

Prudenzia suddenly craned her neck and Mirelle realized she had seen her. Her aunt said nothing, but her eyes narrowed.

"So," Turko continued, "you want one of your own to manage the shop. You want this man"—he looked Narducci up and down—"and think he'll do a better job than I will. You are Narducci?"

Narducci took another step forward. "Indeed."

"And you've been here how long?"

"I was apprenticed at the age of six. Thirty-three years, I've worked here."

"And you know people who I—how did you put it?—'brought to the brink of death' in Rome?"

"I do." Narducci nodded. "Isaach Piattelli."

"Piattelli? That pitiful excuse for a man? He's your example?" Turko threw back his head and laughed.

"He was the best craftsman in Rome," Narducci said. "Before you broke him."

"Of course he was." Turko's face was drawn up in sardonic lines. "Because he always took three times as long as anyone else." He turned to Prudenzia. "Is that what you want? Men who put artistry above production? Because if so, this is clearly the right man for you."

Prudenzia glared at Narducci. "My son said you insulted him. You think because your wife is friends with my sister-in-law that you can rile up the men and oppose my decisions? Signor Turko, I want you to make an example of this man."

"You can't do that!" Mirelle heard her own voice crying out.

All eyes turned to her.

"Who is this?" Turko demanded of Prudenzia. "What's this girl doing here?"

"My name is Mirelle d'Ancona," Mirelle said, swallowing down her fear. "I am the daughter of Simone d'Ancona, the man who made this shop the most celebrated ketubah manufactory in the world." She glanced around quickly, meeting every man's gaze, struggling to keep her voice from breaking.

Turko's jaw hardened.

"And he did so because of men like Signor Narducci. A man my father respected." As she spoke, resolve stiffened her spine. She raised her voice. "You would rob my father's legacy of everything that made this workshop special. You would destroy it."

"Signora Fermi." Turko looked at Mirelle's aunt.

Prudenzia raised a hand. "Mirelle," she said in a soft, even tone of voice, like a hissing snake, "you forget yourself. Your father is dead. Your brother is dead. My son owns the workshop. You have no place here."

"You are destroying my father's work," Mirelle said, holding her head high. "My father didn't know how terrible you were until you came to live with us. But I know. My mother knows. And I will make sure all of Ancona knows."

She walked up to where Turko stood, his whip in his hand. "I do not think you dare strike this man—any of these men—for defending my father and grandfather's good name and the place they've dedicated their lives to."

Turko looked at her with cold fury, the whip clenched tight.

"You will not strike this man," Mirelle repeated.

Turko lowered the whip, but growled, "Your aunt wants you to leave. Don't think because you are a girl that I won't lay hands on you."

The men gasped and Narducci stepped up again. "Even *you* wouldn't dare."

Turko laughed deep in his throat, his face disfigured by a sneer. "Well, perhaps not. But nothing will stop me from whipping you or another man to punish her, if she persists in coming here. Do you hear me, girl?"

Mirelle tossed her head up, still defiant. "We'll see about that."

As she exited, she was cheered by the sound of clapping. Her heart was in her throat; every inch of her buzzed. The men's applause rang in her ears. *Papa would be so proud.*

But Turko and Prudenzia were right. She had no rights in the workshop any longer. She could not help the men.

# 46

# MAY 25

Daniel and Christophe moved quietly through the scrub. They kept the girl in their sights, never drawing close enough to alarm her.

*Not that she seems worried*, Daniel thought. She was singing at the top of her lungs, a children's song that he translated as "Goat, Little Goat."

"*Capra Capretta*," she warbled, "*che bruchi tra l'erbetta, vuoi una manciatina, di sale da cucina?*"

More than a month had elapsed since the olive-throwing incident. While Daniel tried to keep watch over Francesca daily, their conversation had turned her cautious. She continued to deliver food and supplies to her husband, but having lived in the shadow of these mountains all her life, she was adept at finding her way. More than once he had trailed and lost her.

This morning, however, Daniel had received a stroke of good luck. Together with Christophe, he'd arrived at the tiny farm just as two women left the house. The soldiers had ducked behind some trees to listen.

"The baby needs a doctor," the younger one said.

"Nonsense," said the elder. "It's just the croup. The string of garlic will help him breathe. And he certainly isn't lacking for prayers."

With Francesca distracted by the baby's sickness, it was the girl,

Barbara, she'd sent to deliver supplies to her father. Daniel and Christophe had watched from the trees as Francesca kissed her daughter on the forehead, looking around cautiously.

Now, with Barbara singing her ridiculous song, it wasn't hard to keep up with her.

"*Il bimbo é nel prato, la mamma é alla fonte, il sole é sul monte, sul monte é l'erbetta, capra, capretta!*" she trilled.

"What is she singing?" Christophe muttered.

"Some nonsense about a goat and the mountain . . . in the grass? That can't be right."

"Why not? This mountain is in the grass," Christophe said, moving around a giant boulder in their path.

After a half hour of steady climbing, Barbara stopped in a clearing before a rocky face that jutted upward toward the mountain peak. She put the basket down, stuck two fingers in her mouth, and whistled sharply. The whistle—two short, one long, and one short—was clearly a signal.

In a moment, Emilio emerged from a cave carved in the face of the rock.

"Barbara!" he cried, opening his arms. "My girl!"

As they hugged, Daniel observed the man he'd hunted for more than a month. Emilio's clothes were stained and torn, his beard and hair wild and unkempt. Daniel expected the same loathsome coward he'd seen at the palace. He was surprised to see love in the man's eyes as he embraced his daughter. Daniel exchanged an awkward glance with Christophe. Then his jaw hardened, thinking of Mirelle and her brother and father.

"Where's your mother?" Emilio asked the child, holding her at arm's length.

"The baby is sick. Mama couldn't leave him. Hug me again, Papa!"

He obliged, holding her to him for a long moment. Christophe started forward, but Daniel grabbed his arm to stop him.

"Wait until the child leaves," he murmured. "I don't want her to see this."

Christophe nodded. Emilio started into the cave with the basket, Barbara at his heels.

"What if there's more than one way out?" Christophe asked. "We could lose him."

That might be true. Reluctantly, Daniel removed the pistol from his holster, poured in powder, and dropped a lead ball in the barrel. Christophe followed suit. They moved swiftly into the cave.

The moment they stepped inside, they realized their fears were unnecessary. The cave was nothing more than a dimpled hollow in the rocky cliff. Well lit by the large opening, there was just enough room for a fire in the middle, a straw mattress on the ground, and a rough table made from a plank of wood suspended unevenly over two stones. The half-unpacked basket stood on the ground next to the table.

"Hands up!" Christophe yelled in French.

"*Mani in alto!*" Daniel repeated in Italian.

Slowly, Emilio turned to face them, hands raised in the air. "Don't harm the child," he cried.

But Barbara had her own ideas. She launched herself at Daniel's legs, trying to topple him. He stumbled but managed to keep his balance. Seeing that Christophe had Emilio covered, he lowered his flintlock, seized her by the arm, and, grabbing her by the scruff of her collar, pulled her off his legs.

Barbara twisted in his grasp, kicking, biting, and clawing. "*Diavolo, demonio!*" she screamed in his face. "*Lasciare mio padre da solo!*"

"My friend will shoot your father if you don't calm down!" Daniel yelled in response.

"Barbara!" Emilio shouted. "For once in your life, hush!"

She pulled out of Daniel's grasp and sank to the ground in a heap, crying.

"It's all my fault," she blubbered. "Mama said be careful. To watch for someone following me. Oh, Papa!"

Daniel and Christophe exchanged glances. Even if he felt a twinge of guilt at using the child to catch her father, it was too late for regret.

Daniel raised his pistol again. "We're heading back to Ancona," he said. "If the girl is coming with us, she has to behave. Tell her, Marotti."

Emilio narrowed his eyes. Daniel could tell that he was trying to weigh his options.

"You killed two of my cousins," he said coldly. "You slaughtered one in front of his parents and sister. The other died slowly and terribly, finally succumbing to the weakness caused by his wound. Look into my eyes and ask yourself if I am lying to you. I will not hesitate to shoot. Not even with your daughter standing beside you."

"Barbara—come here!" Marotti said.

The girl picked herself up and ran to him. He started to lower his arms when she clutched his chest, but Christophe motioned with his weapon for him to keep them raised.

"*Bambina*—be a good girl and listen to these men," he told her, ducking his head to kiss her tangled hair. "They won't hurt you if you do."

"But they'll kill you, Papa!" she cried, gripping him closer.

He stepped out of her tight embrace, eyes hard as iron, and shot Daniel a look of pure hatred. "I am already a dead man."

Daniel would never forget the long trip back to the barracks, keeping his weapon trained on Marotti while negotiating the steep mountain pathways. He had to keep an eye on his prisoner, the trail, and the unpredictable little girl all at the same time.

Before they arrived on the outskirts of Ancona, however, they let

Barbara go, even though Daniel knew she'd run to alert her mother and possibly every other Catholic in Ancona of her father's capture. The cathedral bell chimed noon as they marched Emilio toward the barracks.

Daniel wasn't surprised to find Francesca and Barbara already in front of the building when they arrived, Mario wailing in his mother's arms, a mob of townspeople at her back. A smaller crowd of Jews—including David Morpurgo, Dolce, and Mirelle—stood to one side. A group of French soldiers watched them warily, hands on their saber hilts.

Pushing Emilio forward, Daniel recognized the cardinal in the crowd before him. Then his gaze settled on Francesca. She stood upright, a shawl draped over Mario. As they approached, she handed the baby to one of the women and moved in front of the barracks doorway, arms clenched across her chest.

"Daniel," she said slowly, her black glare unsettling him. "What have you done?"

"Move," Daniel barked.

She didn't. The townspeople stepped closer together, barring them from the door. The soldiers pulled their sabers from their sheaths.

Daniel's heart pounded in his chest. He jerked Emilio before him and raised his flintlock barrel to the back of his head.

"Move," he said. "Now."

He heard Christophe slide his trigger to arm his gun. The second barrel moved alongside his. Keeping his eyes on Francesca's stony face, Daniel cocked his weapon.

She drew in a startled breath. "You wouldn't."

"Don't wager on that," he replied. "You're a good woman, but you married a bad man."

The silence hung heavy.

Finally, Francesca asked, "What will you do with him?"

"That's not up to me, Signora. He'll be questioned, and if it's found he tried to murder one of the councilmen, he'll hang."

Barbara started forward with a shriek of rage, but one of the other women caught the back of her dress and pulled her away. Francesca kept her smoldering gaze fixed on Daniel's face for another moment, then looked at her husband. Emilio was preening like a game cock, clearly enjoying the attention.

Just as they approached the barracks door, Emilio whirled around. With a gleeful expression, he cried, "Hear me, Ancona! I will be free soon enough—and when I am, blood will rain down on the ghetto, on these miserable Jews, every single one of them! I'll take my revenge on these French soldiers, make them suffer, pay for what they've done!"

A ragged cheer rose from the midst of the townspeople. The skin at the back of Daniel's neck crawled.

Buoyed by the applause, Emilio glared at the small gathering of Jews. "You hear me, you pigs? I've killed your kind before—and I will again, as soon as I'm—"

Out of the corner of one eye, Daniel saw a boy—perhaps twelve or thirteen—step out from the crowd of Jews and launch a missile of mud. It struck Emilio squarely in the face, making him reel back.

"Got him!" the boy called out.

Other Jewish boys pushed their elders aside to lob rotten produce and garbage at the captive, berating him: "Murderer! Scum! Dog!"

"You dare!" one of the Christians cried. Men and boys scrambled for projectiles. Insults and curses rang out as both sides pelted one another with whatever they could scoop up from the filthy streets. Women, grabbing their children by the hand, backed away, stumbling over the cobbles and shrieking.

"*Arrêtez!*" The French soldiers, caught in the crossfire, screamed for them to stop. Sabers were raised.

"Ready, steady, men!" came the order from the guard commander.

Any moment, Daniel realized, his stomach sinking, the melee could turn into a riot.

Emilio wiped mud and splattered produce from his face. His lips pulled back in a snarl. He reached deep into his left boot. A dagger sparkled between his fingers. *"Bastardo!"* Ignoring the two pistols still trained upon him, he raced toward the first boy, who was kneeling in the gutter, collecting a new wad of refuse.

Daniel felt the ground shake under his feet, smelled the gunpowder from Christophe's discharged weapon. Emilio gripped his chest with a shocked gasp and tumbled to the ground.

The reverberating echo of the gunshot froze both sides. A scream ripped through the crowd; Francesca thrust Daniel aside and seized her dead husband in her arms. Barbara pulled out of a woman's restraining grasp to put her head into her father's bloody lap, wailing like a wounded animal.

"What have you done?" cried a young man, running to the stricken family. "What have you done?"

Daniel stared at Christophe, whose pistol pointed at the empty space above Emilio's prone body, smoke rising from the barrel. "What have you done?" he whispered.

# 47

# MAY 26

Francesca, robed in mourning black, was genuflecting at her back-yard altar when Father Candelabri found her. She looked up from her fervent devotions.

"Will the French release his body, Father?" she asked.

"I'm not certain," he said, looking at her solemnly. "They might have done so before, but now . . ." He extended a hand and helped her to her feet.

"Now? Did something happen?"

"Yes, my child."

Francesca waited.

"Let's sit down," the priest said. "Perhaps that bench over there?"

Francesca led him to the bench under the magnolia. She was grateful that the baby was sleeping, and that Fiona's mother had invited Barbara to spend the day with them.

"What's happened, Father?"

He pulled a rosary out of his cassock and sat, slowly moving the polished black beads through his fingers. He bit his lip. "I'm sorry to have to tell you this, especially in such a time of sorrow, but you need to know. They've stolen the miraculous Madonna from the cathedral."

Francesca crossed herself in alarm. "The French took it?"

Father Candelabri shook his head. "No. Members of the Catholic

Fellowship. Not the cardinal, but some of the others. We suspect Emilio's cousins Desi and Roberto are among the instigators."

Francesca stared, uncomprehending. "But why?"

The priest returned the rosary to his pocket and took Francesca's hands. "They say they will burn it if the French do not leave Ancona. That Emilio's murder showed how unjust and violent French rule is. A desperate measure, perhaps. But the entire city knows of Bonaparte's fascination with the painting."

Francesca sat rooted to her seat, a loud rushing between her ears. Growing dizzy, she pulled her hands away to grip the bench.

"No," she whispered, sick to her stomach. "They cannot mean it."

Father Candelabri sighed. "They do. I take it you had nothing to do with this, child?"

"Father! How could you even suspect . . ." Francesca sputtered to a halt. "I loved my husband, but I could never countenance an act like this. Never in a million years."

*I loved my husband*, Francesca repeated bitterly to herself. It was a lie, wasn't it? She looked up at the priest and flushed, feeling a damning wave of shame. She had hidden the truth from everyone, excluding it even from confessional. Doing so had forfeited her right to communion. Was she damned for wishing that her husband would die and leave her family in peace—especially now that the wish had been granted? Was his death the devil's work, tempting her? She clung to that part of her that genuinely mourned the man she had married. But another part was glad he was gone forever.

"Bonaparte is somewhere near Milan. They sent a messenger to request his instructions in the matter," the priest said. "Francesca, are you certain you're all right?"

Francesca raised her head. "I'm fine," she said weakly. "Thank you for telling me. I'll pray for the outcome the Lady would want. Surely she will give us a sign."

Candelabri shrugged. "The ways of heaven are shrouded in mystery, child. We still do not know why she came to us as she did."

"But the cardinal . . ."

The priest smiled wryly. "My superior in Christ believes the miracle intended to goad us to action against the French. I am not convinced he was right."

Francesca stared at him, shocked. Priests were supposed to obey, not to question. "How can you say that?"

The priest stood, holding a hand out for her. "Come, let us pray at your altar to Mary. I do not forget your grief. If nothing else, the Lady will bestow peace upon us for a while."

Later that afternoon, Roberto stopped by. He looked nearly as devastated as poor Barbara, who had not stopped crying since her father had been shot. Fiona's mother had brought her home early, saying that neither she nor her daughter could stem the child's flow of tears.

"Come sit, Roberto," Francesca said.

"You should cast me out," he muttered, collapsing in a kitchen seat. "I am sick with shame."

She went over to the cupboard and brought down a glass and Emilio's bottle of grappa. Her fingers trembled around the neck of the bottle, remembering how her husband would grab it off the shelf, the sound of glass scraping the wood. She put bottle and glass in front of his young cousin, and poured out a drink.

"Shame? Roberto, be sensible. Emilio was a prisoner. He taunted the soldiers, murdered Jews, he . . ." She sighed. "You could not have prevented the French from killing him."

Roberto shook his head. "That's not what I mean."

"Not?" Francesca frowned. "Then what?"

"I wouldn't attend the Catholic Fellowship meeting held after the

French captured Ancona," Roberto said. "I wouldn't help him with his plot to kill the Jew. Why, even you were brave enough to sew the uniform for him. Desi visited him when he was in hiding. But me? I am a coward." He downed the glass she'd poured him and poured another himself.

She stared at his hangdog expression, shaking her head. "There's no shame in being afraid. And certainly not in having enough common sense to realize that Emilio's plan could not prosper." She picked Mario up from his basket on the floor and bounced him on her lap. "You blame yourself for not helping. I blame myself for just the opposite. Don't you think I know that if I had not sewn that uniform or"—she lowered her voice, making sure Barbara, sniffling in her bedroom, could not overhear—"sent my daughter to him, he might be alive today?"

Roberto downed the second glass of grappa, and would have taken a third if Francesca hadn't removed the glass from his grasp. He laughed bitterly. "Did you see how that Frenchman shot him down—like a dog in the street?"

Francesca flinched.

"Like a dog, I tell you, Francesca!" he cried wildly.

"*Silenzio*," she hissed, glancing toward the children's room.

But it was too late. Barbara, her face swollen and eyes red, stood in the doorway.

"But we will have revenge, I tell you," Roberto cried, grabbing the bottle by the neck and gulping straight from it.

"Give me that!" Francesca moved the baby to her hip as she reached across the table.

His eyes bored into her. "We've done something for him."

"I heard," Francesca said. "You've stolen the portrait."

Roberto's face brightened, and Francesca felt a shiver. The fanatical light in his eyes felt all too familiar.

"Where is it, Roberto?" she asked. "You must return it."

"Return it? To the French? Are you joking?" He laughed maniacally. "We'd rather see it in flames."

Francesca shook her head. "It's a portrait of God's Virgin Mother. How does burning something that holy help my poor, dead husband?"

"It was his idea," he answered. "Desi told me. It means something to that damn general. Emilio wanted to burn it because Bonaparte demanded his soldiers keep it safe."

"But it's a sin," Francesca insisted.

Barbara burst into the room, fists clenched. "That's just like you," she shrieked, "thinking of sin and God rather than my papa! If Papa wanted to burn it, Cousin Roberto is right—they should burn it!"

Mario started wailing.

"Barbara!"

But it was too late. Barbara pushed past her and raced out the door. Her daughter's angry shouts echoing in her ears, Francesca turned on her husband's cousin. "Do you see what you've done?" she demanded, trying to soothe the now screaming baby. "Stop talking like a madman. Do something useful—go bring my girl home!"

*I can't bear staying indoors*, Mirelle thought. The shocking death in town still lingered in her mind. The wind had picked up, blowing cold off the water, but she decided to walk along the shoreline anyway, past the harbor and the docks. She could be alone there. The hard headwinds invigorated her, drove away her demons.

She tucked her shawl over her head to muffle the wail of the gale. Walking nearly doubled over, she imagined the fury of the elements mocking her, their wild freedom so different from her predicament: forbidden to do the one thing that brought her peace, denied the man she loved.

Nearing the edge of the water, Mirelle thought she saw a shape in the distance. She scrubbed her eyes and drew closer until the figure materialized. It was a small, huddled child.

"Hello," she said, kneeling to the girl's level. "What are you doing here all alone?"

The child looked up, a flash of hatred in her eyes, and Mirelle rocked back on her heels. *I know her*, she thought. She was the daughter of the man Christophe had shot. The girl who had called her and Daniel Jewish devils in the marketplace. *What is her name again?*

"Go away," the girl hissed. "Leave me alone."

For a moment, Mirelle considered it. This child's father had caused so much misery. Emilio had been a demon, a monster—the man who'd slaughtered both her brother and father. Why help his daughter? But then, seeing the girl's dirty, tear-streaked face, Mirelle softened. This child, too, was mourning a father—a father who had been shot dead while she watched. Another family torn apart by hatred, another victim of senseless violence.

*Barbara*, Mirelle remembered. That was her name.

"You can't be out here in this wind, Barbara," Mirelle told her. "Your mother will worry."

"My mother?" the girl spat. "My mother doesn't care. She's glad they killed Papa! She doesn't think I can tell, but I can. She's *relieved*."

Mirelle put out a hand and touched the girl on the shoulder. Barbara hunched away, but Mirelle's hand followed and stroked her tangled hair gently. "You know that's not true."

"What do you know?" Barbara railed. "My papa . . ."

"My father died recently, too," Mirelle said. "I miss him, cry for him at night. Sometimes during the day, too."

Barbara stared at her with baleful eyes. "He wasn't killed, was he? No one shot him down in the streets—like a dog, my cousin Roberto said. They killed my papa like a dog."

"No," Mirelle said slowly, biting back the bitter rejoinder that leapt to her lips. "My papa died in bed. But . . . it was sudden, too."

They stayed there for a moment, Barbara allowing Mirelle to lightly pat her shoulder as she stared out at the horizon. The wind blew sharp pellets of sand into Mirelle's face, stinging her cheeks. The girl wasn't safe out here, she thought. She had to convince her to go home.

"They're going to burn the portrait," Barbara blurted, ducking her head. "Unless the French leave Ancona. Papa wanted to burn it, that's what Cousin Roberto said. But Mama says it's a sin."

"What portrait?" Mirelle asked.

"The Madonna portrait," Barbara said impatiently. "Want to know something? *I* saw the miracle first. Mama keeps saying it was her, but she's lying."

Mirelle studied the child's face. "I don't understand."

"They all say that Mama first witnessed the miracle. Everyone believes her because she's so *holy*, because she's so *special*. But I saw it first!" Barbara shook off Mirelle's hand. "So there!"

"You're angry," Mirelle said. "Have you told your mother how you feel?"

Barbara shook her head. "Mama doesn't care. She loves the portrait more than me."

"I'm certain that's not true." Mirelle knew she couldn't leave the child out here all alone. It was growing late, and the keening wind made her shiver. "I'll take you home," she offered.

Barbara rose, the wind beating at her face. "All right," she agreed. "I'm hungry anyway."

They arrived at the little farm just in time to see a distraught Francesca heading out to search for her daughter. An older woman sat outside in the twilight, holding a baby.

Francesca gasped with relief when she saw Barbara. "Where have you been?" She grabbed hold of her and hugged her fiercely. "I've been so worried."

"I want my dinner." Barbara broke free from her mother's embrace and ran into the house.

Only then did Francesca notice Mirelle. Her eyes widened. "Where was she?" she asked abruptly. "We looked everywhere."

"On the shoreline outside the city. It was pure chance I found her. She's safe now, so I'll take my leave." The last thing Mirelle wanted was to talk to Marotti's widow.

"It seems I have to thank you yet again," Francesca said, more softly this time.

Mirelle shrugged. "No need," she said brusquely. Common courtesy demanded that she offer her condolences, but she couldn't bring herself to say she was sorry. She was glad Marotti was dead, glad Christophe had killed him.

Francesca, though, did not move. She put out a hand. "Nevertheless, I do thank you. It was kind of you—kinder than I had any right to expect."

Mirelle took the widow's hand for a brief second, then let it drop.

Without another word, Francesca turned and went inside to her daughter.

# 48

## MAY 29
## PALAZZA MOMBELLO,
### THREE LEAGUES OUTSIDE OF MILAN

It took Daniel three days of hard riding to reach the Palazza Mombello. Never an intrepid horseman—he left that to Christophe—he'd protested vociferously against being sent. But Captain Bossard, in command of the French contingent in Ancona, had insisted.

"You were with the general when he first saw the portrait," Bossard said. "It only makes sense that you tell him what's happening here."

He'd set forth after tossing a few things into a knapsack, and left a city buzzing with rumor. Who had stolen the portrait? Where was it hidden? The town residents all had their own theories—except when questioned by the French. Then they sat, eyes on the floor or the ground, silent as a tomb.

Daniel rode into an Italy rife with the aftermath of riots—a revolt in Venice in March, a massacre of more than four hundred French soldiers in Verona just over a month earlier. "Death to Frenchmen! Death to Jacobins!" was the cry rising from the pulpit to the streets. Daniel was well aware that this was not the best time to be a lone French rider on a skittish mare galloping through Italy's towns and villages, so he made the best speed he could, wishing he could avoid bustling town squares and lonely roadways alike. Neither felt safe.

He was relieved to reach the château where Bonaparte had set up his headquarters to negotiate treaty terms with the Austrians, the pope, and sundry Italian leaders. His first view of the palace made him catch his breath: a building golden in the afternoon sunlight, surrounded by tall cedars, nestled in Lombardy's rolling hills. Everything about it spoke of grandeur.

Entering the château, he felt unequal to his task. He was muddy, exhausted, and, despite days of mumbling to himself in practice, still unsure how to address the general.

Luckily for him, the first person he saw upon entering the palazzo was Bourrienne.

"Daniel!" the secretary cried. "Why are you here?"

He grasped the back of a chair. After riding nonstop for three days, he felt almost seasick, his legs wobbly and weak. "I've been sent as a messenger."

"Let's get you some food and drink," Bourrienne said. "And clean you up. You don't want to report to the general looking like that."

The secretary brought him into a vast flagstoned kitchen and called for some bread, meat, and a glass of wine. Daniel gulped down his repast, desperate to dispatch his message and head back to Ancona. When he was finished, he asked, "Where can I clean up?"

"I'll take you to my quarters," Bourrienne said. "We'll arrange for your lodging later."

The general was relaxing with his family in a glassed-in sunroom just off the château's courtyard when Bourrienne brought Daniel to see him. Daniel was curious to see his wife face-to-face. Josephine had always provoked a good deal of gossip among the soldiers, not all of it savory.

But as she moved forward to greet him, he was struck by the sweet and gentle grace of her manner. Her dark curls clustered around her face, and her black eyes were large, expressive, and welcoming. She was slender, dressed in a white dress that fell from just under her chest in a column to the floor. A gold chain was clasped around her milky white throat, two pearl drop earrings dangling from her ears. She might have served as a model for a Roman goddess, Daniel thought.

She glided toward him, extending a hand out from a shawl of crimson. "Welcome, Sergeant," she said, her tones dulcet.

Not knowing what else to do, Daniel bent and kissed the back of her hand.

The general, who was listening to a young girl play a harp, turned sharply and glared, first at Daniel and then at his secretary. "What now, Bourrienne?" he demanded.

"Sergeant Isidore is here from—"

"Listen," Bonaparte snapped. "I need to dictate a letter to Barras."

The smile on Bourrienne's face faded. He slipped a small notepad from his breast pocket and opened it, ready for the general's direction.

"Director Barras. You've written me about the public's desire for peace," Bonaparte barked. "Said they weary of war and feel France is no longer endangered by outside forces. But you know how untrue that is. England alone . . ."

Perplexed, Daniel glanced from one man to the other. The last time he'd seen them together, they had acted more like equals than commander and subordinate. Something must have shifted in their relationship.

". . . that pirate nation, bent on ruling the waves, defrauding us of rightful colonies, blockading trade to assure our destruction, cannot be left to militate against us. Nor can we give in to the peacemongers who want us to surrender our due compensation, our reward for blood and glory."

Bonaparte was clearly in a foul humor.

"You chide me for offering the Austrians Venice so that France may keep Belgium. Are the rumors true that you were paid to protect the Venetian Republic's interests? Did you betray France to line your own pockets?"

Daniel fought hard to keep his expression neutral.

"Finally, you blame me for the complaints of rape and pillage coming from Verona. I would have you know I paid my soldiers a bonus of twenty-four livres to prevent just such looting. Surely you trust me more than those officials who encouraged the massacre of our citizens?" Bonaparte finished his dictation and, waving Bourrienne away, turned to Daniel. "What is it, Sergeant?"

Daniel straightened and saluted. "I'm sorry to disturb you, sir, but I bring urgent tidings from Ancona."

"From Ancona . . . Wait! Weren't you with me at the bridge at Lodi?" Bonaparte's face changed instantly from impatience to pleasure.

"I had that honor, sir," Daniel stammered. "You were—that was—"

"Hortense! Josephine! Pauline!" Bonaparte interrupted. "This soldier worked the artillery with me during that glorious battle! Josephine, I wrote you! I recognized my destiny that day. From that moment"—he rose and paced the sunroom, hands gripped behind him—"I saw what I might be. Already I felt the earth flee from beneath me, as if I were being carried into the sky."

Hortense, Josephine's daughter, giggled, then hid her face behind a fan. Josephine's eyes, however, seemed to glow brighter as she clapped her hands together.

"You were honored, indeed, Sergeant," she said, smiling upon Daniel.

Daniel felt light-headed. He didn't want to break the mood, but he knew he had to. Before he could speak, however, a captain burst into the room.

"News from Venice," he cried.

Bonaparte took the man by the arm. "Come tell me," he said, leading him away.

Josephine smiled sweetly at Daniel, who realized he was gaping. He closed his mouth.

"I'm so sorry, Sergeant. I'm sure he'll see you later," she said, waving him out.

Daniel backed hastily from the room, but not before he heard Bonaparte in an inner room growl and say, "Their delegation is coming to see me tomorrow. We'll see what they say then!"

Daniel wasn't allowed back into Bonaparte's presence until the next afternoon. As the morning progressed, he sat in the antechamber and watched as the great general received supplicants.

Bourrienne joined him for a quick word before disappearing into the drawing room. "It's like a royal court," he whispered. "And here I thought we'd disposed of the king."

Daniel didn't respond. After all, what could he say?

Daniel watched as the Austrian delegation was ushered inside, then representatives from the pope. A courier from General Moreau, bringing news about his advance into Austria, was ejected bodily from the room by a furious Bonaparte.

"I proposed this to Moreau and the Directory months ago!" Bonaparte raged, following the frightened man into the hallway. "They're jealous! Frightened of my ambition! So this is how they treat me—denying my counsel and advancing behind my back, long after it does me any good!"

The antechamber door was left open when a delegation from Venice was admitted. They, too, endured rough treatment. Daniel winced as Bonaparte's shouts echoed through the hallway. "Your government is nothing less than treacherous! And those rascals shall pay for it. Your republic has had its day, and it's done. You hear me? Done!"

By the time Daniel was brought in, he felt sick to his stomach. Bonaparte sat at a small table with a midday meal before him. Josephine had entered through a back door and sat with him, though she wasn't eating.

"Sergeant," Bonaparte said brusquely, not looking up from the plate of roast chicken and beans he was wolfing down. "I'm sorry we were interrupted yesterday. The affairs of state . . ." He shook his head. "What news from Ancona?"

"I'm sorry to report, sir, that the portrait of the Madonna has been stolen," Daniel said, his words tumbling over one another in a rush.

Bonaparte's fork stopped midway to his mouth. "It has—what?"

As quickly and clearly as he could, glad he'd had three days' ride to practice his speech, Daniel recounted Marotti's capture and death after almost inciting a riot—followed by the plot to burn the portrait if the French refused to leave Ancona.

The fork clattered to the table; chicken splattered the tablecloth. Bonaparte threw back his chair and rose, pacing the room, footsteps echoing on the marble.

"The portrait . . . has been *stolen?*" he bellowed.

Daniel could only nod dumbly.

"What portrait is this?" Josephine asked.

The general waved an impatient hand and kept striding up and down the room.

"What portrait?" Josephine asked again, turning to Daniel.

"It's a portrait of the Madonna, Citizeness Bonaparte—the—the miracle portrait. The one reported to have moved her eyes and wept."

"A miracle portrait . . ." Josephine breathed. She glanced at her husband.

Cold sweat ran down Daniel's back. Bonaparte was beet red, his eyes stormy.

"You will recover that portrait, Sergeant—you hear me?" Bonaparte barked.

Daniel straightened to attention. "Yes, sir! Of course, sir!" He turned to leave.

Josephine grasped his forearm, stopping him. "But Napoleon," she asked, not seeming a whit disturbed by her husband's rage, "what's one more portrait of Mary? Let them burn it!"

"Not this portrait," Bonaparte hissed.

"But why?" she persisted. "Because it is—what did the boy say? A miracle? Surely you don't . . ."

Daniel admired her courage. He quailed before Bonaparte's fury, as men of superior rank had done before him. But the general's wife remained cool, as though they were discussing books or roses or dinner.

"Why? You ask why?" Bonaparte waved a finger at her. "You, with your fortune-tellers and your tarot cards? This portrait . . ." His voice hushed. "It spoke to something within me. Do you understand?"

Josephine stood there calmly, playing with the ends of her shawl, waiting.

"She glared at me," Bonaparte said. "Until that moment, my destiny was clear—liberate Italy from the Austrians, make France's borders safe forever. But the Virgin *saw* me. She turned to me, turned her eyes . . . God's own mother . . ." The general shivered. "I do not question myself lightly, madame."

Josephine put a hand up, as if in surrender.

"I swore to protect the portrait," Bonaparte continued. "I gave orders to hold it safe, until I could understand the truth behind its portents. Now this soldier tells me it is in the hands of thugs, miscreants who would use it as a weapon, a Damocles sword suspended over my head. I will not permit it! It is an omen, I tell you, Josephine. When I consider the bad luck in Italy lately—the riots, the massacre of our soldiers . . ." His lips twisted. "I will have that portrait safe and the men involved executed!"

The general turned to Daniel, who had been standing motionless, wishing he were invisible. "What are you still doing here? Get back to Ancona and find it!"

# 49

# JUNE 10
# ANCONA

Christophe and Daniel were walking through the marketplace one morning when they ran into Dolce, a servant trailing behind her with an armful of packages. She told the servant to go home, then greeted Daniel with a melting smile and turned to Christophe. "I'm so glad to see you. Can you spare me a few moments? Daniel, do you mind?"

"Of course not—"

"Why, exactly?" Christophe asked. "I don't mean to be ungracious, but . . ."

Dolce surveyed him coolly. "We haven't talked since Mirelle and her mother came to visit. Trust me, this won't be a waste of your time."

Daniel bowed. "I'll take my leave."

Dolce watched him go. "He's not in favor of your suit, is he?" Her mouth twitched in amusement.

"No one is," Christophe said, eyes on the pavement. "Not even Mirelle."

"Don't say that," Dolce said. "Come, let's walk to the harbor."

As they made their way through the market stalls, Dolce mentioned that Mirelle was paying an early-morning visit to Abrianna Narducci.

"She's been banned from the workshop itself," she said, "so she visits Signora Narducci daily instead." Briefly, Dolce explained the situation with Turko, how much the men were suffering under his iron rule, and how Mirelle's aunt had already left Ancona for Rome, putting the sale of the family home into the hands of a local agent.

"Mira and her mother weren't even allowed to take furniture from the house," Dolce concluded. "It's breaking their hearts."

"Couldn't they buy the house back?"

"With what money?"

For a moment, Christophe wished he'd been less heedless with his pay. He pictured himself buying the property, being lauded as a hero when he presented the deed to Mirelle's mother, who would instantly approve their wedding as a result. But even had he been as frugal as Daniel—who sent most of his meager salary home to his parents—it would never have been enough.

"Your father could do it," he said.

"He could if he chose to," Dolce agreed.

Christophe breathed in the fresh salt smell of the harbor. The troops drilled alongside the bay. Seagulls flew above them, scavenging for food, arguing with wild cries. On the docks, men unloaded cargo from one ship and prepared another to sail. People sat drinking coffee at the cafés on the side of the water.

"It's so peaceful," Christophe said. "I can hardly believe that my company is probably fighting somewhere right now."

"It must be hard for you, stationed here." Dolce put a hand on his arm.

"I thought it would be wonderful. Time to be with Mirelle. But now she refuses to see me. Listen, signorina, I enjoy your company, but is there a point to this walk? When I told you your father had won, you said to trust you. Was that a mistake?"

Dolce squeezed his arm. "Not at all. My father remains on his best behavior—I've heard no talk of marriage since Mirelle came to stay." She looked around. "Let's sit in that café. You can buy me a coffee."

They settled in seats overlooking the harbor. A waiter took their order: coffee and pastry for them both.

"Signora d'Ancona has been helping me manage the household," Dolce said. "She's both very willing and very good at it. Better than I am."

"Oh, I doubt that, signorina."

Dolce waved a hand at his polite rejoinder. "I know my strengths and weaknesses. I'm an accomplished hostess, brought up in a political household." She thought for a moment. "Perhaps what first attracted Papa to Mirelle was how artless she is. We're very different, she and I. She means what she says. I don't always." Dolce looked at him under lowered eyelashes. "I shouldn't admit that, should I?"

"Say what you wish." Christophe was taken aback by her direct-ness. "It's not my place to judge you."

Dolce shrugged. "Anyway, I'm not a good housekeeper. Since Pinina took over many of my duties, the house runs like clockwork. And believe me, Papa notices."

"What are you saying?" Christophe asked, watching the waiter return with their coffee and almond pastries. "That he's falling in love with Mirelle's mother because she's a good housekeeper? That's ridiculous. If he marries Mirelle, he'll get the best of both worlds: a lovely young wife to bed and a fond mother-in-law to manage his household."

Dolce nodded. "Perhaps. But if Mirelle agreed to marry you, her mother wouldn't be left bereft. My father might not marry Pinina—but I'd convince him to keep her as housekeeper. After all, I'll proba-bly wed myself within the year."

"Will you?" Christophe grinned at her. Daniel was a lucky

bastard—if he could be brought to understand his luck. "Who's the fortunate man?"

Dolce's deep blue eyes seemed to laugh back at him. "Time will tell."

# 50

# JUNE 12

Mirelle dragged herself into the Morpurgo mansion with slow footsteps. The news from the manufactory was bad, had been bad for days. Yet whenever she tried to confide in her mother, Pinina merely shrugged and turned away.

"There's nothing we can do," Mama said. "Don't upset yourself."

Mirelle was pleased her mother was managing her grief. But she didn't understand how she could ignore the terrible plight of the workers, men who had put food on their table and clothes on their backs for so many years. She tried to think of a way to free Papa's workers from the nightmare of Turko. He made them work inhuman hours, flayed the skin from their backs when they disobeyed, and took bread out of their families' mouths with fines. When the men protested at the city council or appealed to Rabbi Fano, they were stymied by one irrefutable fact: Their articles of employment tied them to the manufactory for five, ten, fifteen years to come. Not one of them could afford the sum it would take to set them free.

"I can't bear to look at Sabato when he comes home at night," Abrianna Narducci had moaned to Mirelle just that morning. "He's a broken man."

Mirelle felt the pinch of her own poverty acutely. She was imposing on her best friend's hospitality because she had no place else to go. And now her birthday was just a week away. *What am I waiting for?* she thought, untying her bonnet strings. *Why do I pretend I've any sort of choice?*

"Mirelle." David stood in the hallway. "You look tired, child."

"Just a headache." She touched her forehead. "I'm going to lie down."

"Before you do, if you're well enough, would you come with me into my library?" David asked. "I want to ask you something."

Could he possibly want her answer now? As a guest in the man's home, she couldn't say no. "Certainly," she said dully.

David took her arm and ushered her down the hall to the library, a room lined with bookshelves that reached the ceiling. He led her to a corner where red velvet chairs were arranged around a low ivory-inlaid table. She sat, hands lying in her lap, waiting.

He seated himself across from her. "It's a week until your birthday," he said. "I've been patient, respectful of your wish and your mourning. But I want to have a suitable betrothal present ready for the day you say yes."

"A betrothal present?" Mirelle was surprised. "Surely—"

"Just listen," he said, leaning forward. She smelled tobacco and coffee rising off his coat. "I can't afford both gifts I'm considering. So you'll need to choose between them."

Mirelle's heart began to pound. What could be so expensive?

"My first thought," he said, "was to buy your old home for you and your mother. I'm informed that Prudenzia's agent still hasn't found a buyer. Of course, your mother would be the only one living there, since you would soon grace my home. But I know how much it would mean to you both, for your mother to live in her own house again."

"My God." Mirelle found it hard to breathe.

David put up a hand. "The second gift is even more expensive. In truth, there'd be some financial maneuvering necessary. It would take several years to pay off—and you would have to help me do so."

Mirelle stared at him. She had no idea what he was talking about. The house she could understand. But what could he offer her that she could help pay for? How in the world did he expect her to do that? If they wed—*when* they wed—she would be nothing more than a penniless bride. Before he died, her father would have dowered her generously. But because everything had been tied up in the entail, she had been left without a scudo.

He smiled at her. "I know how much you care about your father's legacy, of the welfare of the men at the ketubah workshop. How you spend every day inquiring after their well-being and despairing at their current condition."

Mirelle hung her head. "I only wish I could help. The men—it's terrible what they're going through. If only . . ."

David patted her hand. Mirelle looked up, tears in her eyes. She hadn't expected sympathy, not when no one else understood or cared. She let the tears drop down her cheeks, not bothering to hide them. She hunted in her reticule for a handkerchief.

"My second idea—which I suspect you'll accept—is to buy out the workers' articles. All of them."

Mirelle felt herself turned to stone. She stared at him, unbelieving.

"I'll create a new manufactory," he continued. "One we'll entail upon our firstborn son. We'll put Narducci in charge as manager and head scribe. I've consulted with the rabbi, and so long as you are owner in name only, you won't contravene Jewish law. I only wish your father had taken this step rather than blindly trusting that a woman could not inherit . . . but it's worthless to repine. You'll pay me back from the profits over the next several years. In the end, we could both end up richer as a result."

He smiled and leaned back in his seat, watching her.

"You can't mean it," she finally whispered, light-headed.

"I do mean it," he replied. "Am I right? Is this the gift you want?"

She forced air into her lungs, felt her breath expand beneath her heart. She exhaled slowly. "This will beggar you," she said. "Even you can't be that rich."

"It will stretch me"—he nodded—"but I am that rich, sweetling. And I want to give you everything your heart desires."

She took a deep breath, but he put up a hand to stop her from speaking. "But there is one condition, Mirelle. You will no longer work in the shop. As I explained to you once before: my betrothed wife will hold a certain position in society. She must turn all her attention to being a hostess to my guests, my wife—and, hopefully soon, the mother of my children." He studied her with a level gaze. "You must agree to this stipulation before you agree to marry me. And certainly before I expend my money in this way."

Mirelle sat back. For one heady moment she'd thought David's generosity meant everything—not only delivering the men from their tyrannical manager but also granting her the position she deserved, bestowing the legacy of her father's business upon her. But it was not to be. And she knew David Morpurgo well enough to recognize that she could not persuade him otherwise. He was not her gentle father. As kind as he'd always been, David was a hardheaded businessman. Once a bargain was struck between them, he would demand that she honor the terms.

But it still meant salvation for the workers. And that meant everything.

She reached out blindly, groping for his hands. She clutched them, dry and powdery beneath her fingers. She wanted to pull away. Instead, she leaned forward. "David Morpurgo," she whispered, "I will marry you."

# PART FOUR

## July–October 1797

# 51

# JULY 20

"They burned the Venice ghetto gates, just as we did here," Daniel told the Morpurgos, Mirelle, and her mother. "And in Padua, the general made the city fathers tear down the gates with their own hands. Bonaparte posted a declaration saying Jews could reside anywhere they wanted."

"I'd love to read that," Mirelle said, remembering what it was like to be locked behind Venice's gates. She knew Daniel understood what she was feeling, far more than Christophe ever could.

When Daniel's cheeks flushed, she felt an odd thump of her heart. *I'm betrothed to David*—she reminded herself—*and still in love with Christophe.*

He looked away, rustling in a pocket. "Here: 'First, the Hebrews are at liberty to live in any street they please.'" His voice echoed loudly in the small salon; he moderated it as he continued. "'Second, the barbarous and meaningless name of Ghetto, which designates the street they have been inhabiting hitherto, shall be substituted by that of Via Libera.'" He handed the paper to David Morpurgo.

"Wonderful," David said. "Will it be in tomorrow's papers?"

Daniel nodded.

"It's the beginning of a new era for us Jews." David's hands gestured grandly in the air. "To be free to conduct our lives like any other citizen." His chest expanded. "A new age, a new epoch—not only for us but for Jews throughout the world."

Mirelle's shoulders hunched as her fiancé pontificated. She hoped she would eventually grow used to his public persona, making speeches without provocation, a diplomat promising everything to everyone. She noticed Dolce nodding as her father spoke. Of course, she had years of practice as his dutiful daughter.

Mama interrupted Mirelle's reverie. "What a beautiful way of describing this miracle, David. Such stirring words!"

"Let's celebrate this glorious occasion," Dolce cried gaily. "I know— we'll throw a ball!"

"A ball!" David raised his eyebrows. "You'll beggar me, daughter!"

But of course, if Dolce wanted to throw a ball, a ball there would be.

As Mirelle and her mother entered the ballroom, the violinists were playing a waltz, the new German dance where couples embraced as they whirled about, scandalizing half the dowagers present. Glittering candlelight reflected off crystal chandeliers, flowers adorning the room.

"It's a wonderful night, isn't it, Mama?" David planned to announce their wedding date that evening. Mirelle wished she felt more pleasure at the idea. More emotion of any kind, instead of this empty longing.

"A wonderful night. You look like a dream." Mama slyly eyed Mirelle's exquisite gown, another gift from David.

Mirelle stepped carefully, unaccustomed to heels, onto the black-and-white parquet tiles of the ballroom, which was crowded with Jews and Gentiles, Italians and Frenchmen. An orchestra played on a raised platform in one corner. Mirelle had festooned the room with candles and flowers that morning, sprinkling the floral arrangements with water every hour so they wouldn't wilt.

Dolce sashayed into the room, her dress an unusual shade of tangerine, its long train sweeping the floor. Tawny lilies were caught in her blond curls and draped in the folds of her gown. Her neck and wrists shone with amber mixed with seed pearls. "Oh, a waltz!" she cried in delight, eyes twinkling. "I must find a partner immediately!"

"Allow me," said a tall blond soldier who appeared before her, bowing low. Dolce caught her train over her arm in a practiced gesture and stepped onto the dance floor. Christophe put an arm around her waist, pulled her close, and whisked her away.

Mirelle looked after them, blinking quickly. *He didn't even glance in my direction.*

"My dear, how lovely you look," David said. "May I invite you to the floor?"

To Mirelle's relief, Mama put out a hand. "Not to this," she protested. "I'm surprised you allowed the waltz to be played. And let Dolce dance it. It's shocking!"

David glanced at Mirelle's mother, annoyed and amused in equal measure. "Do you think I had a hand in ordering the music?" he asked her. "Pinina, you've lived with us long enough to know better."

"Dolce." Pinina sighed. "We must find her a suitable husband, don't you think? Before she does something foolish."

David laughed. "I wish you joy of the endeavor."

Mirelle was pleased at how fondly he looked at her mother. And Mama, arrayed in soft dove gray, a black cap set on her silver head, seemed almost happy.

"I'll have a word with the musicians and make sure this is the last waltz they play," David said. "For I won't be forestalled from dancing with my beautiful bride—and I hope you'll honor me as well, Pinina!" He strode off toward the musicians' platform.

A flush stole up Mama's neck.

"Why did you stop me?" Mirelle grumbled. "Everyone dances the waltz, unless they're dreadfully old-fashioned."

"I guess I must be, then," Mama retorted. "And stop tugging at your skirt, Mira. It's too sheer!"

Mirelle glanced down at her skirt, layer upon layer of the thinnest gauze. The dress, which cast a silver sheen in the candlelight, was probably the most expensive garment she had ever owned. But she felt trapped in it, its folds irritating her.

"I'm surprised not to see you on the floor." Daniel stood before her, bowing low. "Would you finish this dance with me?" He extended a gloved hand.

Quickly, so that Mama couldn't interfere a second time, Mirelle allowed him to lead her out. The warmth of his arm radiated through the layers of her skirt as he clasped her waist. She put her gloved hand in his and they began to whirl around the ballroom. Before long, Mirelle grew dizzy. She felt him pull her closer to him and nestled into his arms, hoping Christophe would notice.

Across the room, Christophe was complaining to Dolce. "Trust you, you said." He turned her so that his back was to Mirelle. "And now I can't even dance with her. Daniel is dancing so close, he's practically embracing her. And you tell me your father will announce their engagement tonight? What good has trusting you gotten me?"

Dolce grimaced. "I didn't expect him to win her heart by saving the ketubah workshop," she said. "He appealed to her sentiment over her father's legacy. Astute move."

"Astute move? Do you think this is a chess match? My life's at stake!"

Dolce's lips pursued. "You're being dramatic. Your life will go on if you don't marry Mirelle."

He glared at her. "And what of your idea that he'd fall in love with Mirelle's mother? What happened there?" His lips tightened. "I shouldn't have listened to you. Who would consider a poor widow when you could bed her beautiful daughter instead?"

Dolce's eyes flashed. "Careful, Sergeant. That's my father you're speaking of."

They moved down the ballroom. Just as they reached the orchestra stand, Dolce touched his sleeve. "Take a look at my father and Pinina and tell me I'm wrong."

Christophe turned so he could see them. Signora d'Ancona and Morpurgo were sitting close, heads nearly touching. Morpurgo wasn't even watching Mirelle. Instead, he was talking earnestly with his prospective mother-in-law, who nodded at him with a gentle smile.

"But what difference does it make?" Christophe said, whirling Dolce back around. "He's marrying Mirelle."

The waltz over, Mirelle started dutifully back to her mother. But before she could reach her, Dolce intercepted her and ushered her into an empty room set aside for card players.

"Enjoying yourself?" Dolce asked, studying her face.

"The evening has barely begun," Mirelle replied, plopping down in one of the gilt chairs. Her new shoes were already pinching her feet.

"You know that poor boy is in love with you, don't you? It's unkind to dance with him just to make Christophe jealous."

"Daniel? In love with me?" Mirelle shook her head. "You're joking."

Dolce's harsh laugh trilled in the empty room. "What is this power you have over men, Mirelle? Christophe, my father, now Daniel . . . Didn't you notice how closely he held you? Christophe certainly did."

"Daniel?" Mirelle paled. *Can it be true?* She thought back to the many times he'd taken her for walks, visited the family, helped her through the difficult days following her father's passing. But that was just because he was family. Wasn't it?

"You don't deny you wanted Christophe to notice. Don't worry. I won't tell Papa."

"And what if I did?" Mirelle asked, goaded. What game was Dolce playing? "I can't do anything about it. Isn't marrying your father what I've been brought up to do? Haven't I been told since childhood that I'm supposed to become a rich man's wife?"

"What about your heart?" Dolce leaned over the small table. "Don't you see you're trying to evade your fate? That you and Christophe were destined to meet and fall in love?"

Mirelle stared at her friend, eyes narrowed, distrustful.

"I admit," Dolce continued, "the apple doesn't fall far from the tree. You talk about sacrificing love for duty—while your mother does the same."

"Mama is what?"

"Yes: Mama. So clearly falling in love with my father. Don't you see it? And she might let herself—if it weren't for you."

Mirelle rose, indignant. "My mother adored my father. He's only been buried three months."

Dolce laughed. "Do something for me. Watch them when they don't know you're looking. Then tell me I'm wrong."

Mirelle shook her head. "David's announcing the wedding date tonight. The last day of October, right after the High Holy days. None of us can change that, Dolce. It's too late."

"What are you talking about?" Daniel burst out, astonished. He stood in the tiny courtyard under the stars, where Christophe had led him after Mirelle disappeared with Dolce.

"Don't think I haven't seen you mooning over her!" Christophe flared. "And then to dance with her like that."

"You're crazy! She's my cousin!"

"Not that close a cousin, though, is she? Her grandfather and yours are cousins—what does that make you?"

"I don't know and I don't care! Honestly, Christophe." Daniel shook his head. "You've gone mad."

"Have I?"

"Besides, it makes no difference who dances with her. She's marrying Morpurgo."

Christophe took three wild strides and found himself hemmed in by the garden wall. "If they're so rich, why is this garden so damned small?" he raged.

"This is still the ghetto, you fool. Morpurgo used up most of his land for the house."

Christophe groaned. "Why did I even come this evening?"

"Don't ask me. Because Dolce bade you?"

"Dolce!" Christophe's hands balled into fists. "She's treating this like a game. I'm done listening to her."

"Good! And stop thinking about Mirelle. Even if she were free, she would never marry you. You know that." Despite the shadowy gloom of the garden, Daniel saw Christophe's face darken, but he persisted. "Her religion still matters to her. Her brother died because he was Jewish. Her father too. How could a Christian win her heart?"

"I know she loves me. She just needs to be reminded of it."

"Reminded of it? How?"

But Christophe was already striding toward the ballroom. Daniel stood in the blue twilight, watching him go.

When Mirelle reentered the room, the musicians were resting as David stood on their platform, addressing his guests. She lingered next to one of the three-quarter windows open to the night breeze, enjoying the soft draft, as she listened to her betrothed's speech.

"General Bonaparte's dismantling of Venice's ghetto—the first ghetto ever established—is a milestone for Jews the world over," he said, hands clasped behind his back in the manner of a French officer. "Some history for our Christian friends: in the 1500s, the rulers of that noble city-state decided to isolate its Jews to a cramped and dirty island, the site of a foundry—*il ghetto*—which gave the ghetto its name. Surrounded by water, secured by heavy gates manned by Christian guards, Venice's Jews were forced to move to the island and were henceforth imprisoned there after nightfall." He scanned the faces of his guests. "The ghetto assuaged Gentile fears that Jews would contaminate their population. They allowed the Jews in the city during the day to transact trade, but banished them after sunset to miserable, crowded streets. Soon, other ghettos sprang up all over Italy—we're standing in the remnants of one right now—as well as throughout Europe. We Jews were also forced to wear distinctive hats and badges, so there could be no mistaking what we were when we walked among Gentiles."

Mirelle looked around. Fans hid the reactions of the Gentile women. Many of the men looked at the floor or up at the ornate mural on the ceiling.

"But General Bonaparte changed all that. His Hebrew nickname, Helek Tov, is a playful Hebrew adaption of his French name—a good part. His actions throughout Italy have—"

Someone suddenly took hold of Mirelle's wrist and pulled her backward, behind the long silk curtains. Before she could cry out, she was trapped by a strong pair of encircling arms. Any shout that might have issued from her lips was muffled by a firm mouth covering hers.

*Christophe*, she realized, a thrill pulsating through her body. *Is this really happening?* For a moment she tried to pull away, but the teasing thought that this memory would have to last her lifetime permitted her to melt into his embrace. Her knees turned to water, and her arms wrapped about his neck. Her lips trembled under his. They clung together, and desire surged through her. She molded herself to him, felt his body respond to hers.

And then, it was over. He released her just as she heard the muffled clapping of gloved hands, followed by David saying, "But this is not the only reason we have to celebrate," he announced. "At an earlier event held in this very room, I proposed to the most beautiful Jewess in all of Europe. She recently accepted me, and—Mirelle, where are you?—tonight we announce not only our betrothal but also our wedding date."

Mirelle leaned against Christophe's broad chest, unable to move, scarcely breathing. She didn't dare step out from behind the curtains. *Dear Lord, the scandal!* She raised her head, a plea for help written plainly across her face. Christophe reached behind her and threw up the window so she could climb out. She reached down for her skirts, blushing as she raised them high enough to clear the sash. His eyes flickered involuntarily over her exposed calves. She clambered over the window frame and stumbled into the narrow path that encircled the house. Her delicately layered skirt caught on the thorns of a rose bush and ripped, and she—tripped up by her new heels—landed on the ground. She snatched them off her feet and ran shoeless, ruining her silk stockings, toward the servants' door at the back of the house.

Luckily, no one was there; the servants were all either in the ballroom or the kitchen. Using the back stairs, she fled to her room. There, with shaking hands, she lit a single candle on her dressing table. By its dim light, she looked at the damage to her dress and stockings and peered at her flushed face in the mirror.

She heard footsteps coming up the stairs. Panting, she stared at her eyes in the mirror. *What can I say to them? What lie will they believe?* Her mind was a blank. She turned to face the door. A knock would mean it was Dolce or David. Her mother would walk right in. She stood there, paralyzed, waiting.

# 52

# AUGUST 30

It had been a month since Mirelle and Christophe first kissed at the ball.

Since then, she'd felt like she was living on a cloud, fully alive only when they met. She frequently stole out—for a walk, to visit a friend, to buy a skein of thread—and met Christophe in the woods. Twice she even let him sneak her into the French barracks when they were empty.

The liberties she permitted shocked her. Every day they went just that much further. Eventually, he would pull back, or she would. But the attraction between them was uncontrollable. He rained kisses on her mouth, her neck, her throat, the tops of her breasts. She stroked his close-cropped hair, moved her hand down his neck to nestle it in his lawn shirt, rested her palm against the hard muscles of his chest. His hands ran over her body, moving closer and closer to the furnace that resided in her lower belly. Her fingers were drawn irresistibly to his breeches, and she felt *him* through the heavy cloth. As she swooned under his fingers, his mouth, he unfastened one more button on her shirtwaist, reached a little farther under her skirts.

When she left him, she felt sick to her stomach—riddled with shame. But she was helpless at the thought of him. Sitting in the late summer garden or wilting in the heat in Dolce's blue salon, her limbs would turn languid, her pulse race. She replayed their encounters endlessly, resting a hand on her chest to slow her rapid heartbeat. *He* must *be my soul mate*, she told herself. *How could I feel this way otherwise?*

Dolce had been her confidante since the night of the ball when she, thank goodness, opened Mirelle's door. Dolce had helped devise the necessary lies, telling their worried parents that Mirelle's heel had broken and she'd taken a bad spill. The exquisite gown was declared beyond repair, but Mirelle wouldn't dispose of it. David smiled when he heard that, and Mirelle could only suppose that he thought it was out of affection for his gift.

Mirelle realized that Dolce was only helping her to prevent her marriage to David, but her friend never said so out loud, or asked Mirelle to break off her engagement—which confused Mirelle. She wouldn't blame Dolce for making such a demand; after all, it was the honorable thing to do, the thing God, with His strictures against wantonness, would demand of her. And Mirelle would have if she weren't worried about two things: Mama and the ketubah workers. The thought of betraying either made her stomach churn. *If I marry David, I can save them both*, she told herself. *I'll keep Christophe a secret.* A secret to look back upon fondly once she fulfilled her duty to her family.

Christophe didn't want to hear about her duty. He pressed her to run away with him. "Let's go to the Cisalpine Republic," he said as they sat in the woods, referring to the republic Bonaparte had established in Northern Italy. "They allow civil wedding ceremonies there. It wouldn't take long to travel to Bologna. Less than a day by horseback."

Mirelle bit her lip. "I can't do that to my mother. Or to David. I'm promised to him."

Christophe's eyes turned stormy. "How can you consider marrying him, when it's me you love?"

"I have to." Tears choked her throat. "I agreed to marry David. Please understand."

Christophe reared back, fuming. "Understand?" He jumped up, standing over her, his hands clenched at his sides. "You ask too much of me." In one swift motion, he hauled her to her feet, pulled her to him, and kissed her with a fierceness that seemed to brand her very soul. Then, just as wildly, he thrust her backward so she stumbled and almost fell.

"Do you really think I'll let you marry him?" he demanded.

She reached back blindly and, finding a tree trunk, straightened herself with a hand that trembled. "Would you force me?" she asked, suddenly furious.

"You know I won't."

"Well, then—"

But he didn't let her finish speaking. Instead, he seized her to him once more and kissed her passionately. When he finally broke off the caress, he held her at arm's length, his eyes searching her face. "You'll come to me of your own free will. Because you love me. Deep down, you know it's true. We're meant to be together."

Dolce encouraged their rendezvous, even when Mirelle wished she wouldn't. She knew what her friend wanted—for Christophe to carry her off and free David. Mirelle knew she shouldn't confide in her, but she ached to share her wild, uncontrolled feelings with someone who wouldn't condemn her. Dolce was her only real choice.

"You go along," she told Mirelle one afternoon as she stood before her, twisting her fan.

"Why don't you come, too?" The company would shield Mirelle from the danger of yielding, once and for all, to her desires.

"Nonsense. If I came, who would distract your mother and my father?" Dolce gave a conspiratorial laugh. "Go on now, Mira. Your swain awaits."

Mirelle let herself out of the house, stepping into the sultry summer sunlight. A breeze blew off the water and caught her bonnet. To her dismay, it flew clear off her head and skipped along the wooden dock. Hampered by her narrow skirt, she hobbled to catch it. It was nearly in the water when a hand reached out and grabbed it.

"Yours, I believe, cousin?" Daniel asked, handing it to her with a bow.

"Daniel!" Mirelle could hardly contain her delight. "How long has it been?"

"Since the ball, I believe."

"Thank you." She shook out the bonnet, readjusted the ribbons, and tied them tightly under her chin. "Where are you going?"

Daniel's shoulders slumped. "I've been helping with the search for the miraculous portrait. No luck yet, I'm afraid."

"Is that why you haven't been to see us?"

Daniel nodded, looking away from her and toward the harbor.

Mirelle wondered: Had Christophe told her cousin about their meetings? She bit her lip. If Christophe had even hinted, what must Daniel think of her?

"Why are you helping with the search?" she asked, striving for a normal tone of voice. "What do you care if the painting is recovered or not?"

Daniel shifted from one foot to the other. "The general has ordered it recovered. If it isn't—I fear for Signora Marotti and her children."

"But he wouldn't . . . ?" Mirelle looked into Daniel's face, reading the truth there. "Is your general that ruthless?"

"Bonaparte?" Daniel asked. "Once, during an insurrection in Paris, he fired grapeshot into a crowd of Royalists. Live ammunition on French men, women, and children. No one else would have dared. He's a general, Mirelle. A strategist. He does what he must to ensure victory."

"And you admire that?"

Daniel glanced at her. "It is the mark of a great man, and perhaps one reason I could never hope to be one. Yes, I admire it. But I don't think I could emulate it."

"There are other ways to become great," Mirelle said, patting his arm. "Helping a woman whose husband has done you harm, for instance."

Daniel shrugged. "It's not her fault she married a villain."

"Still . . ."

"I plan to go there tomorrow—to convince her to help us find the portrait. Perhaps you could come and translate for me. She told me you brought Barbara home. She might listen to you." He laughed, wryly. "I could use the help."

Mirelle didn't want to see Marotti's widow ever again, but Daniel looked at her with so much hope that she couldn't deny him. "All right."

They fell into a companionable silence. Mirelle still wondered how much he knew about her and Christophe. As they walked past the French army barracks, Christophe emerged from the building.

"There you are!" he said, taking her arm. "I wondered if you were coming today."

Mirelle felt the flush sweep through her entire body. Glancing at Daniel, she saw he, too, had turned bright red.

"Daniel, you can hand her over to me now," Christophe said gaily, not seeming to detect the embarrassment the other two felt.

Without a word, Daniel bowed to Mirelle and walked swiftly away in the opposite direction.

"What's the matter with him?" Christophe asked, sounding amused. "He's turned strange lately. I know he disapproves of us, but—"

"Disapproves of what? What have you told him?" Mirelle asked, pulling her arm out of his.

He looked at her, eyebrows raised. "He's been a friend of mine since we were nine years old. Of course, I've told him I hope to marry you."

"And what we do together? Have you told him that, too?" Wanting to sink into the ground, Mirelle could barely voice the question.

"What kind of cad do you take me for?" Christophe exclaimed. Then he thought for a moment and chuckled. "Of course, he knows of my luck with the ladies. Perhaps he speculates."

"And you enjoy it!" Mirelle flared. "Why do I allow you . . . What's wrong with me?"

Christophe blinked in surprise. "Mirelle, my love, you're over-wrought. There's nothing to be ashamed of."

"I am ashamed," she whispered. "What we're doing is wrong."

Christophe took her arm, pulled her into a shadowed corner of the barracks, and gathered her in his arms. He cupped her chin and covered her mouth with his. All resistance ebbed from her; her body grew slack. He lowered his lips onto her neck, kissing the nape, then moving to her shoulder. She felt his heat through the thin fabric of her dress and shivered.

"Are you still ashamed?" he murmured in her ear. "Is it still wrong?"

"Yes," she whispered, her voice husky. "I am. It is."

But as he began to pull away, she put up her arms to hold him fast.

# 53

# AUGUST 31

Francesca was cleaning the morning dishes when a pounding at the door startled her. Tentatively, she creaked it open. A contingent of French soldiers stood there, with Daniel at their head, Mirelle at his side.

"I brought my cousin along to translate for me, Signora Marotti," Daniel told Francesca. "We need to search the house. *Permesso?* May we come in?"

Francesca bit her tongue. Could she refuse him? Mario was crawling at her feet. She reached down and picked him up.

"He's gotten big," Daniel said.

She backed away to let the soldiers inside. Barbara was God knew where. She hoped the child wouldn't return before she'd had a chance to return everything to order. She knew from past searches what chaos the soldiers would leave in their wake.

Daniel chucked the baby at his throat, making him laugh. "He's sweet," he said. "Listen, signora, I must ask you some questions."

She stuck up her chin. "I've told you, I know nothing about the portrait. Yet still you plague me, frighten my children. What more do you want from me?"

Daniel looked toward Mirelle, who spoke to him in French. *Why did he bring her along?* His Italian was perfectly passable.

"I asked to lead this detail," he replied. "They want to bring you in for questioning, signora, put you behind bars. I told them you'd answer me."

"Why should I?" She spat the words, tasting bile. "You French have ruined my family's life. I'd rather talk to anyone but you."

His lips thinned. "The general orders us to find that painting if we have to turn the entire city upside down. If the soldiers think you know anything, they'll throw you in chains. Whip you. Starve you. But you can tell me what you know, and I'll protect you."

Behind them, one of the soldiers overturned a kitchen cabinet, sending the wood crashing to the floor, dishes smashing. The baby wailed in Francesca's arms. She and Mirelle both flinched. Daniel reached out and touched her elbow; she pulled away.

"Take me in, then," she said, eyes blazing with scorn. "Torture me. What do I care? I've nothing left to live for anymore."

Daniel stared at her, wide-eyed. "That's not true," he whispered.

"Isn't it?" She heard the hysteria rising in her voice. "My husband is dead. His cousins are holding the portrait hostage—the Lord only knows where. My daughter runs around like a hoyden and hates me. When I pray for solace, the Lady remains silent, indifferent. I'm all alone and you—" Her voice broke, and a torrent of weeping flooded out from the deepest part of her. The baby, who had been whimpering since the crash of furniture, turned red and started screaming.

Daniel stood as if turned to stone. Mirelle stared, openmouthed, silent.

Finally, Daniel reached for the child. "I'll take him," he said, speaking loudly over her sobs. "Let me get you something to drink."

She clutched the baby to her for a moment, wondering if she could trust him, but gave in and placed Mario in his arms. The boy screeched even louder, reaching out plump arms past Daniel's shoulders for his mother as he carried him away. She collapsed on the step and leaned against the doorjamb, hiccupping as she tried to stop crying. Behind her, the soldiers, seemingly indifferent to her anguish, continued to tear her house apart.

Mirelle sat beside her and placed a hand on her knee. Another crash made the Jewess's shoulders shoot up around her neck. "Is it like this every time they search?"

Francesca whisked her tears away with the back of her hand. "Yes."

The two women sat silent for a moment, then Mirelle spoke again. "I'm sorry. If you truly have no idea where the portrait is . . ."

"I don't," Francesca said shortly. "I've said it a hundred times. I say it again and again, and it makes no difference."

"But your family took it, didn't they?"

"My husband's family, not me. What they threaten to do is a sin."

"Then why not help us find it?"

Francesca almost wanted to laugh. How innocent she was!

Daniel returned with a cup of water. The baby sucked on a spoon, dribbling honey on her floor. His little face was still beet red, but at least he'd stopped wailing.

Francesca took the glass and tried to drink it, but her throat had closed. She returned it to Daniel, shaking her head.

"Francesca," he said. "Listen to me." He sat beside her and put the baby on the stone step just outside the door. Mirelle moved aside to give him room. Mario grabbed hold of his mother's foot, smearing it with his honeyed spoon, then abandoned both to toddle off into the yard.

"Listen," Daniel repeated.

She stared at him.

"You must help us."

She plucked the sticky spoon from her foot and threw it carelessly into the grass. "I don't know where the portrait is. And how could I tell you if I did? Betray my people?"

"No one has to know." Daniel touched her gently on the arm. "But it would be over. Don't you want this to be over?"

"Devil," she whispered, staring at him. "Satan, get thee behind me."

Daniel shook his head. "We're not the devil. Your miracle painting is in danger. All we need is a clue. Because the alternative . . ."

"The alternative?" Francesca kept her eyes on his face.

"The general has sent new orders. If we don't find the painting in three days, we are to begin executing the suspects. Starting with Emilio's cousins, whom we've already incarcerated."

Francesca slumped against the doorframe. She thought of Desi—how he loved a girl in a fishing village near Ancona, planned to marry her once he'd saved up enough money. Of Roberto, who still hadn't enough hair on his face to be considered a man, and who'd always been the kindest of Emilio's cousins, despite the anger he now carried as though it were a living thing. Both with lives yet unlived.

"This portrait," Francesca said, sitting up. "To us, it's a miracle. Why does your general care so much about it?"

Mirelle shifted closer. "You cannot tell anyone. He told me this in confidence." She took a breath. "He said . . . the portrait glared at him."

Daniel started. "You knew that?"

Mirelle glanced at him, equally surprised. "He told me the night of Dolce's salon—but swore me to secrecy."

Francesca shook her head. "So what? The Lady smiled at me. She wept. Hundreds of the faithful and unfaithful witnessed the miracle."

"A glare is different," Daniel said. "Bonaparte is a great man, to be sure, but a superstitious one. Not unlike yourself, signora. When I told him it had been stolen, his wife asked the same question you just asked. He told her that the portrait rattled him—shook him to his core. Forced him to question his destiny. And for a man like Bonaparte, destiny is everything." Daniel looked at the clouds scuttling overhead. "Until he can unravel its portents, he wants the portrait safe and under guard. And he will do anything to get it back."

"Anything? Kill people?"

"He's a soldier, signora. He's used to killing to get what he wants." Daniel lowered his voice. "You'll be executed, your children left motherless *and* fatherless. You can't want that."

*The children.* Francesca shut her eyes, then stood with an effort, gripping the doorjamb so she wouldn't fall. She watched Mario playing in the dirt of the kitchen garden, wondered again where Barbara might be. *My first duty is to these children.* Another crash echoed through the small house.

"All right," she whispered. "I'll help you find it."

# 54

They'd stuck Roberto and Desi in the basement of the French barracks. When Francesca entered, her heart in her throat, Roberto stood next to the window of the cell, looking out at the shoes and boots of passersby. A dusty, warm breeze filtered through the bars.

Desi sat, looking desolate, on the single cot in the room. Francesca sat next to him and put her arms around him in a hug. He squeezed her shoulders, but Roberto ignored her and glared at Daniel, who stood by the open cell door.

"Why is *he* here?" Roberto grated.

"They won't let me see you alone." Francesca reached out her hands to him, but he ignored them.

"So they sent you with that Jewish bastard?" Roberto hissed. "The one who gunned your husband down in the street?"

"That wasn't Daniel," Francesca countered, "that was his friend." Even as she said the words, she regretted them.

"What difference does that make?" Desi spat. "He hunted him down, didn't he? He marched him like a criminal through the streets. Might as well have pulled the trigger himself."

Francesca threw Daniel a desperate look.

"I can send in another guard if you want, Signora Marotti," he said impassively.

Father Candelabri slipped past Daniel and stood in the center of the cell, taking in the scene with careful eyes. Francesca had asked him along in hopes his presence would help.

"One French pig is as bad as the next," Desi sneered. "What difference does it make?"

"This one is a Jew as well as French," Roberto said, narrowing his eyes. "Emilio was right. We should have killed them all when we had the chance."

Daniel stiffened, and a chill chased up Francesca's spine.

"Roberto, what's gotten into you?" Father Candelabri admonished. "What are you saying?"

Roberto's lips thinned. "Emilio died because of them—the French and the Jews." He pointed at Francesca. "Why defend these pieces of filth?"

Francesca struggled to find the right response. "They're going to kill you," she finally said. "You know that, don't you?"

Desi spat on the sawdust-covered floor. "So we'll die as patriots. So what?"

But Francesca noticed how young Roberto froze at the thought of death. She pressed on. "They'll shoot you or hang you in the market square."

Roberto squared his shoulders, trying to seem brave, but Francesca saw through it.

"And then," she continued, "they'll kill me. And leave the children orphans."

"You?" Desi burst out. "But you had nothing—"

"Nothing to do with it. I know. But that doesn't matter. Bonaparte wants the portrait back and doesn't care who he has to kill to get it."

Francesca paused to let her words sink in.

"Is that true, Father?" Desi looked toward the priest, eyes wide and frightened.

"It's true," Father Candelabri said. "You have a choice, men. I pray you make the right one."

Silence weighed down the room. Daniel stood stock still, as if any movement could sway the two cousins.

Roberto glared at him. "Fuck the painting," he declared. "I'm dead whether I tell you or not."

"No. There's still a chance," Francesca urged him. "Daniel, tell him."

"Roberto," Father Candelabri said, "please. For Francesca's sake. For Emilio's innocent children. For the sake of your soul. Tell us where the painting is hidden."

"We're dead whether we tell you or not," Roberto repeated.

"What if you're not?" Daniel asked.

The two men stared at him.

"Do you think we're fools?" Desi snapped. "Hang us and be done with it."

"The entire city is in an uproar," Daniel said. "The general wants the situation resolved as quickly as possible: the portrait returned, and calm restored to Ancona. If he gets both, he's willing to concede your freedom. On one condition. You must leave Italy. Forever."

"Leave Italy?" Desi asked Daniel. "Never. Your general is a liar and this is a trap. Why would Bonaparte let us go?"

"Because the general saw the miracle of the blessed Madonna when he looked at it," Francesca murmured. "Because he knows how holy it is."

Roberto glared. "Bullshit. You betray your husband's memory by colluding with the enemy."

"I'm protecting my family," she responded hotly. "And protecting you as well, from sin and damnation. Tell them what they need to know and live." She swiveled toward Desi. "You must want to live! Think of all you have to live for!"

"Think of Francesca and the children," Father Candelabri added.

A moment of silence followed.

"I'll tell you," Desi said.

"Desi!" Roberto broke out, anger blistering in his eyes.

"You'll thank me someday," Desi said. He turned to Daniel. "Your word is good? You will not double-cross us on this?"

"You'll leave Italy forever?" Daniel asked.

Desi shut his eyes, then nodded. Roberto groaned loudly, turning his back on the room.

Daniel shivered as they descended the steep stone steps to the crypt. "I can't believe the portrait's been in the cathedral this entire time," he said.

"They were ingenious," said the priest. "We never would have thought to look here."

It was cold and dank, and somewhere water dripped into a bucket with a monotonous drip, drop, drip. Daniel shivered at the penetrating sound and turned toward Francesca, who'd insisted on coming. "Are you all right, signora?"

She shrugged, clearly still upset. Roberto had cursed them all as they left the cell. Once they found the portrait, Daniel would give orders for the two men to be put on a boat sailing for a port far from Ancona.

Francesca drew in a sharp breath. Daniel followed her gaze . . . and shuddered. In a glass coffin set deep in an archway decorated with a thick pediment of stone angels and ivy lay the remains of a saint.

"Saint Ciriaco," breathed Francesca, crossing herself and kneeling before the crypt.

Daniel couldn't believe what he saw. The skeleton was dressed in a rich, flower-embroidered tunic. On his head was a bishop's miter. Daniel swallowed hard, noticing the saint's feet, shorn with red plush slippers that turned upward, banded in gold. He looked away, attempting to conceal his scorn for the skeletal display.

The priest crossed himself and genuflected before the entombed saint. "A legend states Saint Ciriaco was originally Jewish and converted after he restored the True Cross to the Church," Candelabri said. "A martyr to Julian the Apostate." The priest paused. "It would be ironic, don't you think, Sergeant, if history repeated itself? You, a Jew, instrumental in recovering our prodigious painting—not unlike Ciriaco's restoration of the True Cross."

"I've no plans to convert, Father," Daniel said.

The priest smiled. "I'm sure Ciriaco had no intention to either, when he helped Helena, Constantine the Great's mother, find the Cross. And yet, here he lies, a sanctified saint in our pantheon of the faithful."

Daniel felt impatient. Staying any longer than necessary, surrounded by the damp walls of the underground cell and the strangely garbed skeleton, didn't appeal to him. "Desi said they stored the picture behind one of the urns."

"The urns are there." The priest extended an arm toward the ancient stone archways protecting them.

Daniel walked over to the bronze receptacles and reached down, feeling in the narrow space between the urns and the damp stone wall. "Ah!" He drew a tube of brass from behind one of the urns.

"Desi made that container," Francesca said, drawing near. "He didn't want the portrait damaged."

"Not unless they burned it," Daniel said dryly. He handed the tube to the priest. "You open it, Father."

"They wouldn't burn it." Francesca shook her head. "Desi is a good man underneath his bravado. And Roberto's a gentle soul."

"That's a gentle soul?" Daniel asked, incredulous.

Francesca sighed. "He was."

The priest opened the tube and slid the painting out. He carefully unrolled one edge. "It's the Madonna." His relief echoed through the ancient chamber. "Thanks be to Christ."

"Take charge of it, will you?" Daniel said. "The general wants it returned to the chapel it came from, kept covered. I'll assign a guard within the hour."

The priest nodded and turned to leave. Francesca started to mount the stairs behind him. Daniel looked about, staring for a moment at the glass tomb, feeling the cold of the ancient crypt creep into his own bones.

"Jesus, too, was a Jew," he muttered. "To think of all this superstition—relics, saints, miracle paintings—every bit of it created in his name." He turned toward the steps. "I think he'd be horrified—he and his mother, both." Sighing, he started up the narrow stairs, eager to reach the warmth of the late summer sunshine.

# 55

## SEPTEMBER 25

Mirelle couldn't keep her eyes open. It didn't matter if she'd slept a full night or had dozed off in her chair earlier that day, she craved sleep even more than food—despite being hungry most of the time. She found herself drowsing through the long day of prayers during Rosh Hashanah. She invented excuses not to go shopping with her mother, who, armed with David's purse, was busy accumulating Mirelle's trousseau. She told Dolce to take walks alone, then slipped between the covers of her bed and dreamed the afternoon away. Even when she met Christophe she spent most of their time together fighting slumber, once even falling asleep with her head deliciously perched in his lap.

Then she couldn't fasten the back buttons of her blouse. She called one of the maids to help her, but Nina couldn't stretch the fabric over her chest.

"Have you gained weight?" Nina asked as they searched for a less constricting shirtwaist.

"Maybe," Mirelle said ruefully. "I can't seem to stop eating these days."

The maid looked at her suspiciously. "You look bigger. Is your chest sore? Tender?" she asked, gesturing with open palms, as though hefting Mirelle's breasts.

"No," Mirelle answered, biting her lip. *Is it?* She wasn't sure.

A few minutes later, Dolce entered her room. Mirelle was standing in front of her mirror, looking at herself sideways.

"Nina said you couldn't button your blouse," Dolce said. "Are you feeling all right?"

"I'm fine," Mirelle said. "The food here is just too delicious."

Dolce pursed her lips. "Let's go for a walk."

Mirelle sank back onto her dressing chair, almost woozy with weariness. "Oh, no, Dolce. I don't want to."

Dolce tilted her head, thinking. Then she brought another chair over to the dressing table and took Mirelle's hands in hers. "This is important," she said. "When did you have your last—visitor? Your courses?"

"When . . ." Suddenly, Mirelle realized what her friend was asking. Her mind went blank as she tried to recall. She, who had always kept a mental count of her courses, couldn't remember when she'd last had her monthly flow. The distractions of the last few weeks had overwhelmed her heretofore practical mind. Her hands grew icy as she withdrew them from Dolce's grasp and raised them to her cheeks. "My God," she said, stomach churning.

Dolce was still sitting close. The glint in her beautiful blue eyes made Mirelle suspicious.

She pushed her chair back. "You wanted this," she accused her friend.

"Seriously? You're blaming me?" Dolce's laugh was a bell-like tinkle. It made Mirelle wince. "I'm not the careless one."

A wave of mortification washed over Mirelle. Dolce was right. It wasn't her fault; it was Mirelle's. Her recklessness had ruined her life.

After Dolce left, Mirelle sat on the edge of her bed, frozen. Eyes closed, she thought back to the afternoon she had finally surrendered to him. Though, to be fair, she had been as eager as he. More eager, in fact.

It was only one time. They had lain on a bed of moss in the woods, caressing one another, growing more and more heated. She let him undo the buttons of her shirtwaist, reach into her chemise to softly cup her breasts. Her own hand, almost of its own accord, had reached down to feel his manhood through his trousers, straining toward her through the material. The buttons slipped easily out of the button-holes, and he sprang out to meet her questing fingers.

She nestled closer, their breaths mingling. His hand left her breasts.

"Oh," she moaned. "Don't move."

But he ignored her, snaking his hand down to the edge of her skirt, bunching it up as he followed the line of her leg upward. He folded the skirt over her stomach and reached inside her undergarments. She felt hot and slick as he slowly inserted his fingers inside her.

"I want you," she muttered into his neck, her hand gripping him, feeling him grow even harder as she caressed him. "Christophe, I want you."

"We have to stop," he panted, pulling away. "If you're going to remain a virgin, we have to stop. Or I won't be able to control myself."

*Now* he was acting like a gentleman, a man of honor? The thought spun crazily in her overheated mind. *Isn't this what he wants? What we both want?*

"No," she cried. "No, don't stop. Don't stop."

He moved away. "Mirelle. You must be sure. If we do this—there's no going back."

Mirelle reached for him again. "I need this. To remember you. To remember you always."

Christophe froze, eyes sparking in anger. "You mean—after you marry that old man? One afternoon of bliss in exchange for . . ."

It sounded awful. Mirelle reached out and kissed him anyway. "Please," she pleaded with him, her lips against his neck. "Please."

He remained still for a moment longer. "This isn't what I want," he told her. "I've had this: a dalliance with a willing wanton. I want you,

Mirelle—in my heart as well as in my bed. But not if you're going to leave me."

Mirelle sat up. She knew she should listen to him. But every vestige of common sense appeared to have fled. "You won't do this for me?" she pleaded. "You've been begging me to love you for weeks, now—and now you won't?"

"I've been begging you to run away with me," he said. "To love me, not sleep with me. There's a difference."

"I can't marry you. You know I can't. If you loved me enough—"

"I'd sleep with you—just once? You don't think much of me, do you?" His tones were harsh, his bitterness sharp as a blade.

She closed her eyes. How had this gone so badly wrong? "Christophe, I love you," she whispered. "If things were different, I'd fight to marry you. But I can't. You must see that."

He opened his mouth to speak, but her fingers flew to cover his lips.

"Listen," she said, "I've longed my entire life for someone to put me first. I'm asking you to do that for me. Every time I think of sleeping with David—as a virgin, a woman never truly touched by love . . ."

It was enough. Christophe pulled her into his arms. His mouth came down on hers, his hands cupped her body. Their moans mingled as he took her, whispering his adoration for her. When it was over, they lay intertwined, Mirelle weeping against his shoulder.

And now? What would he do now? Would he discard her, the way Mama said unworthy men did once they'd taken their pleasure?

A sudden chill rocked her as she considered Christophe as her life partner. All the reasons for her infatuation—his swagger, the glint in his eye—what kind of husband would that make him? This possible pregnancy was a cold splash of reality, waking her out of a dream.

He wanted her to be his wife and nothing more—to abandon her life in Ancona without a second thought, leave behind her religion, her promises to the dead, her father's legacy.

How foolish she'd been! Playing with fire, holding fast to the thought that she would eventually bid Christophe farewell and marry David. It was no one's fault but her own that she'd been scorched.

Later that afternoon, Christophe held Mirelle to him, trying to find words to comfort her. They sat in the same secluded spot where she had convinced him to take her virtue. He remembered how she had wept for a long time afterward, sheltering in his arms. Her tears hadn't alarmed him; even the lustiest of his bedfellows had sometimes wept in release.

Now she was sobbing again against his chest, and he felt both triumph and panic. She would marry him now, be his wife. They already had a family on the way.

But now that Christophe had what he'd longed for, he found his victory had a hollow ring to it. *What's wrong with me?* he wondered, pushing the desperation deep inside so he wouldn't alarm Mirelle. His conversation with Daniel, back when they first came to Ancona, flashed into his mind. *She's something you'll never have*, his friend had said. *You like the challenge more than the girl.*

Was it true? Had his avowed love for Mirelle simply been frustrated desire for a prize he never thought he'd win?

But then he remembered what he'd told Daniel during that same conversation: "I would never hurt her." He would keep his promise, no matter what it might cost him. He would make all the necessary arrangements, save her from recrimination. Send her home to Paris. But how would they convince someone to marry them? Or find money for her travel expenses? The army did owe him several months of back pay. He'd have to borrow against it.

It was a busy night, with news about an aborted coup d'etat in France taking up the bulk of the paper. As in so many other articles published in the two newspapers Daniel and Christophe printed, Bonaparte played a leading role. As he proofread the first page off the press, Christophe was momentarily distracted from his own troubles. Bonaparte's soldiers had captured the Royalist Comte d'Antraigues and brought him to the general in Milan. While interrogating him, Bonaparte had discovered a plot by some of the Directors to betray the Republic. Acting swiftly and heroically, Bonaparte had dispatched General Augereu to support those Directors who were still loyal. One of the traitorous Directors escaped, but the others and their conspirators had been exiled to Guyana.

Christophe made a few corrections to the copy, then approved the page. As he lifted his head, Daniel approached him.

"Something wrong?" his friend asked. "You seem distracted."

"I'll tell you later," Christophe said, relieved by the prospect of unburdening himself. Daniel was smart. He'd help figure all this out.

As he and Daniel walked together from the municipality toward the barracks, Christophe drew in a deep breath of sea air.

"Mirelle's pregnant."

The punch came from nowhere, a sharp blow to his chin, followed by another to his gut. He doubled over.

"What the hell?"

He straightened painfully. Daniel stood with raised fists, his jaw jutting out and teeth clenched. He moved in for another clout, but Christophe jumped out of the way.

Daniel swung again, this time connecting only with air. "I'll kill you!"

"Daniel—stop! I'm going to marry her, you fool!"

Daniel did not look appeased. "Not if I can help it, you won't."

When they were younger, Uncle Alain had taught them to wrestle and box so they could best the bullies from rival printshops. Christophe had won every tussle then. But he had never seen this murderous light in Daniel's eyes before.

He stepped back, out of reach of his friend's fists. "Stop," he protested. "I didn't mean for this to happen."

"How could you?" Daniel demanded, furious eyes pinned to Christophe's face. "She's my family—someone you should have respected." He narrowed the space between them and swung again, connecting with Christophe's nose. Blood rushed from it. Daniel slammed his entire body into Christophe's, knocking him backward, making him stumble and fall.

"You bastard." Daniel followed him to the ground, pummeling him with his fists. "You *salopard, salaud . . .*"

Christophe wrenched himself into a sitting position and butted his head against his friend's stomach, then grabbed him under the arms and about his neck. He twisted him to his back and scissored his leg between Daniel's, cradling him so his shoulders couldn't move.

"Listen to me," he panted, pulling Daniel tighter against him. "I'm going to marry her! And nothing you"—he tugged his arms again, slamming the back of Daniel's head against the ground—"or anyone else says will stop me." He battered his friend's head once more, and then, with a fluid motion, let go and jumped up and away, watching Daniel cautiously in case he didn't accept defeat.

But Daniel remained prone on the ground, breathing hard.

Christophe watched as his friend's eyes stared at the starry sky, as if searching for some kind of answer.

After a moment, a look of resignation crossed his face. Seeing it, Christophe kneeled beside his friend, keeping out of arm's reach.

"She's having my baby, and no, it's not what we wanted. But otherwise she'd have kept her promise to that old man. And I couldn't allow that."

"That *Jewish* old man," Daniel muttered, refusing to look at him. "Do you think she's going to be happy, marrying out of her faith? And you're a soldier. Where will she live once you're married? With Odette? Can you imagine what your mother will do to her?"

Christophe felt an uncertain qualm. "Mother will grow to love her. Can you imagine not loving Mirelle?"

Daniel's laugh was full of sour memories. "We're talking about *your mother*, Christophe. The woman who still thinks I'm the scum of the earth because I'm a Jew. And now you're going to send the poor girl home to her—and pregnant besides? Odette will explode."

"Alain will be there," Christophe said. "He'll protect her."

Daniel shut his eyes. "I'll marry her," he said slowly. "You know I care for her. I'll raise the child."

Christophe felt his hands balling into fists. He took a deep breath. "She doesn't love you. She loves me. We're getting married. It will all work out."

Daniel sat up, brushed himself off, and clambered to his feet. "For her sake, I hope so. But I think you're both making a huge mistake."

With that, Daniel turned on his heel and walked off into the darkness.

# 56

# SEPTEMBER 30

The long day of prayer during Yom Kippur was especially hard for Mirelle that year. Pregnant women were excused from fasting, but where did that leave her? *One day won't matter*, she told herself as she dressed that morning, already famished. *The baby can survive one day.*

The time would soon come when she could no longer conceal the truth. Better to break the news early, she thought, than have them discover it on their own. But Christophe had asked her to wait until he had made the necessary arrangements.

Was she sensing reluctance in him—the same reluctance she felt? Or was he just being practical? "I can't afford to pay for your lodgings, *and* a wedding, *and* your passage to Paris," he'd said. "And you can't stay in the barracks."

"But I don't want to go to Paris," she'd wailed. Once the idea had excited her. Now it just seemed frightening. "I want to stay with you, here in Ancona."

He held her to him, stroking her hair. "Darling, I won't be here forever. Besides, think what your life would be like. Your family and friends will shun you when they learn you've married a non-Jew and had his baby. You'll be friendless and alone."

"But to go to Paris without you!" She wept against his shirt, staining it with her tears.

"Uncle Alain will be there," he said. "I don't know what we would have done without him, after my father died at the Bastille. How we would have survived the Terror. You'll grow to love him like I do."

Mirelle noticed he didn't say anything about his mother. She wondered what living with her mother-in-law would be like. She suspected the worst.

"I'll request some leave," Christophe said soothingly. "Think how happy I'll be to come home and find you there!"

She'd smiled tearfully at him, thinking, *He's doing his best. I'll never tell him how I really feel.*

Christophe wasn't trying to delay the inevitable, she reassured herself now. He just wanted everything in order before they upturned everyone's lives. She had to trust him, rely on him. But her emotions were riding a runaway horse, terrifying and uncontrollable. She'd heard from young matrons in the ghetto that such feelings were natural when you were expecting, but simply knowing that didn't help. The effort of hiding her pregnancy from her mother, David, and the servants was exhausting. She'd already had to take Nina into her confidence. *Thank goodness for Dolce*, she thought, pinning up her hair. Her friend was cunning as a fox, capable of turning anything out of the ordinary into a jest.

Dolce agreed with Christophe about saying nothing until all the arrangements were finalized.

"Our parents are so happy, planning this wedding," she told Mirelle, combing her hair and braiding it one night before bed. "Let's give them a few more days of joy."

"But it's wrong to let all these arrangements go forward—expensive, too," Mirelle argued. "And what about the ketubah workshop? I can't just abandon the men."

Dolce shrugged off the expense. "Papa can afford it. And we'll sign over the workshop to your mother."

Mirelle's eyes widened. Why hadn't she thought of that?

"One of my father's clerks can draw up the papers." Dolce grinned as she concocted the plan. "I know just the one—Bartholomo. He'd do anything for me." She dimpled mischievously, then continued more thoughtfully, "Pinina will have a secure living. My father will help her run it. And I'll insist your mother stay here as housekeeper, besides."

"Do you think she will?" Mirelle wondered. "After all this?"

"Mira'la," Dolce said, sounding amused. "How could she say no? To me? Don't you know that when I want something, I find a way?"

Mirelle couldn't help a frown at that—a frown she quickly hid. She was grateful to Dolce for her help. But she was well aware that what Dolce really wanted was for Christophe to carry her off so her father couldn't marry her.

Later that morning, Mirelle sat in the women's balcony at synagogue, bitterly reflecting on her hypocrisy in being there at all. She put a hand on her rumbling stomach. At least in Paris she would have family. Daniel had stopped by during the days of Atonement, offering the traditional apology for anything he might have said or done to upset her during the year. When she offered him the same, his blush told her he knew her secret.

"It's all right," he murmured, moving out of her mother's earshot. "I understand."

"Did Christophe tell you?" she whispered, and hunched when he nodded. "Oh, Daniel."

"He says you'll live with his mother and uncle in Paris," he said. "It's difficult to be a Jew in France these days, to observe any religion openly. But you can always visit my parents in Le Marais. They're the kindest people on the face of the earth. They'll welcome you and . . ." His eyes flickered to her belly; she slid a surreptitious hand over it.

"At least for the holidays," he added. "Keep some of our traditions alive."

Remembering that, her prayer book seemed to scorch her hands. Where would she be next year? At a secret prayer service in Paris? Or, worse yet, absent from synagogue altogether?

The cantor began to intone the Al Chet—the list of sins one might have committed during the year for which one begged forgiveness. Mirelle followed along, mouthing the catalogue of iniquities with the other women, her conscience squirming within her.

*For the sin which we have committed before You with immorality,* she repeated, cringing. How everyone would condemn her, once they learned! *For the sin which we have committed before You by improper thoughts. For the sin which we have committed before You by a gathering of lewdness.*

She felt faint. It was hot in the synagogue, the crush of bodies pressed together stifling. At the first interlude in the Al Chet, she begged the Lord, "For all these, God of pardon, pardon us, forgive us, atone for us."

The list continued. Some of the sins Mirelle felt lightly, but others battered her like blows:

*For the sin which we have committed before You by a glance of the eye.*

*For the sin which we have committed before You by running to do evil.*

*For the sin which we have committed before You by a confused heart.*

Next to her, Dolce, dressed elegantly in black silk, recited along with ease, "For the sin which we have committed before You by scheming against a fellowman."

Mirelle glanced toward her friend. But Dolce never lifted an eyelash.

The long, doleful service wasn't even half over. Mirelle rose and crept through the crowded benches to the balcony railing for some air. Her body, constricted by a too-tight bodice and corset, made it hard to breathe.

As she looked down, a plume of sunlight lit the very spot where her father used to stand, wrapped in his prayer shawl, swaying back and forth to the cantor's melodies. Jacopo would stand next to him, dark curls threatening to dislodge his *kippa*, earnestly following along. Daniel stood in their stead, her father's tallit draped over his shoulders. Mama had given him the prayer shawl during the shiva. He looked lit from within, the sun dancing over his dark hair, illuminating his intent expression. His mouth moved together with those of the other men, eyes fixed upon the altar.

Mirelle wondered why her pulse was suddenly racing. She forced herself to turn away.

When she did, she nearly jumped at the sight of Dolce's piercing blue eyes narrowed upon her face.

"They sit today in their synagogue," Cardinal Ranuzzi cried from the pulpit, "wallowing in transgression, speaking of wrongs done this past year, praying for forgiveness. But they can never be forgiven for the worst sin of all. Christ died on the cross for our sins, and still they deny Him. They turn away, as did their people more than a thousand years ago, forsaking His love, nailing Him to the cross every day with bloodstained hands. How can the Lord God, Christ our Savior, or the Holy Ghost do anything but cast them into a hell of their own making? All of Mother Mary's tears cannot stop them from wandering the Earth, forever homeless, a foulness upon our city, a blot upon the holiness of Italy itself."

Francesca shifted uncomfortably in her seat, looking out from under lowered eyes at the rest of the congregation. The cardinal's description of the Jewish people didn't match what she knew of Daniel. But all around her, people in the pews were nodding.

"And the godless French marauders? They come to conquer, to spread their so-called Enlightenment, to blind our nation with false wonders. They've cast off Catholicism, beheaded their king and his family, executed their nobles, sentenced thousands to the merciless edge of the guillotine. They've dispatched their armies to empty our churches and cities of our precious religious objects, take our food, and rape our women." The cardinal's face was purple with fury.

"Is it any wonder that they have joined forces, these godless French and sinful Jews? That we have aldermen of Jewish blood sitting on our city council, contaminating our laws, grabbing greedily at everything they can pillage? Is it any wonder"—and here Cardinal Ranuzzi's eyes rested on Francesca's averted face—"that they have killed or banished the men of the Marotti family—not just Emilio but also Desi the blacksmith and gentle Roberto? For did these men not defy them, say that we must take arms against the Jews and the French, rid our country of their scourge?"

Everyone turned to stare at Francesca. She struggled to keep her face neutral. How dare the cardinal use her husband and his family for his own purposes? Hadn't he banished Emilio from the Catholic Fellowship, forcing him to act alone? Prayed publicly for the return of the painting, damning Emilio's cousins for endangering it?

"We must act," the cardinal bellowed, winding toward the close of his homily. "Honor the Marotti men, show these enemies that we will not tolerate their reign of blasphemy and sin. We cannot—will not—stand idle while such wrongs go unpunished!"

Suddenly, Francesca saw them—Roberto and Desi, sitting in

a pew in a dark corner behind the altar. Her heart thudded with sudden fear. Why were they back? What did the cardinal intend for them? Didn't anyone else see them?

Ranuzzi cast his eyes to heaven. Francesca knew he had won the hearts of everyone in the church. Everyone but her.

Father Candelabri stepped forward. *"Credo in unum Deum,"* he intoned as the congregation stood for the Apostle's Creed. Francesca kept her face closely guarded as heads bent and eyes closed.

# 57

## OCTOBER 15

When Christophe and Daniel entered the printshop at noontime, they were surprised to find Lucien Bourrienne waiting for them.

"We need to talk," said Bonaparte's secretary. "Dismiss your men for an hour."

While Daniel went to tell them, Christophe asked, "Is this about the letter I sent you? About my wedding?"

Bourrienne smiled. "No, Sergeant. But my news may help."

Christophe's eyebrows rose. Bourrienne turned toward the door, waiting for Daniel. Christophe heard the soldiers laughing and shouting, as if they were schoolboys released for an unexpected holiday. "Be back in an hour," Daniel called after them. A door slammed, and boots clattered up the stairway.

Daniel had barely reentered the room when Bourrienne started to speak. "I've several stops to make today and must be back in Campo Formio without fail in two days' time."

Christophe leaned against the tall table where they loaded the forms.

"This is confidential, men," Bourrienne continued. "Revealing what I'm about to tell you is a court-martial offense." He stopped for a moment. "To anyone. Even your fiancée, Sergeant Lefevre. Yes?" At Christophe's curt nod, he sat on one of the tall stools. "The army is leaving Italy. General Bonaparte, so victorious in war, has proven an adept peacemaker as well—despite the Directory's interference. In three days' time, we'll sign a treaty with the Austrians. We have won all we were fighting for—the Austrians admit our victory—so hostilities can cease. You two were on the front lines and have done much since to keep the peace here in Ancona. So, on behalf of General Bonaparte, I congratulate you both!"

Christophe grinned. Looking over, he noticed a similar smile lighting up Daniel's face.

"Now, you must—discreetly—prepare to leave. At the same time, your printing activities must continue until you announce the treaty in the military press. The day after, you will pack up the equipment and we'll provide transport for you to Paris."

"And our staff?" Daniel asked.

"The general feels you will find more skilled help in Paris. The men will remain here as part of Ancona's guard. But you have proven efficient and effective, so we want you to continue to manage the military press. And for that reason, we are giving you a second battlefield commission—to go into effect after you reach Paris—making you both Sous Lieutenants."

With that, Bourrienne rose and stood at attention. Christophe and Daniel followed suit. Christophe felt his chest swell. Second Lieutenant! Who would have thought it two years ago, when they were both half starving over a paltry campfire? How proud his uncle would be at the news!

Bourrienne kissed them on both cheeks and handed them each a small drawstring bag. "Epaulets befitting your rank. You'll be issued new uniforms when you arrive in Paris, but I wanted to present these to you myself. With the general's thanks and best wishes."

"Where do we report in Paris?" Daniel asked.

"You'll be sent orders before you leave Ancona. We may establish the military printshop in Les Invalides, but that remains unconfirmed.

In all events, you'll be stationed in Paris until it's decided where Bonaparte will be sent next. Perhaps England—but that, I'm sure you realize, is not to be shared with anyone." Bourrienne turned to Christophe. "Now: your fiancée. I am arranging transport for military wives to leave Venice on the twentieth. If you marry the girl and she can arrive in Venice by then, I can make room for her."

Christophe's heart dropped. "I can't marry her in Ancona," he said slowly. "Could I have two days' leave, so I can bring her to Bologna?"

"Now?" Bourrienne frowned. "Impossible. Why can't you marry her here?"

"In Ancona, weddings are purely religious affairs."

Bourrienne shrugged. "So find a priest."

"A priest would not marry them, sir," Daniel chimed in. "Mirelle is Jewish."

"A Jewess?" Bourrienne frowned. "And you, Christophe? Not Jewish with that first name, are you?"

"No, sir."

"I see." Bourrienne thought for a moment. "This is highly irregular. I can't put her on the wives' transport unless you are legally married. Nor can I grant you leave until you reach Paris."

"I couldn't possibly afford to send her to Paris," Christophe protested, then remembered he was speaking with a superior. He strove to make his tone respectful. "We haven't been paid in months. Sir."

"Let her parents pay for it," Bourrienne said. "Or borrow the money." He cleared his throat. "I must go. Remember: what I've told you is a military secret. Understand?"

Christophe and Daniel nodded, saluting. Bourrienne returned their salute and walked swiftly from the room.

The cathedral bells were chiming two o'clock when Mirelle was handed a note by one of the Morpurgos' servants.

"It just arrived, signorina," he said. "One of the French soldiers delivered it."

She waited for him to leave before tearing open the seal and unfolding it. The note was scarcely two lines long: *We need to talk. Today. Can you come to the municipality? I can't leave the printshop. C.*

Mirelle pursed her lips, annoyed. This summons brought her in direct proximity of the man she was still promised to wed. Didn't Christophe realize that she might easily bump into David there? If that happened, how could she explain why she was there? Time was flying by—the wedding was a mere two weeks away!—and still Christophe refused to allow her to confess the truth. Did he expect her to abandon David at the chuppah? As she adjusted her hat in the mirror, she made a decision: either he came with her tonight to tell them, or she'd do it herself. Her conscience wouldn't let her wait another day.

Mirelle made her way to the printshop. As she entered, Daniel looked up from the plates he was examining, and she felt the same tingling of her pulses that she'd felt in the synagogue. She swallowed, hard, then forced a smile on her lips as he welcomed her.

Christophe emerged from the back room. "Good girl," he said. "Daniel, can you give us a few minutes?"

Daniel nodded curtly. Mirelle wondered at his grim expression. But then Christophe drew her into the inner room and shut the door.

# 58

## OCTOBER 18

Mirelle decided that they should reveal their plans to her mother and David at the printshop. David, Christophe, and Daniel would all be in the building, so it would be simplest if Mirelle brought Mama there. While she dreaded making the announcement, Mirelle was relieved that her secret would be a secret no more. Even Dolce agreed.

That day, not wanting to see David before their meeting, Mirelle remained in her room until the clock chimed twelve. She slipped on a plum-colored dress with a matching pelisse suitable for travel, grunting a little at the effort of fastening the back herself.

She walked slowly downstairs, trailing her fingers on the banister. Mama sprang up as she entered the sitting room. "Darling," she cried. "Feeling better?"

Mirelle had stayed in bed this long, pleading a headache. Now her fiction turned real, pounding her temples and making her feel sick. "I'm fine, Mama," she lied. "Let's take a drive. Dolce, too. I'll feel better with some fresh air."

"If Dolce joins you, I'll stay home," Mama said. "I have too much to do."

"No, Mama," Mirelle insisted, taking her mother's hand. "I want *you.*"

"Are you certain you're feeling all right, sweetheart?" Mama asked, studying her face.

"Yes, but I'll be ill if you don't come. Dolce, tell her she must."

Mama patted the hand atop hers. "Of course I'll come. I'll change into a hat and get my cape."

When she left the room, Dolce turned to Mirelle. "You're pale. Can you manage this?"

Mirelle sighed. "What choice do I have? I can't disappear without telling them. Or just leave a note. That would be the coward's way."

Mama was surprised when the carriage rolled up at the municipality. "Why are we stopping?"

"I thought you'd like to see where Papa works," Dolce said.

"And Daniel, too," Mirelle added dully. "In fact, why don't we go down to the printshop first? You've never seen a printshop."

"Are they expecting us?" Mama asked, frowning. "I don't want to disturb them at work."

"Daniel knows we're coming, Mama—and it's a surprise for David." Mirelle did her best to sound lighthearted.

Mama, still looking reluctant, followed her daughter and Dolce down the steps to the basement. She flinched when the doors sprang opened and three soldiers almost collided with them, chattering about more unexpected time off. Seeing the women, the soldiers cut short their bantering and stood aside.

"What's going on?" Mama asked, suspicious.

"Welcome, Cousin Pinina." Daniel was at the door; he ushered them in with a bow.

A circle of chairs was set up in the front room near a high table. The frames that generally lay there were tucked into a corner. The table served as a sideboard, with a tea tray containing a porcelain pot of tea and several unmatched cups.

"I'll fetch Papa," Dolce said, slipping out.

Christophe bowed to Mama, leading her to a chair. "Thank you for honoring us with your visit, Signora d'Ancona."

"What's going on?" Mama repeated, her question high-pitched with anxiety.

"Just wait, Mama." Mirelle's voice quavered. Her mother cast her a worried glance and Mirelle tried to smile. But the corners of her mouth wouldn't cooperate.

David entered the room with Dolce following close behind. "Pinina!" he cried, sounding both surprised and upset. "Mirelle! What are you doing here?" He bowed, face creased with annoyance. "You called me out of an important meeting. Can't this wait?"

"I'm afraid not, Signor Morpurgo," said Christophe. "May I ask you to take a seat? Would anyone like tea?"

No one wanted tea.

Christophe stood behind Mirelle's chair, his hands on her shoulders. Mama and David glared at the possessive gesture.

"What's this about?" David growled.

"Signor Morpurgo," Mirelle started. "Mama." She had insisted that she be the one to tell them. Now she wondered if she could. She stared at them, willing the words into her mouth, but they wouldn't come.

"So formal!" David's smile didn't reach his uneasy eyes. "*Piccola*, we'll be wed soon enough. Call me by my given name."

"I'm afraid we won't," Mirelle said. "You see . . . I'm with . . . with . . ."

"With child," Dolce said, unable to keep quiet. "Papa, she's pregnant."

Mirelle shut her eyes to blot out the look of horror that crossed her mother's face.

"It's my child," Christophe said. "Sir, I've wronged you."

"Wronged me!" David roared, jumping from his chair, which fell, clattering behind him. "And what of her?"

"Wronged her as well," Christophe agreed. "But I plan to do right by her."

Mirelle looked at her mother. She was staring at her, face working, white-knuckled hands gripping the arms of her chair. "You . . ." she moaned. "You . . . How could you?"

Mirelle hung her head.

Christophe turned to Mama. "Signora d'Ancona. It's not Mirelle's fault. We love one another. She promised to marry Signor Morpurgo out of duty to you. Because he could provide you both a home. But she couldn't withstand what we are. We are—what's the word, Daniel?"

"*Beshert*," Daniel whispered, his eyes on the ground.

Mirelle cast an anguished look toward him, but he didn't see it.

"*Beshert*," Christophe said. "Soul mates fashioned for one another by God for eternity."

The silence in the room was palpable. Finally, David spoke, his jaw clenched. "God does not pair Jews and Gentiles. I don't care how you try to excuse this—you seduced the girl. You should be horse-whipped. Caned. Drummed out of the service."

Mirelle reached up and compulsively clutched Christophe's hands.

Mama's eyes narrowed. "Mirelle. I trusted you. And you . . . you . . ." She paused a moment, swallowing hard. "I'm glad your father isn't alive to hear this. Or your brother."

"Mama!" Mirelle protested, tears streaming down her cheeks.

But her mother turned away, shoulders shaking.

"And you, daughter?" David turned on Dolce, black fury evident on his face. "Do you want to pretend you didn't know about this?"

"Of course not!" Dolce said smoothly. "How can you accuse me?" Her eyebrows rose in pretended affront.

But David scoffed. "Don't think I didn't know you opposed my marriage to Mirelle. I'm certain you had a hand in this."

"Papa!" Dolce's look now was one of genuine alarm.

But David swiveled sharply away from her and stared at Mirelle.

"And what of the workshop? What would you have happen to the poor men whom I rescued at tremendous expense—for no other reason than to please you?"

Mirelle raised her head, her face soaked with tears. "I know. I've lain awake nights, thinking of the debt I owe you. That the men working in the workshop owe you. Dolce helped me sign over ownership of the workshop to Mama. The papers are back at home—I mean, at your home. In an envelope on my dressing table." She looked at her mother, her voice pleading. "I've left you provided for, Mama. With Sabato Narducci in charge, you'll never know want. And Dolce says that you should stay with the Morpurgos, as their housekeeper. I wouldn't leave you to starve."

"How can you possibly think I'd be able to stay there, Mirelle?" Mama whispered, still refusing to look at her. "In such shame?"

"But, Mama—"

"Dolce helped you, Dolce says," David muttered. "So you knew nothing, daughter?"

Dolce turned pale. "It's not what it seems. Of course I knew—after Mirelle told me. Do you think I wasn't as shocked as you? But someone had to think about poor Pinina." She pointed at Mirelle. "*She* certainly wasn't."

"Dolce!" Mirelle cried, aghast.

Christophe stepped around to hover threateningly over Dolce. "What do you think you're doing?" he demanded. "Pretending you didn't have a hand in this? You plotted against your father's marriage from the start. You said you would help me—and you did. And now you play the innocent?"

Dolce clenched and unclenched her hands. "Don't dare utter such lies."

"Enough!" David shouted. "I'll deal with you, Dolce, in my own time and my own way. As for Mirelle . . ." He hesitated a moment, looking at Pinina with concern. She was bent over in her seat, sobbing in great, heartrending gulps. He stepped over and put a hand on her arm. "All will be right," he murmured. "I won't desert you, my dear."

She just wept louder.

He bit his lips. "Perhaps you should tell us your plans, Lefevre."

"We can't be married here—and for reasons I can't share, I won't be in Ancona much longer."

"The Treaty of Campo Formio," Morpurgo said, nodding. "My sources say it will be signed today or tomorrow. You'll return to Paris?"

"I should have realized you'd know." Christophe shrugged. "I borrowed enough money to send Mirelle to Paris. She'll live with my mother and uncle until we can be married."

"Married?" Mama burst out. "In a Catholic church?"

"In a civil ceremony. That's how marriages are conducted in Paris nowadays."

"That's not a marriage," Mama said. "Not for my daughter."

"Mama." Mirelle rose and knelt in front of her. "It's the only way."

Her mother hunched her shoulder, ignoring her.

David looked down at her. Mirelle saw the regret in his eyes. Her heart twisted.

"When do you leave?" he asked.

"Will you let Mama stay with you?" Mirelle pleaded. "Keep her safe?"

"If she wishes," David said.

Mama reached up and took hold of the neck of her linen dress. She tore it at the neck. The sound of ripping echoed through the room.

"*Yit'gadal v'yit'kadash,*" she began, praying the mourner's Kaddish, "*sh'mei raba . . .*"

"Mama!" Mirelle cried. "No!"

But Pinina was relentless: " *. . . b'al'ma di v'ra khir'utei . . .* "

Christophe gaped. "What is she doing?" he asked Daniel in a low whisper.

"Praying the prayer for the dead," he muttered. "Because she's marrying a Gentile—you—she no longer recognizes Mirelle as her daughter. She is dead to her."

Christophe stepped over to Mirelle, who had collapsed at her mother's feet. He reached down a hand to her. "Come," he said.

But before she could take his hand, two people raced into the room, jostling one another. Through her agony, Mirelle barely recognized Dolce's uncle Ezekiel and . . . was that Francesca Marotti?

"Daniel!" Signora Marotti cried. "They are gathering to attack the ghetto!"

"Brother!" Ezekiel shouted at the same moment. "They're going to cast the cathedral bell into cannon to defend against the French!"

# 59

The room erupted in confusion, shouting voices clamoring and overlapping.

Daniel regained his senses first. "Everyone—shut up!" He turned to Francesca in the abrupt silence. "Who's attacking the ghetto?"

"The Catholic Fellowship," she panted.

"Ezekiel!" David grabbed hold of his brother's arm. "What do you mean, they want to cast the cathedral bell into cannon?"

"Father Candelabri sent one of the village women to tell us." Ezekiel wiped beads of sweat from his forehead. "They're going to melt the bell to forge a cannon and fire on the French."

David shook his head. "Fools!"

"Melt it down?" Francesca asked, swerving to stare at Ezekiel. "That means Desi." She covered her mouth with both hands.

"What? Who? Tell us what you mean, signora."

She spoke through her fingers, voice muffled. "My husband's cousin. He's a blacksmith. They'll use his forge to melt the bell."

"We'll stop them," David said decisively. He thought for a moment, eyes shut. "We'll need French support."

Daniel reached for the bayonet he always left in the corner of the room. "Christophe, let's get to the barracks and tell the captain what's happening."

Christophe cupped Mirelle's shoulder. "You stay here, *chérie*—you and your mother and Dolce. You'll be safest here."

"But you?" Mirelle's eyes widened with fear. "Will you be safe?"

Daniel felt his heart twist. He wished that Mirelle would look at *him* that way, would worry about *his* safety. He could only wonder what Morpurgo thought, watching them.

"I'm a soldier. You know that. But I promise to return." Christophe turned to Daniel. "You'll need to head to the ghetto—they'll want someone who can speak to the people."

"You'll be careful, won't you?" Dolce asked him softly, touching Daniel's arm.

Daniel shifted out of her reach. "Let's go."

"I'm coming, too." Francesca tugged on Daniel's sleeve, face strained.

"Absolutely not! It's dangerous, signora."

"I'm not asking you," she said firmly.

"You can't!"

But before he could stop her, she turned and ran from the room.

"Signora Marotti! Wait!" Daniel ran to the door, calling up the stairwell. His voice echoed back to him.

"We'll go with the soldiers to the cathedral," Morpurgo told Christophe as Daniel returned. "They'll need the authority of the Council to stop them from taking the bell."

"We're going where?" his brother asked.

"To the cathedral," Morpurgo replied.

"No!" Ezekiel blurted, alarm clouding his eyes. "I must make sure Speranza is safe."

"Don't worry, brother. The French will make short work of the rioters. Speranza and the rest of the ghetto will be fine." Morpurgo looked at Pinina, who had stopped praying and now sat quiet, hands limp in her lap. "Pinina, I'll take you home when this is all over. We'll talk about the future then."

"I'll take care of her, Papa," Dolce said, her eyes on his face. "Count on me." She drew herself up to full height and stepped in front of Pinina, arms outstretched. "Come back safe." She tried to hug him, but he pushed her aside. Daniel saw a quick flash of hurt cross her face.

Mirelle was clutching Christophe's hand with both of hers, knuckles white. Daniel locked eyes with his friend and tipped his head to the door in silent command.

Gently, Christophe extracted his hand and kissed Mirelle's forehead. "There's no time to waste," he said quietly. "I'll return for you soon."

At the barracks, Captain Bossard was already mustering the men to head to the ghetto. The stomping of boots and the clanking of weapons as the men formed ranks was deafening. Daniel and Christophe took the captain aside and explained the situation at the cathedral.

Bossard looked annoyed. "It's not as if we have hundreds of men to call out," he said, shaking his head. "Or as if taking the bell were as dangerous a situation as the ghetto. Sergeant Lefevre, take five men. Stop them."

"Yes, sir."

Bossard's second-in-command, Lieutenant Paget, offered a soft-spoken objection. "We don't really have a say in what they do with the bell, Captain. Not if the cardinal permits it."

Bossard shrugged. "We do if they plan on casting it into cannon. Besides, two members of the municipal council have requested our aid. We're just lending our support."

Christophe watched his fellow soldiers, Daniel among them, march toward Via Astagna. "We'll take your carriage," he said, turning to Morpurgo, as the last soldier passed out of sight. "Quicker than the climb."

"You're in charge," Morpurgo muttered. "At least for now."

Christophe could sense the anger simmering beneath the older man's words. After a moment's thought, he snapped his heels together. "Begging your pardon, sir," he said, standing at attention. "I request the use of your carriage in the name of the French army."

Morpurgo waved an irritable hand. "Let's just get on with it."

They crowded inside; two of the soldiers climbed onto the box. The men lurched as the coach clattered over the uneven road, heading up the steep mountainside toward the cathedral.

Captain Bossard stationed men on either side of the road at the entrance to Via Astagna, flanking the open space where the ghetto gates used to be, then sent Daniel to reassure the inhabitants.

"Don't be afraid," Daniel called out, in Hebrew, Yiddish, and Italian, his boots echoing loudly as he walked the empty streets. The residents of the ghetto already knew of the imminent attack, he realized. Doors were locked, shutters closed, the narrow avenue deserted. "We'll protect you. No one will burn your homes or attack your families. The French army won't permit it."

Eyes followed him as he walked past the crowded homes. Window curtains fluttered.

"Stay inside," he called out.

"God bless you," someone called back.

Mirelle didn't know what to do. As the seconds ticked by, she grew increasingly anxious. Her mother turned her back, refusing to utter a word. Mirelle still couldn't believe that Mama had declared her dead. Dolce seemed more concerned about her father's mood than her friend's welfare. And David hated her. Why wouldn't he? She had broken her promise to wed him, deceived him in the ugliest way possible. *And what if Christophe is killed? I'd be pregnant, penniless, and alone.*

Yet, even as these thoughts chased through her head, she reproached herself. The men were facing real danger. What did her personal concerns matter when compared with what Christophe and Daniel—even David and Ezekiel—were facing?

Dolce stood by the presses. Mirelle approached her.

"Dolce. Talk to me."

"What do you want now?" Her friend averted her face. "I've nothing to say to you."

Mirelle backed off and moved a chair to one of the other rooms, a room crisscrossed with laundry cord. Christophe had once explained how they'd mimicked the system of ropes his uncle had devised in Paris to dry the pages after they came off the press.

She sat down heavily, wondering what would happen after the day was over. Would Christophe send her off to Paris? When would he be able to join her? And what kind of reception would she receive from his uncle and mother? Did they even know about her? About the baby? Would she have to be the one to tell them? She shuddered at the thought.

The sound of weeping tore through her; the pang of her mother's misery was growing unbearable. Why wasn't Dolce comforting her? She was as complicit in this secret as Mirelle herself. Why had she denied it? Mirelle strode back into the other room.

"For the sin which we have committed before God by scheming against a fellowman," she said, turning Dolce by the shoulder to face her.

Her friend glared, stepping back. "Leave me alone."

"You are the schemer who sins that sin. I see it and God sees it. You did everything you could to divide your father and me. You used me. Used Christophe. And you won." Mirelle's laughter was tinged with hysteria.

"I did win," Dolce said. A momentary twinge crossed her face. Was it shame? Guilt? But then she squared her shoulders. "I always win."

Mirelle stepped forward again, practically nose to nose with her friend. "For the sin which we have committed before God by scheming against a fellowman," she repeated.

Dolce turned on her heel and walked away.

The carriage pulled up alongside the narrow bell tower, a white stone edifice as tall as the cathedral, capped with a red slate roof and, at its peak, a single cross. Between arched windows, Christophe could make out the enormous bell.

It made Christophe remember a recent letter from his mother. *The church bells ring out again in Paris*, she'd written. *Not all of them and not regularly. But after years of silent services, of huddling in corners to worship the Lord, it is a blessed sound.* The church bells had been a fixture of his youth before the Terror stilled them. He hadn't realized until now how much he'd missed them.

Two distinct groups stood at the base of the tower. Christophe recognized the two women he'd seen at the Marotti house the day they'd captured Emilio. Behind them stood a priest, several other women, and a few old men, faces bronzed by years of toiling in the sun. Facing them down was a large man with thick, blackened forearms. A cadre of noisy young men massed behind him, brandishing weapons fashioned from farm implements.

As Christophe neared, their conversation became clearer. During the months he'd lived in Italy, particularly in Ancona, he'd picked up enough Italian to get by. He might not understand every word, but he could grasp what these plainspoken peasants were saying.

"Back off," the older woman demanded, arms crossed on her chest. "Bad enough you threatened to burn the portrait of the Madonna. Thank Our Lord and all the saints it was saved, even if it is under French guard. Now you threaten to take the cathedral bell? No and no."

"What's gotten into you, you old . . . ?" The next word the heavy-set man used was some kind of unintelligible insult. He continued, sounding bewildered. "You were the first to say no to the French. Driving us crazy with your prayers that they wouldn't take Ancona. But they did, and now that we want to do something about it, you say you'll stop us." He thought for a moment. "If it's the church you're defending, Cardinal Ranuzzi sent us."

"Of course I didn't want the French here, Desi!" she barked, forcing him backward. "But what's one cannon—even two—going to do for us?" She turned to the priest. "Father Candelabri, the cardinal didn't tell you to let them have the bell, did he?"

"It doesn't matter what the cardinal said," Morpurgo said, stepping forward. "I'm a member of Ancona's municipal council and I'm ordering you to stop."

Both groups turned to stare at Morpurgo. Christophe moved behind him, bayonet at the ready. The men he commanded fell into line.

"A member of Ancona's council, Jew?" Desi jeered. "With the cursed French at your back? Why should anyone listen?"

"Because, like it or not, I've the authority to stop you."

"Authority given you by the enemy," Desi sneered. "Traitor! Collaborator! Jew!"

Ezekiel had remained behind the line of soldiers, but now he moved to stand beside his brother. "We insist that you leave the cathedral grounds," he said. "And we've brought these soldiers to make certain you do."

"What do you care, anyway?" someone else called up from the pack of men behind Desi. "You're Jews. What does it matter to you if we remove the bell?"

"It matters," Morpurgo said. "The cathedral is one of the import-ant"—Christophe thought the next word must mean *landmarks*—"of the city, and the bell tower and bell are part of that. For that reason alone, we are here to defend it."

"For that reason alone?" Desi scoffed. "All you Jews care about are your own people, your own greed. The French are probably paying you to stop us. And while you stand here, defending a cathedral bell, you've no idea what's happening in your homes."

David's mouth twisted. "Don't we? You'd be surprised, blacksmith."

Daniel came around the corner, still calling out to the Jews of the ghetto to remain inside—and stopped short. Francesca stood hud-dled in the center of a small cul-de-sac, ineffectively shielding her face and body from stones pelted by a group of teenage boys from the upper windows of the local yeshiva.

"Go away!" one of them shouted.

"Come to watch us die?" another shrieked, letting a rock fly. "*Vai al diavolo!*" His missile smashed into Francesca's chest, making her stumble.

"Stop!" Daniel bellowed up at them, stepping in front of the now-weeping woman. Seeing Daniel's raised musket, several boys ducked their heads back inside. Windows slammed shut. But a few didn't scare so easily.

"What's she doing here?" one cried out. "Don't think we don't know who she is!"

"I don't mean any harm," Francesca quavered, looking around the shield of Daniel's body.

"Don't you?" cried another. "You and that fake portrait of the so-called Virgin Mother! You and that husband of yours!"

"It's not fake," Francesca shouted, crying out as another rock hit her forearm.

"Stop!" Daniel pulled her more securely behind him, then pointed his musket toward the open windows. "You're the pride of your yeshiva, aren't you—attacking a defenseless woman?" he called up to the boys in Yiddish. "*Heldish mentshn!* Such brave young men!"

"Get her out of here!" the boy who threw the rock retorted, waving a fist.

Daniel turned to Francesca, who was tying a handkerchief around her arm to stem the trickle of blood. "What did I tell you?" he rebuked her. "Didn't I say it was too dangerous to be here?"

She shrank back against the stucco wall.

Daniel looked around. "And now it's too dangerous for you to leave. Let's find a place where you'll be safe." His eyes lit upon the synagogue building. "Come."

"There?" Francesca shook her head. "I can't go there."

Daniel reached for her arm. "I haven't time for this. You'll be safe there."

As they entered, she looked around, wide-eyed. The room was long and narrow, the ark and windows supported by pillars gilded in gold paint. Chairs were covered in red velvet; glistening wood pews lined the sides of the room. Chandeliers of bronze hung from the ceiling, filled with fresh candles.

Daniel led her up the stairs to the women's balcony.

"The cardinal is right," Francesca murmured. "You Jews are wealthy beyond belief."

"Don't be foolish," Daniel told her. "Think of your own cathedral. Are you rich because your church is adorned with gold and silver?"

She looked unconvinced, but said nothing as Daniel deposited her in the balcony.

"Stay here and pray," he instructed. "I'll come get you when it's all over."

# 60

Roberto scowled as the cardinal addressed the men. Ranuzzi had mustered dozens of them, equipped with daggers, muskets stolen from the French, even a few pistols. They passed bottles of grappa around for courage. Roberto grabbed one from the man standing next to him and took a long slug.

"The Jews are a disease," the cardinal was saying. "A blight on our city. They have not changed from the days of Christ, when they delivered Our Lord for execution. Judases all. Trust me, they've collected their thirty pieces of silver—and then some."

"Thirty!" called one of the men. "More like three hundred! I've seen the mansion of the Jew councilman. You've seen it too, Roberto. Tell them!"

Roberto nodded, thinking back to that dreadful day. "The man drowns in silver," he snarled. "Every inch of the place is marble, every wall thick with artwork, servants crawling in every corner. That's where our money has gone—to the Jews. They've grown fat on our misery."

"And this Jew and his brother rule over us now." Ranuzzi sneered. "Should we stand for this? Nonbelievers, traitors to true Italians, who will someday tell us that we can't worship in our churches? Collaborators with the French, who've stripped their entire nation of its Catholic ways? Do you want the same done here?"

"What are we waiting for?" one of the men asked, taking another swig of grappa. "Enough blather! Let's move!"

"Father Candelabri, isn't it?" Christophe asked the priest through Morpurgo, who translated for him. Father Candelabri nodded. "Did the cardinal instruct these men to take the bell?"

Morpurgo glared at him, appalled. "Don't ask him that!"

The men's grumbling diminished as they leaned in to hear the priest's answer.

Candelabri's lips thinned. "I may be severely punished for not obeying my superior, but he is wrong in this instance," he said in uneasy French.

"What do you mean?" Desi cried. "Speak Italian, Father!"

The priest looked at Christophe, eyebrows rising.

"Go ahead," Christophe said. "I'll tell you when I don't understand."

"Plainly then—yes, the cardinal said the men could take the bell—"

A roar of victory erupted from the men's throats, countered by shrill shouts of protest from the other group.

"And just as plainly," the priest shouted above the tumult, "I forbid it!"

"What?" Desi shrieked. "You can't!"

The old woman stepped up, raising her arms for silence. Christophe noticed with surprise how swiftly she subdued both sides.

"Desi, you should be ashamed," she scolded. "Think how often you heard the church bell ring—when it was time for school and prayers, at your confirmation, and for every wedding and funeral in the city. How can you think of robbing Ancona of it?"

"If the French have their way, they'll still it soon enough," Desi argued. "They'll forbid us the cathedral, deny us the worship of Our Lord. Father! Ask this French soldier if he can still kneel in prayer at Notre Dame—or at any other church in Paris."

Christophe felt the weight of their collective gaze. How had this conversation swerved into such a dangerous philosophical debate? He shouldn't allow these insurgents to bandy words with him. "This is neither the time nor place for religious questions," he said to the priest, who translated with a frown.

"Isn't it?" Desi demanded. "Where better than here and now?"

"My son," the priest told him. "I won't stand by and watch blood being shed—no, nor sacred property turned to an instrument of war."

"Leave the bell where it is today," David said. "I promise the council will discuss whether or not we should forge a cannon to defend our city after the French leave."

"After the French—do what?" Desi turned to Christophe. "Are you leaving, Frenchman?"

Christophe knew they would still be leaving a force behind in the city, but if these men thought they were leaving, it might help their cause. The Italians stared at him, waiting.

As time ticked by in the dusty, still air of the synagogue, Francesca grew increasingly perturbed. Fiona's mother had taken the baby but said she couldn't tend Mario for more than a couple of hours. "I have my own family to care for," she'd said. "Especially if the rumors are true and there's more trouble."

"I'll be home soon," Francesca replied. "Before the girls return from school."

But the hour grew late. Fiona's mother had probably handed the baby over to Barbara, grumbling about broken promises. Would Barbara venture out with Mario to find her mother? *What am I doing here? Why did I go running to Daniel with news of the attack?*

Yet what else could she have done? Her husband's hatred of Jews had polluted his soul. If only his father had not lost his fortune to a

Jewish moneylender, squandering Emilio's inheritance. If Emilio had not tried to cheat the Jewish merchant in Venice, wounding his arm. If the cardinal had not convinced him to join the Catholic Fellowship, given him absolution to kill and maim. If the wealthy Jewish merchant who'd wounded him had not been such an attractive target—yet somehow survived Emilio's stabbing attack. If it hadn't been a Jew—Daniel himself—who'd captured Emilio and plunged them all into the intrigue of the stolen Madonna. And a Frenchman, Daniel's friend, who'd dispatched her husband to the fires of hell.

Francesca closed her eyes, remembering everything that had brought them to this moment. How could her husband not hate the Jews after everything that had happened to him? And yet—how could Mother Mary excuse him from the destruction he'd wrought, the sin of murder and pain, even upon unbelievers?

Francesca felt a qualm, wondering what the priests would think of her sitting in this house of infamy, this place of worship of the people who'd crowned Christ with thorns and bedeviled him on the road to crucifixion. She pulled her string of rosary beads from her pocket. *Mother Mary, protect my soul from evil and guide me to do right*, she thought, beginning to pray.

But as the minutes passed, her prayers echoed menacingly within these foreign walls. *What am I doing?* Francesca asked herself. She couldn't pray to the Madonna here.

Daniel returned to the ghetto's entranceway. "I've instructed them to remain inside, Captain," he told Bossard.

"Good. Stay close, Isidore, so you can translate."

"Captain!" one of the men ran up. "They're on their way!"

Daniel heard a determined tramp of feet. He took a deep breath, his weapon at the ready.

Mirelle wiped her tears with the flat of her palms. She struggled to breathe. She wouldn't stay here in the printshop, not if neither Mama nor Dolce would speak with her.

And then she felt it—a sudden tug low in her stomach. She crept into a back room, behind a screen, and, wrestling with her clothes, peered down into her undergarments. *Blood.* Why was there blood? *It's not possible*, she told herself. *I'm not bleeding, I'm pregnant. I have Christophe's baby inside me. Blood, how can there be blood?*

Again the familiar ache in her gut. Eve's curse, that monthly visitor, which so often drove her to curl up in a tight ball under the covers.

*Why was there blood?* The answer was irrefutable. *Because there is no baby*, said a voice inside her. *You're late, not pregnant.*

For a moment, Mirelle clung to the feelings that had sustained her for the past weeks—*You and Christophe are meant to be, you and Christophe are having a child together, there it is, the proof of your union, growing inside of you.* She stared at her undergarments, trying to make sense of it, but the red stain remained.

No baby. There was no baby. She felt a pang, her heart breaking, as she thought of the tiny being that had only existed in her mind. It had felt so real, growing inside her, forcing her to give up everything she'd ever known. All for nothing—a phantom, a mistake of timing. A mathematical anomaly. How could her body have betrayed her so? She stood there, staring blankly at the spot ruining her linen. Perhaps ruining her life yet again.

Pulling herself back together, she crept back to her mother. "Mama . . ."

Her mother turned away. "Leave me alone," she hissed. "You're dead to me."

Mirelle felt sick. How could she have been so wrong? Wrong about so much—even loving Christophe, the man who would soon be her husband. But they'd confessed their lovemaking and she still had to marry him. Would he be angry when she told him she wasn't pregnant? She felt panic at the thought that he might cast her aside, leaving her ruined and alone. And if she did marry him? What would Christophe's mother think of her, penniless and destitute? Didn't she already have reason enough to despise her—an unmarried woman who wasn't even carrying her son's child? Mirelle urgently wanted to return to her room, to bathe and change. Before she confessed to Christophe. Before David returned and denied her the door.

But it would be fatal to stroll openly into the ghetto now, while riot raged in the streets. She paced the room. How could she find her way back to the Morpurgo house undetected?

The image of Jewish gravestones on the hillside overlooking Ancona popped into her head. She remembered the day she had snuck out to visit Jacopo's grave, back when the entire Jewish community had locked themselves inside the ghetto for their own safety.

The tanner's yard. She could slip through the fissure in the wall. No one would see her if she kept to the alleyways and entered the Morpurgo mansion through the servants' entrance. She'd go and return the same way. No one would know. And when Christophe returned, she would leave Ancona. They would have other chances for children.

"Well, Sergeant," Desi demanded again, "is it true? Are you leaving?"

Christophe bit his lip. He'd been ordered not to report the French withdrawal, but desperate times, he knew, called for desperate measures. Defusing the situation was more important than a possible court-martial. "The French *are* leaving Italy soon," Christophe replied, as both David and the priest translated. As he spoke, both sides broke out into cheers. Christophe knew it would be useless to ask them to keep the news secret. It would spread through Ancona like wildfire.

Desi shook his head, clearly unconvinced. "Very convenient lies you're telling me."

Morpurgo spoke up. "It's true. Bonaparte may be signing the treaty with the Austrians at this very moment. The French troops will be leaving—in mere days, at most."

Desi glanced at the men. "What do you say, fellows? Why strip our cathedral of its bell if the invaders are leaving?"

A familiar twinge of fear coursed through Roberto as they approached the ghetto. He curled his fingers, opening and closing them around his stiletto hilt.

"They're waiting at the ghetto entrance," someone whispered frantically. "The French are ready for us!"

The cardinal turned a sickly shade of green. "How many?"

"Dozens!"

Roberto swallowed hard, trying to think what Emilio would have said to rouse the men. In a gritty voice, he cried, "Never mind! We'll cut through the French like a knife through butter! Show them what true Italian fighters can do. And then"—his throat was dry, but he forced himself to say it—"we'll kill every Jew in Ancona!"

"Hush, Roberto," the cardinal growled. "Be still. So many soldiers? I didn't expect . . ."

Roberto closed his eyes. Why had he come back from Greece at the cardinal's bidding? The islands had been warm, the sea calm, the people friendly. He'd been safe there. "Let's go!" he cried, loudly enough to banish his fear. The men echoed him with a wordless roar.

Daniel saw them coming, moving up the street in a disorganized pack. Not a trained soldier in the bunch. He stayed by the captain's side, prepared for battle. With silent intent, the captain held his men back, waiting for the Italians to make their first move.

As Daniel waited, he remembered the stories his cousin Ethan told about riots in his little village in Alsace soon after the Bastille. No one had protected the Jews then. Nor during the riot that had taken place not so long ago on these very streets—a massacre the Jews had been powerless to stop.

His lip curled. They were defenseless no longer.

The captain stepped forward, gesturing for Daniel to follow. "Halt!" he called. "What is your business here? Why are you carrying illegal arms?"

Daniel began to translate: "*Fermi! Perché state—*"

A sharp cry from the Italian brigands cut him off mid-sentence.

"Return to your homes," the captain commanded. "No one is allowed in the Jewish Quarter today."

As Daniel translated, a sudden shot from the unruly mob made him rear back. A second musket ball whizzed by his ear.

"Arrgh!" The soldier three paces behind him fell to his knees, clutching his shoulder, blood gushing to the cobblestones below.

"Attack!" a man shouted, and ran straight at Daniel. *Roberto.*

Mirelle pushed and pushed, wedged tightly between the two walls of the fissure. *Come on*, she urged herself. With a gasp, she squeezed through.

She heard gunshots, shouts, and groans coming from the main

street. For a moment, she considered turning around. But then she thought of Christophe. She couldn't have her future husband think her a coward. Heart thumping, she ran in the shadow of the back alleys, heading toward the safety of the Morpurgo mansion.

Francesca heard the skirmish approaching. Pulse racing, she groped down the dark narrow stairs to the main floor. She pulled back a red velvet curtain and clutched both hands to her mouth, horrified. Men lay in the streets—some screaming in agony, others fearfully still, eyes wide even in death. Blood from both sides mixed as it flowed in a crimson river to the gutter. As she watched, a French soldier stabbed a man she knew from the market, plunging a bayonet in his stomach. Tonio sank to his knees, mouth foaming as he retched in pain, and tumbled headfirst into a heap. Whimpering, Francesca watched the soldier take his red-stained weapon and thrust it again in Tonio's back. She gasped, a sharp, sympathetic pain radiating through her. The soldier yanked the bayonet out, twisting viciously, and ran to aid one of his fellows, who was hard-pressed fighting another Italian, a stranger.

Trembling, Francesca looked through the haze of dust and gunpowder for friends and neighbors. Hunched over a stone step was the barkeep, Mattia, clutching his stomach and shrieking pitifully for his mama. Nicolò, a fellow farmer, fought hand to hand with a soldier. Francesca gasped as he pierced the soldier's neck with a stiletto. The Frenchman fended Nicolò off, slashing at his arm with a sword. Nicolò cried out, wrenched his dagger from the man's neck, and plunged it into his left eye. As the soldier reeled back, howling, Francesca gagged and turned away.

Her attention was seized by the sight of Cardinal Ranuzzi hiding behind a stone wall. *Coward*, she thought, lips curling in disdain.

Then, glancing back at the main street, a shock jolted her.

Roberto and Daniel stood at the center of the mob—Roberto with his dagger trembling in his grasp and Daniel with his bayonet. They circled one another, feinting, eyes fixed. Both trying to find a vulnerable spot, waiting for a weakness.

Her hand flew to her heart.

"Let's go straight to the ghetto," Ezekiel said as he climbed back into the carriage. "I need to make sure Speranza is all right."

David nodded.

Christophe groaned inwardly. Captain Bossard wouldn't be pleased, but how could he refuse Morpurgo now?

Roberto was breathing hard. His stint in French prison, the days of wandering through Greece and scrounging for food, were taking their toll. Sweat dripped in his eyes, stinging, making him blink uncontrollably. Unable to stop himself, he swiped at his forehead with his knuckles—and the Jew soldier's bayonet sliced into his dagger arm.

His stiletto fell with a clatter on the cobbles. The pain throbbed up his arm. He fought the urge to collapse. Grunting, bent nearly level to the ground, he loped away.

They heard the screams and smelled the gunpowder long before reaching the ghetto. Christophe shouted for the driver to stop the carriage several yards away. The soldiers on the box slid down and ran to support their fellows.

"Stay inside!" Christophe ordered the two brothers as he scrambled out, grabbing his weapon. "I'll get you when it's safe."

He hurried, tripping over bodies, and arrived to the melee just in time to see Daniel chasing Roberto around a corner toward the alleyway. He started to follow, only to be stopped by a crazed Italian who faced him down with bared teeth, swinging an axe. Christophe aimed his musket and fired straight at the man's head. Bits of bone and blood flew into the air.

Mirelle crept around the back of the ghetto buildings, heart thumping. The odor of gunpowder and blood caught in the wind, and the vile smell almost overpowered her. Once she reached the safety of the Morpurgo villa, she'd wait out the fighting there. Then she would return to the municipality, and together she and Christophe would decide what they would do next.

*But, oh God, what if Christophe dies in the fighting? What will happen to me then?*

*No, Christophe will survive. He must. He promised he would.*

She turned a corner. *Almost there now. Almost safe.* She breathed easier as the Morpurgo mansion loomed before her.

A man came hurtling around the corner and Mirelle screamed.

He was cradling an arm, dripping blood. When he saw her, he drew back, then seemed to propel himself forward. The breath fled from her chest.

"Why are you here?" he gasped, moving unsteadily toward her. "Are you a fool, outside right now?"

Mirelle trembled. "Don't touch me!" she shouted, backing against the stone wall of the Morpurgo rose garden. Rough rocks scraped through her dress. "Leave me alone!"

"How can I?" the man demanded, sounding anguished. "I'm sorry, but . . ." He drew himself up. "You're a Jew," he declared loudly. "One of them. Nothing more than a leech, a rat, a . . . a—"

"Look at me!" Mirelle cried. "I'm not any of those things!"

"You're a Jew, aren't you?" the man said through gritted teeth. "All Jews are the same." He raised a hand to strike her.

His fist came down on her like an iron bar; she doubled over in agony.

"Stop! Please stop!" she cried. The world spun, and she fell against the wall. Pain ripped through her. *Christophe*, she thought wildly, and then—*Daniel, where are you?*

Francesca couldn't watch the carnage any longer. She pulled open the synagogue door and crept from the building. All around her, men slashed at one another. She put hands over her ears to block the screams of the wounded and dying.

*Barbara*, she thought. *Mario. Keep me safe, Mary. Holy Michael, Archangel, defend us in battle . . .*

And then she stopped praying, because she didn't know whom she wanted the Archangel Michael to defend.

She found herself lost in a warren of shadowy alleyways. *Just go home.*

Then, turning a corner, she gasped, and her hand flew up to stifle the cry that leapt to her throat. Roberto! He was raining blows upon a young woman, his face twisted almost unrecognizably.

Francesca wanted to run, but the sight of the child beneath the man's brutal fists stopped her cold.

"Please!" the girl called out in anguish. "Help me!"

"Roberto!" someone screamed.

Roberto recognized the voice. *Francesca?* He pushed the Jewess against the building, slamming her head against the wall in a fury, and turned.

"Why the devil are you here?" he growled. "Go home!"

Beside him, the Jewess was moaning, slumped, hands cradling her head. Roberto raised another fist to strike. But Francesca caught him by the arm and pulled him away.

"Are you all right?" she asked the woman, leaning down.

"What are you doing?" Roberto raged. "What would Emilio say to you? She's a godforsaken Jewess! Emilio would have killed her, wouldn't he? If I still had my dagger . . ."

Francesca turned on him, eyes blazing. "The devil has taken your soul," she cried. "You will burn in hell forever! How can you do this to a defenseless girl?"

Roberto felt his fists clench again. *Someone must pay for what they did to Emilio. The Jews, the French, they're the ones who belong in hell. Not me.*

"Get away!" He grabbed Francesca's hair and yanked hard, ignoring her cry of pain.

And then, out of nowhere, he heard the pop of a musket, a rush of air. He looked down. A searing sensation burned its way through his chest and the world began to whirl. The ground rose to meet him. His legs and arms gave way, and he landed, face first, on the pavement, gasping like a landed fish.

*Someone must pay*, he thought dimly, clawing at the dirt.

Then everything turned black.

"Mirelle!" Daniel ran to her, ignoring Francesca, who stooped, sobbing, over the prone body. He didn't understand why Mirelle was there, battered, crying against the wall.

He cradled her in his arms and she moaned in pain.

Panic rose in him. His mind was a fog. He looked about wildly, hoping someone would help them. "What hurts?" he asked.

"My head, oh, my head," she moaned, her words strangely garbled.

"Mirelle!" Christophe appeared above them and nearly tore the girl from Daniel's arms.

Daniel let her slip into Christophe's embrace.

"My darling! Are you all right?"

Mirelle murmured an unintelligible response. Francesca turned on Daniel, eyes wide with shock. "You killed him!" she shouted.

Daniel looked at her, unable to speak.

She remained crouched next to the prone body. "You killed him," she wailed.

He knelt next to her, striving for calm. But how she could mourn a man who would beat a woman just for being a Jew, bewildered him. "Signora . . ."

"Roberto, oh, poor, gentle Roberto," she said, and collapsed, sobbing, against the dead man's chest.

"Daniel!" Christophe sounded frantic.

Daniel looked over Francesca's dark head. Mirelle lay limp in Christophe's arms, her breathing dangerously shallow.

# 61

## OCTOBER 20

Dressed in black, Francesca knelt beside her husband's burial mound, her daughter and son beside her. She was teaching Barbara Saint Gertrude's prayer for souls in purgatory: . . . *for all the holy souls in purgatory, for sinners everywhere, for sinners in the universal church, those in my own home and within my family. Amen.*

Barbara struggled to memorize the prayer. She had not slept well since the day her father was killed, twitching with nightmares every night. Even awake she couldn't remain still, rocking back and forth on her knees.

"Why is Papa a sinner in our home?" Barbara demanded. "Why do you think he's in purgatory? Surely he's gone to Heaven, Mama."

*Surely he's gone to hell*, Francesca thought. But she couldn't tell her daughter that.

"We can't be certain," she said. "But the Lord Jesus and especially Our Lady will hear your petition, child."

After Barbara finally mastered the prayer, she recited it once more, and the little family rose from their knees. As they left the cemetery, Francesca was startled to see Daniel waiting at the gate.

"Go home," Francesca told her daughter, not wishing her to hear whatever Daniel wanted to say to her. Had he come to gloat over killing Roberto?

Stiff shouldered and red faced, Barbara pushed by Daniel and ran down the hill.

"I've come to say good-bye," he told her, watching the girl's retreating back. "We're ordered back to Paris and leave in a few days."

Francesca stared at the ground, shifting the toddler from the crook of one arm to another.

"I wasn't sure you'd want to see me, signora, but I couldn't leave without bidding you farewell."

She looked up at that, studying his solemn face, wondering what he was thinking.

"We were praying for Emilio's soul," she finally said. Anything to break the tense silence between them. "The girl's mourning her father. It helps her to think her father might be blessed with eternal life."

Daniel opened his mouth as though to respond, then closed it again. After a moment, he said, "What will you do? Will you stay in Ancona?"

"Where else would I go?"

"Your husband's cousin, the blacksmith, requested a passport to Corsica. Funny that, eh? Bonaparte's home island. But I hear they're more Italian than French there, even if their famous son is France's great hero." He looked into her eyes. "I could arrange for you to accompany him, start a new life. What's left for you here?"

Francesca smiled wanly. "There's Our Lady in the Cathedral. I'll stay close to her. She'll help me raise my children and find solace."

"And you still believe in the miracle of the painting?"

"The miracles have stopped ever since I helped you find the painting. The Madonna no longer blesses us with smiles and tears." Her lips curled involuntarily. "You might let your general know he no longer has anything to fear from her."

Daniel again seemed to want to say something but stopped himself.

Francesca sighed. She knew he didn't believe, would never believe.

Harsh though it might be, that lack of belief condemned him to the fires of damnation. Would he and Emilio and Roberto meet in hell, carry on their enmity through eternity? The thought was sobering. "The portrait is still dear to me," she added. "It's home. Miracle or no miracle."

"I'm glad for you." Daniel picked up her worn hand and kissed it. "I wish you nothing but happiness, signora. You deserve it."

Francesca watched as he walked away. When he disappeared from sight, she hefted Mario on her hip and started down the other side of the hill.

Daniel headed back into town, toward the army barracks. As he passed by the marketplace, he heard a voice call him from behind. Turning, he saw a sweetly smiling Dolce, accompanied by a maid.

"Nina, you can return home now," Dolce said, as she extended a hand toward him. "Daniel will accompany me."

Daniel bowed stiffly. "Unfortunately, duty calls."

Dolce shook her head. "Nonsense. You're leaving in the next few days, are you not? Were you not planning to come by the house to bid me farewell?"

"I'm afraid . . ."

Dolce placed her long fingers on his arm, and it was all he could do not to snatch it away. She peered almost uncertainly at him. "Afraid? Surely, I've given you enough encouragement, sir. Don't you have a question to ask me?"

Daniel's face burned. "Very well," he finally managed. "How is Mirelle?"

"Mirelle?" Dolce fired back. "Mirelle, Mirelle, always Mirelle. What magic does she practice, bewitching all of you?" She paused, and when she spoke again, she'd brought her tone back to its usual caressing cadence. "Especially you, Daniel, when you even yet might possess yourself of a far richer prize."

It was time to put an end to this farce. "Far too rich a prize for me, signorina. And, I think if you'd take the time to consider, far too poor a reward for you."

Dolce shook her head, a hectic flush decorating her high cheekbones. "You're a fool, Daniel. A bewitched, befuddled fool."

He bowed once more and half turned away. "Perhaps so."

Dolce stared at him with raised brows for a moment. Then she turned on her heel and, with a sharp bark at her servant, walked away.

# 62

# OCTOBER 20

Mirelle's eyelids were fused together. She wanted to wipe them clean, to open her eyes, but her hands wouldn't obey her. She felt weak. So weak.

"Is she awake, doctor?" someone asked.

*Mama?* Mirelle thought dimly. Hadn't Mama declared her dead?

"Barely, Signora d'Ancona. She's regained consciousness, but we should let her sleep."

*Sleep*, Mirelle thought. She stopped fighting and sank back into darkness.

When she opened her eyes again, it was black outside, and she was alone. She tried to shift position, but every part of her body hurt. She groaned.

Her mother appeared out of nowhere, leaning over the bed, kissing her forehead. "Mira'la," she murmured. "Let me help you drink some water."

Mama reached behind and supported her. Mirelle felt as if her head would explode. She closed her eyes, trying to stop from moaning. Mama raised a cup to her lips and she sipped obediently, barley water trickling down her throat.

"Shhh, now," Mama said, settling her down. "Back to sleep, darling."

Now it was day. The sunlight hurt. A maid sat next to her. "You're up," she said. She rose to leave the room.

Mirelle was back in her room in the Morpurgo mansion. But how? She remembered the man hammering her with his fists, smashing her head against the wall. She remembered pleading with him to stop.

Mama came into the room and adjusted the curtains.

"What day is it?" Mirelle asked.

"Shabbat."

"Shabbat? But that means . . ."

"It's been nearly four days," Mama said. "I was afraid I would lose you, too."

"Too?"

*Like Jacopo or Papa?* Then she remembered what had happened right before the attack. "Mama, I have to tell you—I'm not . . ."

"Pregnant. I know."

"You know?"

"I helped undress you, sweetheart."

Mirelle shut her eyes, trying to shield them against the too-bright light. Tears leaked from under her closed lids. Mama patted them away with a scrap of linen.

"Christophe?" Mirelle whispered.

"He's outside, waiting to speak to you. Are you strong enough?"

Mirelle tried to sit up; her head throbbed as she shifted position.

Mama eased her against a bank of pillows and smoothed her hair. "You don't need to see him right now, you know," she said, the backs of her fingers tracing down Mirelle's cheek.

"Now, Mama," Mirelle insisted, her voice a mere thread. She closed her eyes and waited.

Her mother went to the door. "She's still weak," she warned the man standing outside. "Don't tire her."

"I won't, I promise." Christophe sounded solemn.

Mirelle heard him move softly into the room and sit in the chair next to her bed. Her eyes still closed, she felt him take her hand.

"Mirelle?"

Her eyelids refused to open. Why did the light hurt so much? When she finally managed, he was peering uncertainly into her face. "I'm so sorry," she murmured.

"Sorry? Why sorry?"

"I really thought I was pregnant. I wasn't trying to fool you."

Christophe clasped her hand to his heart. "Don't you think I know that?"

"When I found out, I panicked." She pulled her hand out of his grasp. *Why didn't I just stay where I was? Safe?*

Christophe patted her arm. "Did your mother tell you? The doctor says you'll be fine soon."

A tear escaped her eye, traveled slowly down her cheek. He brushed it away with a thumb.

"Listen, we need to talk. The French garrison leaves Ancona in three days. You'll follow me to Paris . . . when you're well enough to travel."

The words stuck in her throat. "Follow you to Paris?"

"Of course. What else?" He shifted back in his chair.

*What else?* Mirelle took a short breath. "There's no baby. Do . . . do you still want . . . ?"

Christophe looked away, stared out the window. "Of course," he said, but there was no conviction in his voice. "If you do." He waited a beat. "Do you?"

*Do I?* Mirelle asked herself, closing her eyes again. Darkness enveloped her and she slipped back into slumber.

When she woke again, Dolce sat by her side.

"Well, finally," her friend said.

Looking out the window, Mirelle saw the sun was near to setting. She remembered Christophe's words in a flash of panic. He had three days left in Ancona and she had slept one of them away.

"How are you feeling?" Dolce asked.

"Thirsty," Mirelle croaked.

Dolce rang a bell and a maidservant bustled in. Following Dolce's pointed finger, she poured some water and helped Mirelle drink it.

"Enough?" Dolce asked after a few seconds. She dismissed the servant with a brisk nod and pulled her chair closer. "Papa will speak with you himself, but I wanted to make some things clear first."

Mirelle waited, too exhausted to protest.

"My father could never marry an impure woman. Even if you were never pregnant, you're still ruined. You know that, yes?"

Mirelle nodded.

"You'll leave Ancona, marry Christophe. That's what you want, isn't it?"

Mirelle stared at her. *No*, she thought. *You don't choose my future for me. Neither does your father, my mother—not even Christophe. I will decide.*

But Dolce, being Dolce, interpreted her silence as acquiescence. She rose briskly, looking calm now, as though their friendship had been restored. Mirelle knew better. They were not friends, not anymore. Perhaps they never had been.

"Don't worry," Dolce said. "I'll help when you're well enough to leave. And just think—I'll be able to visit you in Paris!" Her silk skirts swished on the marble floor as she left the room.

The candles were lit and Mirelle had managed a light supper of chicken broth and whey wine when her mother ushered Sabato Narducci into the room. David followed.

"A friend to wish you well." Mama backed away to stand with David.

"Signorina Mirelle," Sabato said, doffing his hat and bowing. "We were heartbroken to hear of your attack."

There was a slight, uncomfortable pause. Did the entire ghetto know she had slept with a man while still unmarried?

"I am happy to see you, Signor Narducci," Mirelle said slowly, wondering why he was here. "How are things in the workshop?"

Sabato told her of commissions won, ketubot completed, happy customers. "And happy workers, too," he added. "Signor Morpurgo visits almost every day, ensuring the quality your father and grandfather were so proud of. We are relieved to be free of Turko." Sabato bowed in David's direction. "After so much tragedy and unhappiness, it is paradise to have everything settled so satisfactorily."

"I'm glad," Mirelle said. But her heart sank within her. What would happen to these men when her betrothal to Morpurgo was officially severed? Had she really ever stopped to consider their fate?

"I brought you a gift—actually, a few gifts," Sabato said.

He placed several pieces of parchment on her bedside table. One by one, Mirelle picked them up and exclaimed over their beauty.

They were ketubot—her ketubot, made out in her name. The name of the bridegroom had been left blank. She looked at David in astonishment.

"I decided," he answered her questioning glance, "to allow space for the groom to be filled in later."

She studied the beautiful marriage certificates. There were five in all—one with ancient animals, a veritable Noah's ark of a ketubah; one drawn with delicate pastel flowers curling in and around the block of dark-lettered text; one richly decorated with gold curlicues around the edges; one with Biblical figures dancing in celebration. And last was a magnificent ketubah that placed two love birds above the text, set off by marble columns, flowers intertwined throughout, drawn in gold and silver and jewel tones.

"We thought that would be the actual marriage certificate," Sabato said. "You shouldn't have more than one, but we all wanted to have a hand in making these—even if only a pen stroke or hue."

Fresh tears rolled down Mirelle's cheeks. She reached for her handkerchief, but it eluded her grasp and slipped to the floor. David stepped over and handed it to her.

"Look at the amount," he hissed in her ear, leaning close. "See what you were once worth to me."

She glanced at the price that her bridegroom would pay if he ever divorced her. Her eyes widened. "One hundred thousand scudi?" she whispered, unbelieving. It was a fortune.

"One hundred thousand scudi," David repeated, anger tinging his voice.

Sabato averted his eyes, sensing the discomfort in the room. David dismissed him and Mama with a commanding wave of his hand, Mama glancing back anxiously as she left.

David sat down and Mirelle shrank against her pillows.

"How could you have just abandoned them?" he asked. "After I paid for their articles?"

Her face burned.

"You've wanted to carry on your father's legacy since you were a child," he continued. "And you gave it all up to sin with a Christian. Do you think I'll marry you now that you've disgraced yourself before man and God?"

Knowing he didn't expect an answer, Mirelle's lips tightened.

"Think about the price I put on my bride. Can your Christian lover match it?" David's lip curled. "Take those ketubot to Paris and no court will honor those certificates. The civil courts would laugh at them, the Jewish courts disregard them. And he'll never have such wealth, will he? Marry Christophe and those beautiful documents will be nothing more than wallpaper in your wretched home."

"It was just—"

"You are not what I thought you were. You made a fool of me in front of the entire community, cost me more money than I could easily afford. Despite your being punished by God for your misdeeds"—he glared at her, and she raised a hasty hand to her face—"I'll never forgive you. But what does that matter? You'll leave, I'll recover, and only your mother will be left, mourning the loss of her family. You might spare her a thought as you abandon her."

He looked at her for a long moment, then rose stiffly and walked out the door. Mirelle watched him leave, clutching the ketubot against her chest, heart aching.

# 63

Mirelle lay in bed, sleepless. David had made it clear: she had to leave Ancona with Christophe, no matter how little she wanted to. All the reasons she'd wanted him seemed idiotic now, when weighed against her home, her heritage, her father's legacy. Everything she was being forced to abandon. Christophe must realize it, too. Their infatuation had been fleeting, foolish. If they married, if she moved to Paris, they would be miserable together.

But she couldn't stay here, could she?

Could she?

She suddenly remembered the papers that signed the workshop over to her mother. The original agreement between David and herself was in the same envelope. Where were they? She'd left them on the dressing table near the window. Getting out from under the covers with an effort, she gripped the edges of the dressing table. The envelope was gone.

She slid open the table's single drawer and there it was, unopened. She took it in both hands, glad her pounding headache had subsided somewhat, and collapsed in the chair next to her bed.

"Mirelle!" Her mother rushed in, looking appalled. "You should be in bed!"

"I needed to see the terms of the workshop agreements," she said. "I told you, didn't I, back at the printshop, that I would provide for you?"

Her mother looked at her blankly. "Did you think to ask if I wanted it?" She pushed aside the rumpled covers and perched on the bed. "Did you stop to consider that it would only bring me pain—make me miss your father even more? Or Jacopo? Or even you?"

"But you need an income," Mirelle said. "Unless you stay here. Dolce talked of your becoming Signor Morpurgo's housekeeper. You may feel that's awkward now."

Mama's eyebrows rose. "An understatement, don't you think?"

Mirelle allowed herself a faint smile. "Well, perhaps if I stay here, manage the workshop myself. . ."

"If you *what?*"

"You know it's what I've always wanted."

"Aren't you leaving with . . ." Mama's voice petered out, as if she couldn't bring herself to say the name.

"When I thought I was pregnant, it was different." Mirelle sighed. She knew how it must look—how flighty! how irrational!—but she no longer cared. "But he doesn't want me, not really. And I don't want him. It was all a mistake, don't you see? A terrible, terrible mistake."

Mama laced her hands in her lap, hope flashing across her face. "But then why not marry David?"

"David?"

"You acted like a child," Mama continued. "True. But now you've a second chance at a golden future: A man who cares for you. Who can provide for you. Who even found a way to answer your childish dream to own the workshop. He'll give you a second chance, I know he will. I'll speak to him!"

"Mama, he won't! He's humiliated, says I'm unworthy. And even if he *did* listen to you, I won't marry him. I didn't want to before and I certainly don't now."

The hope that had shone so brilliantly was snuffed out. "*Still* acting like a child!" Mama clenched her hands in her lap. "Just throw it all away. Selfish. Stupid. What *do* you want, Mirelle? Don't you care about me at all?"

"Care about you?" Mirelle pulled the second agreement out of its envelope and extended it to her mother with an outstretched hand. "Look what I did for you!"

Mama snatched the sheaf of paper. "This?" she spat. "What *is* this?"

"The agreement granting you ownership of the workshop," Mirelle replied. "Dolce and I drew it up when I thought I was leaving with Christophe."

Mama took a moment to consider the document. Then, without a word, she tore it in two.

Mirelle watched the pieces flutter to the ground.

Mirelle woke up resolved the next morning. Her head still throbbing slightly, she rose and washed. She wished she felt better, but there was no time to stay in bed, no time for recovery.

*Why didn't I stay in the printshop?* Mirelle wondered. *If I had, I'd be well now. Even now, I might be on my way to Paris.*

She felt a guilty sense of relief that she wasn't.

She dressed slowly, every movement stabbing at her temples. She brushed her hair and gingerly placed a hat on her head, struggled into a warm pelisse.

The morning air was crisp and clean. It had rained while she lay unconscious, and all remnants of the battle in the ghetto had been washed away. Mirelle felt the sun's beams tease her eyes as she walked toward the French barracks.

As she mounted the shallow steps, several soldiers emerged, arms full of kitbags. She was glad she hadn't delayed. Preparations to leave were clearly underway.

"Is Christophe Lefevre here?" she asked one of the guards.

"I'll find him. Wait there." He pointed to a bench just outside the barracks.

Mirelle walked to the bench and sat. Grateful that it stood in the shade of an olive tree, she shut her eyes, waiting.

"Mirelle? What are you doing here? I would have come to see you before we left!"

She opened her eyes and smiled. He was as handsome as ever, though the glint in his green eyes had now been replaced with worry.

"I didn't want to talk to you there," she said. "It's better away from that house."

He sat next to her and she couldn't help but think of another bench, in the Morpurgo rose garden, when he had made her heart beat faster just by sitting close.

"I've made arrangements for your journey." He pulled a thick purse out of his jacket and handed it to her. "There's money and instructions."

She felt the heft of the purse and tears prickled her eyes. "Christophe, you're a good man."

He kicked at a stone. "Nonsense."

She handed him back the purse. "I'm not coming to Paris. We're not getting married."

The sudden flare of relief in his eyes was masked just as suddenly by shock. "What do you mean? Mirelle, let me do the honorable thing. You can't stay here, and you certainly can't marry Morpurgo now."

"I won't marry him," she said, putting a hand on his knee. "As for staying here, here in Ancona—well, we'll see. But I release you from any promises you made me. You're a free man."

"But . . ." He seemed too bewildered to go on. Then he found his voice. "I would have always cared for you. Cared for our children." He looked at his boots. "We'd have had a good life together."

"I know," Mirelle said. "And I'll never forget what we shared. I know it's not as important to you, a man who has loved other women."

"Never one like you, though." Almost in wonder, he asked, "Why wasn't that enough?"

She sighed. "Because we're from two different worlds, I suppose. If we'd truly loved one another, we might have bridged the gap. But what we had—it only tricked us into thinking it was love. It wasn't real."

He nodded slowly.

She rose. "I must go. Will you be all right?"

He put his arms around her. "Will *I* be all right? Will you?"

She smiled up at him, and, rising on her toes, gently kissed his cheek. "I will. Farewell." She took a step back, and repeated herself, this time separating the two words. "Fare well, my dear friend."

Her heart heavy, Mirelle made her way to the ketubah workshop. She paused by the blue-and-green enamel mezuzah attached to the front doorpost, just as she had the day they told her she could no longer work there. Now, as then, she reached up to touch it, then kissed her fingers.

The men's faces swiveled curiously in her direction as she entered. Focused on her task, she approached the office where Narducci sat. The sight of him in her father's old chair did not upset her as it once would have.

"Mirelle!" he cried, rising quickly.

"Good morning," she said.

"It's wonderful to see you, but . . . what are you doing here?"

Mirelle smiled patiently. "I've come back to work, if you'll have me."

"But . . . aren't you going to Paris with your young man?"

Her smile faded a little. It would take a long time to live down the scandal—if she ever did. But she wouldn't let it stop her. "No longer. Nor will I marry Signor Morpurgo."

"I don't understand."

Mirelle pulled the original agreement out of her reticule. "Did you ever see this? When Signor Morpurgo bought out your articles, Prudenzia realized that she'd own nothing but an empty shell of a building. So she let him buy the entire works and he put it in my name. As owner."

He studied the page. "With him as trustee," he said, pointing to the clause. "Entailed on your firstborn son."

"Yes. And as owner, I feel it's in my best interest—and yours—to come to work. Every day."

Narducci nodded slowly, and she felt her heart lift.

"I'll need to find someplace to live. I don't need much—just a place to rest my head at night."

He stared at her. "You're serious?"

"As serious as I've ever been," Mirelle declared with a grin.

"The men will be delighted. And you'll stay with us." He waved a hand toward her father's chair. "That's your seat now."

Gently, Mirelle lowered herself into her father's seat and reached for the ledger. The prospect of doing real work again nearly banished her headache. Narducci gathered up his notes and headed to the workroom.

Mirelle had been checking through the accounts and orders for an hour. When she heard the cathedral bell sound, she rose to make workshop rounds.

She was bending over Anselmo's ink work, discussing his ideas for the commission, when the thud of the door swinging open made her heart skip a beat.

David Morpurgo, Dolce, and Rabbi Fano were clustered at the entrance. Mama stood behind them, wringing her hands; Daniel stood at her side.

"Mirelle d'Ancona!" the rabbi barked, making her jump. "What are you doing here?"

Her chin rose as she turned to face him. "Well, I would think that was obvious, Rabbi Fano. I'm working."

"Is that not forbidden? How many times must I tell you? Your parents forbid it—your erstwhile fiancé forbids it"—the rabbi cast a sheepish look at David—"and *I* forbid it! A maiden working where holy work is done, among scribes . . . I have been far too lenient with you. You have not a shred of reputation left in Ancona. Why are you still here? Here in this town where you've made a mockery of common decency? Here in this workshop where you contaminate God's holy word?"

Mirelle's fists clenched as she straightened to full height. "This is my workshop."

"*Your* workshop?" the rabbi sputtered, incredulous.

"In name it is, Rabbi," David agreed, one eyebrow rising. "Legally, Mirelle owns it."

The rabbi stared at him.

"*My* workshop, just as Ancona is my home," Mirelle said. "Yes, I've made mistakes, and I beg pardon of those I've hurt because of them." Mirelle glanced at her mother, who hunched a shoulder; at David, who watched her with his mouth agape; and at Daniel, who nodded in response. She refused to look at Dolce. "But no one will tell me I cannot stay in Ancona—or work here."

Narducci moved to her side and put a hand on her shoulder. "Every worker in the d'Ancona Ketubah Workshop adds their voice in our owner's support. We'll proclaim to all Ancona if need be: she has earned her place here among us."

"A ruined woman, working hand in hand with young scribes? Are you a fool, Narducci?" The rabbi shook his head. "Don't you see what disaster may come of this?"

"We do not hire men of loose character to work here," Narducci said scornfully. "And any man who approaches Signorina d'Ancona with sinful intent will bear the brunt of our wrath and be turned off without a character. Trust me, she is safer here than anywhere else on earth."

A murmur of agreement rose from the men.

"And heed this," Narducci added, "we don't forget what she's done for us. Her counsel to Beniamino. Her defense of the workers against Turko, trying to stay his hand from the whip. Her sacrifice at surrendering the work she was born to do, agreeing to marry a man older than her father—solely to secure our well-being." He stood firm by her side. "No, we won't let you dismiss her."

Mirelle blinked hard, eyes smarting. A thick silence followed, stretching for what seemed like minutes.

Finally, David turned to her. "Is this truly what you want?"

"Yes, Signor Morpurgo. What I've always wanted."

"And your Christian lover?" He lobbed the question at her like a missile.

She took a breath. "That was wrong. But we realized our mistake in time." She looked straight at him, buoyed by Narducci's warm words. "Will you forgive me? I never wanted to marry you, would never have agreed had my family not needed it so desperately. You've been nothing but kind to me, and I treated you dreadfully. But we should not wed."

"No," he agreed slowly. "And perhaps, in time, I'll forgive you. Besides"—his mouth twitched—"you owe me quite a sum of money, don't you? This way, you'll be able to repay me."

"I plan to," Mirelle said solemnly, putting out her hand to shake his.

"No!" the rabbi cried, his face almost purple with rage. "I do not agree!"

David, still clasping Mirelle's hand, looked at him, an amused expression crossing his face. "But I do, Rabbi. And if you attempt to place an interdict on the workshop once more, you'll find I have more influence in the community than you do."

Rabbi Fano swallowed; a bead of sweat ran down his forehead. For a second, it looked like he might mouth another protest, but then he grunted in frustration and pushed out of the shop.

The men cheered his exit.

Mirelle squeezed David's hand. "Thank you."

"Come by my office tomorrow and we'll make this arrangement official," he said. "Pinina, Dolce, we'll go home now. Mirelle, you are welcome to stay as my guest until you can find somewhere to live."

"I'll be staying with the Narduccis until I can find lodgings," Mirelle told him. "But I'm glad Mama has a place to stay."

Mirelle glanced at her mother's face and realized, her heart twisting within her, that it would be fruitless to approach her just then. Pinina's eyes bore a hole in the ground. *Someday*, Mirelle thought, *she will understand.*

"You go, Papa," Dolce said. "I want to talk to Mirelle."

Mirelle watched her mother and David file out of the shop. Daniel hesitated, unsure whether to follow or not. She stopped him. "Daniel, please stay. Whatever Dolce has to tell me can only take a moment."

Dolce drew herself up. "That is, if you've a moment to spare," she seethed. "You are certainly fortunate, aren't you? What did Christophe say your name meant in French? Admired one? Admired by all these men you've jilted or wronged—my poor father, your Christian lover, even the men in the workshop, and who knows how many others?"

"What exactly do you want, Dolce?" Mirelle asked. "You never wanted your father to marry me. You never cared if Christophe married me—only that he'd ruin me for your father. So *you* got what you wanted, no?"

Dolce waved her words aside impatiently. "I want to understand. You're a woman who has defied all decency, who slept with one man while promised to another, who pretended to be pregnant to entrap him. No better than a common slut. And yet . . ." She threw a hurt glance at Daniel.

"Dolce." Mirelle's voice was sharpened by the rage building inside her. "You pushed me into Christophe's arms. Saying it was romance, fate—anything but sin."

Dolce opened her mouth to retort, but Mirelle flung up a hand, stopping her.

"For once in your life, be satisfied. Go home."

Dolce stared from Mirelle to Daniel. Her mouth opened. But then she shut it again and stalked off.

Mirelle glanced around the shop. The men looked to be hard at work, but she could tell every ear was tuned to hear what came next. "Come into my office," she told Daniel.

They settled in the chairs, Mirelle stifling a groan as she sat.

"You need rest," Daniel said, concerned.

"Soon enough. Daniel, did Christophe . . ."

"He told me that you'd broken off the engagement. He left Ancona this morning, went with the first convoy to Paris."

"Is he—all right?"

Daniel leaned back. "He will be. And you?"

Mirelle sighed. It had been such a short time, even though it felt like years had passed, since she and Christophe were together. The baby, the attack—everything felt like a whirlwind. Days ago, she'd thought she loved Christophe with all her heart, but now? It was as if a weight had been lifted from her chest. *Still, I am a ruined woman*, she thought bitterly. *No man will ever want me again.*

"I'll be all right," she said. "When do you leave?"

"Tomorrow," Daniel said slowly. "We leave tomorrow."

Mirelle smiled sadly. "I wish you didn't have to go."

He laughed, and she detected a bitter tinge to the laughter. "I wish we didn't, either. But I'm a soldier, with no say in where or when I go. Not for years to come."

She sat silent for a moment, wrestling with her feelings. And then she had an idea. "Would you write? It wouldn't have to be much—maybe a letter every month or so. I just wouldn't want to lose you altogether."

Daniel's bitterness evaporated and he smiled. "You could never lose me, Mirelle. Of course I'll write."

The next day, the French garrison left the city. As Mirelle watched Daniel march off behind the cart that carried the printing presses, she couldn't help but think of how much had changed since they'd met. Mama might still not understand, the rabbi might yet oppose her, and Dolce, well, Dolce would require careful watching. But all of that was unimportant. She had a workshop to run.

Once Daniel disappeared beyond the bend of the road, Mirelle walked toward the stone archway that had once housed the ghetto gate. She paused for a moment and reached out to where she'd wound her fingers through the ironwork curlicues that had imprisoned her nightly. All her fingers touched now was the morning mist—and the open world before her.

Without looking back, she walked through the entrance, heading toward her future.

# Acknowledgments

My thanks to both early and later readers: Stephanie Cowell, Sipora Coffelt, Caprice Gavin, Laurie Lico Albanese, Meg Wiviott, Beverly Jackson, and Mally Becker.

Judith Lindbergh, my partner in The Writers Circle, gave me the means to earn a living while "living the writing life." I am continually inspired by the energy and enthusiasm of our student writers, particularly the kids, teens, and my aspiring novelists. Judith served as sounding board, long-suffering reader, and someone on whose shoulder I could both cry and exalt as I worked on this book.

Alex Cameron was instrumental in making this novel all it could be—from working through plot points to honing my pitch to editing an early version to working through radical changes throughout a lengthy revision process. Sorry for playing the "mother card" so often, Alex—and I hope the book's dedication makes up for it!

Agent Heather Schroder worked tirelessly to improve the novel. Independent editor Susan Dalsimer challenged me to make some significant changes, including a fundamental shift in the novel's conclusion. Julie Maloney introduced me to She Writes Press and gave me the push I needed. The publisher of She Writes Press, Brooke Warner, along with Lauren Wise, Krissa Lagos, Pamela Long, and Julie Metz, have all been a joy to work with. And at an important juncture in the publishing process, my brother, Matthew Kreps, meticulously proofread the novel.

Frederica Heiman, a native Italian speaker, vetted my Google Translate Italian. I thank Liz Samuel for introducing us.

My family has never failed in their support throughout the long process of writing, revising, revising again, and then many more times. While Alex had a special role in the making of this book, I am also grateful to my son Geoff and husband, Steve, for so generously rooting for me throughout.

# Author's Note

As a historical novelist, I have been blessed by discoveries—gifts, in a manner of speaking—made during my research. When I started writing *Beyond the Ghetto Gates*, I possessed only a few historical facts. I wanted to focus on Napoleon's campaign in Italy, especially his tearing down of ghetto gates in the country in which they originated. I placed the novel in Ancona, a harbor city previously unknown to me, because that was where Napoleon's Jewish soldiers first dismantled the gates. I learned about the riots that took place just before General Bonaparte arrived on the scene. And in reading the story of Napoleon's involvement in Ancona, I discovered the Morpurgo brothers, Jews whom Bonaparte appointed to the newly formed municipal council.

But that was all I knew, before further research showered me with two substantial gifts.

The first was learning about Ancona's reputation as Europe's foremost ketubah makers. The idea that this small city contained some of the most talented scribes and artists in the Jewish world, producing exquisite marriage licenses, gave me both a home and a passion for Mirelle. Her desire to further her family's legacy, blocked by the city's rabbi and her parents' wish to see her wed well, provided a starting point. Mirelle—like so many young women of the time—was raised to marry to enrich her family, a duty that would run counter to her own happiness.

The second gift was stumbling upon the miracle of *La Madonna del Duomo*. Ancona lay claim to a miracle portrait of Mother Mary—purported to smile, cry, and turn her eyes upon the congregation. Who could resist Napoleon's alleged reaction to seeing the portrait in person? Bonaparte, like conquerors before and after, was denuding the treasures of Italy and sending them to fill France's empty coffers, and this made his encounter with the portrait all the more compelling. And accounts of the "prodigy," the term the Church uses to describe miracle art treasures, introduced me to the historical characters of Francesca Marotti and her daughter Barbara. Emilio, Francesca's Jew-hating husband, is, however, wholly my invention.

The young General Bonaparte, his staff, and his family are all historically based, though naturally I've embellished their characters. However, there is no reason to believe that a military press was ever established in Ancona. Nor was the miracle portrait ever stolen or held hostage.

Aside from the two Morpurgo brothers, Francesca, Barbara, Father Candelabri, and Cardinal Ranuzzi, most of Ancona's cast of characters here are fictional. While a riot did take place in Ancona's ghetto before Napoleon arrived, and there was a surge of indigenous fellowships throughout Italy to combat the perceived French threat to the Catholic religion, Emilio and his cohorts in Ancona's so-called Catholic Fellowship are imagined. I owe Cardinal Ranuzzi an apology, as there is no historical evidence to support the rabid anti-Semitic beliefs I thrust upon him.

I made a concerted attempt to accurately follow Bonaparte's military campaign and political maneuverings as he conquered Italy, though I'm certain errors abound. And while there was a second riot in Ancona, as well as an attempt to seize the church bell to cast a cannon—a plot historically foiled by the Morpurgo brothers—these events took place a few years later than portrayed. I deliberately condensed the history for dramatic effect.

Mirelle's dilemma—to marry David Morpurgo or her dashing Gentile French soldier—highlights a theme I've explored in
nearly all my writing. The intersection between assimilation and
safeguarding religious belief is a muddy one, and it's difficult to
know where to draw the line. This was why I was so drawn to
the story of the Jews during the French Revolution. The question
of surrendering the traditions you were born into to pursue a
secularized life is fraught equally with guilt and exhilaration. I
hope my portrayal of the challenges Mirelle faced does justice
to the depth of the quandary faced by many individuals during
both this era and others.

I also wished to convey how difficult it is to overcome taught
prejudice. Jews and Catholics in Ancona lived separate lives before
the ghetto gates were torn down, and the resulting clash of cultures
contains echoes of our modern-day experience. How does one tran-
scend deeply held beliefs about a group of people who are different? Is
getting to know someone personally enough to overcome prejudice?
Can you ever fully discard bias imbibed from people you trust, such
as family or clergy? Francesca and Daniel's relationship gave me the
scope needed to explore this issue in all its messy complexity.

I owe an immense debt to Michael Goldfarb, whose impeccable
book, *Emancipation*, gave me both the backdrop and the details
needed to begin this novel, while Franz Kobler's *Napoleon and the
Jews* provided further insight. I consulted too many biographies
about Napoleon to mention, but books specifically dealing with
his Italian campaign included Desmond Gregory's *Napoleon's Italy*
and Guglielmo Ferraro's *The Gamble*. Philip Haythornthwaite and
Richard Hook's *Napoleon's Campaigns in Italy* not only detailed
the battles but also illustrated in full color what the well-dressed
French soldiers and officers wore. One of my students, fellow SWP
author Eileen Sanchez, helped me locate a translation of the Catholic
Church's juridical examination into the prodigy of Ancona. And I

would be remiss if I failed to mention one of my favorite childhood books, Annemarie Selinko's *Désirée*, where my fascination with Napoleon originated.

# ABOUT THE AUTHOR

© Peter Vidor

Michelle Cameron is a director of The Writers Circle, a New Jersey-based organization that offers creative writing programs to children and adults, and the author of works of historical fiction and poetry: *The Fruit of Her Hands: The Story of Shira of Ashkenaz* (Pocket, 2009) and *In the Shadow of the Globe* (Lit Pot Press, 2003). She lived in Israel for fifteen years (including three weeks in a bomb shelter during the Yom Kippur War) and served as an officer in the Israeli army teaching air force cadets technical English. Michelle lives in New Jersey with her husband and has two grown sons of whom she is inordinately proud. Her website is michelle-cameron.com.

# SELECTED TITLES FROM SHE WRITES PRESS

She Writes Press is an independent publishing company founded to serve women writers everywhere. Visit us at www.shewritespress.com.

*Dark Lady* by Charlene Ball $16.95, 978-1-63152-228-4
Emilia Bassano Lanyer—poor, beautiful, and intelligent, born to a family of Court musicians and secret Jews, lover to Shakespeare and mistress to an older nobleman—survives to become a published poet in an era when most women's lives are rigidly circumscribed.

*Elmina's Fire* by Linda Carleton $16.95, 978-1-63152-190-4
A story of conflict over such issues as reincarnation and the nature of good and evil that are as relevant today as they were eight centuries ago, *Elmina's Fire* offers a riveting window into a soul struggling for survival amid the conflict between the Cathars and the Catholic Church.

*Light Radiance Splendor* by Leah Chyten $16.95, 978-1-63152-178-2
Set in Eastern Europe in the first half of the twentieth century and culminating in contemporary Israel and Palestine, *Light Radiance Splendor* shows how three generations of the Hebrew Goddess Shekinah's devoted mission keepers grapple with betrayal, love, and forgiveness.

*The Sweetness* by Sande Boritz Berger $16.95, 978-1-63152-907-8
A compelling and powerful story of two girls—cousins living on separate continents—whose strikingly different lives are forever changed when the Nazis invade Vilna, Lithuania.

*Even in Darkness* by Barbara Stark-Nemon $16.95, 978-1-63152-956-6
From privileged young German-Jewish woman to concentration camp refugee, Kläre Kohler navigates the horrors of war and—through unlikely sources—finds the strength, hope, and love she needs to survive.

*The Vintner's Daughter* by Kristen Harnisch $16.95, 978-163152-929-0
Set against the sweeping canvas of French and California vineyard life in the late 1890s, this is the compelling tale of one woman's struggle to reclaim her family's Loire Valley vineyard—and her life.